DREAM SIGHT

Book Three of The Dream Waters Series

Erin A. Jensen

2017 Dream Sight
Text copyright © 2017 Erin A. Jensen
All Rights Reserved
Dream Waters Publishing
ISBN: 0997171278
ISBN 13: 9780997171273

To Chris for believing in my dream. None of this would have happened without you.

To Maggie —my "super fan" across the pond who became a dear friend —for encouraging and supporting me as only a fellow writer could.

To Emilie for sticking with me through even the most painful moments. This one's for you because, as you once said, Bob is your homeboy.

To Kate, Amy, Emilie and Al —my original beta readers —for your continued input, support and encouragement.

To Shannon, BillieJo, Stacy, Cyndi and Linda for beta reading, helping with signings and all your feedback and support. Your book club will always have a special place in my heart.

To Missy, Robyn, Barbara and Marsha for helping me spread the word during book signings.

And to my Wegmans family for supporting me in so many ways.

The fury of a demon instantly possessed me. I knew myself no longer. My original soul seemed, at once, to take flight from my body; and a more fiendish malevolence...thrilled every fibre of my frame.

–Edgar Allan Poe / The Black Cat

1

BOB

Watching Nellie dredge up all the heartache from her past was torture. What was the point of this? Hadn't this bastard caused her enough suffering? What purpose could forcing her to pour her heart out to Charlie possibly serve? Even at a distance, I could feel how much it pained her—but hard as I fought against it, I couldn't free myself from the spell that bound me. I couldn't move a muscle, couldn't call out to Charlie and warn him of the danger. I couldn't do a damn thing to help the woman I'd vowed to protect with my life. Keeping me immobilized just inside the forest, close enough to witness her anguish but powerless to help her, seemed intentionally cruel. Not that Henry Godric's cruelty came as a surprise. Nellie had shared her story with me soon after Charlie brought her to my shore. I knew what a monster her ex-husband was, and it killed me that I hadn't prevented him from getting to her.

Laughter danced in Godric's cruel eyes as he watched me. "You're a noble man, Robert. I can see why Nellie is so fond of you."

"Why are you doing this?" I managed to choke out through gritted teeth.

"That doesn't concern you, my friend."

"You're no friend of mine," I whispered, sweat beading on my brow from the effort.

Henry's amused grin widened. "I suppose that's true."

Exchanging words with this monster was a waste of energy, so I ignored him and focused on fighting the invisible bonds that held me frozen in place.

My life had become something magical the night Charlie washed up on my shore with Nellie and her daughter, Lilly. Before them, I walked that shore alone and my life had lost all sense of purpose, but they breathed new life into me. They became my purpose and my one goal in life was to keep them safe from the dragon that Nellie believed was coming for her, but after enough time passed without incident, I suppose we both got careless. There didn't appear to be anything to worry about. Neither man nor beast had come searching for Nellie or her sweet child so we settled into a comfortable routine, spending our days playing with Lilly and our evenings learning everything there was to know about each other. Nellie was hesitant to share the details of her past at first but as we grew closer, she began to trust that she could tell me anything and eventually she opened up and shared the nightmarish details of her past. A weight seemed to lift from her as soon as she did, and she truly began to enjoy life again. That's when Henry Godric showed up on our shore.

Determined as I'd been to slay Nellie's demon, I couldn't even touch him. The instant I stepped toward Godric, he paralyzed me. Then he took sweet little Lilly and sealed her in an elaborately ornamented cage. If I'd been able to speak, I would've warned Nellie not to cooperate with that monster but he made certain that I couldn't tell her anything. He froze my vocal chords as well as every muscle in my body. Then he told Nellie that Charlie would be paying us a visit soon and if she didn't do exactly as he said, he'd take the lives of the two people she loved most in this world. He didn't ask her to lie or deceive Charlie. He simply instructed her to tell her tale as it had truly happened, but that was torture enough. Nellie kept those memories buried deep inside. Allowing them to surface was agony for her, and for the life of me, I couldn't imagine what reason Godric could have for making her do it.

Utterly spent and useless, I struggled to draw a breath as I watched Nellie drop into Charlie's arms. For a short eternity the two of them wept, locked in that embrace. I spent those torturous minutes fighting to regain control of my voice and holler a warning to Charlie but for all my efforts, I didn't accomplish a thing. They spoke a bit longer after Nellie straightened and shortly after that, Charlie departed none the wiser.

Henry dragged Lilly's gilded cage and my immobilized body out of the forest, and I died a thousand times over as we approached the spot where Nellie's body lay crumpled by the Water's edge. She lifted her head as we neared her, and I wanted nothing more than to take her in my arms and dry her tearstained cheeks.

Henry let out an infuriatingly cheerful laugh. "You did well, Nellie."

I ached to throttle him, but I still couldn't budge an inch or even verbally come to her defense.

"Then leave us alone like you promised," Nellie answered in a hollow whisper.

"I'm afraid there's been a slight miscommunication," Godric murmured as he took a step toward her. "I never promised to leave you alone."

A frail sob escaped Nellie's trembling lips. "What?"

"No, I simply promised to spare the lives of the people you loved."

A tear slid down Nellie's cheek as Godric moved toward Lilly. "What are you saying?"

"Your knight in shining armor truly is a noble man." Henry's grin widened as he turned to look at me. "He's honest and decent and selfless, everything that I despise. Did you really believe that I would allow him to keep what belonged to me?"

Try as I might, I couldn't choke out a response.

Nellie stole a worried glance at me as she numbly repeated her question. "What are you saying?"

"Dragons do not part with their treasures."

Nellie dropped her head as if it had suddenly grown too heavy for her neck to support. "You never treasured me."

"True," he agreed, his voice cold as ice, "but you belong to me, and I can't allow another man to keep what's mine."

"I did what you asked... Please," Nellie whimpered, "let me go."

"I'm afraid I can't do that." Grinning like he didn't have a care in the world, Henry took a leisurely step toward me. "I thank you for your hospitality, Bob. However, I can't allow you to keep on screwing my wife, now can I? What sort of man would that make me?"

"You...are...no...man." As I choked the words out in a broken whisper, Nellie's sobbing shattered my heart.

"Enough tears." Godric took a step toward Lilly's cage and rattled it with his foot. "If you behave, I might consider allowing you to keep this lovely little enchantment."

Nellie instantly stilled at his words.

With hardly any effort, Henry lifted Nellie off the ground and tossed her over his shoulder. Then he picked up Lilly's cage and dipped his head toward me. "It's been a pleasure, Bob."

As they moved toward the Water, Nellie lifted her head to look back at me and mouthed the words, "I love you."

Then Godric stepped into the Water, and the Waters promptly swallowed them.

The moment they vanished, my invisible chains fell away. Heart pounding, I rushed to the Water's edge and dove in after them...

...I startled myself awake with a groggy holler, rubbed my eyes and looked around the room. I musta dozed off on the couch again. I couldn't re-member what the hell I'd been dreamin about, but I was definitely havin a nightmare. My old heart was beatin a mile a minute. Somehow, Nellie'd managed to sleep through my outburst. She was still snorin away with her head on my shoulder. I brushed the wiry pieces of gray hair off her face. That's when I saw the tears on her wrinkled cheeks.

I gave her a little shake. "Wake up, woman. Naptime's over."

She didn't wake up, but her eyelids twitched and she let out a whiny squeak. Guess I wasn't the only one havin nightmares. What the fuck were we watchin when we nodded off? I squinted at the television. Two sour old bastards were flappin their gums about fly fishin, not exactly my idea of quality programmin but it wasn't the stuff nightmares were made of.

Nellie let out another squeak.

"Hey!" I shook her a little harder. "Wake up. You're startin to worry me."

She jerked her head off my shoulder and looked up at me with her eyes wide as hell. "He's planning to take the Princess."

"Shhh." I'd gotten pretty used to Nellie's looniness. In fact, I usually found it kinda endearin, but her face looked too pale this time. "It was just a bad dream, that's all. Everything's okay."

"No, it's not," she muttered. "You need to find Charlie and warn him that Godric's coming for the Princess. You'll find him with the Sarrum. They've been training him at the palace."

I narrowed my eyes at her. "What the hell's gotten into you, woman? You're startin to scare me."

Her crazy eyes widened as she grabbed ahold of my arm. "You need to find Charlie! Tell him Godric took me and he plans to take the Princess!"

I leaned back to get a better look at her. "Charlie checked outta here, remember? The kid ain't here no more."

"Not here," she squeaked, "in the Dream World."

"I think that oversized retard fucked up the dose on your medication." I caught the slow kid's eye and flagged him over to us. "Hey, numb nut! Get your fat ass over here and make yourself useful for once!"

He stomped across the room and dropped down on his knees in fronta Nellie with a blank stare on his retard face. "What's goin on?"

"I'll tell ya what's goin on," I growled. "The old bat woke up talkin nonsense, so either somebody laced her oatmeal with LSD or she's havin a fuckin stroke."

The retard motioned for a skinny broad over by the door to join us, then he turned to Nellie. "Okay, Nellie, we're gonna take you for a walk and have the doctor take a look at you."

"Fuck off, troll," Nellie snarled. Then she grabbed my hand. "You need to remember, Bob! When you fall asleep, find Charlie! Have him take you to the Dragon King, tell him his Princess is in danger and tell Charlie that you need his help because Godric took me!"

"Just relax, Hun." The skinny broad was all smiles as she pulled a syringe outta nowhere and jabbed it into the saggin skin on Nellie's arm.

Nellie looked up at me as she slumped sideways. "Find Charlie… You have to save me… and they need to protect the Princess…"

I felt useless and guilty watchin them wheel in a gurney and lift her lifeless little body onto it. They wheeled her out the door and I dropped my head back against the couch, concentrated on slowin my breathin and tried to convince myself I did the right thing. I'm embarrassed to admit, it didn't take me long to nod off again...

...I bolted upright and sprang to my feet a few inches from the Water's edge. The last thing I remembered was diving in the Water after Godric took Nellie and Lilly. What had I been thinking? I couldn't travel through the Waters like Nellie and Charlie. I was just a simple man with simple memories of a single world and no special abilities to speak of. I had failed the woman I'd sworn to protect, but I'd be damned if I would ever give up searching for her. If the Waters would rather spit me out than take me to them, I'd just have to find another way to reach her.

Adrenaline coursed through my veins as I marched toward the forest. My axe was just inside those trees. I would chop down enough of them to build a raft, travel the Waters and search until I found her. No... not her... *Find Charlie.* I wasn't sure how or why I knew, but I'd never been more certain of anything in my life. I needed to find Charlie. The only trouble was, I had no idea where to even begin looking for him.

Praying for a miracle, I entered the forest, grabbed my axe and swung it at the nearest tree.

2

DAVID

Rage coursed through my veins as I flew over Draumer searching my kingdom for the one creature whom I treasured above all else. Furious as I was with Godric for stealing her from me, I was equally furious with myself. This was my fault. Had I been a less selfish creature, I never would have stolen a Princess of Light on the day she was born and kept her locked away in the Darkness with me. But I was a selfish creature. Being dragon, I was not inclined to covet from afar. I was inclined to take what I wanted, quite skillfully I might add. Dragons are the most skillful predators in all of Draumer for good reason, there's no need for us to chase our prey. When you instinctively sense the innermost longings of the creature you wish to possess, it will willingly come to you once you offer what it desires most.

Emma and I spent fifteen blissful innocent years in the mirage I'd created to protect her from the Darkness that lurked beyond. I raised her like a daughter, guided her and taught her everything she needed to know about being Sighted. I fashioned her mirage after a clearing in the forest where we'd vacationed in the waking world. It was heavily warded and protected by spells that were woven with the magic of childhood innocence, a purity that no Dark beast was capable of penetrating. This was all well and good, but childhood cannot last forever and neither can the innocence that stems from it.

I kept my eyes peeled to the forest below as my mind drifted to the day that everything began to change...

...*A wide grin spread across my face as Emma stepped into the living room with her slender arms wrapped around a massive bowl of popcorn. Now that she was a mere week shy of her sixteenth birthday, opportunities for us to spend time alone together had become something of a rarity in the waking world. So, when Albert and Judy spontaneously decided to go off for a romantic weekend, I gladly offered to stay at the house with Emma in their absence. As far as her Unsighted parents knew, Emma was uncomfortable staying home alone after dark. It was a fib that had served us well as she grew older and was scarcely in need of a babysitter, considering she was old enough to be one herself. Feeling frightened on her own overnight*

ERIN A. JENSEN

was still believable enough at her age, and her parents were thrilled that I was willing to stay at her house whilst they were on holiday. Though I saw her every day in Draumer, my waking self still missed her and I struggled when there were long bouts of absence between us, as did she—especially since the parents who conceived her were usually far too busy tending to their own selfish needs to concern themselves with hers.

Emma flashed me a radiant smile as she rounded the couch and sat down beside me. "So, what's the surprise you brought me?"

I raised an eyebrow. "I've no idea what you're talking about."

She sat the popcorn bowl down on the coffee table and grinned at me as she sank against the couch cushions. "Liar."

I grabbed a handful of popcorn and popped it in my mouth as I stood from the couch. Then I moved across the room to my overnight bag. "A little bird informed me that you've been dying to watch a certain horror movie that's all the rage amongst your classmates."

She rolled her eyes as I pulled the DVD from my bag. "Yeah, but mom says I'm not old enough to watch it."

"But your father disagrees." I flashed her a devious grin as I walked to the DVD player and inserted the film in question. "Who do you think told me about it?"

She narrowed her eyes at me as I sat down beside her on the couch. "He never goes against her."

I picked up the remote and turned on the television. "I suppose that's why he told me rather than supplying you with the offensive material himself, plausible deniability." Her hushed giggle was music to my ears. Nothing pleased me more than providing whatever it was that my Princess desired. Smiling to myself I added, "And in all fairness, I believe I ought to have equal say in what you are and aren't allowed to do. It seems only fair considering I'm every bit as much your guardian as they are."

"True," she murmured as her attention drifted to the screen. As the opening credits rolled to an eerily discordant tune, she glanced back at me. "Thanks."

I wrapped an arm around her and planted a kiss atop her head. "Anything for you, my dear." A pang of sorrow gripped me when she dropped her head to my shoulder and snuggled closer as her eyes returned to the screen. Each precious moment with her was bittersweet these days. Benjamin was constantly reminding me that our time together was drawing to an end, and I couldn't deny it much longer. My sweet child was blossoming into a lovely young woman, a fact that simultaneously filled me with parental pride and broke my heart. Childhood innocence was crucial to the spells that protected her dwelling place in Draumer. Once she shed that innocence and entered adulthood, the walls that shielded her from the Darkness beyond would falter and fail and my sweet little bird would have no choice but to leave the nest and head to the Light Forest. I wasn't worried for her. The Light creatures would welcome my Princess with open arms, but I would ache from the loss till my dying breath. It was my own fault for stealing an infant fairy from the Light in the first place but if I had it to do over a thousand times, I'd do it again every time.

The first horror scene snapped my attention from my melancholy musings back to the moment at hand. I felt the racing of Emma's heart and the shallowness of her respirations. Her fear instinctively lit a fire inside me, despite the fact that a harmless form of entertainment was the only cause. I grabbed the remote and paused the movie. "Would you like to stop watching it?"

Emma tilted her head to look up at me without lifting her head off my shoulder. "No."

I nodded and resumed the movie but a few moments later, her hand reflexively clutched my arm as she buried her face against my chest. "Don't stop it," she whispered. "Just tell me what's happening. Then I can still say I watched it, right?"

I touched my chin to the top of her head. "Your secret is safe with me."

I proceeded to narrate the more frightening parts of the film and she listened attentively, but her grip on my arm never loosened. Whenever a gruesome scene concluded and I confirmed that it was safe to look, she'd turn her head and watch until the next horrific scene began.

"You can look now," I whispered for the umpteenth time as a violent scene gave way to a quiet one where a young couple awaited their inevitably gruesome fate in a vacant barn.

I focused more on her than the screen, only half listening to their painfully predictable discussion about how terrified they both were and how much they regretted all the things they would probably never live to do.

"I don't want to die a virgin," the actress whispered.

"Me neither," her male counterpart rasped. It wasn't difficult to surmise where this scene was headed and I couldn't help but feel slightly awkward viewing this with my child tucked beside me. However, fast forwarding the scene would only amplify the awkwardness so I resigned myself to patiently awaiting the predictable conclusion.

"You know," the doe-eyed actress whispered, "we don't have to die virgins."

I raised an eyebrow in silent distaste as the second rate actors fell into a passionate embrace. That's when my Princess's proximity to adulthood barreled into me with all the subtlety of a freight train. The unmistakable scent of female arousal bled through the air as her grip on my arm twitched so slightly that anyone else would've missed it. Her respirations grew shallow as her heart beat quickened and blood rushed to the parts of her innocent young body that were aching to be touched. Tears blurred my vision the instant the sensations hit me. This was it, the beginning of the end for us. It was time to let her go.

It only took seconds for my dragon instincts to trample my parental grief. A primal desperation to satisfy the needs of my most precious treasure was genetically hardwired into me. Those needs were no longer the needs of a child, but my feral urge to please her was unconcerned with the trivial fact that I had raised her as my daughter. The wrongness of it tore at my heart, but the rest of me didn't care. She was in need, and I was more than capable of satisfying those needs.

Eyes glued to the screen, I fought against every innate inclination howling inside me. I had to distance myself from her body. The need to do unforgivable things to her was unbearable and if I gave in to it, I would be no better than the monster who sired her, but I didn't trust myself to move. My body was far too inclined to betray the intentions of my heart. I was libel to pounce on her the instant I permitted my muscles to work. So, I sat there with the pounding of my heart echoing in my head and the overwhelming need to act coursing through my veins, and I didn't move a muscle till the closing credits rolled and her desires had long since faded. As she hopped off the couch, I cleared my throat and fought the desperate need to take her and make her mine in every possible way.

She tugged a hand through her tousled hair and smiled at me, such an innocent gesture. Yet, all I could focus on was the perfection of each sweet curve of her body and the fullness of her lips. "I'll be back in a minute. I'm going to brush my teeth and grab a blanket from my room."

It took too long for her words to register over the echo of my pounding heart. When they did, panic gripped me. Why hadn't I listened to Benjamin? This was inevitable. A part of me had always known that but I'd suppressed it and denied it, refusing to recognize the woman she was becoming because I couldn't bear the thought of losing the child she had always been. My child. My world. My dearest treasure. She was everything to me and I would cherish her until my dying day, but I'd endangered her by letting it come to this. I should have distanced myself when Benjamin first suggested it, but I couldn't let her go. Now she was no longer safe from the demons in the Darkness, no longer safe from me. I closed my eyes and focused on keeping my voice steady. "You should sleep in your room tonight." Dear God, how was I going to stop myself from going in there?

Uncertainty danced in her gorgeous green eyes. "Why?"

"I'm afraid," I cleared my throat, searching for innocent words to conclude my sentence, "I'm afraid I've got quite a bit of work to finish. I won't be drifting off to sleep anytime soon."

She smiled, but I felt the hurt she was concealing. "I won't bother you. I'll just fall asleep on the couch."

"You aren't a little girl anymore, Emma," I whispered hoarsely. My control was failing. I had to get her away from me. "You need to go to your room."

Tears glistened in her eyes as she whispered, "I can't be alone after watching that movie. My imagination will be playing tricks on me all night."

She took a step toward me and my body shook with need. "Go to your room!" I growled. "Lock the door and don't come out till morning!"

"What?"

Flames flared in my eyes as I leapt off the couch, struggling to suppress the urge to throw her down and pin her beneath me. As if all of this wasn't despicable enough, dragons were by no means gentle lovers. We were predators who took what we wanted, claiming and devouring until every unholy urge inside us was thoroughly satisfied. "Go!" I snarled as my feet stepped toward her without me consciously willing them to do so. Necessary as my bluntness was, the fear in her eyes struck me like an arrow to the heart as she spun around and raced toward her room.

I waited until I heard the lock slip into place, then moved to her door. The lock would scarcely block me from entering. I could rip the door from its hinges without even breaking a sweat. The lock was simply a deterrent, a reminder to the waning portion of my heart that still sensed how wrong this was.

Listening to the muffled sobs that emanated from her room was agony, but I sat down on the floor with my back against her door because I couldn't bear to leave her alone.

When the Waters finally came to carry her off to the world of dreams, I sped through them and beat her to our clearing.

3

CHARLIE

I flopped down on the ground with a bone-weary sigh, and a gust of steam spewed from my monstrous mouth. *Crap.* This dragon body was gonna take some getting used to.

Benjamin narrowed his eyes at me. "What the hell do you think you're doing?"

"Sitting," I growled, startling myself with the thunderous quality of my voice. Like I said, this would take a while to get used to. "What the hell does it *look* like I'm doing?"

"Listen, smartass," an icy tone crept into Benjamin's deep Dark voice as he stepped toward me, "just because you've finally figured out how to bring out the dragon in you, it does not mean you can talk to me like that."

"Sorry," I muttered. Even my apologetic mutter sounded menacing. "Guess I'm just feeling a little overwhelmed. How the hell did the Sarrum hold all this together twenty-four seven? I'm exhausted, and I've only been shouldering the weight of the mirage for a few hours."

"Don't you remember my warning the day the Sarrum slammed you against the wall and choked half the life out of you for calling him a pedophile? All the power that you witnessed back then was just a small fraction of what he's truly capable of." Benjamin sat down on the grass beside me. "You're a dragon, so you have the ability to hold the Princess's mirage together but it's gonna require your full effort. You've never even flexed your dragon muscles before today. The Dragon King was trained since birth and on top of that, he had the benefit of an extremely potent genetic makeup. He was bred to be more powerful than every other creature alive, and he absolutely is."

I let out another frustrated sigh, unintentionally blasting Benjamin in the face with a shot of steam. He glared at me but didn't comment. "So, what am I supposed to do? Stay here in dragon form until the Sarrum gets back? My body can't stay asleep in the waking world forever. At some point I'm gonna need to eat." A loud rumble echoed from my enormous gut, as if it was agreeing with me.

"Actually," Benjamin replied pensively, "that's exactly what the Dragon King is going to do. He won't wake until he brings Emma back here safe and sound."

My insides knotted as a horrifying thought occurred to me. "What about Emma? The Sarrum told Isa to go back to the waking world and keep her awake, but how long can Emma go without sleep and what's to prevent Godric from hurting her even when she's not conscious in this world?"

Benjamin closed his pitch black eyes. "Thankfully, fairies don't exist in Draumer when they're up and around in the waking world. They disappear the moment their bodies wake, so that son of a bitch won't be able to lay a finger on her as long as they keep her up."

"But how long can they keep her awake?" I muttered. "At some point her body's gonna be too exhausted to keep going."

"Then we need to get her back here before she reaches that point," Benjamin snarled as his eyes snapped open.

Not all that long ago, the Darkness's snarl would've made me piss myself, but now it didn't faze me a bit. Besides, I knew his anger wasn't really meant for me. He was just venting in my direction.

"Think again," the shadow growled.

"What?"

"*Plenty* of my fury is directed at you right now. None of this would be happening if you hadn't let

Godric trick you into trusting him and transported him into the Princess's clearing."

Damn it. He was right. *This was all my fault.* "I know," I whispered. "I don't deserve to be here. Why did you trust me to hold down the fort for the Dragon King after what I did, and why the hell did he agree to it, for that matter?"

"I trusted you because I knew you fucked up out of stupidity."

"Thanks," I muttered.

"I know you'd never intentionally allow any harm to come to the Princess. Obviously, the Sarrum knows it too or he never would've allowed you to shoulder the weight of her mirage in his absence, but a big part of his decision stemmed from the fact that *I have faith in you.* So, keep that in mind the next time you feel like pissing me off."

"I will." I looked up at the dome that concealed the mirage in the heart of the Dark Forest. The fractures were still smoldering from the fire I'd breathed to seal them back together. "And thanks for believing in me."

The Darkness gave me a swat to the back of the head. "Don't get all touchy feely on me, dragon."

I let out a thunderous chuckle, and for a moment I almost forgot about the excruciating pain screaming through every muscle in my gigantic body. "I'm not sure how long I can keep this up," I whispered.

An obscenely grating hyena-like laugh echoed through the night sky. When I looked up, the winged demon it originated from grinned at me from his perch atop the ceiling of the dome, displaying a nasty mouthful of jagged teeth. I leapt to my feet with a rage-fueled bellow. **"What the hell are you grinning at, you filthy insignificant creature?"** When the creature continued to grin, I opened my mouth and basted the ceiling of the dome beneath his feet with fresh flames. **"I will roast you alive, then rip you to shreds and eat you before your heart stops beating!"**

The hyena's demonic eyes widened as he let out a yelp and jumped back from the heat.

"Still think I'm funny, asshole?" I roared. **"Why don't I come out there and show you just how funny I am? I could use a good meal right about now! You may not be good, but you'll do."**

The demon hyena's body was trembling but he still stood his ground.

"You're really starting to piss me off!" I exhaled another fiery breath and took a flying leap toward him with a flap of my monstrous wings. Luckily he jumped out of sight before I tumbled out of the sky and landed on my massive scaly brown ass.

"Your strength should be solely focused on holding this place together," Benjamin snarled. "This task is too important to let yourself get distracted. Or is teaching that little bastard a lesson more important to you than maintaining the integrity of Emma's safe haven?"

"Of course it isn't," I muttered. *Why the hell did I even let that puny demon get to me?*

"Everything's gonna get to you," Benjamin replied in answer to my unspoken thought. "Now that you've embraced what you are, you're gonna have a hard time controlling your actions for a while. Dragons aren't known for their ability to hold back. They plunder and take and do whatever the hell they please."

"The Dragon King doesn't."

"He's had a lifetime of practice suppressing those bestial urges, and there have been instances when even his impeccable self-control crumbled. Which reminds me, you need to understand that the stronger you feel an emotion and the more you desire to do something or take something, the harder it'll be to restrain yourself. Dragons are instinctually inclined to take what they want whenever they feel the urge to do so." Benjamin smiled as my stomach rumbled again. "And right now, you're ornery because you feel the need to eat."

"And the need to take a break," I whispered. "I seriously don't know how long I can do this."

"I know," Benjamin answered with an unconcerned nod.

"So, why don't you sound worried?"

"Because," a female voice replied from behind me, "you don't have to do it alone."

I grinned and turned toward the familiar voice. "Hey, Rose."

Laughter danced in her eyes as she moved toward me. "Hey, yourself."

There was a radiant confidence about her that seemed pretty out of character. She was usually much more timid and soft spoken.

"Is that so?" she murmured, answering my thought.

"Sorry," I muttered. "There's just something really different about you tonight."

"Yes, there is," she agreed, eyes glistening with amusement. "I'm not suppressing my dragon nature either. Why should you get to have all the fun?"

I'd almost forgotten Isa's daughter Rose was a dragon, too. She'd never unmasked around me, and she always seemed so meek and uncertain.

Her gleeful laughter echoed through the clearing as she unmasked, transforming from a petite girl with chocolate brown eyes and sleek black hair cropped to frame her sweet young face to a gorgeous beast with violet flames dancing in her monstrous eyes, luminous gray scales and silvery wings that shimmered with just a hint of iridescent purple. *She was magnificent.*

I took a step closer to her and the mingled scents of honey, sugar cookies and freshly mowed grass started leaking from my pores. *What the hell?*

A smack upside the head knocked me back to my senses...sort of. Everything went dark as Benjamin's voice thundered inside my head. *Just focus on shouldering the weight of this mirage, dragon! And keep it in your fucking pants!*

I'm not wearing any pants! Man, I was hopeless. Why was *that* the first thought I'd ever successfully managed to direct toward a single individual? Couldn't I have thundered something cooler back at him?

Don't fuck with me, dragon! You may think you're stronger than I am and in some aspects that may well be, but you won't be any good to anyone if I don't restore your senses.

Fear flooded through me before I could answer, overpowering everything else until there was nothing else. The last conscious thought I managed to think was, what an asshole Benjamin was for making me piss myself in front of the female I wanted to claim.

4

EMMA

No one would give me an honest answer about what was going on. Isa and Dr. Price said I had to stay awake till the excessive dose of medication that the doctor accidentally gave me wore off, but he hadn't given me any medication. He could claim that I couldn't remember because short-term memory loss was a symptom of the overdose all he wanted. I knew it was a lie. I wasn't a mind reader, but there were times when I swore I could hear what they were all thinking. It was possible that I was just a crazy person because more often than not, the things I heard them thinking didn't make a lick of sense. The fact that I'd recently spent time in a mental facility—and was currently under house arrest because of the temporary insanity verdict I received for stabbing my housekeeper—was fair proof that I might be a lunatic, but there was more to it than that. The housekeeper who I'd stabbed was still watching out for me. Isa came back to us shortly after waking from the coma that I put her in. If I was crazy enough to nearly kill her, why would she come back to work for us?

Tristan kissed the top of my head and flashed me a dazzling grin when I looked up at him. "Movie time," he announced in a silky whisper.

I didn't want to watch the horror film Isa had dug out of the bureau in my bedroom. I hated horror movies—especially this one—but they all insisted that it would be an excellent distraction to help keep me awake.

Tristan draped his arm across my shoulders as the movie started, and I dropped my head to his shoulder with a resolute sigh as I tightened my grip on the cup of coffee the doctor had given me to help me stay awake. As the opening credits drifted across the screen to an unnervingly eerie tune, an unsettling bought of déjà vu struck me and a blinding burst of pain exploded in my head. I squeezed my eyes shut as the cup slipped from my hand, but I didn't feel hot liquid spill on me or hear the porcelain shatter. Someone must've caught the cup. I was about to thank them when everything slipped out of focus as the music took me back to the night David and I watched the movie together...

...I'd been dying to watch the horror movie for weeks. Everybody else in my class had seen it, but my

mom still insisted that I wasn't old enough to watch that sort of film. The fact that my sixteenth birthday was only a week away wasn't good enough for her, but she wasn't home. She and my father had gone away for a spur of the moment romantic weekend. Thanks to David's brilliant plan—that I pretend to be afraid to stay home alone overnight—we had a chance to enjoy some time together in the waking world. It didn't matter that I saw him every day in Draumer. My waking self still missed him. He was the only parent who put me above everything else. My mother and father had always chosen to give all their love to each other, but David had always chosen me and I loved him more than anything.

Watching the movie didn't turn out to be as fun as I expected. I couldn't handle the scary parts because my imagination was too overactive. David didn't tease me about it though, he just talked me through the scary scenes while I clutched his arm for dear life and buried my face against his shirt. There's no way I would've finished the whole movie if he wasn't sleeping over. Knowing that I could look over at any point during the night and see the most powerful Dark creature in existence beside me was the only thing that made the fear bearable. Of course, you might argue that I could always do that—his blood was inked into my scalp when I was a child, so I could call his enchantment forth whenever I wanted to—but that wouldn't be enough tonight. *I needed the real thing beside me after a movie like that, not an enchantment but living, fire-breathing flesh and blood.*

I wouldn't admit it out loud, but I was glad when the movie finally ended. It took me a few seconds to steel the courage to get up to brush my teeth and grab a blanket from my room, but I wasn't pathetic enough to ask him to come with me. Although, the thought did cross my mind. What happened next is too painful to recount in detail. Long story short, David said he had work to do and told me to go sleep in my room. When I promised to settle quietly onto the couch near him, he growled at me and said I wasn't a little girl anymore. Then he leapt off the couch as he hollered at me to go to my room and lock the door. There were flames in his eyes as he snarled at me. I'd never seen him so furious before, and certainly never at me.

Terrified that he might actually hurt me, I raced to my room and locked the door like he told me to. Then I sunk to the floor in tears. After crying for God knows how long, I drifted off to sleep curled up in a ball on the floor and woke in the middle of our clearing.

Rain was pouring down and the night sky was filled with almost constant flashes of lightning and claps of thunder that shook the ground beneath me. It never stormed in our clearing. Storms weren't a natural phenomenon in Draumer. They were the byproduct of a dragon's emotions. David was so angry that he felt the need to vent

ERIN A. JENSEN

his fury into the atmosphere. I stood up and hesitantly started toward the cave, but I didn't get far. An invisible barrier blocked me from getting near the cave. But why? What did I do?

"Go to the cottage, Princess!" his voice thundered in my head.

The cottage at the far end of the clearing was a replica of the one we stayed at on vacation when I was a little girl, but we didn't live in it. I went there to work on my paintings or read when the Sarrum was attending to kingdom business. My room was in the palace and the palace could only be accessed through the cave. Why on earth would he ban me from it? What was he punishing me for?

You're not a little girl anymore, Emma. That's what he said when he told me to go to my room. Why would that make him so angry? That's when it hit me. I was the child he'd always wanted, but I was growing up. Did he have no need for me now that I was too old to be his precious little girl? The thought turned my stomach and made me feel like a pathetic idiot. The Dragon King didn't treasure me. He treasured the little girl he'd played daddy with and now that I was growing up, he had no use for me. That couldn't possibly be true…could it?

I pressed my body against the invisible barrier as I stared at the dark entrance to the cave. He was in there watching me. I could feel it. "Please come out!" I hollered into the night. "I'm afraid!"

The only answer was the clamor of the storm that raged above me as I stood there achingly and utterly alone...

..."Emma," the doctor's voice took a minute to register.

Eerie laughter echoed from the television as if that stupid movie was mocking me. A chill crept down my spine as I opened my eyes and watched the room gradually come back into focus. As soon as I could see straight, I grabbed the remote and turned off the television. "I don't want to watch any more of this."

Seated on Tristan's other side, Brian leaned forward to get a better look at me as he murmured, "Emma."

"No!" My heart was racing. I couldn't catch my breath. They were all staring at me, and it was starting to piss me off. "Leave me alone," I muttered as I jumped off the couch a little faster than I probably should have.

The doctor stood from his chair and touched my arm. "Relax, my dear. The medication is affecting your mood, that's all. You need to give it time to dissipate."

I pushed his hand off and started toward the door. "I just want you all to leave me alone."

"Trust us, Emma." Tristan stepped up beside me and put a hand on my shoulder, stilling me somehow. "We're here to help."

I wanted to argue, but another burst of pain throbbed inside my head with an intensity that threw me off balance and would've knocked me to the floor, if Tristan hadn't caught me the instant I faltered. "What's happening to me?" I whimpered as he lowered me in his arms.

The doctor crossed the room and knelt down beside us. "You're starting to remember, Princess."

5

DAVID

It didn't take long to reach the Dragon's Lair at my rage-fueled pace. Thanks to Tristan's tireless intelligence gathering efforts, I knew Godric's supporters often frequented the tavern that was situated on the border between the Dark Forest and the Forest of Light. Fortunately, the Purists were not all rocket scientists. It wasn't difficult for an incubus like Tristan to garner information from them once they were sufficiently intoxicated. Quite frankly, extracting secrets from them whilst they were stone cold sober would be child's play for Tristan, but it eased their shoddy consciences to have a substance to blame for their disloyalty in the morning.

Since Godric's trail had gone cold during the moments I wasted chastising Charlie for his idiocy, my next best option was to interrogate supporters of the would-be king. I landed on the ground with a thunderous impact that sunk the earth beneath my clawed limbs several feet. It was an unnecessary entrance—as I was more than capable of landing without so much as a snapped twig to show for it—but I had neither the time nor the inclination to arrive at the border stealthily. Rage crackled through every fiber of my being and I planned to make that abundantly clear to anyone who had the misfortune of crossing my path. I announced my presence with a thunderous bellow, then scorched the sky with a fiery exhalation. The flames immediately coalesced into massive rage-filled clouds, smothering the moon and stars and blanketing the heavens with my fury. I let out another bellow as lightning lit the darkness and a monstrous clap of thunder shook the Dragon's Lair at its foundation. A chorus of startled gasps and screams confirmed that my arrival had been duly noted by every creature within the establishment. Satisfied with their response, I unmasked, moved toward the tavern and ripped the door open.

I stepped inside, and every eye turned to me as a collective hush settled over the room. **"Where is the owner of this establishment?"** I roared both aloud and inside the heads of everyone present.

Muffled whimpers and the scent of fresh urine were the only responses to my question.

Every second these inebriated miscreants wasted with their silence further fueled my rage. Each squandered breath marked one less second I would have to reach Godric before my Princess succumbed to exhaustion and fell into his clutches. I fed my fury into the storm that raged outside the tavern walls. A deafening clap of thunder shook the floor beneath our feet, the lights flickered and the high-pitched squeals of gin-soaked fairies echoed through the room.

The terrified patrons parted and knelt as I made my way toward the bar at the other end of the room. I stopped a few paces short of the bar where a fairy barmaid cowered behind two bartenders—a male shadow with a pasty complexion, greasy hair and Dark emotionless eyes and a female sorrow with a drool-soaked apron and a belly that bulged with the miseries of her drunken patrons.

I locked eyes with the pale fellow. **"Step out here and face me, shadow."**

His heart hammered in his chest as he stepped out from behind the bar and stopped several paces shy of meeting me face to face.

"Are you the owner of this establishment?" I knew full well that he was because of Tristan, but I didn't intend to inform him of that.

The shadow swallowed and took a trembling breath. "No, Sarrum."

I took the remaining steps to close the gap between us, and he cringed as I opened my mouth to speak. **"Would you care to rethink your answer, Galen?"**

The shadow winced at the sound of his name. "Yes, my King, I am the owner."

Another crack of thunder shook the floor so hard that several of the patrons' drinks toppled from their hands. **"You waste precious time with your lies, shadow. If you have half a brain in that greasy head of yours, you will answer truthfully the first time I ask a question. Are we clear?"**

The shadow nodded without uttering a syllable.

"Now, I want you to give me the names of the Purists who frequent this establishment and point out the ones who are present this evening."

Behind me, several creatures bolted for the door. I mentally extended, slammed it shut and held it firmly in place, ignoring the shrieks from the troll who was unfortunate enough to have his hand in the doorway when I slammed it. Galen's eyes drifted in their direction, and I stepped a bit closer to regain his attention.

His Dark eyes widened as they locked with mine. "I swear, I don't know who the Purists are—"

I gestured toward the bar with a slight flick of my wrist and four shelves' worth of decorative glass bottles exploded, filling the room with the echoes of shattering glass and startled screams. I narrowed my eyes at the shadow whose trousers were now soiled with a mix of liquor and piss. **"I'm sorry. Did I disrupt your train of thought? I believe you were in the midst of signing your own death sentence."**

Tears dripped from the shadow's pitch black eyes as he cowered before me.

Each tear that this pathetic creature shed marked another wasted second. I wrapped my fingers around his neck and lifted him off the floor by his throat. **"I'm done with you."** Pressed for time as I was, I had no intention of giving any creature multiple chances to cooperate. I tightened my grip till his wheezing stopped and blood gushed from his mouth and nose. Then I tossed him aside and sent him crashing headfirst into a table surrounded by red-faced dwarves. As the resulting gasps and screams subsided, I turned toward the door and a fresh rush of piss soured the air. The creatures I'd barred from exiting bolted to blend into the crowd as I stepped toward them, deserting the troll who was still frantically working to free his crushed hand. I allowed them to scurry just far enough to assume they were safe, then I snapped my fingers and drew them all back to the door. All but the hysterical troll dropped to their knees as I approached.

"As you may have noticed, I am not feeling particularly patient this evening. My Princess was taken from me less than an hour ago, and I intend to burn as many souls as I have to in order to determine Godric's whereabouts. So, it's entirely up to you. Tell me what I want to know or burn."

6

BOB

The more I thought about it, the sicker it made me. Nellie'd gone downhill fast. One day she just fell asleep on my shoulder her loony old self, and she woke up an empty shell of a woman. They'd been druggin the shit outta her since then cause she kept gettin all agitated and ramblin about some fuckin princess and some asshole who she kept insistin had kidnapped her. Whenever they brought her out to spend time with the rest of us she'd start beggin me to find Charlie, the kid who'd gone home weeks ago. She couldn't seem to sort out her dreams from real life. She was convinced that I could just hop in her dreams, save her, find the kid and rescue this imaginary princess she wouldn't stop goin on about. I tried to calm her down the best I could so they'd stop pumpin her fulla drugs, but she just wouldn't let it go.

My heart sunk a little as I watched them wheel her into the room cause I knew it wouldn't be long before they were stickin her with a needle to numb the crazy outta her again. She shot me a phony smile as the retard parked her wheelchair nexta my couch. It'd been days since she'd come into a room on her own two feet, her cheeks had gotten hollow since she kept refusin to eat and her milky old eyes were even duller than they were before she started all this nonsense.

I knew it wasn't my fault, but that didn't stop me from blamin myself for bringin the numb nuts in white into it. I shoulda just kept her quiet and calmed her down on my own. Maybe it wouldn'ta gone this far if I'd done that. The retard helped her onto the couch, and I took her hand and gave it a squeeze.

She squeezed mine back like she was holdin on for dear life. "He's killing me, Bob."

I'd give anything to go back to the days when her nonsense just irritated the shit outta me. *This* nonsense… this just broke my fuckin heart. "Who's killin ya?" I muttered as I watched the retard wheel her chair outta the room.

"Henry," she whispered, "my ex-husband. I told you all about him in the Dream World. Please remember, Bob. Please. I need you to remember. I need you to find me before my heart gives out."

"I don't have to find ya." I gave her hand another squeeze. "You're right here nexta me, sweetheart. Ain't that enough?"

"No," she squeaked. "I'm dying in the Dream World. You need to find Charlie and get help, and you have to warn the Dragon King that his Princess is in danger."

This was killin me, but arguin with her hadn't gotten us anywhere. So I decided to play along this time. "Okay, Nellie. How do I find the kid?"

Her wrinkled lips curled into the first genuine smile I'd seen her crack in days. "You'll never find him by going through the Waters. Go into the forest, tell any creature you meet that you need to get to the Dragon King and warn him that his Princess is in danger."

I let out a tired sigh. "Okay." It fuckin killed me to lie to her insteada tryin to pull her outta this, but all that'd accomplished lately was gettin her stuck with a syringe fulla tranquilizers and wheeled back to wherever the fuck they were keepin her. "I'll find the kid. I promise."

Her cloudy eyes filled up with tears. "You promise you'll go into the forest and find the King?"

I narrowed my eyes at the skinny bitch across the room who was just hoverin and waitin for Nellie to act up so she could pump her fulla chemicals. "Yeah. Sure. I'll find the King and the kid."

"You have to go into the forest," Nellie whispered as she dropped her head to my shoulder. "Promise me that's where you'll go."

"Yeah." I touched my head to hers. "I'll go in the forest and find them, soon as I start dreamin."

"Thank you." She let out a big yawn as her eyes drooped shut.

"Anything for you," I whispered. Then I closed my eyes and nodded off...

...I woke to the melodious chirps of morning birds and cringed as I opened my eyes, because I knew exactly where I'd find myself. With a frustrated sigh, I sat up and took in my painfully familiar surroundings. I was inches from the Water, fragmented remnants of my latest raft littered the ground around me, I could tell without inspecting myself that I had a fresh bunch of bruises to show for my efforts, and I was exactly where I always was—exactly where I'd started the night Godric took Nellie and Lilly. I hopped to my feet with a frustrated grunt, and kicked the battered pieces of my raft into the Water. Useless as my efforts had been thus far, I refused to give up. However, it was becoming abundantly clear that traversing the Waters by any means would get me absolutely nowhere. So, where did that leave me?

A howl echoed somewhere deep within the forest, and a twinge of remorse struck me. The solution was just beyond my reach. I could sense it on the periphery of my brain, as if I'd just dreamt it. Dreams weren't just dreams. I knew that much, thanks to Charlie and Nellie so that vague sense that I'd dreamt the answer was worse than having no answers at all. The life of the woman I loved was at stake and the answers were inside my head, somewhere just out of reach. A tear slid down my cheek as I smacked my head in frustration. That useless old man that I was in the other world, he had all the answers I needed. I hit my head a little harder. "Remember! You stupid old bastard! You're the only chance she has! Tell me how to help her—"...

... "Help her!" I shook my head and rubbed my eyes. Jesus. I woke myself up screamin like a snot-nosed kid. What the fuck was wrong with me?

Nellie lifted her head off my shoulder. "Bob?"

My head ached like a son of a bitch, and my heart was beatin too damn fast. What the hell had I been dreamin about? I flashed Nellie a smile and touched her wrinkled cheek. "Sorry I woke ya."

"Did you do it?"

"Did I do what?" I muttered, still strugglin to get my bearins and stop actin like a fuckin pansy.

She let out a squeaky little sob. "Did you go into the forest?"

I was still too disoriented to play along with her craziness. "What?"

"The forest." She leaned back and searched my eyes. "Did you enter the forest and look for somebody to help you find the King?"

"Wha…" I was about to ask her what the hell she was ramblin about, but I remembered just in time. She'd lost her marbles and I had to play along to keep her from gettin worked up. "Yeah." My heart ached a little more every time I lied to her. "Yeah… of course. I went in the forest just like you asked."

She nodded and dropped her head back to my shoulder. "Then you should get back to your nap so you can keep looking."

I rubbed a hand over my face. "Sure." At least she was stayin calm. This was the most time I'd gotten to spend with her since that first outburst of hers. So, why didn't that make me feel any less guilty about bein dishonest? And why in fuck's name did I feel like I was failin her?

7

CHARLIE

I woke to the tantalizing sound and mouth-watering smell of bacon sizzling on the stove downstairs. Practically on the verge of orgasm, I sat up and wiped a thin trickle of drool off my chin. The morning sun was just beginning to brighten the cheery guestroom on the second floor of the Talbots' palatial home.

Keen as my dragon senses were, Benjamin's presence didn't even register until his deep Dark voice startled the crap out of me. "Rise and shine, virgin."

I sat up and stretched. "Why don't you give me a break?" *Virgin* was the Sighted term for an individual who never learned the ways of the Sighted as a child, but considering the word's *Unsighted* definition, it was also a term that irritated the crap out of me. "I've tapped into my inner dragon now. Can't you drop the humiliating term of endearment and give me a nicer nickname, like ass wipe or shithead?"

There was no trace of amusement on Benjamin's stoic face as he stood from the chair across the room and approached my bedside. "How about dumb ass?"

"Better," I muttered. The sad thing was, I wasn't even joking. I'd way rather be referred to as a moron than an inexperienced lover, especially around Rose. An image of her unmasking into her gorgeous dragon form popped into my head and I instantly stiffened.

Benjamin's eyes narrowed as a muted growl reverberated in his throat.

I growled right back at him. The whole mind reading thing was really starting to piss me off. "What the hell's your problem, shadow?" *Shit. Did I really just say that out loud to the Darkness, the Sarrum's shadow and right hand man?*

"Yes," fear flooded through me as the Darkness snarled, "You did."

That was my cue to back off and apologize, but I didn't give a crap. "This is stupid! If you'd stay the hell out of my head, we wouldn't even be having this conversation! I shouldn't have to answer to you for things I didn't even say out loud! My thoughts are none of your fucking business!"

"Then don't shout them," he snarled. "Keep them to yourself or don't think them at all, dumb ass."

I let out a frustrated sigh, and a puff of smoke scorched my nasal passages as it billowed from my nostrils. "Shouldn't you be a little nicer to the dragon you're counting on to hold things together until the Sarrum gets back?"

Benjamin answered in an icy tone that was even more terrifying than his usual deep Dark voice, "Do I need to remind you *why* that's necessary, *virgin*?"

Shit. It felt like somebody had coated my lungs with gasoline and dropped a lit match down my throat. My chest was on fire. I squeezed my eyes shut and whispered, "What the hell's wrong with me?"

"Like I said in the clearing," Benjamin replied in his normal deep Dark tone, "everything is gonna get to you for a while. Dragons aren't exactly famed for their impulse control."

I opened my eyes as he sat down on the edge of the bed. "If this's normal, why are you so pissed at me?"

"Rose is my soul mate's daughter, dumb ass. She's off limits to you. No matter how weak your impulse control is, remember that. You don't want to fuck with me where my family's concerned."

I focused on suppressing the genuine hurt that I felt so it wouldn't leak into my tone as I whispered, "Am I really *that* horrible that the thought of me getting close to Rose is so unthinkable?"

"You're a dragon."

"So is the Sarrum, and you bound yourself to him for life."

"I did."

"So...help me out here," I muttered. "What am I missing? Why am I such an undesirable match for your girlfriend's daughter?"

Benjamin cleared his throat. "Most fathers worry about their daughter getting knocked up by some horny little moron because it'd fuck up her life."

"Aren't you kinda jumping the gun a little? I've never even held Rose's hand."

"And I'm not about to let it even get that far," Benjamin replied coldly. "You and Rose are both dragons."

"So?"

"So, you getting her pregnant wouldn't fuck up her life. It would end it."

I raked my fingers through my mussed-up hair. "What?" Then I remembered what Henry Godric taught me before I found out that he was a monster. *The odds of a Sighted mother surviving a dragon birth were only twenty percent.*

"Yeah," Benjamin lowered his voice as he added, "those aren't odds I'm willing to risk."

How could I argue with that? "Understood." I glanced around the room without really taking it in. "Don't I need to get back to the clearing?"

Benjamin shook his head and for a second, I could've sworn I saw regret in his eyes. "Rose's got it covered."

"Do you have any idea how heavy that burden is?" I muttered, finally realizing that I wasn't shouldering any of the weight.

The Darkness narrowed his eyes at me. "Yeah. I do. I hate to break it to you kid, but she's a lot stronger than you."

"Awesome," I whispered. "That's just awesome."

"I'm not saying you'll never match her strength, but she learned from the best of the best alongside the royal dragon children at the Talbot estate in England. So, you've got a lot of catching up to do."

There was no point in wasting time wallowing in self-pity over my lameness. "How long can she shoulder the weight of the mirage on her own?"

"Long enough for you to get some food in your belly and fill your lungs with fresh air."

"Then what?"

Benjamin let out a slow sigh. "Then we go back and wait it out until the Sarrum finds Emma and brings her home."

Distressed hollers echoed from the floor below us, and my body instinctively shifted into defense mode. *That was Emma's voice.* I leapt off the bed, bolted for the door and made it halfway down the stairs before Benjamin's calm voice brought me back to my senses.

"She was never lost to us in this world."

Right. I'd been racing toward her like I could rescue her from Godric, but he didn't have her in the waking world. He stole her from the clearing in

Draumer. She was only his prisoner in the Dream World—and only if she fell asleep—but that realization didn't stop me from rushing to her. The fact that she was shouting meant something was wrong in this world too, and I had to help her.

My heart was racing as I rushed into the living room and found her on the floor in Tristan's arms with Doc kneeling beside them. An involuntary growl rumbled in my throat at the sight of the incubus's muscular arms wrapped around *my* Emma.

The Sarrum's wife. I could tell by the expressions on their faces that Benjamin's thought was only directed at me. *She's not yours, dragon. She's HIS, and only HIS. Do not ever forget that.*

Fuck off! As I mentally hollered the thought, every male set of eyes in the room locked on me. Time seemed to slow as their accusatory stares burrowed into me. My heart was pounding, my chest was heaving and sweat was dripping from my brow.

Tears glistened in Emma's gorgeous green eyes as she looked up at me. "Charlie?"

I didn't care that the rest of them were staring at me. None of them mattered but her. I steadied my breathing as I moved to Emma, sat down on the floor and focused my thought toward Tristan. *Let her go!* The incubus glared at me. His fury did nothing to detract from his beauty, but his physical perfection didn't arouse me like it usually did. It enraged me. *Get your hands off her, Tristan!*

Tristan put a hand on my shoulder without lessening the intensity of his smoldering glare. *You should go, dragon.*

Tranquility flowed through me as his gentle touch and silky whispered thoughts warmed my insides. *No, damn it.* I was a dragon. His charm couldn't sway me unless I allowed it.

My nostrils flared as Brian and Benjamin closed in on our foursome on the floor. *Go ahead! Try and take me away from her!* "Give her some space," I growled, without taking my eyes off Emma, "and let me talk to her."

"I don't think that's a good idea," Brian murmured as he knelt down beside us. "Why don't you go get something to eat, Charlie?"

Fire roared inside my chest. *Fuck off, all of you!* I saw the fear in their eyes as the flames ignited in mine. Good. They *should* fear me. I was a fucking dragon, and I wasn't about to take orders from any of them.

But you WILL take them from me! Benjamin's voice thundered in my head, filling me with dread and a desperate desire to flee.

The flames in my eyes intensified, and the three men on the floor scooted back to give me some space. Let them scurry off in fear. I was taking Emma. One of them had spooked her, and I wasn't about to let it happen again. Tristan slid back a little farther as I reached out to take Emma in my arms.

That's when the Sarrum's dragon enchantment appeared out of nowhere and towered above me. Before I could consciously choose to back off, he opened his monstrous mouth and let out a deafening bellow. Then he exhaled and bathed my arms in blue flames.

I fell back with an agonized whimper as the world went dark.

8

EMMA

I was still trying to get my bearings and bring the world back into focus when Charlie came storming into the living room. His clothes were wrinkled. His hair was a tousled mess, and his widened eyes blazed with a disoriented rage that suggested he'd rushed out of bed in the throes of a nightmare. It didn't make sense. What logical reason could there possibly be for Charlie to be in my house at the crack of dawn? Nothing that was happening lately made any sense.

No one spoke. They all just glared at each other, though an entire conversation appeared to be wordlessly taking place among them. Charlie stood motionless, glaring at everyone but me. All of them glared back at him. I couldn't help wondering if I was actually the one in the midst of a nightmare. "Charlie?"

Charlie squared his shoulders as he crossed the room. Then he sat down beside me and glared at Tristan. Tristan glared right back at Charlie as he touched a hand to his shoulder. For a moment, Charlie seemed to calm but the fury in his eyes reignited the second Brian and Benji moved toward us. "Give her some space," Charlie growled as his eyes fixed on me, "and let me talk to her."

"I don't think that's a good idea." Brian cautiously knelt beside us as if Charlie was a bomb that might detonate at any second. "Why don't you go get something to eat, Charlie?"

Rage flared in Charlie's eyes and they all backed away, *which made no sense.* These weren't timid men. They didn't back away from anything, except maybe my husband on the rare occasion when he was in an exceptionally foul mood.

Charlie slid closer to me as Tristan backed away, but something about this just didn't feel right and I couldn't stop myself from cringing when he reached for me. The second I recoiled, Charlie let out a whimper and crumpled to the floor.

Without uttering so much as a syllable, Brian and Benji picked Charlie up and carried him out of the room. *What the hell is going on?* That was my last conscious thought as Tristan and Doc stepped toward me, but my mind slipped back to the past before either of them reached me...

...I woke in the morning, curled up on the floor of my bedroom beside the door. I sat up and combed my fingers through the disheveled locks of my hair. David left me out there alone in the rain all night. *At the drop of a hat, I'd gone from being the creature David loved more than anything to someone who wasn't even worth sheltering from the storm. My stomach lurched at the thought and I sprang to my feet and rushed to my bathroom, barely making it in time to vomit up the popcorn I'd eaten just hours ago—when everything was still right with the world. Now everything was all wrong. I needed David. He was the only person in my life who loved me more than anything else. A throb of pain blossomed in my chest as I realized how untrue that was. I'd obviously been nothing but a temporary diversion for the Dragon King—someone for him to play daddy with for a few years—but now, what did he need with a stupid teenager who'd grown too old to play the part of his precious little girl? I felt like such a pathetic idiot. The change in the way he looked at me had come on so suddenly without any warning. What'd caused it? The movie? Did the realization that I was old enough to watch those films strike him at some point while we watched it? Or was it the babyish way I'd acted, unable to handle the scary parts? Was he disgusted by my childishness now that I was no longer a child? Whatever the reason, I just wanted to shrink until I disappeared.*

The dull clinking of metal against metal sounded down the hall as David moved around the kitchen collecting pots and pans from the cupboards. How could I face him after what'd happened? **I considered hiding in my room till my parents came home and David was gone, but I knew him well enough to know he wouldn't leave things like this...at least, I thought I did. Maybe I'd never truly known him at all.**

My humiliation still bore the sting of a fresh wound and the vision of those flames in his eyes would be forever seared into my brain and yet, as soon as I finished brushing my teeth and combing my hair, I opened the door to my room because some pathetic part of me was still desperate to see his face and hear his voice. *Maybe it was all just a big misunderstanding.* **As much as I wanted that to be true, I knew in my heart that it wasn't. Still, I walked to the kitchen as though some invisible force was drawing me to him.**

He stood at the counter with his back to me as I walked in the kitchen. I regretted leaving my room the instant he turned around and smiled at me. "Good morning."

What was good about it? **The center of my universe had shunned me. Now he was greeting me as if nothing had changed. I choked back a surge of queasiness as I headed for the coffeepot and concentrated on keeping my hands steady as I poured myself a cup. "I've got a paper to write today and I know you've got a lot to do, so don't let me keep you. Mom and Dad will be home soon," my throat constricted around the next words and I had to force them out in a hoarse whisper,** *"and I'm not a little girl anymore."* I dropped my gaze to the floor and focused on the tiles as I moved past his feet. My eyes were swimming with tears by the time I reached the door. Stepping through that doorway seemed so final, like I'd be walking away from him forever.

"Emma," he murmured behind me, "we need to talk.

"There's nothing to talk about." I stepped out the door, loathing myself for the pathetic way my voice trembled. "Please go home." It only took a few steps to realize I'd left my coffee on the counter, but there was no way I was going back into that kitchen.

"Come back and talk to me, Princess."

Princess. I stilled for a moment, paralyzed by the ache in my heart that the term of endearment prompted. When I heard him step into the hall behind me, I shook myself out of immobility and hurried toward my room.

"Get back here." A day ago, I'd have bet my life that he'd never speak to me in such a harsh tone.

Tears stung my eyes as I whispered, "Please go."

A wave of molten fury washed over me as he growled, "Benjamin was right. I've allowed you to get away with far too much. When your King commands you to do something, YOU DO IT."

The rage in his voice sent my pulse racing, but I couldn't bring myself to turn around. What good would drawing this out do? Tears spilled down my cheeks as I clutched my doorknob with a trembling hand and opened my bedroom door.

An instant later, David was behind me. He braced one broad palm against the door on either side of me and slammed it shut.

"Please." My breath hitched as I tightened my grip on the doorknob. "I feel pathetic enough as it is. Please don't humiliate me anymore."

He drew a deep breath and for a second, I thought he was going to back away but his hands stayed firmly planted against the door on either side of me, caging me where I stood. His mouth moved closer to my ear as he whispered, "Why on earth do you feel pathetic?"

"Please." My stomach churned and I squeezed my eyes shut and touched my forehead to the door, terrified that I might puke on my own feet and make an even bigger fool of myself. "Just let me go. Don't make this hurt more than it already does."

"Turn around."

I shook my head but didn't say a word.

"It's not a request." There was an odd strain to his voice as he added, "It's a command from your King. Turn around."

Afraid to disobey after his unprecedented display of fury the night before, I turned around without opening my eyes.

"Look at me."

I reluctantly opened my eyes and fixed them on the buttons of his crisp blue shirt.

He repeated the command in a deeper voice, "Look at me."

I tilted my head back, and my breath escaped me in an anxious rush as his eyes met mine. Brilliant blue flames blazed in those eyes but it wasn't fury fueling the fire. It was something Dark and entirely foreign to me.

The muscles in his jaw tensed as he repeated his question in a more insistent tone, "Why do you feel pathetic?"

"Because I was stupid enough to believe you'd always love me," I whispered, the ache in my heart throbbing as each word left my lips.

He exhaled an unsteady breath and touched his forehead to mine. "And what makes you think that I don't?"

"You yelled at me and made me lock myself in my room," I muttered in a small uncertain voice, "then you blocked me from the cave and left me out in the storm all night."

Wisps of blue smoke wafted from his flared nostrils and swirled through the air around us. "That was to protect you."

Smoke no longer seeped from his nostrils but the heady scent lingered, clouding my mind and making it nearly impossible to focus. "I don't understand."

"I know."

"You're the strongest creature in existence. You could protect me from anything."

"Yes, but who'd protect you from me?"

The only response my addled mind could manage was a perplexed frown.

"Think back to your lessons, Princess." A tear slid down my cheek. He brushed it away with his fingertips

and his scent intensified till it was so potent I could practically taste it. For a moment, there was nothing but our measured breaths to mark the silence. "Why are dragons the most skillful predators in all of Draumer?"

What was he talking about? What did that have to do with anything? Irrelevant as his question seemed, I answered, "They don't have to chase their prey."

"And why is that?"

"Dragons sense the desires of their prey," I muttered, mesmerized by the flames dancing in his eyes. "They lure their prey by offering whatever the creature most desires."

"And does prey always equate with victim?"

"No," I answered in a breathless whisper.

"The more we dragons treasure a creature, the greater our need to satisfy that creature's desires. However, we do not simply sense those desires. We feel every sensation that accompanies them and our urge to satisfy those longings becomes just as desperate as our prey's desire, sometimes more so."

"What does that have to do with anything?"

"You are what I treasure above all else, Princess."

I didn't know what he was getting at or how to respond, so I just watched him and focused on remembering to breathe.

He lifted his head from mine without breaking eye contact. "When you were a child, it was simple. What you needed more than anything was a parent who placed you above everything else. Filling that role was the most natural thing in the world for me because I wanted nothing more than to dote on you and shower you with love."

The ache in my chest throbbed as I lowered my eyes to the buttons on his shirt. "*But I ruined it by growing up.*"

"*No, my dear.*" *He let out a slow exhalation and I breathed deep, drinking in his scent.* "*You've ruined nothing. I'm the one to blame. Think back to the movie last night. How did you feel while you watched it?*"

"*Terrified.*"

"*Yes, but what else?*"

I took a trembling breath and shrugged.

"*Think back to the scene in the barn,*" *he commanded in a thicker voice.*

An image of the actor and actress's sweaty bodies tangled in the hay flashed through my mind and a twinge of excitement flared inside me.

"*Yes, that's the scene.*"

I trudged through the mental fog, retracing the steps of our conversation in a sorry attempt to piece together what he was trying to tell me. He could feel what I felt watching that scene. Did that make him uncomfortable?

"*No.*"

What then? I tried to think back through everything he'd said. He felt a desperate need to satisfy my desires. What could that possibly mean in this instance? My cheeks flamed as I muttered, "*Do you…feel the need to find me a boyfriend?*"

"*My sweet innocent girl.*" *He reached up and swept a stray tendril of hair off my cheek with a tenderness* that brought fresh tears to my eyes. "When you needed a loving parent, did I go out and find another man to be a proper father to you?"

He stroked the backs of his fingers over the cheek he'd exposed, setting fire to the blood that rushed through my veins. He couldn't possibly be saying what I thought he was...could he? I tilted my head back to search his face for answers. Something carnal flashed in his beautiful blue eyes as they locked with mine, and my breath caught in my throat.

"Ah. There it is," he whispered, "Comprehension." He cocked his head to one side and studied me through narrowed eyes. "But no fear, nor disgust."

A rush of heat pooled in my belly as I stood there under the scrutiny of those fiery eyes.

"No," he whispered, "quite the opposite."

I opened my mouth to respond, but nothing came out. I'm not even sure what I meant to say.

"I feel it, Emma," there was a hoarse rasp to his voice that I felt deep inside me. "I don't simply sense your desires. I feel the racing of your heart, the change in your breathing, the way you attempt to steady it and the rush of blood that heats the parts of your body that are aching to be touched."

Consumed as I was by the fire his words ignited inside me, it was a wonder my legs didn't buckle. But it made no sense. He couldn't possibly want me in that way.

"Yes," he growled in a primal tone that summoned a gush of heat between my legs. "That's exactly what

I want." He touched his head to mine again, and I ached to feel more of his flesh against mine. A sigh of frustration escaped his perfect lips. "Had you been frightened or repulsed by my words, we might've continued as we were a bit longer. My urges would've been tempered by the knowledge that this wasn't a desire I could satisfy. However, we both know that isn't the case." His thready exhalation washed over me, heating me to my core.

I reached up and gripped his arms without consciously intending to. Empowered by my own boldness, I whispered, "If it's something we both want, what's the problem?"

"You're an innocent young girl who has never been touched."

"So," I murmured, "touch me."

It was the first time I'd ever seen David look shocked. "I raised you as my daughter, Emma."

I gripped his arms a little tighter and thrilled at the feel of his muscles tensing beneath my hands. "But you aren't my father."

"No," he rasped, "I'm his best friend and I'm old enough to have fathered you."

"I don't care," I whispered. "No one has ever loved me as much you do, and no one else ever will. You're the only one I want to touch me."

"For now," he murmured, leaning closer despite his words, "but you're too young to make a commitment of that magnitude."

"If I'm old enough to feel this way, shouldn't I be old enough to act on it?"

"I'm talking about more than your virginity, Princess."

My entire body flushed at his unabashed statement. "What do you mean?"

He shifted, narrowing the gap between us even more and another pulse of heat gushed between my legs. The fire in his eyes blazed brighter as he answered in a voice more feral than human, "Do you honestly believe I could ever let you go once I had a taste of you?"

A taste of me? His scent washed over me, melting my insides as I answered in a trembling whisper, "Why would I ever want to go?"

A thrill coursed through me when his powerful body trembled at my words. "Dragons are not gentle lovers, Princess. Dragons are predatory creatures. We are possessive, our appetites are ravenous and our desires are often quite Dark. You have no idea what you're asking for."

Embarrassed by the throbbing need that his words ignited inside me, I whispered, "That doesn't sound like you."

"I am a gentle guardian and a gentle teacher," he murmured, shifting so close that there was barely any gap left between us, "but I am by no means a gentle lover. You've no idea what I would take from you, the things I would do to you. You couldn't begin to fathom how Dark my needs are—"

"I don't care," I whimpered, terrified that he was about to pull away. "Whatever you want, take it from me. Whatever you need to do, do it to me. I'll be anything you want me to be."

"My sweet girl, I'd never ask you to be anything but yourself." He leaned back, widening the gap between us. "You are perfect just as you are, and I have no desire to take your innocence."

I clung to his arms for dear life. "We both know that isn't true."

He straightened so our heads no longer touched and planted a soft kiss on my forehead. His mouth lingered a moment, unwilling to break the contact between his lips and my flesh. "You were right," he whispered hoarsely as he backed away, "I should go."

Too confused and disoriented to move, I just stood there with my heart fracturing as he gathered up his things and left. The moment the front door closed, I raced to the window and watched him walk to his car. He hesitated as he reached for the door handle but he never looked back. He just shook his head, got in his car and drove away.

I couldn't tell you how long I stood there staring out the window, but it was long after his car had driven out of sight. When I finally stepped away, my eyes were drawn to a shirt he'd left draped over a chair in the living room. I moved to it and picked it up. Lifting it to my face, I breathed in his scent as I walked to my room. Then I shut the door, locked myself inside *and tossed the shirt to my bed. Hoping a cold show-er would snap me to my senses, I stripped out of my pajamas and took a few steps toward the bathroom. When I caught sight of myself in the mirror, naked and flushed, I stopped dead in my tracks and tried to look at my body through his eyes. I smoothed my hands over my skin, noting its softness like I was feeling it for the first time. I touched the places where I wanted him to touch me, and my eyes drifted to his shirt on my bed. I moved toward it, trembling as if it was him I was approaching. Then I picked it up and slipped it on, heating at the feel of it against my skin as his scent enveloped me.*

I'd die if he didn't touch me—maybe not right away, but eventually I'd die if he didn't touch me the way I need-ed to be touched. He'd woken something inside me and there was no undoing it. No one would ever love me the way he did, and there were no other hands I could ever imagine taking the place of mine...

...Emma. Wake up. Faint voices echoed in the distance, calling me. *Emma, come back to us...*

...They slipped away as an elegant voice mur-mured, "Ah, there you are."

Something wasn't right. My eyelids felt too heavy. I struggled desperately to lift them, to lift any part of my body. *What's wrong with me?*

"Give it time," the male voice replied in a lovely British accent—an accent I associated with David and Charlie, with safety and comfort.

With a great deal of effort, I managed to lift my eyelids and a hazy room coalesced around me with all the opulent furnishings of a Victorian noble-man's parlor. Disoriented dread flooded my veins as I took in the foreign surroundings that made me feel as if I'd slipped into a bygone era. "Where am I?"

"Welcome to my humble home, Princess," the voice murmured behind me. "I realize it's much less than you're accustomed to, but I'm afraid it will have to suffice."

I spent several minutes straining against the pa-ralysis in my muscles before mustering the strength to shift toward the voice.

A handsome man with pale blue eyes was seated on a sofa with blood-red velvet upholstery and an or-nately carved mahogany frame. He was dressed in an untucked white linen shirt with gray pants and bare feet. The skin around his crystal blue eyes crin-kled in the most charming way as he smiled at me. "Do you know who I am?"

Panic saturated my thready whisper as the mem-ory of my abduction from the clearing rushed back to me, "Godric."

He nodded and gestured for me to come sit on the sofa with him. "Please have a seat."

Until then, I hadn't noticed I was lying on the floor. "I don't want to."

His deceptively charming grin widened. "There's no need to make this more unpleasant than it has to be."

"Please let me go," I pleaded in a desperate whisper.

"I'm afraid I can't do that."

"Why are you doing this?"

"I do apologize, Princess. You must understand, I have no quarrel with you but the only way to hurt an invincible creature such as your husband is to harm what he treasures most." His charismatic smile coupled with his cruel words magnified my overall state of disoriented confusion.

A muted chorus of growls echoed behind me, and I shifted toward a wall of windows dressed with blood-red velvet curtains. The world beyond the windowpanes was dark—not dark like the night sky, but dark like a void where no light had ever been and no light could ever be. Yet somehow, I could still see the creatures snarling in the void. There were hundreds of demons, maybe thousands, in all manner of shapes and sizes— some almost lovely in their own macabre way, some so hideous that my eyes refused to rest on them.

"They're quite anxious to meet you," Godric murmured behind me.

I was too shocked by the horrific scene beyond the windows to turn back to him. "I don't under-stand what's happening."

ERIN A. JENSEN

"That's the trouble with a scrambled mind," Godric murmured with false sincerity. "It makes for very frustrating conversations."

Scrambled mind? Confused, I turned back to look at him.

"Fortunately, I can fix that." He picked up a silver goblet from a mahogany table beside the sofa. "Drink this. It will help."

An ache flared at my temples. "No."

He stood and crossed the room, then knelt down in front of me and held out the glass. "I'm afraid I must insist."

A blinding burst of pain exploded inside my head. "I don't want to."

His charming smile faded and all the warmth in his eyes dissipated along with it. "I didn't ask what you wanted." He pressed the glass to my lips, and a gust of wind—laden with the Sarrum's scent—erupted between us. A slew of curses spilled from Godric's mouth as the goblet fell from his hand, bleeding its contents across the floor and onto the hem of my dress.

I looked up and a monstrous pair of sapphire eyes blazed above me. The beast towering over me looked identical to my Dragon King, but he only felt like a piece of him...

...*Emma.* A chorus of faint voices called my name as the room melted away...

9

BOB

I woke with a screaming headache. My lungs were constricted, making every breath a labored one. My muscles ached with an unparalleled intensity. Every fiber of my being was begging me to turn back. This was how each day had begun since I entered the forest. How many days had I been wandering aimlessly amidst these impossibly lofty decaying trees? I couldn't even wager a guess. Time had no meaning in this ungodly place. I stood up and brushed the dirt from my clothes. It felt like a lifetime ago that Nellie and Lilly had been taken from me. After God knows how many fruitless attempts to travel the Waters in search of them, I'd woken with a vision one morning. It was nothing but a frail wisp of a dream really, but dreams were every bit as real as the ground I stood on. The image of a shriveled

ERIN A. JENSEN

old woman with milky eyes had stuck with me that morning. Though she bore almost no physical resemblance to my Nellie, there wasn't a doubt in my mind that it was her. *You have to go into the forest, Bob.*

She'd been determinedly persistent about it but my stubborn older-self had been too pigheaded to listen, so eventually she began speaking to me as the old fool was drifting between worlds. I awoke hearing her feeble whispers in the breeze. *Go into the forest. Find anyone who'll listen, and tell them you need to find the Dragon King to warn him that his Princess is in danger. You'll find Charlie with the King. Tell Charlie that Lilly and I were taken and you need his help to find us.* It was the same every morning. For all I knew, I'd just been wandering in circles all this time. The forest poisoned your mind—whispering of unfathomable dangers, filling you with terror—demanding that you turn back before it was too late. I ignored the voices and clung to the whispered words that came to me each morning as I woke, an aged version of my Nellie's melodic voice. I would not let her down more than I already had. I'd never give up searching these woods till I found her.

"You're lost," observed a voice behind me, making me practically jump out of my skin. It was the first real voice I'd heard since I entered the trees.

"I'm not." I turned slowly with my hands in the air, making it clear that I came in peace. The voice

72

didn't respond and I saw no creature in the direction it'd come from.

"The hell you aren't," the voice replied.

I squinted, searching the rotting forest for any sign of life that the voice might have originated from. "Where are you?"

"Turn back, old man," the voice grumbled from a different direction. "It's time for you to give up and go home."

I turned again without much hope of spotting the fellow with whom I was conversing.

"Down here, you big fool," the voice grunted.

I crouched and searched the forest floor. "Where?"

A pebble pegged me in the back of the head with barely enough force to detect. I turned carefully, afraid I might squash the creature the voice belonged to. Again, I saw nothing.

"I knew the Unsighted were dim, but this is ridiculous."

"I hardly think that's fair," I retorted without even attempting to turn toward the voice. "You're clearly much smaller than I am. It isn't my fault that you're too cowardly to show yourself."

"Easy for you to say, you daft giant."

I inspected the ground beneath me, then sat once I was certain that particular patch of earth was unoccupied. "Is that the best retort you can come up with?"

ERIN A. JENSEN

"You're no fun at all," the voice grumbled.

I exhaled a sigh of frustration. "I've no time for fun."

"You'd think the first Unsighted bloody human that happened into my section of the forest would be a little less boring," the creature grumbled.

"Sorry," I muttered, scanning the forest floor for signs of movement. "I'm a little busy trying to rescue the love of my life from the bastard who made off with her."

"Well, that's a bit less boring."

I shivered as a chill crept up my spine. Something flicked my left ear and I slowly turned my head in that direction. A shriveled creature no larger than a mouse grinned at me, displaying a mouthful of rotten teeth. His sagging skin was a sickly shade of gray and his eyes were a dull lifeless brown. He stood with hunched posture and drooping shoulders, dressed in tiny clothes that might've been adorable if they weren't so threadbare and filthy. He narrowed his dull eyes at me and extended a hand with four long spindly fingers.

I took hold of his tiny hand and gently shook it. "Pleased to meet you, friend."

He let go of my hand and wiped his own hand on his earth-stained pants, as if I had gotten *him* dirty. "I haven't decided if you're a friend or foe yet."

"Well, can you please decide quickly? I'm in a bit of a hurry."

"No fun at all," the creature grumbled again.

"My name's Bob, by the way. Who might you be?"

"I might be somebody who could help you." The wrinkled creature scratched his scruffy chin. "What the hell kind of nonsense name is Bob, anyway?"

"It's *my* name," I tried my best to keep the irritation I felt from leaking into my voice. After all, he did say he might be able to help me. Nellie's older-self had instructed me to ask anyone who I happened upon for help. "I didn't catch your name."

The tiny, albeit hugely annoying, creature sat himself down on my shoulder with a loud huff. "I didn't throw it."

I couldn't stop myself from scowling at him. "Well, that's just bad manners."

He let out a sound that was something between spitting and laughter. "Do I look like I give a troll's ass about manners?"

Despite the urgency of my mission and the creature's irritating nature, I let out a chuckle, which almost knocked the little fellow off my shoulder. I steadied him, earning another grumble. "Tell me your name or I'll just have to make one up for you."

"Is that so?" He crossed his arms over his chest. "And what would you call me?"

"Pipsqueak has a nice ring to it." I grinned at the glare he shot me. "I could call you Pip for short."

"Joking about a man's height isn't funny, you overgrown clod. How about I call you Mammoth man?"

"Or you could call me by my name, which I gave you because it's the polite thing to do when you meet someone."

"Whatever, Mammoth. I didn't ask for a lesson in politeness."

"You said you could help me," I reminded him. "So will you help me, Pip?"

The wrinkly little creature let out an entirely non-threatening growl. "My name's Melvin. Now, stop calling me Pip."

I shot him a sly grin. "I think I like Pip better."

"Do you want my help or not, Mammoth?"

I dropped the grin. "I truly do."

He nodded and the annoyed expression slipped from his face. "So who took your woman?"

"A dragon."

He scurried down my arm and climbed onto a nearby rock so that we were almost face to face. "Does this dragon have a name?"

"Yes," I replied in a gravelly whisper. "His name is Godric."

Pip let out a pained gasp as if I'd struck him. "Well, why didn't you say so?"

"Does that mean you'll help me?"

"It does," he agreed. "What exactly do you need me to do?"

"I need you to help me find the Dragon King." It felt odd saying it aloud for the first time. "I have to warn him that his Princess is in danger. Godric plans to take her, too."

"Shit," Pip muttered. "Yeah Mammoth... I mean Bob, I can help with that."

The tension knotting my muscles eased a bit. "You know where to find the Dragon King?"

"No," he muttered, scratching his chin. "No one does."

"Then how can you help me?"

"I can take you to someone who can bring you to someone who works for the King."

I raised an eyebrow. "That sounds marginally promising."

"Have you got a better plan, big guy?"

"No, Pip," I cleared my throat, "Sorry, I mean Melvin, I don't have a better plan. How do we proceed from here?"

The creature motioned for me to lift him up to my vantage point. "You can call me Pip. It's kinda growing on me."

A grin spread across my face as I lifted him to my shoulder and steadied him as I stood up. "Alright then, Pip. Lead the way."

10

DAVID

"Please don't kill me," the sorrow-eater sniveled, "Have mercy, Sarrum. Please. I beg you."

If I had a nickel for each time I'd heard such whimpered pleas, I would have drowned in useless coinage a lifetime ago. I released him from my hold and the loathsome creature hit the floor with a wet thud and a wounded shriek. He cowered at my feet, whimpering like an infant as my pitch black venom trickled from his blistering lips and oozed from his nostrils.

I stood there for several minutes, watching the molten liquid drip from his chin and singe his flesh as it bled its way down his swollen belly. Pressed for time as I was, it was crucial not to rush such things. Successful interrogation required time for the interrogee's agony to crest, then subside enough for the mind to clear. Given sufficient time, a desperate desire to bring an end to the suffering could break even the most steadfast of souls. This pitiful creature before me was no such soul. Destroying him would be child's play, but he was the only Purist within the tavern walls who still drew breath. I'd attacked the first several in a fit of blind rage. The ones after that were stubborn, and by the time I broke their spirits, their minds were too damaged to be of any use to me. Now it all came down to this one last despicable creature.

As his whimpering tapered, I crouched in front of him and spoke inside his fractured mind. *My patience is spent, sorrow. Tell me what you know or I've no further use for you.*

"Okay." He wiped my venom from his lips with a trembling hand and smeared it in blotches across the front of his shirt, fashioning himself into a living breathing inkblot test. "I'll talk."

Have I given you the impression that I am not pressed for time? Out with it.

"There's a couple that works for Godric," he sniveled. "They were in here a few weeks ago, bragging about how they'd soon be in possession of a Princess of Light that men would pay anything to bed."

An infuriated growl rumbled in my chest as I grabbed him by the collar and stood, yanking him off the floor. *Did this Princess have a name?*

"Yes." Piss trickled down the sorrow's pant legs as he whispered, "*The* Princess. They were talking about *your* Princess."

Flames blazed in my eyes as smoke began to billow from my nostrils. *And you felt no need to report this?*

"The female is a shadow," the sorrow whimpered, "and she scares the shit out of me."

I released his collar and let him free fall for a moment before catching him by the throat with my other hand. *And I don't?*

"Of course you do..." Another gush of piss rushed down his legs. "Nobody thought they were serious. The male demon is a sweet-talker. We all just thought he was trying to impress his woman. If I'd thought—"

Whether or not you believed they were serious is irrelevant. Where did these creatures say they would be taking the Princess?

The sorrow hesitated for a moment as he eyed the burnt remnants of the tavern door behind me.

I shook him to recapture his attention. *Think carefully about your next words, sorrow. They may well be your last. Make them count.*

The simpleton was too petrified to mute his thoughts. *Why? What can you do to me once I'm dead?*

You'd be amazed what I'm capable of. There are fates far worse than death. Would you care to find out what those are?

"No," he replied in a barely audible whisper. "There's a cabin in the woods a few villages from here where the Purists sometimes congregate. That's where they told the bidders they could find her."

A monstrous crack of thunder shook the Dragon's Lair with such force that several of the windows shattered. *Where is this cabin?*

"I don't know." Mucous-like tears oozed down the sorrow's cheeks and mingled with my venom as he sobbed, "I've never been invited to one of their gatherings."

Then you've outlived your usefulness. I tossed him aside like a useless rag. He struck the bar headfirst and his lifeless body crumpled to the floor.

I picked up a towel from the bar and wiped the collective blood of the Purists from my hands as I moved toward the doorway. The moment I stepped through it, I unmasked and took to the sky. As I took flight, my mind wandered to the morning after Emma and I watched the horror film—the morning I left her standing in front of her bedroom door...

...I scarcely remembered driving home from the Reeds' house. Every ounce of strength I possessed had been focused on fighting the overwhelming urge to turn around and go back to her.

Benjamin was waiting for me in the foyer when I entered the house.

I narrowed my eyes at him. "Go ahead and say it."

He answered with a stoic expression and a subtle shake of his head, "I don't need to."

I kicked off my shoes and headed for the lounge.

Benjamin followed me in silence. When we entered the room, he stepped behind the bar and poured two drinks as I moved to the fireplace. He crossed the room and handed one of the glasses to me.

I took it with a nod and downed a sip before speaking. "How the hell did I let it come to this?"

"You didn't want to admit how little time you had left with her," he whispered, "so you chose not to see it."

"See what?"

Benjamin took a slow sip of his drink before answering, "That she'd grown up."

A snarl barreled up my throat as I threw my glass against the wall. "I've endangered her."

"You can still fix this."

A humorless chuckle erupted from my mouth. "And how exactly shall I do that? Instead of gently coaxing her from the nest, I've no choice but to shove her from it and hope she figures out how to fly."

"She's a smart girl," Benjamin whispered. "She'll figure it out."

"She's still too young." I exhaled a puff of smoke as I moved toward the window. "I haven't had enough time to protect her properly, to teach her how to protect herself out in the world. My enchantment will fade over time without my touch to reinforce it."

Isa's calm voice drew my eyes to the doorway, "I can help with that."

"How?"

"We can give her a talisman to reinforce it."

I stopped moving. "I'm listening."

"The pendant you bought for her birthday?" Isa whispered. "I can infuse the diamond with your blood. As long as she wears it, it will strengthen the enchantment."

"A blood diamond?" Isa never ceased to amaze me. Such Dark magic was forbidden and yet, she didn't hesitate to suggest it. Perhaps all these years in our presence had corrupted her. Whatever the reason, it was the surest protection I could offer my Princess before casting her out. "Are you confident you could produce one? A mishap during the process could have disastrous repercussions."

A wicked smile curved Isa's full lips. "I have no doubt that I could make one. I watched my Grandmother do it when I was a child. There's no forgetting a process like that."

"Then we should pick the pendant up from the jeweler's today."

Isa grinned at me as she pulled a small box from the pocket of her jacket and handed it to me. "I already did."

I opened the box and brushed a finger over the intricately woven metal vines that caged the brilliant heart shaped diamond. The jeweler had crafted it precisely to my specifications and it was lovely, exactly as

I'd envisioned it. Though, I had imagined gifting my Princess a pure diamond of perfect clarity, not a Dark gem impregnated with my venomous blood. I met Isa's eyes with an appreciative smile. "We might as well get started."

11

CHARLIE

I opened my eyes with an agonized groan and a blinding ache flared inside my head, the sort of ache I imagine you'd get after head-butting a brick wall for a few hours. I squinted at my blurry surroundings. As the space around me came into focus, I found myself lying on the cold stone floor of a dimly lit cave. Just once, couldn't I wake up in a luxurious bedroom in the palace when they forced me through the Waters to Draumer?

Benjamin's deep voice echoed from the shadows in a corner of the cave, "This isn't a vacation, dumb ass."

I rubbed my eyes, but my inferior vision couldn't penetrate the darkness in the corner. "What the hell did I do this time?" I muttered to the voice shrouded in shadow.

"You reached for the Princess."

"So?" I sat up and squinted at the corner Benjamin's voice was emanating from. "I've put my arm around Emma hundreds of times and the Sarrum's enchantment never stopped me before."

Benjamin stepped toward me and the shadows slipped from his body like a cloak of black silk. "The Princess wasn't in mortal danger before."

I grimaced and pressed my fingers to my temples. "The enchantment can sense that?"

"Yeah. That's the entire purpose of the enchantment, to sense and eradicate potential threats before they ever touch the Princess."

Brilliant orange flames blazed in my eyes, obscuring my vision as I glared at Benjamin. "Since when am I a potential threat?"

Beyond the hazy curtain of fire, Benjamin extended a hand and yanked me to my feet the instant I accepted it. "Since you frightened the Princess."

"Shit." His words were the verbal equivalent of a bucket of ice water, dousing the fire in my eyes and extinguishing the flames. "I did?"

Benjamin's expression softened a little. "Yes. You did. She has no conscious memory of her abduction when she's in the waking world, but she still feels the dread she experienced when she was taken from the clearing. On top of that, Doc and Isa gave her a dose of the memory potion they cooked up and her buried memories are beginning to surface. In the fragile state she's in, it doesn't take much to spook

her and your psychotic behavior enhanced her confusion. You're supposed to be her rock, remember?"

A wave of nausea washed over me, and it was all
I could do to keep from painting the floor of the
cave with the half-digested remnants of my dinner.
The last thing I wanted to do was scare Emma. I
swallowed and choked back the queasiness. "Am
I ever gonna figure out how to control my dragon
impulses?"

"In time," Benjamin answered with a sympathetic
frown, "but for now, it'd be best to keep your distance from Emma and Rose."

The queasiness flared again. "But Rose needs
my help to hold up the clearing."

"I'll be there to keep you in line."

"By scaring me senseless?" I glanced down at my
pants. *Fabulous. I pissed myself again.* I was hopeless.
"You should just shoot me now and put me out of my
misery. I'm a total failure as a dragon."

"Don't be so fucking selfish," Benjamin growled.
"Emma needs you to hold her home together until
the Sarrum returns with her."

"Rose can do that," I muttered to the stone floor
because I was too embarrassed to meet Benjamin's
eyes. "She's stronger than me anyway, isn't she?"

"Yes," Benjamin agreed, "for the moment, she
is. But she's nowhere near as strong as the Sarrum.
She may be better at controlling her abilities than
you currently are, but you've got more raw potential

power and she's gonna need your help soon. So we need to get back to the waking world, put some food in that gut of yours and get you back to the clearing."

My stomach gurgled at the mention of food. "And I'm guessing I need a shower in the waking world, too?"

"Already taken care of."

A vision of Tristan stripping me naked and soaping me up flashed through my head, and I focused like hell on not getting aroused. "By who?"

Despite the dire circumstances, Benjamin let out a spine-chilling burst of laughter. "Wrong brother."

"Awesome," I muttered. That actually did make me feel a little better. Still, the thought of being undressed and bathed like a toddler by another man didn't exactly make me feel like a winner.

"Get over yourself," Benjamin growled. "Brian hosed you down like a farm animal and threw some clean clothes on you so we could get back to business. Pissing yourself is inevitable when the Sarrum knocks you on your ass."

"His enchantment set my arms on fire," I muttered. Maybe it wasn't that pathetic to piss yourself when your arms were covered in flames. I looked down at my arms. They looked perfectly fine.

"Remember that feeling," Benjamin whispered, "the next time you feel like touching the Princess or thinking of her as yours."

"Don't think I could forget if I wanted to."

With a satisfied nod, Benjamin started toward a Waterfall at the other end of the cave. "You've had enough time to cool off. Time to get back to the waking world."

Was that Waterfall there the whole time? I followed Benjamin across the cave, stepped into the Waterfall after him and sat up on a couch in an unfamiliar guestroom. I stole a glance down at my clothes. They were obviously Tristan's. Didn't anyone with a less Greek-godlike build keep spare clothes at the Talbots' house?

"Nobody gives a damn what you're wearing." Brian was seated in a chair beside the couch, and a tray of food had been set on the coffee table in front of me.

"Thanks for the food," I muttered, trying my damndest not to picture Brian stripping me out of my piss-stained clothes and hosing me off.

Brian looked utterly calm as he nodded. "You're welcome."

Since he didn't seem embarrassed, I decided there was no point in worrying about it. Besides, they'd all seen me piss myself before. *Except Emma.* "Crap. Did I—"

"It happened after we carried you out of the living room," Brian whispered. "She didn't see anything."

I took an egg and cheese bagel sandwich from the tray in front of me and stifled a moan as my teeth sank into it.

"Don't hold back on our account," Tristan's silky voice murmured from the doorway. He winked at me as he stepped in the room and shut the door behind him.

That vision of Tristan lathering me with soapsuds resurfaced and my cheeks flamed.

Tristan must've noticed, but he didn't comment on it. He just sat down on the coffee table next to the tray of food, picked up a slice of toast and tore a bite off with his perfectly white teeth. The man even managed to make eating toast look sexy.

Brian scowled at his brother. "That's not for you."

Tristan ignored his older sibling but didn't flash his usual *I'm too sexy for the rules* smile. Instead, Tristan's expression was all business as his gorgeous green eyes locked with mine. "What do you say, dragon—no hard feelings about what happened in the living room?"

"No," I whispered, "I get it. I was acting like a psycho."

"No," Tristan lowered his eyelids in a way that made my body temperature skyrocket. "You were acting like a dragon." His eyes raked over me and he finally seemed to notice I was wearing his clothes.

My cheeks flamed even hotter. "Sorry."

"Don't be." He flashed me a grin that melted my insides. "I like you in my clothes."

Brian extended a foot and prodded his brother in the back. "Cool it."

Tristan turned and grinned at his brother.

Then for no apparent reason, Brian hopped to his feet and yanked Tristan to his. "We've gotta go."

Tristan tossed his half-eaten slice of toast on the tray. "Why?"

"The Sarrum needs our assistance."

Tristan nodded and touched a hand to my shoulder. "Be strong, dragon. You've got this."

"Thanks," I muttered, but Tristan was already halfway out the door. I looked up at Benjamin. "How did Brian know the Sarrum needed them?"

Benjamin grabbed a banana from the tray and sat down on the other end of the couch. "Those tattoos of his are more than just decoration."

"Okay?" I raised an eyebrow as I took a bite of my bagel sandwich.

"They were inked with the Dragon King's blood."

"Isn't that kinda messed up?" I mumbled around a mouthful of bagel and egg.

"That's how an enchantment is created."

"So... where is Emma's tattoo?" Tattooing a gorgeous woman who shared your bed seemed a lot less messed up, and more hot as hell. A thrill rushed through me at the thought of marking Rose's flesh with my blood.

Benjamin narrowed his eyes at me. "It's a small mark at the base of her scalp beneath her hair, not that it's any of your business."

"I didn't see any dragon enchantment appear in the room. How did Brian know the Sarrum needed him?"

"He felt it. The tattoos heated, and he heard the Sarrum's voice in his head."

"Did you hear it too?" I muttered. "Because I didn't hear anything."

"I heard it because I'm bound to the Sarrum."

An encouraging thought suddenly occurred to me. "Do you know why the Sarrum needs their help?"

"He hasn't found her yet," Benjamin whispered. "Eat up. We need to get back to the clearing.

12

EMMA

When I woke up on the couch in the living room, the opening tune of that damn horror movie was playing again, but my heart was racing too furiously to make a fuss over it. Whatever I'd been dreaming about had terrified me. The gist of the dream had escaped me the second my eyes opened, but the feeling of dread stuck with me. I sat up and looked around the room. Charlie was gone. *Right. Benji and Brian carried him away after he passed out.* Tristan was also gone, but I didn't remember him leaving the room. Isa and Doc were sitting in chairs across the coffee table from me. *Did I pass out, too?* I was almost positive Isa wasn't in the room when all the commotion with Charlie started. She'd been in the kitchen fixing us an early breakfast. A tray of food sat on the coffee table in front of me, confirming what I thought I remembered.

Isa met my eyes with a cheerful smile as she hopped up from her chair. She grabbed a mug of coffee from the tray as she rounded the coffee table and held it out to me as she sat down on the couch beside me. "The medication seems to be doing quite a number on you. You should drink some more coffee."

Numb and exhausted as I was, it was sheer reflex that prompted my hands to reach out and take the mug from her.

"Drink," she whispered.

I didn't need more coffee. I needed sleep, but the dread that had clung to me as I was waking up made that option equally unappealing. Too tired to argue, I sipped the coffee. It was delicious. Isa had added cinnamon and vanilla to the cream. I'd almost forgotten how good her coffee was. I lifted the mug to my lips, took a larger sip and muttered, "Thanks."

"You're welcome," she whispered as she adjusted the blanket that someone must've draped over me while I was unconscious. "Do you trust me, Emma?"

"Of course." If one of us had trust issues, it ought to be her. After all, *I stabbed her* in the midst of my grief-stricken hysteria and put her in a coma for months.

"I need you to do something...even if it seems wrong to you." Her smile slipped for a moment, belying her cheery demeanor. "Can you do that for me?"

I took another sip of my coffee, stalling for time. What on earth could she want me to do that would strike me as wrong? *She came back to work for us after what I did to her*—the level of trust that must've required was mindboggling. How could I not trust her entirely? "Sure," I muttered, "What do you want me to do?"

Her forced smile widened as she slipped a hand in her pocket and pulled out the heart-shaped ruby pendant David gave me for my sixteenth birthday. "Put this on."

I'd proudly worn the pendant every day of my life since the day David gave it to me—until the day Sophie Turner informed me that he'd given her one too, one he only let her wear *when he fucked her*, as she so crudely put it. My stomach churned as I sat my mug down on the coffee table. "No."

"Please, Emma. I wouldn't ask if it wasn't important." When I looked up at Isa, there were tears in her eyes.

Witnessing her tears made it nearly impossible to hold back my own. "What reason could you possibly have for asking me to wear that?"

"Don't question it," she whispered, "Please. Just trust me and put it on."

A tear slid down my cheek as I reached out and touched the intricately detailed metal vines that caged the massive heart-shaped ruby. Odd as it sounds, it almost felt as if I was touching my husband.

ERIN A. JENSEN

The sensation of his presence warmed me, comforting me. Then an image of Sophie jeering at me in the bathroom mirror at the party that night sprang to mind, and I pushed Isa's hand away. "I can't."

"You have to, Princess." Tears streaked down Isa's cheeks as she unclasped the chain and leaned forward to put it around my neck. "We're running out of time."

I was going to protest and question why she called me Princess, but everything slipped away as the weight of the pendant settled against my chest...

...It'd been a week since David left me standing in front of my bedroom door. Each day since, I'd hoped he would show up at dinner or stop by the house to drop papers off for my father. David had been working from home all week. My father said it was because he was fighting off a cold and he didn't want to spread germs, but that was a lie. The Dragon King didn't get colds. He didn't ever get sick. The blood that flowed through his veins had the power to heal not only him, but others as well. David was keeping his distance from me. I'd never spent this much time away from my Dragon King. There had occasionally been bouts of absence between us in the waking world, but never in Draumer.

I hadn't been handling our separation as well as David obviously was. He consumed my thoughts, day and night in both worlds. I'd spent an unhealthy portion of my week in the waking world locked in my room, wearing David's shirt and imagining that my hands were his. *In Draumer, the storm had stopped raging in our clearing but the barrier remained intact, and I'd spent most of my time absently staring at the cave I couldn't get near. I could've gone to the cabin like David told me to, but I wanted to prove that I could be just as stubborn as he could. Eventually, he'd come out of the cave and talk to me. He had to.*

Today would finally bring an end to all of that. It was my birthday. I'd already celebrated my sweet sixteen with my friends—friends I could only share so much with, friends who had no inkling what sort of agony I was being forced to endure. Tonight we were celebrating with a quiet family dinner—just me, my parents and David. He'd never missed any of my birthdays and he certainly wouldn't skip such an important one.

By the time my father came home from work, my stomach was so full of butterflies I doubted I'd be able to stomach my dinner. Although, I couldn't have cared less about the meal. Seeing David was all that mattered.

My father smiled at me as he stepped into the dining room. "How's my birthday girl?"

"Good," I muttered, watching his hands rather than meeting his eyes. My father's mood could change at the drop of a hat for no apparent reason. A tremor in his hands was a sure sign that I should make myself scarce or at least keep my distance. His right hand plunged into a coat pocket and emerged holding a small box wrapped in black and white silk ribbons. It was almost too beautiful to unwrap. My heart sank as he held the package

out to me. My father had never been one to bother with extravagant wrappings.

"David asked me to tell you that he's sorry," he whispered with an apologetic frown, "but he won't be able to join us for dinner. He's still feeling under the weather."

Tears spilled down my cheeks as I took the box from my father.

My father took a step toward me and for a moment, I actually thought he was going to hug me. He hesitated for a few awkward seconds, then recoiled without laying a finger on me. Regret flickered in his eyes as he whispered, "Dinner smells delicious."

I nodded and wiped the tears from my cheeks.

My birthday dinner was a blur. I couldn't stop staring at the box wrapped in black and white silk—Dark and Light intertwined and yet, entirely separate. The minutes ticked by at a torturous pace as I went through the motions of eating without really tasting the food. When the meal finally ended, my mother placed my presents on the table in front of me. I opened the other gifts first—new clothes and some books from my parents, a sweater from an aunt who lived on the other side of the country and rarely visited.

When all the other gifts had been unwrapped, I picked up the only one that mattered. My parents watched me, oblivious to the fact that my heart was crumbling inside my chest. Their attention was never really focused on me. When I was a little girl, David explained that my parents felt there should only be one person you chose to give all your love to. My parents chose to give their love to each other, and that had been tolerable because David had always chosen me. I concentrated on keeping my hands steady as I unraveled the layers of black and white silk till I reached the black velvet box at the center. My eyes welled with tears as I unhinged the lid and opened it.

My mother let out a gasp as the light hit the heart-shaped gem caged by a pendant of elaborately detailed intertwining metal vines. "My God, look at the size of that ruby. That thing must be worth more than every piece in my jewelry box, combined."

"Damn it, David," my father muttered under his breath, "A giant fucking ruby is too much to give a sixteen year old child."

My father's bitter voice barely registered as I lifted the pendant out of the box. I touched the jewel and felt David's presence as surely as if his arms had wrapped around me. My father was still ranting but my focus was on the Dragon King's enchantment that had appeared without me willing it to. The gorgeous beast dipped his head so his face was just inches from mine as his intoxicating scent filled the room.

My mother's voice was just a distant echo, "It's not as if he can't afford a ruby that size."

My parents might as well have been a million miles away as I unclasped the chain and put the pendant around my neck. The two of them had no clue how valuable the jewel truly was. It wasn't a ruby. It was a diamond. *Never mind what a regular diamond that size must've cost. A blood diamond of any size was a rarity because the Dark magic required to create one was forbidden. The wearer of such a jewel fell under the irrefutable protection of the creature whose blood impregnated the stone. It was a priceless possession no matter who the blood donor was, but this diamond was massive and it'd been infused with the blood of the strongest creature in existence. Sighted creatures would kill to possess a stone like this.*

I spent almost an hour sitting in the dining room watching the dragon tower over us as my parents bickered about how to deal with such an inappropriate gift. When I couldn't stand to listen to their argument any longer, I stood from the table and walked out of the room. I moved down the hall at a snail's pace, expecting my parents to notice my absence and call me back. They were bound to realize that my cake was still sitting on the kitchen counter, unsliced and unblemished by birthday candles. I had no desire to blow out candles or eat cake as I stepped in my room, locked the door, undressed and slipped into a nightgown. No one called me back to eat cake while I was washing my face, or when I turned off the lights and crawled into bed. I clutched the pendant that hung from my neck and watched David's fiery-eyed enchantment stare at me until my eyelids grew heavy and I drifted off to sleep with my parents' muffled voices still bickering beyond my door...

...The melodic chirps of songbirds welcomed me to the clearing as I opened my eyes. I wrapped my fingers around the pendant, stood up and moved to the invisible wall that prevented me from going near my home. "Thank you for the gift," I whispered. He'd hear, even if I only thought the words.

Benji's deep voice startled me when it sounded behind me, "It's a parting gift, Princess."

Dread gripped me, latching its talons onto my heart at the cruelty of his words. "Why would you say that?"

Benjamin stepped beside me and took hold of my arm. "Because it's true." It must've been a ridiculous sight—a teenage girl who didn't possess the strength to break free from a sock monkey's grip. Of course, anyone who might've been around to see it knew that monkey was one of the strongest creatures alive. Benjamin released my arm with an exasperated sigh. "It's time for you to leave the Darkness, Princess. This place isn't safe for you anymore."

The sock monkey in front of me grew blurry as my eyes filled with tears. "If he wants to get rid of me, why did he give me this?"

"So you'd have something to remember him by."

I took a step back from Benjamin. "This is my home."

"It's not safe for you here, Emma."

"How can you say that?" Panic bled into my words as I sobbed, "You guard me. You're strong enough to protect me from anything."

The monkey's eyes darted to the cave beyond the in-visible barrier. "I can't protect you from him."

I followed his eyes to the cave and searched the dark-ness at the entrance for any sign of my Dragon King. "He'd never hurt me."

"I vowed to guard you with my life," Benji whispered, "and that's exactly what I'm trying to do. I'm begging you to turn around and jump in the Waters, Emma. You belong in the Light with your own kind. If you stay, these walls will crumble and this place will kill you. You have to leave now while you still can." He took my arm and practically dragged me toward the Water. I tried to re-sist, but he was too strong.

At first, I was just irritated but by the time we neared the Waters' edge, my heart was slamming in my chest. In a fit of frantic terror, I swung a hand back and struck the creature who had vowed to lay down his life to protect me. "Let go of me!"

Benji's Dark eyes glistened with tears as he yanked me closer to the Water. "I won't stand by and watch you wither away in the Darkness."

I let out a strangled cry as my toes touched the Water.

"LEAVE US!" The instant the Sarrum's command echoed across the clearing, Benji dropped my arm and vanished. A second later, David was standing beside me in human form. I took one look at the sapphire flames roaring in his eyes and expected him to throw me in the Waters and be done with me.

"I'll never force you out of here." His voice was gentle, but the flames that blazed in his eyes were violent and furious.

I'd spent so many hours rehearsing what I would say when David finally came out of the cave but now that he was standing in front of me, I felt lost. I wanted to prove to him that I wasn't a child anymore. Instead, I broke down in tears like an infant.

A mix of tormented emotions flickered across the Dragon King's face, but the intensity of those flames in his eyes never lessened. *"This is my fault."* He stepped closer and wrapped his arms around me, and I sunk against his powerful body and wept. I felt him shudder as he tightened his hold on me and whispered, *"I should have prepared you for this."*

I lifted my head off his chest and took a step back. *"For what?"*

"For the day you'd have to leave."

The world slipped out of focus as dread sunk its talons into my heart. *"Leave?"*

"The protections that guard this dwelling were woven with the magic of childhood innocence, and you are no longer a child." David's pained expression made me wonder if dread gripped his heart, too. *"Can't you feel the walls of this mirage weakening?"*

A terrifying burst of laughter drew my attention to the walls of the dome that encompassed our clearing. I could see them now—the walls that protected me from *the Darkness, and the ungodly beasts lurking beyond them. There were far too many demons to count and their voices all echoed inside my head, they were all desperate to get into the clearing, desperate to get to me. Terror flooded through me as I looked up at the only man I would ever love. "You can protect me from all of them."*

"Yes," he whispered, "but who'd protect you from me?"

"You said that at my house last week." I took a step back and searched his eyes. "But you'd never hurt me."

"Not intentionally." He took my arm and stepped closer to the Water. When I jerked away from him, he didn't stop me. He simply waved a hand, and a motionless wall of Water appeared before us. I took a step back from it, but he stepped behind me so there wasn't much space between me and the Water. "Trust me when I tell you I'd never force you out," he scolded in a harsh whisper. "Look at your refection."

I met his eyes in the Water's mirrored surface and watched him lift a hand to the nape of my neck. His reflection placed a knuckle between my shoulder blades, but I felt the solid bone of a massive claw. He slowly traced the knuckle down my spine and every fiber of my being sang in a way that it never had before. I closed my eyes and surrendered to the sensation.

He drew a tense breath and allowed me to lose myself in the ecstasy of the moment till his knuckle halted midway down my spine. Then his mouth moved to my ear, "Look at your reflection."

The ache in my heart coupled with the euphoria from his touch enveloped me in a haze of disoriented confusion as I opened my eyes and blinked at the girl that the Waters reflected. She looked almost identical to me, but this girl had a dazzling pair of gossamer wings that caught the sunlight and sparkled like new fallen snow on a winter morning. I scowled at the false image and turned my head to ask why he'd created it, but the glistening corner of a wing made the words catch in my throat. Confused, I met David's eyes in the reflection.

He smiled at me as if he were appreciating a fine work of art. "Lovely, aren't they?"

"Where," I swallowed, searching for words, "where did those come from?"

His fiery breath heated my ear and resonated deep inside me as he whispered, "Those wings signify that a fairy has reached maturity, much like other physical changes signify adulthood in the waking world."

"What?" Why hadn't he ever prepared me for that?

"You are no longer a child, which means that the protection afforded to you by childhood innocence no longer applies."

The talons sunk a bit deeper into my heart. "You can still protect me. Why does anything have to change?"

He lowered his head so we were cheek to cheek, and I melted at the feel of his flesh against mine. "Darkness and Light were never meant to coexist. One will always eclipse the other in the end, and there will either be Light or Darkness."

My reflection responded with a furrowed brow.

"Night adores the sun," he whispered in my ear, the heat of his breath licking places much lower. "She is more radiant than anything he has ever set eyes on. Each night, he pursues her and for a brief glorious moment, they join and magnificent color floods the sky but that brilliant explosion is the onset of the sun's demise. However much the night loves her, his touch is the very thing that swallows her until she is no more and he's left alone in the dark."

My reflection opened her mouth to speak but didn't utter a sound.

"Dusk and dawn are the meeting places of impossible lovers, Princess. For those brief, shining moments, they mingle and shower the sky with their brilliance. We've already had our dawn. Raising you was the most magnificent pleasure of my life. You lit this Darkness and filled me with more joy than I'd have ever imagined possible, but if you were to stay, it would soon become dusk and I would devour every trace of you. However much I'd fight against it, in the end my Darkness would extinguish your Light and I cannot have that."

"That doesn't make any sense," I whimpered as the talons punctured my heart, "It's just a beautiful bit of poetry, a pretty excuse for getting rid of me."

He gently took me by the shoulders and spun me so we were standing face to face. Before I had time to question what he was doing, he slipped a hand into my hair and cradled the back of my head in his palm. Then he lowered his head and planted the sweetest whisper of a kiss on my lips. I closed my eyes as the warmth of his mouth heated my blood and rushed through my veins, overwhelming me so entirely that I barely noticed when my legs gave out. His lips moved to my ear as he caught me by the waist. "Open your eyes, Princess."

I followed his voice like a lifeline back to consciousness till I remembered how to open my eyes. I looked up at him, and he tipped his head toward my left shoulder. My gaze obediently followed the movement and found my perfect glistening wing marred by an ugly black spot, reminiscent of the ones that once sullied the leaves of a diseased maple tree in our yard. When I looked up at David, he unmasked for just an instant so I could see the magnificent spot of shimmering brilliance that dotted the leathery pitch black flesh of his massive wing, mirroring the splotch of damage on mine. Horrified, I looked up at him in wide-eyed disbelief.

"I would devour you if you remained here," he whispered as his fingertips circled the decay on my wing. "Your weakness would become my strength."

"Why should I care about losing something I never even knew I had?"

"It wouldn't stop there." There was an odd rasp to his voice as he added, "I would take from you until there was nothing left to take."

Dread spilled from my punctured heart and blossomed inside my chest as he took a step back from me. This was it. He was leaving me. "I don't care," I muttered in a strangled whisper. "I'd rather live one day in the Darkness with you than a million days in the Light without you."

He reached up and stroked my cheek with his finger-tips. The finality of the gesture coupled with the determined set of his jaw delivered the death blow to my heart as he murmured, "I could never live with that."

Tears spilled down my cheeks as I clutched his blood diamond to my chest. "But you promised you'd always choose me."

"I do choose you." He planted a tender kiss on my forehead, and a fresh blotch of decay immediately tarnished my other wing. "That's why I'm letting you go." At that, he turned and started toward the cave.

I moved to go after him, but the barrier reformed directly in front of me. The breath escaped my lungs in an agonized rush and an ache like nothing I'd ever experienced flared inside my chest as I watched him walk away from me. I dropped to my knees and screamed at the top of my lungs, pleading with him to come back to me, but he just kept walking. With each step he took, those talons tore another piece from my heart.

I would willingly endure an eternity of breaking bones to escape the agony I felt as I watched him step inside the cave and disappear.

13

BOB

We had walked until I couldn't walk anymore, several hours after the sun went down and the woods around us filled with the whispers of beasts that you couldn't see with your eyes or hear with your ears. No. These were beasts that you *felt*, who whispered threats inside your head until you were certain you'd gone mad. Thankfully, I didn't have to suffer alone any longer. Of course, my new traveling companion couldn't exactly fight at my side if something were to attack us outright. Pip wasn't much bigger than a field mouse. In fact, he wasn't large enough to make the trip on foot. He spent most of our trek standing in my shirt pocket. After attempting several methods of carrying him, we'd finally decided this way was best. Standing with his arms resting on the edge of my pocket and his face peeking out made him feel more dignified and it put him at the perfect vantage point to navigate. Though Pip wasn't a knight or a fighter of any sort, he made the journey less lonesome and offered a glimmer of hope that I might actually find this Dragon King I was searching for and meet up with my friend Charlie again.

A meager fire warmed our feet while it roasted the rabbit I'd killed for our dinner. We weren't planning to sleep all night, just long enough to rest our bones for a spell. I didn't want to waste more time than we absolutely had to, and Pip had surprised me by agreeing that rest was of minor importance until we accomplished our mission.

I handed Pip my flask, and had second thoughts about the gesture the instant he accepted it. How much liquor could a body that size handle? I imagined a thimbleful would be all it would take to get such a small fellow rip-roaring drunk. I watched him steady my flask against a rock, stand at the opening and tip some liquor into his mouth. Not wanting to be rude, I waited until he'd downed a few drops before speaking. "Mind if I ask you a question?"

He tipped the flask upright, wiped his mouth with the back of his grubby hand and rubbed his hand on his equally dirty pant leg. "Would it stop you from asking if I said I did mind?"

I grinned at him as I picked up the flask and capped it. "I'm not sure."

Pip shook his head as he settled onto the ground with his back against a log. "Just ask your question, giant."

I leaned toward the fire and turned the spit so the flames could roast the underside of our rabbit. "I've never encountered a creature quite like you before. What exactly are you?"

He frowned and scratched the scruff on his chin, and paused for so long that I was certain I must have offended him. "Not sure I'm *exactly* anything. I'm a bit of a mutt, I guess. My mother was a troll and my father was an imp."

I opened my mouth, then closed it and prodded the fire with a stick.

He picked up a pebble, tossed it at the back of my arm and grinned when I looked over my shoulder at him. "Go ahead and ask. Everybody does."

"Alright." I leaned back against a tree trunk, uncapped my flask and took a swig before asking, "How exactly does that work? Seems to me, it'd be a bit like mating a mouse with a bear."

I got the distinct impression that his burst of laughter was at my expense, which was fair enough considering my questions. "I almost forgot you were Unsighted. How the hell did you even end up in the forest or learn anything about the Dragon King?"

"Sighted friends," I murmured. "I suppose I know more than I ought to. But you're changing the subject."

"No," he whispered, "I'm really not. If you were Sighted, you'd know you asked a stupid question."

I scowled at him, but in truth, I was grateful for the temporary distraction from my worries. "Well, thank you very much. And why exactly is my question stupid?"

"A week ago, I'd have died laughing if somebody told me I'd be sitting at a camp fire with a big brave knight, having *the talk* about the birds and the bees."

"I know all about how babies are made, thank you."

He shook his head. "That's just it. You think you do, but you actually don't have a clue."

"Enlighten me then."

"Storks bring them."

I didn't really intend to laugh because he seemed so serious, but a hearty chuckle burst from my mouth before I could contain it.

"I'm not kidding." There wasn't a trace of amusement on Pip's face. "You've got the mechanics of the process right, but babies aren't ever conceived in this world. They're conceived in the waking world and delivered by bird-like creatures who wait by the Waters for newborns to enter this world. A fair percentage of the time, the storks even manage the deliveries without fucking up and the baby goes to one or the other of its actual parents."

I took a slow sip from my flask and considered that for a second. "You've got to be joking."

"No joke." Pip stood and moved closer to the fire to inspect the progress of our dinner. "It's one of the many perks of this world, no consequences to casual sex—no diseases, no unintended pregnancies."

"You wouldn't be pulling my leg to see how gullible the Unsighted fool you're traveling with is, would you?"

"Scout's honor." Pip traced a cross on his chest with a long filthy finger. "It's the God's honest truth."

"That's a bit much to wrap my brain around." I leaned toward the fire, grabbed the spit and pulled our perfectly cooked rabbit off the fire. "So, your parents conceived you in the other world. Why would their parts fit together any better there?"

"They're the same size in the waking world. Their *parts* fit together just fine. It was just their personalities that didn't mesh." He shook his head with a melancholy grin. "That's me in a nutshell. Two halves that were never meant to come together as a whole."

"I'd have to disagree with that. If they had never come together, I wouldn't be sitting here sharing a meal with you."

"Yeah," Pip muttered, "Most creatures would say you'd be better off eating alone."

"Well," I whispered, "They would be wrong."

Pip stood and dropped his eyes to the rabbit as he moved to it and tore off a piece of meat.

"So…imps and trolls are the same size in the waking world?" I helped myself to a chunk of meat and licked my fingers as I settled back against the tree trunk. "What a strange place that must be."

Pip chuckled and almost choked on his rather greedy mouthful of meat. When he finally managed to swallow it, he cleared his throat. "It's not so strange—just really boring. We all look like you in the waking world."

I studied the tiny creature through narrowed eyes. "You all look like me?"

"Well, not exactly like you." He looked me over like he was noticing me for the first time. "You're kind of a freak with all those overinflated muscles. Are you that ripped in the waking world?"

"I'm not sure what ripped means," I admitted, "but even if I did know, I couldn't answer your question. I don't know what I look like in the other world."

Pip's expression immediately shifted from jovial to somber. "Sorry."

"Nothing to be sorry about." I uncapped my flask, took a sip and then handed it to him. After all, his limit was his business and I didn't want to be rude. "It's as it should be. I know far more than I was ever meant to."

"The woman you're looking for," Pip's voice grew thicker as he whispered, "Is she Sighted?"

An ache settled in my chest at the mention of Nellie's abduction, and just like that, the diversion from my troubles vanished. "She is."

"We'll find her, my friend," Pip assured me in a softer tone, as if he regretted having asked. "She's lucky she has a man like you to protect her."

My windpipe constricted as I muttered, "I didn't exactly come through for her when she needed me."

Sorrow pooled in Pip's eyes for a second, but he blinked it away the instant he realized I was watching him. "It's not over, Bob. She still needs you, and you're going to come through for her. There's no doubt in my mind about that."

"Thank you, my friend." I didn't dare speak my thoughts aloud, but I wasn't fool enough to believe that finding Nellie and Lilly alive was a certainty. I had looked into the eyes of the monster who took them, and I was no stranger to that look. I'd seen it in the eyes of madmen before, and I was painfully aware of the horrors men like that were capable of. There were fates far worse than death, and certain traumas were impossible to recover from. I had witnessed too many of those outcomes to be naïvely optimistic.

However, there was one thing that I did know for certain—if my Nellie didn't come back from this, neither would Henry Godric.

14

DAVID

I'd never been a particularly patient man, but now that my Princess had been taken, even a single wasted second was unacceptable. Fortunately, Brian and Tristan were well aware of the urgent nature of our exchange. It took less than a minute from when I summoned Brian for the brothers to emerge from the Waters and join me at the edge of the forest.

Brian nodded as they reached me. "How can we assist you, Boss?"

My eyes darted to Tristan. "Were you aware that a pair of Purists were recently in the Dragon's Lair, boasting that they'd soon be in possession of a Princess of Light that men," I snarled the last words through gritted teeth, "would pay anything to bed?"

Tristan recoiled as if I'd struck him. "Of course not. I would've killed them on the spot if I'd heard that."

My gaze remained fixed on the incubus. "Apparently, they are a couple. The female is a shadow and the male is a sweet-talker."

Tristan's eyes widened. "That's gotta be Plezur and Payne."

A puff of smoke wafted from my nostrils as I growled, "How adorable."

"Yeah, I know. Stupid names," Tristan muttered, "but that shadow is pure evil. I've heard some pretty disturbing rumors about the creative methods of torture she's administered to females she caught Plezur bringing home."

"Then the sweet-talker is an idiot," I growled, "Why take them to his home?"

Tristan's eyes were distant as he whispered, "It's kinda their kink. Either they're both in on it, or he does it because he enjoys getting Payne worked up."

"And where might we find these miscreants?"

As always, Brian's tone was calm and rational, "Did they say where they'd be taking the Princess when they were bragging about selling her?"

A furious growl rumbled in my throat, prompting a crack of thunder that shook the ground beneath our feet as it echoed through the forest. "Apparently, there is a cabin in the forest a few villages from here where the Purists sometimes congregate. That's where they instructed the interested bidders to meet them."

"Plezur was in the Dragon's Lair last week," Tristan muttered.

Brian gripped his brother's shirtsleeve in an uncharacteristic display of impatient frustration. "Who was he with?"

Tristan squeezed his eyes shut. "Payne wasn't with him. He spent most of the night talking to a female demon with gorgeous green eyes, mocha skin and a headful of braids."

I unclenched my jaw enough to growl, "Was this female a regular at the tavern?"

"No," Tristan whispered, "I'd never seen her before that night, and I haven't seen her since."

Another puff of smoke billowed from my nostrils. I had no time or patience for useless bits of information. "Do either of you know where to find this cabin they plan to take the Princess to?"

Brian glanced down at his hand and released his brother's sleeve, as if he'd just noticed he was holding it. "We could question the patrons at the Dragon's Lair."

"I've already done that." I turned to Tristan. "Your workplace is in need of a new owner, and some restorations."

Tristan nodded without saying a word.

"I imagine the female troll would relish the promotion. Find her and inform her that the tavern is hers. I will fund whatever renovations she deems necessary."

"Can't that wait till we've found the Princess?" Tristan whispered.

"No, it cannot," I growled. "I want you there in case a patron shows up with information that might aid our search."

"Of course, Sarrum," the incubus muttered as he rushed toward the Waters.

Brian let out a heavy sigh as he watched his brother. The instant Tristan disappeared, he turned to me. "What now, Boss?"

"Now, you and I find this cabin."

Brian nodded. "Just tell me where you want me to go."

"I'll search north of here, you search south and inform me the instant you suspect you've found anything."

"On it, Boss." With a quick nod of his head, Brian disappeared.

As I unmasked and took to the skies to search the forest below for any hint of this cabin, the ache in my heart was almost unbearable. It brought to mind a similar ache that I'd felt as I walked away from my Princess and left her screaming in the clearing with her heart torn to shreds...

...Her cries were like arrows. Each time she screamed my name, the desperation in her voice pierced another hole in my heart. If she only knew what it cost me to walk away from her, to keep from turning back and taking her into my arms. Though, how could she not doubt my sincerity? In her eyes, I was abandoning her. In actuality, this was killing me. With each step away from her, I grew weaker. The weight of the mirage was a crushing force that had steadily grown heavier as her innocence waned—it fractured while we watched the movie that had started all of this, and again when I confessed my desires and her perfect young body responded with arousal rather than fear or disgust. Now that I'd kissed her, the weight was unbearable. If it were my health and my life on the line, there would be no issue. I would eagerly drain every ounce of my strength to be with her. However, the cost would not be my strength. Her strength, her health, her very life would be the cost of our union. I could never be so selfish as to demand that from her. All I'd ever wanted was to give to her—my love, my protection, my knowledge, my kingdom—I would give all of it to fix this, but her life was too great a price to pay. I reminded myself of this over and over, with each step away from her, with each new fracture of the mirage, each time she screamed my name. This was for her, whether she understood that or not, I would not be the death of her.

Given enough time, she would come to understand that I had done this for her. She would relocate to the Light Forest and meet a nice boy. My heart throbbed at the thought of another male's hands on her, another male bedding her. She was mine. She had always been mine, and she was always meant to be mine. How in God's name could I let another man touch her? None of them would know how to love her as I did. It was me that she wanted, my name she kept screaming. How could I walk away and allow some other man to take her virginity? A growl resonated deep in my throat and a deafening crack of thunder shook the ground. I fed all of my fury and grief to the heavens, and the resulting storm reached every corner of Draumer—all but the clearing. I would force her hand no more than I already had. She would leave on her terms, after taking as much time as she needed to process this and understand that there was no alternative. Until then, the sun would continue to shine in the clearing but she would remain confined to the shore of the lake.

A desperate cry from her sweet lips stopped me dead in my tracks. My chest was heaving and smoke billowed from my flared nostrils, but I didn't turn around. Every molecule in my body was fighting against this. My treasure was behind me. Dragons do not give up their treasures, and they certainly do not leave them in need. I could turn around so easily, and give her everything she was pleading for. She wanted to stay in the clearing.

More specifically, she wanted me. Even in agony, her body was crying out to me. It had been since the moment I stood at her door and explained why it was imperative for me to keep my distance. The scent of her arousal was screaming to me, louder than any cry that escaped her precious lips. Her body did not simply ache to be pleasured. It ached for me—and me alone. My primary purpose as a dragon was to satisfy the wants of my precious treasure. How could I deny her what she so desperately desired? I wasn't fool enough to truly believe that she would ever love another man the way she loved me. I had been everything to her all her life, and she would always be everything to me.

Every bone in my body ached to go to her as her words echoed inside my head. I'd rather live one day in the Darkness with you than a million days in the Light without you. I would trade every breath in my body to take her to my bed just once, but I could not trade hers. Her breaths were too precious.

"Please, David! Don't leave me!"

The dome fractured and my heart shattered.

"I need you!"

My muscles locked, refusing to take another step from her.

Her cries grew louder, as though she sensed that my resolve was crumbling. "I love you!"

Tendons tore and bones splintered as I trudged forward, fueled by an urgent need to protect her from me.

"I'll never love anyone but you!"

The cave was just a few meters away. Yet, the strength to cover that distance escaped me. As her strangled pleas echoed across the clearing, I felt the walls of the dome start to give. The demons beyond were pushing against it, slamming their bodies into it, desperate to reach the fragile creature of Light. The walls had thinned to the point that they could not only see her, but hear the desperation in her cries and catch the frantic scent of her arousal.

I pushed back at the walls and the demons beyond with every ounce of strength I possessed, as I focused the lightning from my storm toward the exterior of the dome. The covetous demons fell back, howling in agony. The Princess's desires might be the desires of a woman, but she was still an innocent girl. I focused on the purity within her and fed it into the protective enchantment that warded the clearing, strengthening the walls. Once I was satisfied that I had adequately repaired the damage, I took the final steps and entered the cave.

Benjamin was waiting in the shadows as I stepped inside. "I'll stay here and keep an eye on her, so you don't have to watch this."

I turned my back to Benjamin and watched my Princess collapse to the grass, weeping. "I will not leave her."

"This is for the best," my shadow whispered, "You know it is."

My focus was entirely on her. I felt every ache that she suffered. "Leave me."

"Wouldn't it be easier to—"

"There is nothing easy about any of this," I snarled as I spun toward him. "Do not make me ask you twice. This is where I will remain until my Princess steps into those Waters."

15

It felt like I'd aged a hundred years since Henry Godric stole Lilly and me from our sanctuary on Bob's shore. All the progress I'd made because of Bob—all the sanity that had been restored—all of it melted away the second Henry appeared on our shore. One look at him, and I was nothing but the broken shell of a woman that Henry had left screaming in a psych ward all those years ago. I fought like hell to stay awake so Henry couldn't get his hands on me or Lilly, but there are only so many waking hours you can endure before the Waters come for you. It was impossible to stay awake forever. How damn ironic was that? I'd spent a lifetime wishing I could spend every second in the Dream World. Now here I was, desperately struggling to hold my eyes open and remain in the waking world.

Bob's gruff voice snapped me out of my sleep-deprived mental fog, "You gotta eat somethin."

I smiled at him as I covered his wrinkled hand with mine. What a bastard fate was, to finally let me find happiness and then wrench it away like this. I shook my head and whispered, "Not hungry."

He picked up my fork with a determined sigh, stabbed a bite of macaroni and lifted it to my mouth. "Doesn't matter if you're hungry. You gotta eat. That bitch by the door is just waitin for some excuse to wheel ya outta here and pump ya fulla more drugs."

"I don't care." Tears stung my eyes as I looked at Bob, my honest-to-goodness knight in shining armor. If his mind wasn't so damn fractured, he could be coming to my rescue. I'd tried explaining what I needed him to do in the Dream World so many times, but he was Unsighted to begin with and his mind was full of holes in this world. Once it'd become painfully obvious that he'd never remember in the Dream World what I asked him to do in this world, I decided to try a different tactic. I started whispering in his ear as he nodded off on the couch, hoping to God he'd somehow hear me in the Dream World and go into the forest to find help. The only trouble was, I had no idea whether I was getting through to my knight in the Dream World or just wasting a crapload of time.

Bob stubbornly pressed the forkful of macaroni to my lips until I opened my mouth and ate it. "Well,

I care. You can't let yourself fall apart like this, woman. Who the fuck am I gonna spend my time with if they cart ya off to some nursin home?" He pointed a shaky finger at the man-shaped horde of insects at the next table. "You expect me to hang around with Dipshit?"

I stared at Frank as I shook my head. Something was really off with that freak show lately. He'd gotten fifty times weirder than he'd already been. Instead of blabbering nonstop, he'd stopped talking altogether. The change in his behavior started the day after Emma left, the same day Dr. Spenser had his stroke. The toad-man had been sitting in our group therapy circle, scolding Bob for cursing at Frank when he suddenly slumped sideways in his folding chair. Of course, I knew it wasn't really a stroke, but the Unsighted doctors didn't know what I knew. I saw it the instant they took him. His waking body slumped, but his Dream form's features contorted into a horrified mask of terror, then something that I couldn't see dragged the toad out of our circle, leaving his empty shell of a body drooling and slumping against the nut-bag to his left. I missed having Charlie around. With him gone, I was the only Dream Sighted patient in the facility. So, there was nobody to corroborate what I'd seen, but I'd bet my life that the Dragon King took both of them in the Dream World. I was dragged through the Dark Forest by the King's shadow once, when he came to warn me to be respectful to the Princess. That experience was terrifying enough. I woke up soaked in piss and feeling ten years older than I felt when I went to sleep. I could only imagine what they might've done to the doctor who'd made Emma's life hell and denied the King the right to visit his own wife in the facility, or the buggish freak-show who'd gone after her in the common room. To tell you the truth, I was surprised the two of them were still breathing.

Bob's voice snapped my exhausted mind back to the cafeteria, "What planet are you on, woman?"

The rest of the meal was pretty much the same. The sour-faced girl by the door stared at me like I was the one who had shoved the stick that was clearly lodged up her ass. Bob tried to spoon-feed me lunch, and my thoughts drifted to what would happen when I couldn't keep my eyes open any longer.

After the meal, they wheeled me into the big common room and the troll helped me onto the couch next to Bob. Ten minutes into the morning news, Bob's eyelids started to droop. I waited till his eyes were shut, then whispered in his ear, hoping somehow my knight in shining armor would hear me in the Dream World. After that, I sat and watched the news until I couldn't fend off the Waters any longer…

…"There's my lovely wife," Henry's charming young voice murmured. I never stood a chance against that British accent and those gorgeous eyes way back when.

"I'm not your anything," I whispered. "You threw me away a lifetime ago."

He flashed that charming grin of his, the one that made the skin around his lovely blue eyes crinkle and made me weak in the knees back before I discovered what a monster he was. "But I came back for you, Nellie. Doesn't that count for anything?"

"You're a sick man," I whispered.

There was a twinkle in his eye as he murmured, "No sicker than you."

I blinked as the room solidified around us and found us seated on opposite ends of a plush red velvet couch. "What?"

Henry shifted closer to me and the room suddenly seemed warmer. "Do you think I can't feel it? The way you still react to me? You despise me and yet, if I were to take you in my arms, you'd come willingly. Tell yourself that you're blameless all you like, but you are the one who drowned our child."

The nausea that had consumed me for so many tortured years came roaring back from wherever I'd buried it. I couldn't deny it. I was the one who killed our Lilly. As much as I'd vowed to stay strong for myself and for Lilly, my eyes flooded with tears. "Why did you make me do it?"

His charming grin widened, as if I'd just asked him why he bought me flowers. That was the worst of it, how little it fazed him, how little he cared. "That's a long story, and I haven't the time, nor the energy

ERIN A. JENSEN

to tell it to you." He leaned over and planted a kiss on my forehead as he stood from the couch. "So, be a good girl and make yourself at home here. I've got other matters to attend to."

The warmth of his kiss spread through my body, rousing all the old sensations I felt long ago, when he was my everything. I loathed myself for still feeling that way. "Where's Emma?"

"That is not your concern."

"It is," I insisted. "What've you done with her?"

The smile slipped from Henry's handsome face as he bent and took hold of my chin. "I told you, that's not your concern. Do not give me reason to move you to less pleasant accommodations, not when I am trying so hard to be a good host to my old girl."

Something in his eyes convinced me not to press him any farther. "Okay."

His charming smile returned as he whispered, "Good girl."

At least I'd kept Lilly suppressed and out of his reach.

He raised an eyebrow as he reached a hand behind my head, slipped his fingers in my hair and stroked the base of my skull—and just like that, our daughter was sitting on the couch beside me.

I blinked at her in disbelief. "Lilly?"

It took me utterly by surprise when Henry backhanded me. He had done unspeakable things to me, but that was the first time he'd ever struck me. Tears spilled from my eyes as I touched a hand to my cheek and looked up at him.

Azure flames danced in his eyes as he growled, "Do not speak that name."

Apart from a sob that I couldn't hold back, I was speechless.

A puff of blue smoke escaped his nostrils and his mouth-watering scent bled through the air. "I never should have told you about my sister. It was a weak moment. I suppose I figured it would make me seem more genuine. You killed our daughter in more ways than you realize."

My chest tightened, squeezing the air from my lungs. "What?"

His eyes were distant as he whispered, "Naming the child after my sister was the first nail in her tiny coffin." He seemed to be talking through me rather than at me.

"Don't blame me for your mistakes."

"*You* were my mistake," he snarled. Then his eyes dropped to Lilly. "You and this little monstrosity."

I stroked a loving hand over Lilly's curls. "She was beautiful."

Another puff of smoke spilled from Henry's nostrils as he lifted one of Lilly's curls and smoothed it between his fingers. "I shouldn't have bothered leaving this little echo behind for you."

I clutched Lilly's hand in mine as I muttered, "How did you do that?"

He dropped Lilly's tendril and stroked the base of my skull again. Suddenly my hand was empty and no one sat beside me on the couch. I had never felt emptier. "I inked her blood into your scalp."

"How?" I opened and closed my empty hand, desperately hoping to feel some echo of my daughter's touch. "When?"

He flashed that look of his that used to melt my insides and despite the horror of all of this, a tingling sensation stirred inside me. "During a moment of passion whilst you were drunk on my blood wine."

"No," I whispered. "I would remember a thing like that…"

Sinister amusement glinted in Henry's eyes as he shook his head. "You would be amazed at the things that transpired that you've no memory of."

I stared at the couch cushion Lilly had been sitting on a minute ago and blinked the tears from my eyes. "You said I was a mistake. Why bother keeping me around?"

"Because you belong to me," he growled, "and dragons do not share their possessions."

As I opened my mouth to answer, I heard old Bob's voice calling me from somewhere distant…

…I let out a startled gasp as my eyes popped open.

Bob shook me a few seconds more before he noticed I was awake. "You were scarin me again, woman."

"What?" I looked at the couch cushion next to me, stupidly hoping to find my daughter there. "Why?"

Bob gently wiped the tears from my cheeks with shaky arthritic fingers. "Musta been a pretty bad nightmare you were havin. You were whimperin in your sleep."

"Thanks for waking me." I wrapped my arms around Bob's neck and concentrated like hell on making Lilly appear, but the cushion next to me remained empty as that old familiar feeling of nauseous terror engulfed me.

16

CHARLIE

Benjamin tossed his banana peel to the tray on the coffee table. "You ready?"

I nodded and the second he touched my arm, we were back in the cave. At least I wasn't lying on the stone floor this time. I was standing next to Benjamin—not sock monkey Benjamin, *scary as hell* demon Benjamin—with solid pitch black eyes that had no discernable pupils. Across the cave, a Waterfall silently spilled from ceiling to floor. No Water pooled at its base and there was no visible source that it was spilling from. That was nothing new. Those Waterfalls were all over the place in the palace, but the fact that I was able to see through the Waterfall into Emma's clearing was definitely new. Rose was still out there in her dragon form, eyeing the ceiling of the dome as she paced by the lake. "How come I can see through the Water now?"

"You've stopped viewing your surroundings through human eyes," Benjamin muttered as he moved toward the Waterfall. "Now that you've unlocked the dragon within, you're beginning to see and hear and think like a dragon."

I followed Benjamin to the Waterfall and watched Rose pace back and forth. "So dragons can see through the Waterfalls?"

Benjamin nodded.

I turned my head toward him. "Can you see through them?"

I realized he could before he answered because his eyes were fixed on Rose. "Yeah. I can."

"So," I muttered, "what now?"

"You go back out there and shoulder the burden that I promised the Sarrum *you* would carry.

I couldn't help noticing that he'd said *you go* instead of *we go*. "You're coming with me though, right?"

Benjamin looked away from the clearing and studied me through narrowed eyes. "Of course. I promised the Sarrum that, too."

My stomach dropped at the thought of shouldering the weight of the mirage again. "So how do I stop myself from acting like a psycho in there?"

"You focus," Benjamin growled as he stepped into the Waterfall.

So much for letting the guest go first. Whatever. I suppose after all that had happened, I wasn't exactly a guest anymore. I let out a frustrated sigh and stepped in after him.

I stepped out the other side, dry as a bone and anxious to join the silver-scaled dragon standing by the lake with Benjamin. *Focus*, I reminded myself. *Rose looks so gorgeous in her dragon form.* I looked down at my body and discovered that it no longer looked human. As I moved toward the lake, something the Dragon King once said to me—when I asked about his relationship with Emma—came to mind. *You have not yet unlocked the dragon inside you. So how would I begin to explain my actions to you?* Dragons were greedy predators who acted on impulse, satisfying their urges at whim and taking whatever they desired. Now I was one of those monsters. All of my recent actions confirmed it. Everything suddenly clicked as I ambled toward the gorgeous female ahead of me. David Talbot treasured Emma more than anything else in either world. How could he *not* take her and make her his? Rose's exotic floral scent greeted me as I neared the lake. How the hell was I supposed to focus with her around? As I reached the twosome, the smell of sugar cookies and honey and freshly mowed grass mingled with Rose's heady scent.

A low growl erupted from Benjamin's throat as he glared at me.

What did I do now?

Benjamin's glare rivaled the one that he hit me with back when we first met at the facility and he saw my arm around Emma's shoulder. ***Don't even think about touching her, dragon.***

What?

Scent mark her and you'll have me to answer to.

What are you talking about? How the hell would I do that? Then I remembered my conversation with the Sarrum the day we met. Scent marking was accomplished through touch. *I won't—*

I sensed what was about to happen even before Benjamin did.

Rose let out an agonized yelp and collapsed as her body reverted to human form, but I took human form and caught her before she hit the ground. A feeble whimper rose from her throat as I lowered her to the grass.

I was so focused on her that it actually took me a few seconds to notice that the weight of the mirage had come crashing down on me. Too preoccupied to marvel at the fact that I'd failed to notice something so monumentally catastrophic, I looked up at Benjamin as he crouched down beside us. "What's wrong with her?"

He swept her hair off her face with his fingertips. "The burden was too much for her to bear any longer."

I choked back a horrified sob. If Rose suffered permanent damage because I'd wasted too much time being an idiot, I would never forgive myself. "But…she'll be okay, right?"

"Yeah," Benjamin's voice was thicker than usual, "She'll be fine, but right now, she needs to rest." He took her from my arms and stood up as if she weighed nothing, which was pretty impressive considering the fact that her human form still felt as heavy as a dragon.

"Good," I muttered, "That's good."

"You're on your own for a minute, kid. I'm gonna take Rose into the palace. Try not to wreck the place while I'm gone."

"Sure." He called me *kid*. It was the first time since I'd acted like a moron in the clearing that he'd called me anything other than *dragon* or *dumb ass*.

Benjamin dipped his head, then started toward the cave.

My heart throbbed as I watched him carry Rose's limp body across the clearing. It was my fault that she'd collapsed.

A hyena-like cackle sounded outside the dome and I instinctively unmasked, looked up and found the same stupid demon I'd chased away earlier perched on the ceiling of the dome. I glared at him and concentrated on fanning the flames in my eyes until he scurried down to the ground.

Benjamin reappeared beside me and grimaced at the hyena-demon. "I see your buddy's back."

"Yeah." I shot the demon a pointy-toothed grin. "My buddy's an asshole."

The Darkness let out a spine-chilling burst of laughter and the hyena-demon backed up a little further.

I peeled my eyes away from the demon and fixed them on Benjamin. "Why aren't you pissed at me?"

"You didn't mean for that to happen any more than you meant for Godric to abduct Emma."

"Yeah," I muttered, "I also didn't mean to scare Emma in the living room or act like an asshole to Tristan, but I still did it all."

Benjamin folded his arms across his chest. "We warned you all along that you'd have a hard time controlling your dragon impulses at first."

I waited several seconds for him to attach a few encouraging words of wisdom to his *I told you so*. When it was clear he wasn't going to, I muttered, "So what do we do now?"

"We wait."

Fabulous—untold hours hanging with the Darkness, with the weight of the world on my shoulders—should be a real blast. "Well, can I ask you some questions to pass the time?"

"Ask away, kid."

I stared at him for almost a minute before muttering, "Why did Rose come here?"

Benjamin levelled me with his classic *you're a fucking idiot* frown, an expression I was all too familiar with. "She was helping you hold the mirage together."

I swallowed and debated whether to abandon this line of questioning before I crossed a line that I couldn't uncross. *Screw it.* "No. I mean...why did the Sarrum bring her here...to America?"

Benjamin's *you're an idiot* frown deepened. "She came to visit her mother because she was lying in a coma."

Several heartbeats passed in silence before I muttered, "Yeah...and now Isa's out of the coma and doing great. So...why is Rose still here?"

A furrowed brow accompanied Benjamin's *you're an idiot* frown. "It's the first time they've been together since Isa left Rose in a foreign country to be raised by a stranger, and Isa was almost on her death bed when her daughter got here. You don't think they deserve some time to visit now that she's conscious?"

"No..." I swallowed again. "I mean...of course, I do. I was just wondering why else Rose is here."

Benjamin raised an eyebrow. "That's not enough reason for her to stay?"

The staggering weight of the mirage was starting to make me feel woozy. I sat down on the grass and shook my head to snap myself out of it. "Yeah. It's plenty of reason...it's just," *Oh, to hell with it.* "It's just... the night Rose and I first talked, she seemed to think there might be another reason the Sarrum brought her here."

Benjamin held me steadily in his gaze as he sat down beside me. "And did she say what that reason might be?"

I could feel my spine crumbling beneath the weight. Stupid as it probably looked, I laid down right there in the grass. *Too late to drop it now, dumb ass.* "Yeah."

"And?"

"She seemed to think the Sarrum might've brought her here to, uh…make himself an heir."

I expected Benjamin to crank up the terror that he naturally radiated, or growl at me, or smack me upside the head. I did not expect his spine-chilling burst of laughter, and neither did the demons pressed against the walls of the mirage. A few of them pissed themselves when they heard it.

The barrier had thinned so much that I could smell the urine as soon as it hit the air, or maybe my sense of smell was just keener now that I was utilizing my dragon senses. I closed my eyes because it took too much effort to hold them open. Every ounce of strength in me was focused on shouldering the weight. "Did I say something funny?"

"You believed that?" Benjamin's voice sounded distant, even though I knew he was still sitting next to me. I could feel his Dark presence there.

"Well…" my voice echoed back at me from some-where far away, making it difficult to follow my own train of thought. "Yeah… I guess I thought it was a possibility. Arthur said—"

"You mean, Godric." I didn't have to look at Benjamin's face. His hatred was clear in the tone of his voice and the fury I felt rolling off of him.

Shit. There was no Arthur. But he knew about Godric now. Might as well finish what I was trying to say. "Yeah, Godric. Sorry. Godric said Emma was too weak to survive a dragon birth."

Sorrow displaced the anger in Benjamin's voice, "She is."

"So…" *What was I trying to ask?* It was getting harder and harder to think straight. The weight was crushing my skull and compressing my brain. I couldn't go on like this much longer.

"Rose isn't here to provide anyone with an heir," Benjamin whispered, or maybe he was speaking normally and I could only catch a whisper of his voice.

"Then…" *Focus.* "…why is she here?"

"Rose is here because we are her family and she belongs with us," Benjamin's tone was practically gentle. That scared the crap out of me more than anything I was feeling, because it had to mean I was dying. "The Sarrum invited her to remain here as Isa's apprentice. Rose is staying to train with her mother. Is that okay with you?"

Good. Mocking me was a good sign. Maybe I wasn't dying after all. "Yeah," I answered in a weak whisper. My throat could barely produce a sound at this point, but there was more I wanted to ask... along that same train of thought...it was just so hard to follow the train and form a cohesive thought. How was I supposed to think when there was a mountain crushing my brain? There was something else I wanted to know. I could feel it, gnawing at my heart and churning in my stomach. Whatever these questions that I couldn't quite grasp were, I genuinely feared the answers. *Emma is too weak to survive a dragon birth.* "So...the King doesn't want to get Rose pregnant?"

"No. He doesn't," Benjamin's voice was just a faint echo.

"Does..." *Focus.* "Does he plan to get some other surrogate Sighted girl pregnant?"

"No."

Tears slid down my cheeks but I couldn't muster the energy to wipe them away. "So...is Emma just fated to die giving birth to the next Dragon King?"

I felt Benjamin's hand touch my arm, lending me strength as his voice sounded loud and clear in my head. *It's time for you to decide where your loyalties lie, dragon.*

Crap. He was calling me *dragon* again.

You betrayed us by consorting with the enemy. I realize you did it out of stupidity, but withholding the fact that you were conversing with a stranger about our operations was still an act of treason. The Princess's life is now in danger because of your actions. You're here to keep the mirage intact until the Sarrum returns with

Emma because you owe them that much. If you intend to stay and continue to learn from us after that, you'll have to swear your allegiance to the Sarrum.

The ache in my heart flared into a searing pain. He was right. What the hell had I been thinking? *I'm sorry.*

What happens between the Sarrum and his wife is none of your business.

I know. I'm just worried about Emma's safety.

You should've been worrying about her safety when you were transporting the King's worst enemy into her safe haven.

I'm sorry. I just don't—

The Sarrum is not the man you think he is.

What does that mean?

It means you should stop making assumptions and pay attention to what's actually going on around you, dumb ass.

17

BOB

After a few restless hours of broken sleep, Pip and I decided it would be best to continue our journey. For a while we conversed about pointless things to pass the time and lighten the mood, but as the forest continued to darken, neither of us were in the mood to talk. For the last several hours, we'd been traveling in silence, save the occasional muttered instruction from Pip to change direction. Unfortunately, silence wasn't truly silent when you were in the Dark Forest. Unseen creatures constantly whispered inside your head—threats, warnings, pleas for help. As much as it pained me to ignore a cry for help, there was nothing for us to do but keep moving forward. After all, we hadn't actually encountered another living creature for at least a day. It was difficult to keep track of time in the forest. The constant whispering messed with your mind till you barely remembered your own name, let alone what day of the week it was or how many days you'd been traveling. My biggest fear was that we had just been traveling in circles all this time. Each new stretch of the forest looked identical to the last. How Pip could possibly keep track of where we were was beyond me.

I was trying to think of a lighthearted topic of conversation to drown out the whispering for a while, but I was having a difficult time concentrating. I contemplated asking Pip if he would care to rest for a spell, but thought better of it when I remembered time was of the essence and we needed to keep moving. I'm ashamed to admit, my thought process had grown so spotty that there were moments when I forgot what our purpose even was.

Pip tugged on my pocket to get my attention as he whispered, "Slow down."

I wanted to ask why, but figured there must be a reason he had chosen to whisper. When I looked down at him, fear glinted in his tiny dull brown eyes.

I could barely hear his soft whisper over the ones inside my head, "Go slow through here. This is dangerous territory."

I chanced a faint whisper of my own, "What manner of danger is this?"

Pip was clutching the top of my pocket so hard that the color had drained from his knuckles. "Trolls."

"Aren't you half troll?"

Despite our dire circumstances, Pip let out a whispered laugh. "Yeah. I inherited the saggy skin and questionable hygiene habits, but in case you haven't noticed, I didn't exactly inherit the size."

"Size is merely a state of mind," I whispered.

"That's a load of horseshit. I could be a hundred feet tall in my mind, but if I encountered a troll with actual physical size, I'd still end up squashed—probably that much quicker for my stupidity."

"I have faced adversaries many times my size and walked away unscathed in the past," I whispered, "and I'm quite certain I could do it again."

Pip shook his head. "You take care of the other threats and leave the trolls to me. With any luck, the one we run into will be a relative of mine. If we catch them in the right mood, I might be able to talk them out of turning us into stew."

"And if the one we encounter isn't a relative?"

"If it goes south," Pip whispered, "then you're up."

"Agreed."

The booming voice of a hefty simpleton put an end to our hushed conversation, "What the hell are you doing here, freak?"

"Hey, Jack," Pip replied in an unassuming tone. "It's good to run into you, too."

Every muscle in my body tensed as a massive troll stepped from the trees onto the path ahead of us. Then the stench hit me. It was so intense that I found myself wondering if this creature had ever taken a bath in his life. Pip's hygiene was impeccable in comparison to this fellow. The troll scratched a puss-encrusted scab on his arm with jagged dirt-caked fingernails as he grumbled, "You don't belong here."

I figured the comment was directed at me, but Pip shook his head as he looked the filthy creature square in the eye. "Trust me, I'd rather be anywhere but here. Unfortunately, I need to find my cousin. The quicker you direct me to her, the quicker we can both get back to despising each other."

The troll peeled the scab off his arm and smudged the puss and blood that oozed from it with filthy fingers. "Enough with the fancy talk, freak. I could squash you like a melon. How'd you like that?"

I tensed, ready to spring into action if the need arose.

"I wouldn't like that, Jack," Pip replied in a remarkably calm voice. "You're bigger and better, just like you always were. Everybody knows that."

The simpleton nodded his big fat head. "And don't you forget it."

"I won't, Jack," Pip agreed. "Now, can you please tell me where my cousin is?"

The dim-witted creature scratched his head, pulled an insect from his matted hair and popped it in his mouth. "What's in it for me?"

Pip seemed unfazed by the troll's nauseating behavior. "We'll leave you to wallow in filth in peace."

"Fancy words," the troll grumbled.

Pip shrugged his shoulders. "Where is she?"

"She's out."

Pip stared at the troll for a moment before asking, "Do you know when she'll be back?"

Jack shook his head. "I ain't her keeper."

"Of course you aren't," Pip agreed in a patronizing tone that the troll was too dense to pick up on. "Can we wait here till she gets back?"

"If you think I'm gonna sit around and entertain ya—"

Pip let out a slow sigh. "We don't need to be entertained. We just need you to keep the other trolls away. That's not too much to ask of a former neighbor, is it?"

The troll plopped down on the ground with a tired grunt. "Like I said, what's in it for me?"

Pip stole a glance up at me. "My friend is an excellent hunter. What if we catch your dinner and fix it for you?"

The troll wiped his nose on his filthy shirt-sleeve. "What's your buddy got in that satchel on his back?"

"His supplies," Pip muttered. "Why don't you give us a break and take the dinner offer?"

The troll's glare shifted to me. "What ya got in there, pretty boy?"

I took off the pack, stepped toward the troll and held it out to him. "Take what you like."

Jack ripped the pack open at the seams and dumped its contents onto the dirt path. "I like this guy."

18

EMMA

I was losing my mind. There was no other logical explanation for the thoughts that filled my head—memories of events that had never happened in places that didn't exist, warped recollections of actual memories. Doc and Isa assured me that it was just another side effect of the medication overdose, but I didn't buy it. They were obviously covering something up. I'd finally lost it. What else could it possibly be? Terrified of what I would encounter when I opened my eyes this time, I stayed still on the couch with my eyes squeezed shut.

"I'm concerned that this is all too much for her," Doc's voice muttered.

There were a few heartbeats of silence before Isa whispered, "What other options do we have?"

ERIN A. JENSEN

Doc exhaled an unsteady breath. "What good will restoring Emma's memories do if we destroy her mind in the process?"

Restoring my memories? What on earth was he talking about?

"This is working," Isa insisted. "We need to stick with it."

"There's no exact way to calculate the dosage on a potion." Doc paused a few seconds, then cleared his throat. "For all we know, we may have administered too much already. I'm afraid any more might be dangerous."

"What other choice do we have?" Isa whispered. "Sacrificing her memory to spare her health is unacceptable."

"I don't think—"

"I don't care what you think! I've known the Princess since she was a toddler. She'd risk everything to preserve those memories. I wasn't able to protect her the night she stabbed me, but I'll be damned if I'll let her down again. Our job is to restore her memory and I don't intend to fail, so you can either help me or step out of my way."

Confused and disoriented, I stopped fighting the exhaustion and drifted off to sleep…

…"There you are, Princess," Godric's elegant voice murmured. "Don't fight it now. Just come back to us."

I opened my eyes and blinked at my blurry surroundings. "Us?"

"Yes." Godric's pale blue eyes twinkled as he grinned at me from the couch. "I thought perhaps seeing the face of an old friend might help put you at ease."

I was still lying on the floor with the life-sized echo of my Dragon King towering over me. "An old friend?"

Godric's charming grin widened. "I assure you, it would all make more sense if you took a sip of wine." He nodded toward a fresh goblet of wine on the floor to my left.

The floor had been cleaned, but blood red liquid still stained the hem of my dress—a silent reminder to fear the man on the couch. The dragon above me exhaled a puff of blue smoke as I whispered, "No thank you."

Amusement flickered in Godric's eyes as he considered the dragon above me. "You know, I am something of an expert on enchantments like that precious bodyguard of yours."

I looked up at the echo of my Dragon King. "What?"

"That's what the creature is," Godric murmured, "an enchantment. That's why he only feels like a piece of your precious dragon."

"How would you know that?"

"Whom do you suppose your dear husband stole the idea from?"

A tightness blossomed in my chest. "Not you."

The skin around Godric's pale blue eyes crinkled in the most charming way as a carefree chuckle tumbled from his lips. "No? Am I not allowed to be clever?" He didn't drop the grin, but something Dark flashed in those lovely blue eyes. "What am I then?"

"I don't know."

"I'm sure you've heard stories of me," he murmured. "So tell me, what do they say when they speak of the Sarrum's mad uncle, the would-be king?"

"I don't—"

Crystal blue flames flared in his eyes. "Do not try my patience, Princess!"

"I really don't know much about you." I looked up as a puff of smoke billowed toward Godric and felt comforted by the familiar sapphire flames dancing in my dragon's eyes.

"Then I have you at a disadvantage because I've heard quite a lot about you. Your beloved Dragon King would tear both worlds apart to retrieve you."

I took a deep breath and slowly exhaled it. "Is that what you think?"

The flames in Godric's eyes flared brighter as he murmured, "Oh, I'm counting on it."

"Why?"

"Tell me, Princess, how do you imagine the world would react to a King who destroyed everything and everyone that stood between him and his precious treasure?"

"He wouldn't…" I couldn't even finish the sentence because I knew that *he would.*

Godric shook his head. "You don't believe that for a second."

"I—"

"You know," Godric whispered, "most creatures are unfamiliar with all the ins and outs of enchantments, and I'd wager that lot includes you."

"What are you talking about?"

"That magnificent beast above you would harm me in whatever manner necessary to keep me from laying so much as a finger on you. He would never heed any threat or instruction from me, nor any other creature he perceived to be a danger to you."

"I know that," I whispered. "I'm not stupid."

If I didn't know how evil the man in front of me was, his charismatic grin actually might have won me over. "I didn't suspect that you were. A Talbot monarch would never waste his time with a less than perfect bride."

Godric's words stung exactly as he intended them to. I was far less than perfect and he obviously knew it. "Then why waste my time telling me things that I already know?"

An amused grin brightened his handsome face. "You are quite a strong willed little creature, aren't you? I can only imagine how much your darling King must've enjoyed breaking you in."

"You're disgusting."

"You and your time belong to me now." Godric's voice was tinged with fury as he added, "Now shut that pretty mouth of yours and listen."

I looked up at my dragon and felt braver because of him. "Or what?"

"You are not as invincible as you believe yourself to be." Godric turned his head toward a closed door across the room and muttered a sentence in a language that I didn't speak. I was almost positive it was a lower demonic dialect. It was too harsh and displeasing to the ear to be anything else.

The door opened and two lanky demons with Dark soulless eyes and oily skin spread taut over protruding ribcages stepped into the room, each pulling a human female in with him. The first female was a little girl with a frilly white dress and a lovely head of coppery ringlets, and I'd have bet my freedom that the second female with an identical head of coppery curls was the girl's mother. The woman looked familiar but when I tried to place her, a burst of pain exploded at my temples.

The woman let out a hopeless sob as her eyes met mine. "Emma."

The pain sharpened when she spoke my name. "Do I know you?"

"Yes," the woman whimpered as the demons led her and the little girl to Godric's couch.

Godric scowled at the woman, and she lowered her eyes to the floor as the taller demon sat her down on the opposite end of his couch. The shorter demon placed the child between the two adults, then both demons moved to the door and stood there awaiting further instructions. Godric grinned at the females for a moment, then returned his attention to me. "You remember Nellie, don't you? She was your fellow patient at the mental facility you were sentenced to after stabbing your female guard."

A gush of molten pain erupted inside my head, and I squeezed my eyes shut as the room began to blur. "What are you talking about?"

"Take a sip of the wine, Princess," Godric murmured. "It will help you remember."

I fought my way through the pain to open my eyes and glare at him. "I don't take orders from you."

"No. I suppose you don't." Godric glanced at the demons by the door with a bemused grin, then turned back to me. "How rude of me, Princess. I just realized, I never finished sharing my insights on enchantments with you."

The woman on the other end of the couch let out a desperate sob as she looked up at Godric. He snarled at her, and she took her daughter's hand in hers as her tear-filled eyes dropped back down to the floor.

I didn't say a word because I didn't know what to make of any of this.

Godric's eyes were cold as ice as they locked with mine. "Every Sighted creature knows there is nothing that I, nor any other creature could say to make that dragon enchantment of yours stand down. However, most creatures are unaware that the soul an enchantment is connected to *can* control it. If you were to command that beast to let us touch you, he would have no choice but to listen."

I looked up at my dragon, and the flames in his eyes flared brighter as he shook his head. "Why in God's name would I ever do that?"

Godric's grin widened as he looked down at the little girl beside him. "Because you could never in good conscience sit by and watch while those demons by the door defiled this child."

The woman's eyes widened in terror as she scooped the child into her arms. "No!"

"Take your hands off that child," Godric snarled, "or I'll destroy her for good right here and now."

A string of broken sobs escaped the woman's trembling lips as she sat her daughter down between them, but kept the child's hand clasped in hers.

My heart hammered in my chest as I glared at Godric. "You deserve whatever fate this brings you."

"Perhaps."

"What's to keep my dragon from hurting whoever touches any of us?"

"That is not the purpose your enchantment was created for," Godric murmured. "He will only protect you—unless of course, you command him to stand down to spare this child."

Emma! Pain exploded at my temples as a distant voice called my name. *Emma! You have to wake up now...*

...I bolted upright on the couch, gasping for breath. "No! Don't touch—"

"You're safe now, Emma." Isa put a comforting hand on my leg as she sat down on the couch beside me. "No one can touch you. You're safe here with us."

"Not me," I muttered as I wiped the tears from my cheeks with trembling fingers. "He threatened to hurt the child if I didn't..." *What was I saying?* "I... uh... I'm sorry. I guess I was having another bad dream."

Doc pushed the tray of food aside and sat down on the coffee table in front of me. "It wasn't a dream, Emma."

I blinked at him. "What?"

"Doc." Isa's eyes were brimming with tears as she shook her head.

Doc lifted my wrist to check my pulse as he whispered, "She can't take much more of this."

19

NELLIE

Emma vanished in the blink of an eye. I was too afraid to ask Godric what that meant for Lilly and me, or to even meet his eyes. Godric growled something to the demons by the door in an abrasive off-putting language. My stomach clenched as I tightened my hold on Lilly's hand, but the demons didn't come toward us. They just nodded their ugly heads, opened the door and left the room. I watched them until the door closed behind them, then dropped my eyes to the floor.

Godric's voice was ripe with amusement, "You played your part well, my dear wife."

I squeezed Lilly's hand a little tighter. "You're a monster."

"A dragon actually."

I kept my eyes glued to the floor. "I hate you."

"But you didn't always," he murmured in that soft sweet tone that used to melt my insides once upon a time.

"I didn't know how sick you were back then."

"I was sick?" I blinked the tears from my eyes, looked up at his handsome face and watched him stroke a hand over Lilly's curls like she was nothing but a pet. "You are the one who drowned our child, Nellie. Whatever excuse helps you sleep at night, it does nothing to change the fact that *you* held our daughter's head underwater till her little heart stopped beating."

Something snapped as I watched him stroke Lilly's cheek, and I reached out and slapped his hand away before I could stop myself.

Flames flared in his eyes as he glared at me. "Do not try my patience when I am trying so hard to be a good host."

"You're insane."

"I couldn't be saner," he whispered. "I accept responsibility for every action I have ever taken, and there is little I would change if I had it to do over again. You on the other hand, are weak and pathetic. This child that you so desperately cling to is nothing but an echo of your daughter, and yet you would sit by and allow a living, breathing girl to sacrifice herself to protect your dusty memory. Tell me, what will you do when Emma returns? Will you caution

ERIN A. JENSEN

her to remain behind her protections or beg her to
let herself be torn to shreds to protect a child who
you killed years ago? Our daughter is not sitting beside us on this couch. That child rotted away a lifetime ago. She is nothing but a pile of bones beneath
the earth in the waking world. Yet you cling to this
empty shell as if nothing matters more. *You* are the
insane one."

He was right, but I needed my beautiful whisper
of a memory. She was all I had left. *No. She wasn't.* I
had Bob, and with any luck, he was out there in the
forest somewhere searching for me. I just hoped to
God he found me soon because I wasn't sure how
much more of this my heart could take. "Emma was
right, you deserve whatever's coming to you."

"Perhaps." Godric turned to the door and said
something in that same harsh language he'd spoken
in earlier. A few seconds later, the demons reentered
the room.

My stomach lurched as I watched them move toward us. Their skin had a toxic sheen to it, like oil
spilled over pavement on a hot summer day. Their
eyes were nothing but hollow sockets and the rest
of their face was featureless, aside from a ragged in-
dentation where their mouth ought to be. They had
nothing to smile with, but I *felt* them smiling at me as
they stopped in front of us.

Godric uttered a command in their demon
tongue, and one grabbed me by the arm while the

other took hold of Lilly's. Godric's laughter filled the room as they dragged us toward the door. "Keep them entertained, Nellie. They bore easily and I'm quite certain you wouldn't appreciate their means of entertaining themselves."

I looked back over my shoulder at Godric as the taller demon pulled me to the door. "You're a horrible person."

Godric grinned at me just as he used to once upon a time. "But I'm a marvelous dragon."

Tears spilled from my eyes as we reached the door. Then the demons tugged us into the Darkness...

...I yanked my head off Bob's shoulder with an ear-splitting scream. "No!"

Bob let out a loud grizzly bearish snort as his eyes popped open. He stared at me for a few seconds as if he had no idea where, or even who, he was. Then his eyes widened with recognition and a sympathetic smile spread across his wrinkled face. "Another bad dream?"

There was no time to waste playing along anymore. I grabbed him by the shoulders and shook him as hard as my frail old hands could manage. "Godric has the Princess! Did you find Charlie yet? You need to find the Dragon King! He's our only hope of getting out of this alive!" I saw the woman by the door moving closer to us out of the corner of my eye, but it didn't matter. We were almost out of time.

ERIN A. JENSEN

Bob gently removed my hands from his shoulders. "Easy now. Don't give that bitch over there a reason to take you away. Just calm down so we can talk in peace."

"There is no peace!" I screeched, "Lilly and I are going to die, and Lord only knows what Henry plans to do to the Princess!"

A pair of strong hands took hold of me from behind the couch. Then that bitch stepped up and jabbed me with a needle.

If they only knew what sort of hell they were condemning me to...

20

MIA

You're probably wondering who the hell I am and why you're suddenly listening to me rather than delving deeper into the tale you're anxious to get on with. I'd have no part in this if it were up to me. This isn't my story, it's theirs. I'm just here to explain how I happened to cross paths with royalty in the most unfortunate way.

I kept replaying the night I was kidnapped over and over in my head. It was pretty much the only thing keeping me sane, tethering me to the life I'd known and hopefully would know again. Reliving the experience countless times was a necessary torture because I was terrified I'd go mad and forget who I was if I didn't keep reminding myself. It had been working so far, but I had no idea how long "so far" actually was. My mind was too muddled to keep track of time, and I was too busy focusing on who I was to calculate how long I'd been a prisoner. I gave my mind a mental slap for wandering and started from the beginning again...

...I'd had the week from hell, but I survived it just like I'd survived every other hellish week that came before it. Although, there were plenty of days when I couldn't decide whether that was a plus or a minus. I unlocked the door to my apartment with a weary sigh, shut the door and immediately started stripping out of my dowdy waitress getup. Honestly, I probably could've started stripping on the bus without earning so much as a raised eyebrow from the other passengers. Yeah. I was that invisible. I always had been. There were times when it wasn't so bad, like when you broke something in public and wanted to slip away unnoticed. I could always slip away unnoticed. All through my school years, I'd been the invisible girl that no teacher or student ever seemed to remember. I guess it could've been worse. At least I wasn't bullied. Kids would've had to notice me to pick on me.

By the time I reached my bedroom, all but my underwear was wadded in a bundle in my arms. I tossed the grease-infused polyester into the hamper as I stepped through the door and headed to a wrinkled heap of clothes on the chair by my dresser. I rifled through the pile till I found a well-worn baggy sweatshirt and my favorite pair of leggings, slipped them on and grimaced at the painfully average girl who stared back at me from the mirror above my dresser. I'd already eaten a lukewarm dinner that some jackass had ordered then ditched the diner without eating or paying for. Yup, free unclaimed room temperature food was just one of the many perks of my glamorous job. Lacking the motivation or energy to shower, I dropped into bed with my hair smelling faintly of french fries, flipped off the lights and fell sound asleep in under five minutes...

...I opened my eyes in a gully near the edge of the forest, hopped to my feet with a stretch and a yawn and took my time walking to the lake. When I reached it, I cupped some Water in my hands and ignored the ugly creature staring back at me as I sipped it. My demon reflection made my waking reflection look like a freaking beauty queen. I splashed some Water on my featureless face and pictured the customers I'd waited on at the diner throughout the day. None of them stood out in my mind as particularly beautiful. Then I remembered the woman in the department store I'd zipped into on my lunch break to buy a pair of stockings because I didn't have the energy to wash the ones I was wearing before waking up and repeating my pointless routine for the zillionth time.

I concentrated on my reflection in the Waters and pictured the woman's headful of exotic braids until they crowned my reflection's head. I watched my blank slate gradually transform to her perfect features—a striking mix of Asian and African traits—full lips, striking green eyes and a body that I doubted anyone had ever ignored. I pictured every detail of the beaded black dress that fit the woman like a glove, showing off every splendid curve. I recalled the tattoo that coiled around her slender upper arm and the matching one around the ankle on the opposite side of her body. Then I stepped back and grinned at the gorgeous creature the Waters reflected. If only I could stay in Draumer and avoid my pathetic waking life altogether.

I was just about to wade into the Waters when I realized my feet were bare, closed my eyes and pictured the death-defying heels that completed my killer outfit. Satisfied with every detail of my reflection, I briefly debated where to spend my evening, but it didn't take long to decide on the Dragon's Lair. Creatures came in every shape and size from every corner of Draumer to frequent the tavern on the border of Light and Dark. It was the place to be if you were looking for someone to make you forget your waking life for a few blissful hours. As if that wasn't a good enough reason, the Dragon's Lair also had an incubus who tended bar on occasion— not just some potluck half-breed, but a pure blooded incubus. He was more than half the reason that the place was so popular. I wasn't fool enough to expect him to notice me, but he was certainly something to look at while I perused the crowd in search of a playmate for the evening. I stepped into the Waters and grinned to myself as I emerged from a lake on the outskirt of town and headed for the path through the forest that led to the tavern.

As I made my way out of the forest, the dragon sil-houette on the tavern's sign glinted in the moonlight as if the establishment itself were winking at me. I straightened my dress, flipped a few braids over my shoulder, then opened the door and surveyed the magnificent assortment of patrons that were present to choose from. A ruddy dwarf whistled at me as I headed toward the bar, but I didn't spare him more than a passing glance. My eyes settled on a pudgy troll as he stepped from the bar with a tankard of mead, sloshing more than a little on the floor as he headed toward his comrades on the other side of the room. I glanced at the spot in front of the bar that the troll had just vacated, and my whole body flushed at the sight of the incubus who'd waited on him. He shook his head as he watched the unsteady troll spill a trail across the floor.

I picked up my pace and miraculously managed to snag the empty space at the bar. The incubus eyed me with a magnificent grin—not a phony customer-service grin like I plastered on my face for eight hours a day at the diner—a genuine I'd-love-to-see-what's-under-that-dress sort of grin. I thanked my lucky stars that I'd crossed paths with the exotic beauty at the department store as he took a step closer and leaned against the bar. "Welcome to the Dragon's Lair."

Every molecule of my body reacted as if he'd done a hell of a lot more than just smile at me. "Thank you."

"Is this your first time here?"

"Why do you ask?"

His eyes raked over me as he murmured, "Because I don't remember seeing you in here before, and I'm pretty sure I wouldn't forget you."

I felt dangerously close to bursting into flames as I pressed my body against the bar and answered in a breathy whisper, "I've been here before, but it's been a while."

The incubus leaned a little closer to me across the counter. "Must've been on my day off."

I was having a hard time remembering how to string words together into a sentence. All I could think about was hopping up onto the bar and tearing off all my clothes. I actually considered doing it for a few seconds. No one would recognize me when I returned in the future if I never took this form again, and this world was all about letting your carnal instincts lead your actions.

I was absently reaching for the tie on my dress when a female troll stepped behind the bar and tapped my incubus on the shoulder. "Hey, sweetie, they could use your help outside." And just like that, the bitch stole my dream man's attention.

He nodded at the ugly troll and winked at me as he stepped out from behind the bar and headed for the door.

The troll stepped up to the bar and flashed me the all too familiar customer-service smile. "What can I get for you, dear?"

I was about to tell her that she could get the incubus she'd just stolen from me when someone leaned over my shoulder. "Whatever she's having, make it two," a deep male voice smooth as satin murmured by my ear.

Still heated from my conversation with the incubus, a spasm of elation rocketed through me as I turned toward the voice. A tall black man with perfect hair and a well-trimmed goatee grinned at me. He was dressed all in black and wearing sunglasses despite the fact that it was dark outside and the tavern was dimly lit. I grinned back at him and whispered, "Why the sunglasses?"

His grin widened. "I like it dark." The words were innocent enough, but they didn't sound innocent in that satin voice of his.

I smiled without really knowing why I was smiling. Then it suddenly dawned on me that I must be flirting with a sweet-talker—a silver tongued demon who could coax almost any creature into doing just about anything with his honeyed voice.

He tipped his head toward the troll behind the bar. "So what are you drinking tonight, pretty lady?"

I'd forgotten all about the bitch behind the bar till he reminded me that she was waiting for my order. I glanced in her general direction without actually taking my focus off the charming sweet-talker. "I'm in the mood for something strong and dark."

The troll nodded and ducked beneath the counter as the stranger leaned closer, pressing his chest against my shoulder so his satin voice sounded closer to my ear.

"I'm not sure they have what you're looking for behind the bar."

The lingering effects of the incubus coupled with this man's delicious voice had me damn near close to trembling. I tipped my head back so it touched the Dark stranger's. "No?"

Amusement saturated his satin voice as he touched his cheek to mine and whispered, "Nah. I'm pretty sure they don't."

"Hmm," I rasped, marveling at the fact that I already felt like I'd been drinking for hours. "Do you know where I can find what I'm looking for?"

The troll slammed two glasses down on the counter and splashed equal portions of a suspiciously murky liquid into both as the man behind me whispered, "Ask me again after a few drinks."

Anxious to throw caution to the wind and embrace my carnal instincts, I picked up one of the glasses and tossed it back in one eager gulp. "I will."

A trickle of laughter as smooth as his voice tumbled from the stranger's lips. "Good." He slid some money across the counter to the troll, grabbed the other drink and winked at me as he downed it.

After that, the details grew hazy. The two of us got cozy in a booth tucked in a corner of the room. There were more drinks, and the rest of the room disappeared as his satin voice murmured in my ear. I'm not sure who kissed who first, but soon after our lips met, we decided to go someplace quieter. Since I *didn't have a dwelling nearby, he suggested we go to his place—which seemed like a fabulous idea at the time. We took our time on the path through the forest that led to the Waters. If I remember correctly, we got sidetracked and stepped off the path a few times. Those details were nothing but a blur of hands and lips, and his satin voice purring in my ear. When we reached the Waters, I hesitated and told him I should probably get going.*

But he grinned and pulled me into his arms, and I distinctly remember how warm his lips felt against mine. Then his mouth moved to my ear, "Come on now. Don't leave me when we're having such a good time."

I felt a twinge of unease as I whispered, "It was a good time, but I think I should go."

His lips brushed my ear as he whispered, "It's okay, baby. I know what you are."

I tilted my head and pulled off his sunglasses so I could look him in the eyes. "What?"

His deep brown eyes watched me closely as he nodded. "I know you're a changeling."

I stared at him for almost a minute because I didn't know what to say. If he knew what I really looked like, what the hell was he doing with me? "Then why did you leave the tavern with me?"

There was a faint smile on his lips as he murmured, "Because you're exactly what I want."

Speechless that he knew what I was and still wanted me, I swallowed and nodded...

...If I could go back and warn myself... *No.* There was no point in letting my thoughts go there. I couldn't change the fact that I left the tavern with the sweet-talking stranger and willingly went home with him. I didn't want to remember anything else that happened in detail, but it was pretty hard not to because my arms were still tied to the bedposts. *I let him tie me to the bedposts for fuck's sake.* What a pathetic idiot I was...

...There was some pleasure before she came in and found me tied to her bed. I'd spent months of my life in the deepest parts of the Dark Forest. I'd dined with creatures that would turn most people's stomachs. I'd slept in damp tunnels with slithering creatures brushing past me in the dark. But none of that compared to this woman. She was lovely to look at—she had long lustrous golden hair, her eyes were a brilliant shade of green, her pale skin was flawless and her features were delicate and perfect, just like her body. Stupid as it sounds, the first thing I felt when the shadow stormed into the room was jealousy. I would've given anything to look like her, but terror quickly replaced the jealousy as she stalked toward me. With each step she took, my fear intensified as I watched her eyes turn a Dark soulless black that I couldn't seem to look away from. By the time she reached the bed, I couldn't see anything else, as if that pitch black Darkness in her eyes had swallowed the entire room and everything in it.

I couldn't see her sit down on the bed beside where I lay bound, but I felt her mouth beside my ear as she spoke in an icy whisper, "Well, isn't this cozy?"

As if the whole situation wasn't nightmarish enough, I lost control of my bladder the instant her breath hit my ear.

The woman let out a growl that wasn't the least bit feminine, or even human for that matter. "Now, who the fuck's going to clean that up?"

The sweet-talker's satin voice sounded distant, "Payne, why don't you ease up and let me handle this?"

Another low growl echoed through the room. "Because you're having too much fun."

"Lighten up, baby," the satin voice murmured.

"Shut the fuck up, Plezur!" the shadow beside me growled. "It's my turn to have fun now!"…

…My mind refused to recall anything that happened after that…

21

DAVID

As I took to the skies to search the forest for this cabin that the Purists allegedly frequented, I listened for Emma's heartbeat and prayed that Isa could keep her from succumbing to sleep. Now that her strength had begun to wane, the Princess tired more easily and I feared she wouldn't be able to hold out for long. As I flew, my mind seemed determined to revisit the past—perhaps because Doc and Isa were working so tirelessly to restore Emma's memories of the events that had bound us together years ago...

...It felt as if time had stopped the instant I confined the Princess to the shore of the lake. There was nothing for me to do but sit in the palace and watch her through the Waterfall, like a perverse voyeur peering at his victim through the fabric of a curtain. The only other viable option was to leave her to suffer alone and although I

was painfully aware that she felt abandoned, I would not leave till she found her way to the Light. After the first week, she stopped crying out to me and took to curling into a fetal position and sobbing till she had no tears left to shed. Silence came after that, but she had made no move to exit the clearing.

She was sitting in the grass by the shore, dressed in a white satin nightgown that tied at the neck—the same gown she had worn on her birthday and continued to wear every day since. Dressed in that gown with those wings that sparkled like virgin snow on a winter morning, she looked every bit the angel she was. Her purity stood in stark contrast to the Darkness beyond her clearing. To any other set of eyes, she sat in the midst of a sunny afternoon, but I could see through the mirage to the Darkness beyond. She and I were as opposite as that sun in the clearing and the Darkness beyond its reach—angel and demon, purity and sin. She was Light, and I was Darkness. It had always been that way, but the differences between us were impossible to ignore now, and there was nothing I could do to change the impossibility of our situation. Had I been less selfish, I could have prepared her for our inevitable separation so it wouldn't have come as such a shock, but I hadn't the heart to darken our time together with the knowledge that it would come to an abrupt end once she reached maturity. I had always known of course, but I wanted to spare her that agony. I wanted her to recall nothing but joy when she thought back on our time together. It wasn't a practical decision, but dragons aren't famed for making rational choices where their treasures are concerned. That being said, dragons are not the monsters that myth and legend make us out to be. We generally choose to live quite peaceably, unless some soul is fool enough to steal our treasure—in that instance, all else be damned. Yet we aren't mindless beasts who keep fair maidens locked away waiting for some brave knight to come and rescue them. Tarnished knights spread those moronic tales to bolster their own egos and compensate for whatever inadequacy it is that leaves them lacking. In actuality, our treasures rarely wish to leave us. After all, it's quite difficult to resist falling in love with a creature who wants nothing more than to satisfy your every desire and be whatever it is that you need.

"You look like hell, Boss."

I twisted in my chair to scowl at Benjamin. "You aren't looking much better yourself."

Benjamin's expression darkened. "Isa's up half the night in the waking world with her infant these days and whenever she does manage to slip to Draumer, our time together inevitably ends with her rushing off to attend to her son."

I exhaled an apologetic sigh, and the room filled with my scent. It was impossible to stopper with Emma so near. "I am sorry, my friend."

Benjamin shook his head. "It is what it is. You and I don't get happily-ever-afters."

I tapped my fingers on the arm of my chair with a melancholy grin. "Monsters rarely do."

"You should at least take a break," Benjamin muttered as he stepped toward the Waterfall.

"Not until she does."

"It's been three months." He turned his head to look over his shoulder at me. "I'm starting to think she never will."

"Then, so be it."

"You look like you've aged ten years in the last three months."

My eyes fixed on Emma as she stood and started to pace. "You're not exactly the picture of health yourself these days."

"I might be miserable, but you're physically exhausting yourself. How long can you keep this up?"

"As long as it is necessary."

"Can't you at least change that sunny day to a starry night to expend a little less energy?"

"She needs the sunlight."

"Then she should go to the Light Forest," he grumbled. "You're draining yourself more than you need to."

A whisper of smoke escaped my flared nostrils and swirled through the air between us. "Do not presume to tell me what I need."

Benjamin took a deep breath and stared at the ceiling of the cave for a minute before responding, "Why don't you let me take her to the Light Forest?"

I studied him through narrowed eyes. "You despise the Light."

"Yes, but I'd suffer it for the Princess, and I've got nothing but free time on my hands lately." Several heartbeats passed before he added, "I wouldn't leave her until she found her place among the Light creatures and started to feel at home there."

"And how at home do you suppose the other Light creatures would feel with you around?"

"I don't give a fuck how the other Light creatures feel." He cleared his throat as he turned back to the Waterfall. "But I do care about her. Let me do what I pledged to do the day she was born. I swear to you, I will protect her until she feels safe enough to remain there on her own."

I stood from my chair with a heavy sigh and eyed my Princess as I moved toward the Waterfall. My desire to devour her purity grew more urgent by the hour, but I fought the urge till my body convulsed with need, and I would continue to fight it until she found her way to the Light. "No one will force her hand. The decision to move on must be hers."

Benjamin squeezed his eyes shut. "What if she never makes that decision?"

"Then things shall remain as they are."

"Your absence is the talk of Draumer these days. People need to see their King on occasion."

"I don't bloody well give a fuck what people need," I snarled, "Her need is all that concerns me at the moment."

"That's exactly what they're afraid of," Benjamin whispered, "that you'll put the needs of your Princess above the needs of your kingdom."

"They should fear that." A pang of sorrow gripped me as I watched Emma skip a stone across the surface of the Water and struggled to reconcile my memories— of lazy days spent teaching my precious child to skip stones—with my bestial desire to strip her of her innocence and bind her to me forever. "Her needs are far more important to me."

22

ROSE

I woke in a guestroom with a splitting headache and a sinking sensation in the pit of my stomach—as if I'd swallowed a ball of lead that was dragging me deeper and deeper into the depths of a despair that I'd never be able to surface from—a feeling with which I was all too familiar. I had let Benjamin down...and the Sarrum. His Princess was in terrible danger, but I'd been too weak and pathetic to do my part to hold her mirage together. Charlie and Benjamin were hardly gone long, yet their short absence was all it took to deplete every bit of strength I possessed. Thank God Charlie was there to catch the weight of the mirage when I collapsed. To add to my embarrassment, Charlie's presence was the reason I'd gotten too overwhelmed to keep it together. He was a beautiful dragon and I wanted a whole lot more than friendship from him. Benjamin had warned me countless times to keep my relationship with Charlie professional because it would be too dangerous for me to get involved with another Sighted creature, especially if that creature was a dragon. I wasn't sure I would ever get used to how different everything was in the Sarrum's court from what I'd been surrounded by my entire childhood.

Louise Talbot had raised me to believe that the greatest purpose I could ever hope to achieve was to bring a new dragon into the world—that is, if any male would stoop low enough to consider me a suitable mother for his child. I wasn't a pure-blooded dragon. I was just a mutt—the unwanted offspring of a promising young sorceress and the shadow who had forced himself on her—and Louise never let me forget it. She had taken pity on me when I was born and agreed to raise me so that I might reach my full potential. At least, that's the story I had grown up hearing.

I flew across the ocean under the impression that I was meant to bear the Dragon King's child because I was expendable and his Princess was not. I didn't question the validity of that for a second. The Princess was royalty—a pure-blooded fairy and the wife of the Sarrum. She was the Dragon King's most beloved treasure, and despite the general opinion of the Talbot family who resided in England—that she was unworthy to be the Sarrum's wife—none of them questioned how precious she was to him. It was an unwritten rule as old as time itself: you do not part a dragon from his treasure, and you certainly don't question the actions of the Dragon King. Louise was thrilled when the Sarrum contacted her to request that I come to America. She was certain that visiting my birth mother was of secondary importance, and that the real reason the King had summoned me was to provide him with a suitable heir to the throne. I obediently accepted the invitation because rejecting an offer from the Sarrum would be unthinkable, and Louise shed no tears when I departed. In fact, she beamed with pride as we exchanged our goodbyes. I suppressed my tears as was expected and gracefully headed toward my inevitable, yet very respectable, death. A day later, I stepped onto foreign soil on the other side of the world, terrified that I had been sent to my death by the woman who raised me.

When Benjamin came to collect us from the airport, I was petrified. My past experiences with shadows had all been less than pleasant to say the least, and the Darkness was the most feared shadow in existence. The first time I was alone with Benjamin, the tenderness in his voice shocked me as he informed me that my birth mother was his soul mate and he planned to protect me as if I were his own flesh and blood. After that, Benjamin took me to meet my comatose mother and permitted me to spend as much time with her as I wanted. I focused on my mother—held her hand, whispered how anxious I was to meet her—and tried not to think about my other purpose for being there. I sat at Isa's bedside for days, watching the doctor and the Darkness come and go.

Charlie also visited a few times, but I focused on my mother and tried not to pay too much attention to him. I was pretty sure he thought I was an idiot because I made a complete fool of myself the first time we spoke. I misunderstood when the doctor called him a "virgin dragon" and thought that he meant *virgin* in the waking world sense of the word. Clueless fool that I was, I said as much to Charlie. Then I proceeded to ask if he and I were meant to conceive a child to provide the Sarrum with an heir. Charlie was probably the most polite dragon I'd ever encountered. He tried to hide his disgust at my question as best he could, but his initial reaction—to spill his drink all over himself—pretty much said it all. The worst part of it all was how disappointed I was to learn that my assumption was wrong. There was a kindness in the lost dragon's eyes that made me believe I could trust him with anything. If I were destined to end my life bringing a new dragon into the world, it would have been nice to at least feel comfortable with the dragon who fathered the child. Charlie did more than just make me feel comfortable. He made me feel things that I never dreamt I'd feel for any male, since a man would likely be the cause of my untimely death. I heated at the sound of Charlie's voice and the kindness in his eyes. Despite the danger, I found myself wanting him to touch me. I began to crave it each time I was near him. Benjamin immediately picked up on that and made it very clear that he didn't approve. At the time, I figured he disapproved because I was meant to bear the Dragon King's child, and the King deserved an untouched female.

The day the doctor finally took me to meet the Sarrum, my heart was hammering inside my chest. When the King dismissed the doctor so he could speak with me in private, it was nearly impossible for me to contain my fear. I was raised among royal dragons, but I had never met one like David Talbot. The Sarrum exuded power, it leaked from his every pore. Damn the dragon's bestial instincts. The Dragon King was born to command respect and elicit fear in the hearts of all who encountered him—and dear God, he did—and I was born to submit to such a magnificent beast's dominance. I thankfully managed to keep it together by averting my eyes and focusing on the floor of his office, but the King surprised me by gently lifting my head to make eye contact. Then he informed me that they did things quite differently than what I was used to. Something in those fierce eyes of his told me not to fear him and somehow I relaxed, but I was still terrified. For all I knew, he intended to make an heir right then and there. I couldn't stop myself from shaking when he informed me that I "could be of great service" to him. Despite everything Louise had taught me about proper behavior, my eyes filled with tears and the Dragon King shocked me by taking my trembling hand and giving it a gentle squeeze. The gesture washed over me like a sedative, calming my body and mind. Once I was relaxed enough to focus on his words, he invited me to stay and train as my mother's apprentice when she recovered. I wanted to ask if he meant for that to happen, when and if I survived the birth of his heir, but I was too afraid of offending him with the fear in my voice. He answered my unspoken concerns with a kind smile and informed me that he had no intention of laying a finger on me or allowing any other man to do so without my consent. He said I'd be under his protection and would be considered a valuable member of his family. After that, I truly began to relax.

Training with the doctor made me feel like a whole new person with a confidence I'd never believed I possessed, and spending all that time training with Charlie was wonderful. The more I got to know him, the more certain I was that he was a genuinely good creature. I also realized how lost Charlie felt among all these people. I could relate to that and I wanted to get closer to him. Unfortunately, it also became clear that his heart belonged to another female. So I focused on my training, first with Doc and then with my mother once she woke. I tried not to think of Charlie as anything more than a friend, but there were times when I swore he looked at me with something more than friendship in his eyes—although perhaps that was just stupid, wishful thinking on my part.

I did my best to suppress my *more than friendship* feelings for Charlie, and I was pretty successful until he sauntered toward me in the clearing, exuding a scent that was somehow both wholesome and decadent. There was no misunderstanding the purpose of that scent, and I was the only female in the mirage. As I became blissfully aroused by that realization, my scent wafted through the air to mingle with his, and I lost focus. The instant my focus became divided, I could no longer shoulder the crushing weight of the mirage. That's when I failed at my duty and collapsed.

23

CHARLIE

It was so dark in the clearing that I could barely see my hand in front of my face, which didn't really matter since I didn't have the energy to hold my eyes open. Benjamin and I had been silent for hours because my attention was entirely focused on the weight that was crushing me to the ground, but I was starting to fade and I needed a distraction from the excruciating pain. Since Benjamin was the only other soul around, he'd just have to provide one.

I turned my head in his direction without opening my eyes. "Tell me a story?"

Benjamin must've sensed how desperate I was to focus on something other than the mountain that was pulverizing my bones because he didn't even mock me. "What kind of story?"

"I don't know…anything." I shifted to one side in a useless attempt to redistribute the weight. "Tell me how you met the Sarrum."

"We met in college."

"Wow," I croaked, "that's fascinating. Really, you should publish that story. Come on man, I'm dying here. Give me something to take my mind off the pain."

He grabbed a fistful of my hair and gave it a swift tug. "There. Focus on that."

I let out a pathetic laugh. "You really do love to kick a man when he's down, don't you?"

"I don't coddle."

"Coddle?" I opened my eyes and squinted at the shadow in the darkness. "Seriously?"

I spotted a brief flash of movement in the dark as Benjamin nodded. "Focusing on the pain strengthens you."

"How do you figure?"

"When you've got nothing else to focus on, you're forced to face the agony and explore your limits."

I gave up on trying to see Benjamin's face and let my eyelids droop shut. "I think I surpassed my limits a few hours ago."

"And yet, you're still here and the mirage is still intact."

"Great, so I'm doing a bang up job. Why don't you reward me with a story?"

"What are you, eight years old?"

190

A vision of my father uncorking a little blue vial and pouring its contents down my eight year old throat came to mind—the vision that'd surfaced when Benjamin drove us off a bridge and the car was filling up with water. The night my father poured that mystery liquid down my throat was the night I jumped in the Waters and left him behind to die. *Screeches from another lifetime echoed in my head.* "Emotionally...maybe."

"Why the fuck do you want to hear about how I met the Sarrum?"

"Because I like to know the history of a family before I pledge my eternal loyalty to them," I muttered, hoping he'd ignore the way my voice wavered.

"Does that mean you intend to pledge your allegiance to the Dragon King?"

"I've got to," I croaked. "I owe him."

"That's not a good enough reason."

"Can we debate that when my brain's not getting squashed?"

"You want to hear my story so you can understand why I aligned myself with him?"

"Yeah." I squeezed my eyes shut tighter as the screeches in my head intensified. "Kinda."

"I had a strict upbringing," Benjamin replied in a narrative tone that suggested this was the intro to a story.

I hoped to God it was, and that his voice could drown out the screeches.

"My parents were both shadows—"

"Wait, then why aren't you a dragon?"

"They weren't both *Sighted* shadows," Benjamin growled. He didn't say it, but I got the message. *Don't interrupt the fucking story.* "My mother was Unsighted and my Sighted father served as my guide. He didn't believe in coddling either."

I wondered what exactly he meant by that, but I wasn't about to interrupt again. I was just thankful he was giving me something to focus on.

"My father started training me to be ruthless and fierce right around the time I started learning how to walk, and he drilled the importance of binding with the most powerful creature I could find into my head on a daily basis. Deep down, he'd always felt inadequate because he failed to bind himself to stronger creature. He had a shot at it when he was younger, but he passed it up and chose to bind himself in marriage to my mother instead. He spent the rest of his life regretting that decision and resenting my mother because of it. After she died, his bitterness drove him to drink and fixate on my training.

I left home at eighteen, eager to be rid of the man and ready to start living my own life, but it didn't take long to realize how deeply his teachings had taken root in me. I craved power, and I was determined to accomplish everything that my father had failed to. The irritating part of it all was that my father tracked me down a year after I left home to send me a news-paper clipping—an article about a new building that was under construction at a university near the coast thanks to the generosity of a wealthy philanthropist in England. The article went on to detail plans for completing construction just in time for the arrival of a new law student who just happened to be the son of the Brit who'd funded the construction. As much as I wanted to toss the article out because it'd come from my father, I couldn't. That wealthy student was a Talbot and his father was the Sarrum, which meant that this dragon would one day take the throne. So I applied to the university and moved to the coast in hopes of aligning myself with the most powerful creature in existence."

I was too curious to stop myself from chiming in, "So, you just walked up to the future King of the world and asked if you could bind yourself to him for the rest of your life?"

"No, dumb ass."

I opened my eyes and discovered that I could see my surroundings in muted shades of gray now.

Benjamin's Dark eyes were glaring at me. "I majored in law, took the same courses as the Dragon Prince and waited for an opportunity to get close to him."

If I squinted, I could just make out the details of Benjamin's face. "How long did it take you to find one?"

"Not long," Benjamin muttered. "A month into our first semester, the head of the university's medical school came into one of our classrooms looking for volunteers for a special case study. He and the law professor who taught the class stood at the front of the lecture hall and announced that they were going on a day trip to observe a psych patient at a hospital a few hours north. They said her case was an interesting study both legally and medically. The trip would involve a review of the records from her murder trial and a visit to observe her mental state, so that we could assess whether we agreed with the insanity verdict she'd received while on trial for drowning her daughter."

A wave of nausea washed over me as I muttered, "Nellie Godric?"

Benjamin's silhouette nodded. "Yeah. Her trial had been a whispered topic of conversation among the Sighted for months."

"So, were the professors looking for Sighted volunteers?"

"Yeah. As soon as they started talking, they unmasked and watched for students who unmasked in response."

"What about Unsighted people who unmask without even realizing they're doing it? I see that all the time. How could the professors tell the difference?"

"There are subtle differences in the way they unmask. The unmasking of an Unsighted creature has a flicker to it that an intentional unmask doesn't."

"Huh." I made a mental note to pay closer attention the next time I watched an Unsighted person unmask.

"The unmasking was a signal to any Sighted creatures present that these professors weren't just going on an observational fieldtrip. This was a visit with a purpose, and they were looking for Sighted volunteers to assist. I didn't know it at the time, but they were really only looking for one additional student. The Prince and his med student buddy from back home in England were already going. In fact, these professors weren't really the ones in charge of the task. They were just there to facilitate the process so it'd all seem logical to the Unsighted, both at our school and at the mental ward. The Prince was in charge and the purpose of the visit was to determine whether to sentence the dragon mother to death for murdering her offspring, but I didn't find that out until after I was selected. I just saw the Dragon Prince unmask after the professors did, figured they'd select him and saw it as my chance to get an in with the future King."

"And the professors picked you to go on the trip?"

"No," Benjamin muttered with a subtle shake of his head. "The Prince selected me. I unmasked right after he did, and watched his fiery gaze scope out the Sighted candidates in the room. When he got to me, he stopped scanning the room and maintained eye contact for several of the longest seconds of my life. Then he gave a slight nod in my direction. The professors pretended to consider all the students with raised hands for a minute, then they "selected" the Prince and myself and instructed us to meet them in the lecture hall that evening for a run through of the details.

I showed up early for the meeting, eager to prove myself to the future King. When I walked in the room, the professors weren't even there—it was just the Prince and that annoyingly cheerful med student he lived with."

I raised an eyebrow.

"Yeah," Benjamin answered without giving me the chance to ask. "You've met that jolly pain in the ass. Doc was studying to take his place as the Talbots' royal healer."

"Wow..." I was about to comment that Doc wasn't kidding when he said they were *old* friends, but I patted myself on the back for refraining from saying it because I realized it'd sound like an insult. I wasn't *totally* unteachable.

Benjamin narrowed his eyes at me, as if he heard what I'd refrained from saying. "I introduced myself to the Prince and offered to be of service to him in any way possible, and he looked at me like I'd just asked him to fucking marry me—and before you make some stupid ass comment, no he didn't look excited. He looked aloof as hell and a little repulsed. I hadn't flat out offered to bind with him for life, but I soon discovered that I didn't need to. The Prince was the most perceptive creature I'd ever encountered, and he wasn't impressed by my eagerness to attach myself to him. After his initial disdainful reaction, he briefed me for our mission with a faint smile on his lips. It became clear pretty quickly that he wasn't as serious as I was."

"Yeah," I muttered, "I'll bet he was the life of the party."

"He was," Benjamin muttered, "Sighted or not, everyone wanted to get close to David Talbot. He was wealthy, and he just had this aura of power about him that made people want to be a part of his circle, but he wasn't really interested in political networking. He was interested in enjoying his carefree youth to the fullest before he took on the responsibility of ruling the whole fucking world. I didn't get that at the time, and I didn't really even like him. I just wanted a piece of his power and he knew it, but he didn't push me away because of it. He patiently pulled me into his circle little by little as he felt I was ready. I didn't find out till much later that he was impressed by my abilities from the start. He immediately sensed what I was capable of and started putting my abilities to the test on that trip we took, but my desire to pledge myself to him for life—just because of his power—wasn't good enough. So, he took the time to get to know me and let me get to know him, and by the end of our freshman year, he invited me to move into the house that he and Doc shared. The deepening of our relationship was a gradual process. I once told you that binding ourselves for life with another creature isn't a decision we shadows make lightly. I was sure I wanted it because of David Talbot's power and importance, but I came to understand that wasn't the right attitude. It took me some time to unlearn all the lessons my father had drilled into me since birth, but in the end I was a better man because of it."

I thought that over in silence for a few minutes before asking, "So, what happened when you went to see Nellie?"

"It was late at night when we got to the hospital—fewer people around to ask questions at that hour. The Sighted doctor on duty had set the whole thing up on the hospital's end. When we got to her room, Nellie Godric wasn't at all what I'd expected. With all the talk, I expected to find a crazed monster in that hospital bed. Instead, we found a broken woman exhibiting sure signs of dragon-blood poisoning. The poor thing was lost and confused and devastated over what she'd been tricked into doing. When we filed into her room and unmasked, she started screaming that we weren't real, we were all just in her head. The sick bastard had not only poisoned her mind and tricked her into murdering her own child, he'd convinced her that she imagined the whole fucking thing. He made her believe that all the conversations they'd had in Draumer about "saving" their daughter by binding her to the Dream World had been in her mind."

I blinked my eyes to fight back the tears I wanted to shed for Nellie. "Why didn't anybody outside her room come to check on her when she started screaming?"

"That was the Prince's first test of my abilities. I can manipulate the minds of those around me so they don't see or hear or register anything that I don't want them to. The Prince tested the extent of that ability by instructing me to block everything that happened in the room from anyone outside it, so no one heard a sound coming from her room. Then the Prince drew her through the Waters to Draumer to make it clear that what she was seeing *was* real and there was no escaping the inquiry they were conducting. I stood by the door the whole time to repel anyone who tried to enter the room with a crippling dose of fear at the thought of opening the door."

"So, why didn't the Sarrum sentence Nellie to death? She *did* kill her own dragon child."

"Yes, but the Sarrum knew it wasn't her fault. That was obvious to all of us as soon as we walked in the room. Draumer law dictated that she be sentenced to death for her actions, but the final ruling was up to the Prince and he took pity on her and softened the sentence. Instead of death, he sentenced her to spend the remainder of her days confined to the mirage Godric had constructed for her. The Prince sealed the mirage so that no one could go in or out, but he allowed her to keep the enchantment Godric had created with their daughter's blood."

I was still stuck on the "no one could go in or out" part. "What do you mean no one could go in or out? I did lots of times."

"Yeah," Benjamin muttered. "We know. Why the fuck do you think the Sarrum invited you to come train with us?"

"I...uh..." I'd come up with about a million theories, but none of them involved the Sarrum being impressed because I got past an impenetrable seal that he'd created. "He invited me to join his family because he was impressed with my abilities?"

"That's one way to put it," Benjamin answered with a bemused grin, "but I'm not sure *impressed* is the word I'd choose. I'd probably go with *intrigued* or *pissed*, but the basic gist is the same. You had more power than you realized, and the Sarrum wanted to explore that to determine your full potential."

"So he could enlist me...or eliminate me?"

"Yes."

"What?" I muttered. "So, he might've decided to kill me? Why didn't you tell me that when I was antagonizing him and insulting him?"

"Don't be an idiot. I warned you a hundred times that you didn't want to make an enemy of David Talbot. I fucking told you the first day we met, when you were a mental patient and you had no idea who or what I even was."

"Why didn't you tell me who you were back then?"

"It wasn't my place to decide whether you should know all that."

"So…where do I stand on the whole live or die thing, now that I'm responsible for getting the Sarrum's wife kidnapped?"

"It certainly didn't strengthen your case."

"Shit."

"Didn't you just criticize me for not cluing you in on the things you didn't understand?"

"Yeah…so?"

"So, listen to me when I tell you that the Sarrum is not the man you think he is. He wasn't the man I expected him to be when I set out to meet him either."

"Then…what is he?"

"A man worth binding yourself to for life."

24

BOB

The troll sucked every bit of flesh and sinew off the bones of the boar I killed and roasted for his supper. I'd been thrilled to snare such a well-fed animal because I figured surely there would be enough meat on its bones to satisfy a hefty troll and still leave enough to tide Pip and myself over for a little while, but I'd grossly underestimated Jack the troll's appetite. After devouring every scrap of meat and even a bit of splintered bone with the sorriest lack of table manners I had ever witnessed, Jack ushered us into his favorite napping spot at the base of a massive rotting tree.

Pip managed his way inside with no trouble at all, but I was considerably larger than he was. As I squeezed through on hands and knees, I couldn't imagine how Jack fit his fat body through the opening. Once I worked my way in, I marveled at how much larger the tree trunk was on the inside. The interior was spacious enough for me to stand upright and even walk around a little. The clever dwelling couldn't possibly be the work of a troll. They didn't possess the magic necessary to create that sort of spatial distortion.

The troll had devoured what little food and drink I'd packed for the journey when he tore my satchel apart at the seams, so Pip and I did our best to ignore our grumbling stomachs as we settled in for the night. Pip seemed oddly at home in our strange surroundings and unfazed when the ground shook as Jack sat down in front of the entrance to our hiding place. He casually drew a hangman's noose and a series of dashes on the dirt floor between us. When I raised an eyebrow, he grinned at me. "Haven't you ever played hangman before?"

"I have not," I whispered, as the troll at the entrance started snoring. "It sounds like a morbid game."

"Nah, it's a child's game." Pip stole a glance at the troll's backside. "But that fat lump stole your flask and we're trapped in here for the time being, so we might as well make the best of it."

I nodded because I couldn't argue with his logic. "How do you play this child's game?"

Pip pointed a grubby finger at the horizontal dashes. "Each line represents a letter. You guess letters and if they're in the words I picked, I fill in the blanks. If you choose a letter that isn't in the words, I draw one of the hangman's body parts. If you guess the words before I complete the stick figure, you win. If I complete the man before you've guessed all the words, I win."

"What an odd child's game." I slid closer to study the dashes he'd marked in the dirt. There were six dashes followed by a space, then five dashes, another space and six more dashes.

"Don't think so hard," Pip muttered. "Just pick any random letter. Once you fill in some blanks, then you start guessing."

"A," I whispered.

Pip's tongue poked from the corner of his mouth as he drew an "a" on the third dash in the second word and another on the third dash of the last word. "See, it's simple."

I nodded and muttered, "B."

Pip looked up at me and shook his head. "Don't just go through the alphabet. You're supposed to pick random letters."

I couldn't help chuckling as he drew the ill-fated stickman's head. "What difference does it make?"

"It's more interesting if you mix it up."

I let out another laugh. "Sorry. I wasn't aware the alphabet was more interesting when recited in a random order."

As Pip scowled at me, a great gust of flatulence whooshed into our hiding spot, courtesy of the napping troll guarding its entrance. It was all I could do to keep from gagging at the odor, but Pip barely seemed to notice.

I tugged the neck of my shirt up to cover my nose. "How the hell can you just sit there scowling?"

"Because you're not making the best of a bad situation."

"The best?" I suppressed a gag. "How can you breathe that foul stench and make the best of anything?"

"It could be worse," he whispered. "At least we don't have to fend for ourselves against any more trolls."

"I think I'd rather take my chances in the fresh air with the other trolls." I let out a cough that probably would have expelled my stomach contents if I had eaten anything recently. "How the hell can you stomach that stench?"

A sorry smile spread across Pip's wrinkled face. "That's the stench of my childhood."

I cleared my throat and tugged my shirt a bit higher as another gust of wind barreled in from the troll's hindquarters. "Earlier…you said you and Jack used to be neighbors?"

Pip looked past me to the slumbering troll who was poisoning our air supply. "Yeah. I didn't exactly fit in around here, but believe it or not, it was even worse trying to fit in with the imps."

"Why is that?"

"I was too ugly to fit in with the imps, and too intelligent to fit in with the trolls...and too small in stature obviously. It wasn't as bad here because trolls are fairly easy to manipulate. Their stupidity kinda worked in my favor."

"I'm sorry." I took advantage of the slight break from the odor and drew a deep breath. "That must have been a difficult way to grow up, never fitting in anywhere."

Pip shrugged his shoulders and didn't even wrinkle his nose when another gust of stench blasted in from the entrance. "I managed alright. I'm guessing you were the life of the party back in your neck of the woods."

I shook my head. "I can't remember my youth. Near as I can tell, I've always lived alone on the shore...that is, until Nellie and her daughter came to live with me."

A sorrowful smile spread across Pip's face. "It's amazing how a girl can come along and make everything better, isn't it?"

I raised an eyebrow. "Have you got a girl back home?"

Pip shook his head as he erased the hangman in the dirt with the palm of his hand. "No. I live alone."

"But you sounded like you spoke from experience just now. There was a woman in your life at one point?"

Pip let out a slow sigh, then nodded without looking up from the dirt.

"Where is she now?"

Pip cleared his throat and hopped to his feet. "That's not a very interesting story." The roughness of his voice suggested that the merit of the tale wasn't the issue. I had clearly hit a nerve.

"Fair enough," I whispered. "But if you want to tell the tale at some point, I'd be happy to listen."

Pip cleared his throat again. "I'll keep that in mind."

I nodded toward the patch of earth where the hangman had been. "What words did the dashes represent?"

Pip looked up at me and grinned. "Knight slays dragon."

25

EMMA

I sat curled up on the couch with a blanket wrapped tightly around me, but I still couldn't seem to get warm. My body temperature had been steadily dropping since I woke from the last nightmare. That stupid horror movie was playing again. Tears filled my eyes as I grabbed the remote from the coffee table and turned off the television. Doc had stepped out to make a phone call and Isa was in the kitchen making hot cocoa. Alone for the first time since they woke me and warned me that it'd be dangerous to sleep, I clutched the blanket a little tighter. I knew Doc would say the drop in my temperature was just another side effect of the medicine I had supposedly ingested, but it wasn't the first time I'd felt this way. I felt chilled to the bone all the time, though normally, all I had to do was curl up beside David with his arms wrapped around me.

My husband was the living, breathing equivalent of an electric blanket, but he wasn't home. Tristan said he'd gone off in the middle of the night to help a client, but I didn't believe that. David hadn't left the house since I came home under house arrest. He might as well have been legally confined to the property right along with me. There was no way he would dash off and leave me to attend to a client's needs. No matter how important the client was, he would pass something like that off to Brian or Tristan. So, where was my husband?

An intense pulse of heat throbbed at my chest, and I looked down and touched the pendant that hung from my neck. I swore I would never wear it again after Sophie told me that David had given her one just like it. Tears spilled down my cheeks as I reached behind my neck to remove the necklace, but a burst of heat scorched my fingers the instant I touched the clasp. I jerked my hands back with a startled shriek, but when I lifted them to my face there wasn't so much as a red mark to show for the pain. I was unraveling. Losing my mind was the only plausible explanation for everything that was happening. I shrugged out of the blanket and stood from the couch with a muffled sob. Charlie had acted like a man possessed when he rushed into the living room earlier, and my husband had deserted me.

I needed David. He was the only constant in my capsizing universe. Without him to anchor me, I was afraid I might drift away. I absently lifted the pendant and brushed it against my lips. Nothing seemed right with the world anymore. Was this just another medication-induced nightmare? Tears spilled down my cheeks as I moved to the door and stepped into the hallway. I didn't want cocoa or coffee. I wanted to silence the ache in my chest. I wanted my husband's arms to wrap around me and make everything better. A bizarre thought struck me as I reached the staircase. *What if I was imagining all of this?* Maybe I'd gone completely mad at some point in the past and had already driven David off. Honestly, how many times could I push him away before he decided he'd had enough? The world around me blurred as I climbed the steps and passed by each happy memory of our life together that was preserved in a frame on the wall. Why was I even fighting the sleep that this serendipitous overdose was so eager to grant me? This could finally be the merciful solution I'd been desperate to find. I reached the top of the stairs in a trance-like daze and shuffled down the hall to my bedroom door. Across the hall, the door of the guestroom David had moved his things into was shut. I moved toward it and stood there with my hand hovering above the knob. If David had gotten home from his supposed meeting with a client, he would have come to check on me. He wouldn't just come home and crawl into bed while everyone else was fighting so hard to keep me awake. He'd be sitting beside me, insisting I drink coffee and watching me like a hawk if he knew about the overdose. I shook my head, but as I started to walk away, a whimper sounded behind the closed door—a breathless female whimper. A rush of fury coursed through my veins as I grabbed the knob. I tried to turn it, but the door was locked.

Heart slamming in my chest, I pounded on the door with enough strength to bruise my fist. "Who's in there?"

Nothing but silence answered from the other side of the door.

I hammered my fist against the door again, too enraged to notice the pain I was causing. "Open this fucking door!"

Soft footfalls approached the door—not my husband's solid confident steps—delicate feminine footsteps. I watched with my heart in my throat as the doorknob turned and a petite young girl with dark skin and dark eyes appeared at the opening. Scantily clothed in fitted pajama shorts and a matching halter top, the girl refused to meet my eyes. Instead, she stared at my feet and muttered, "Hello, Princess."

Nausea barreled up my throat. It was nightmare enough to find this girl in my husband's bedroom, right across the hall from our marriage bed. What sort of sick joke was it to address me by my husband's pet name for me? "Who the hell—"

I never got to finish the question because a blinding burst of pain exploded in my head. Dread enveloped me as the world tilted sideways...

..."Welcome back," Godric's charming voice murmured.

No. Not here. I couldn't be here again. Somehow I seemed to have gotten stuck slipping from one nightmare to the next. A hopeless sob escaped my throat as I opened my eyes.

"It pains me to see you suffer this way, Princess." Godric stood from the couch and moved toward me, briefly eying the dragon above me before his gaze fixed on me. "I give you my word that I will not harm you." There was such tenderness in his voice that I almost believed he was telling the truth. *I wanted to believe that he was.* I swiped at my tear-stained cheeks with trembling fingers as I looked up at Godric. The look in his eyes sobered me, allowing me to process my surroundings with a clearer head. The couch behind him was empty. There was no trace of the woman and child who had sat there earlier. I locked eyes with Godric as he knelt down in front of me. There were tears in his eyes as he whispered, "He doesn't deserve you, Emma."

I looked up at my dragon. Sapphire flames blazed in his eyes as he shook his head.

"You look so lost," Godric's hypnotic whisper drew my attention back to him. "I swear to you, I only wish to help."

I shook my head but didn't speak because I couldn't seem to find my voice.

Tears glistened in his crystal blue eyes. "I promise you, I will do no more than lend a shoulder to cry on."

My head was swimming and I was drowning in a sea of panicked desperation. I needed a warm chest to sink against, and I had no idea where my husband was—or even whether David was more trustworthy than the man kneeling in front of me. I opened my mouth to decline his offer, but the only sound that came out was a ragged exhalation.

"He has hurt you so badly," Godric whispered. "For all my faults, I never harmed the woman I treasured—not once—but the Talbots have always done as they pleased, consequences be damned, and everyone just stands down and allows it to happen. Heaven forbid anyone should question a Talbot's choices."

The ache in my chest throbbed at the genuine sorrow in his eyes.

"Let me comfort you," he whispered. "We can sort the rest out later. For now, just take what I'm offering—a warm pair of arms and a solid shoulder to cry on."

"You're the reason for my tears," I muttered in a small uncertain voice.

His brow furrowed as a sympathetic frown tugged at the corners of his mouth. "Am I?"

He wasn't. David was—the man who meant the world to me, the man who *was* my world and always had been. He'd betrayed me in the waking world. Another woman had taken my place in his bed... more than once.

"The Sarrum has caused us both pain," Godric whispered. "I needn't harm you to get my revenge. Let me comfort you instead. We can commiserate over all the ways that the King has wronged us."

I glanced up at the echo of my Dragon King. "No."

Tears swam in Godric's eyes as he extended a hand toward my cheek. It was the gentlest of gestures and there was a slight tremor to his hand as it hovered there, as though it pained him to be unable to comfort me. "Why allow him to cause you more pain?"

"Because I love him too much to betray him," I sobbed, fighting an inexplicable urge to drop my cheek against Godric's palm. I was so desperate to feel some small measure of comfort.

Godric exhaled a sorrowful sigh. "Even though he betrays you and brings other women into your home?"

I dipped my head a fraction closer to his hand. "No...he wouldn't do that... There must be another explanation..."

"Another explanation for a lovely young woman you've never met to be half undressed in your husband's bed?" Godric's palm inched closer to my cheek, close enough for me to feel its warmth.

"I..." Dear God. I needed a warm body to sink against. "I shouldn't be here."

"No," Godric slid a bit closer to me, "and that young girl shouldn't have been in your husband's room, but there they were...and here we are." He was so close that I could smell the Dark spiced scent of his breath as he spoke—different than David's, but no less exotic. Heat radiated from him, charging the air between us. I wanted to drop my head to his chest and feel the warmth of his arms envelope me. He exhaled again and his scent washed over me. "Let me hold you, Princess. Just once. I'll not harm you. I..." Tears glistened in his eyes as his voice trailed off, and he seemed to consider me in a whole new light as if I had just appeared out of nowhere. He drew a sharp breath then squeezed his eyes shut as he exhaled, bathing me in his scent.

I drank in his scent as I watched him sit there with his eyes squeezed shut. The warmth I so desperately craved was right in front of me, offering itself freely. *This was wrong.* Somehow this moment between me and my captor had taken an intimate turn. Fearing his touch was one thing...but craving it was quite another. Despite the nearness of Godric's warmth, I had never felt colder in my life. I felt so weak and so close to giving in. If my husband had found comfort between another woman's legs, why shouldn't I take comfort in the warmth of this man's arms? I looked up at my dragon.

The flames in his eyes flared brighter as the Waters came and carried me away...

26

NELLIE

The more time passed without any sign that Bob would be coming to save me from Godric, the deeper I sank into a hopeless depression. It broke my heart to see the hurt in old Bob's eyes when he looked at me, but what could I do? I had tried explaining what was wrong so many times. His Unsighted brain just couldn't make heads or tails of it. It was frustrating as hell, but it wasn't his fault. It wasn't anybody's fault.

The sorrow in old Bob's gruff whisper was like a punch to the gut, "We could take a walk down the hall."

I turned toward the old man sitting beside me on the couch and tried to picture him young and handsome like he was in the Dream World. The time we'd spent together on his shore seemed like another life that belonged to some other couple—a couple much younger and happier than we'd ever be. "I don't feel like it."

"That's the closest thing to fresh air I can offer ya," Bob grumbled.

I squinted and tried to blur his features to their younger configuration. "What makes you think I want fresh air?"

"You were mumblin somethin about gettin rescued and bein free when you were sleepin on the couch this mornin. I thought maybe walkin around the halls might make you feel a little less cooped up."

The sincerity in his honorable old eyes made my words come out in a choked whisper, "You make me feel less cooped up."

He touched his wrinkled head to mine. "Good."

"It is good." A tear slid down my cheek and I wiped it away quickly, hoping he wouldn't notice. "We're good, Bob. I'm not sure I ever thanked you for rescuing me."

He pulled his head back and narrowed his eyes at me. "Rescuin you? When the hell did I do that?"

"Oh," I croaked as I wiped another stray tear from my cheek, "about a hundred different times."

He shook his head then tipped it back against mine. "You're losin it, woman."

I let out a throaty cackle. "No. I already lost it...a long time ago."

Bob reached out and took my shriveled hand in his. "We're gonna get you through this, Nellie.

Whatever this is, I'll figure out how to fix it. Just don't give up on me."

"Never," I whispered. "You're my knight in shining armor. I know you'll come through for me in the end."

"The end?"

"Yes." I gave his hand a squeeze. "Whatever the end is, I know you'll be there for me when I get there."

"You gotta get some sleep," he whispered. "They're gonna take you someplace else if you don't snap outta this soon."

"I can't snap out of it without your help."

"Then..." Bob's voice was thick with frustration, "tell me how to help."

"You have to find Charlie and get him to help you."

"You're talkin nonsense." He shook his head, and it gently bumped against mine. "How do I make you see that? The kid's gone, and he couldn't help you even if he was here."

For once, it was the agitation in Bob's raised voice that nabbed the attention of the two staff members by the door. I squeezed Bob's hand a little harder as their heads swiveled in our direction. "Keep it down. You're drawing too much attention."

"Good," he grumbled. "Now you know how I feel. I don't give a fuck how much attention I draw or who the fuck wants to stick me with a needle. You need to snap outta this and if gettin myself drugged is the only way to make you see how loopy you've been actin, then it'll be worth it."

I wasn't getting anywhere with this Unsighted old man, so I spoke to the young knight buried somewhere inside him and hoped to God he'd hear me. "Have you found anybody in the forest to help you yet?"

"I haven't left this fuckin hellhole in years," he muttered. "What the hell forest do you think I've been frolickin in?"

"The Dark Forest."

He twisted sideways to look me in the eyes. "They need to check you for a stroke. Somethin's not right with your head."

"Something's not right with any of our heads, you crazy old fool. Why the hell do you think we're all in here?"

The troll-boy shook his head as he pushed my wheelchair up to our couch. "Time to get you back in here, Nellie."

"Fuck off." I slid a little closer to Bob. "I don't wanna go anywhere."

"Too bad," he muttered as he kicked on the brake. "The new doc wants to have a talk with you."

I didn't want anything to do with doctors. Most of them were clueless Unsighted morons, and the only one I'd ever met who wasn't, turned out to be something much worse. "Tell him to piss off."

Tim hoisted me off the couch and paid no attention to the way my body went limp to make it harder for him. "Tell him yourself."

"I don't wanna tell him shit," I spat as he plopped me into the chair without any semblance of gentleness.

"Behave yourself, woman," Bob whispered as the troll started to wheel me away. "I wanna see you come back here in a while, alright?"

I felt like a pathetic idiot for tearing up. "I'll do my best."

"You're gonna like the new doc," the troll muttered as he wheeled me down the hall toward the toad's old office. "Dr. Weeks is a lot cooler than Spenser."

"I'll believe it when I see it," I grumbled under my breath.

The new doctor was waiting for us in the doorway of his office. He stood there with a dopey grin on his face as he watched Tim wheel me toward him. He looked young and cocky. He also looked like he put a lotta goop in his hair to make it stick up all over the place like he'd just rolled outta bed. What kind of idiot wasted perfectly good time and money to make himself look like a lazy slob? "Hello, Nellie. It's great to finally meet you."

The troll handed me off to the doc and went on his merry way as Dr. Weeks wheeled me into his office and shut the door. The doctor parked me in front of his desk, then scooted around it like he was in some sort of hurry to plop down in his own chair.

I glanced around the office while I waited for him to say something pointless and cliché. The dingy walls had been painted a cheery shade of yellow. Framed charcoal sketches of weathered old fishermen and paintings of ships adrift in harbors beneath fiery sunsets adorned the walls along with the doctor's framed diplomas from colleges that my old eyes couldn't make out the names of. Once I finished inspecting the room, my eyes came to rest on him.

He folded his hands on the desktop and widened his dopey grin. "Can I get you something to drink?"

"No."

He nodded with a thoughtful smile. "The staff tells me you've been giving them a bit of trouble lately."

"The staff can shove it up their asses."

He raised a fist to his mouth and cleared his throat, almost as if he was muffling a laugh. "I might not pass that message on to them."

"I'd be happy to repeat it for them."

"Let's not waste our time with bullshit, Nellie."

That was the first intelligent sentence any employee in the facility ever uttered. I was gonna ask if he felt rushed because he'd already wasted so much time getting his stupid hair to stick up like that, but then I remembered the concern on Bob's face when he asked me to behave. "What?"

"I've come to check up on you because you violated the conditions of your prison sentence when you left your beach."

I sat there in silence for a minute, figuring I must've heard him wrong and wondering if I'd finally lost it for real. When he gave no indication that he intended to say more, I whispered, "You're Sighted?"

"I am," he whispered, "and you're in a world of trouble."

Nervous as that probably should've made me, a burst of laughter hiccupped from my wrinkled lips. "No shit."

27

MIA

If I wasn't trapped in a hellish nightmare, I might've found it comical. I'd spent my entire life wishing somebody would notice me and now that someone had, I was tied to a bed in a sparsely furnished room with nothing to do but go over and over the details of the scenario that'd led me there. I drifted in and out of sleep a lot. If I could have, I would've stayed in the waking world to escape my prison—but something was wrong with me in the waking world. I couldn't even muster the energy to drag myself out of bed. I thought about calling the police when I called in sick to work the morning after I was taken. Then I realized they'd think I was insane and would probably lock me away and pump me full of drugs, which would just keep me trapped in the hellish place even more.

Now and then, I'd hear voices outside the room they kept me in—the satin voice of the man who'd lured me there and the icy voice of the woman he lived with. But I didn't want to think about that female shadow or the things she did to me when she found me tied to her bed. Time dragged on, and other voices joined theirs—deep growling voices, thick demonic accents I couldn't place, voices that sounded like they were snarling no matter what they were saying—but the worst were the voices of the other victims they brought with them. I wasn't sure how many other women they were holding captive, but there were at least four distinct voices I heard whimpering, pleading for mercy and crying out in pain.

I tried to block out all the voices and occupy my mind by revisiting the brief conversation I'd had with the incubus who tended bar at the Dragon's Lair. If it wasn't for that stupid troll, I might've ended up going home with him instead of getting kidnapped. If I ever made it out of this nightmare, I was gonna go back and knife that bitch. Oh hell, who was I kidding? I'd never really do that…and I'd probably never get out alive.

The sound of something shattering against the wall outside my room iced the blood in my veins. *The female shadow liked to break things.* Her ear-piercing screech followed the crash, "What the hell is wrong with you, Plezur?"

"Relax, baby." The sweet-talker sounded closer to my room than her. "I was just gonna check on her."

If I could've stopped my heart from beating, I would have. I didn't want that sweet-talking stranger to come anywhere near me, and I sure as hell didn't want to find out how the shadow would make me pay for it if he did.

"Don't bother," the shadow's voice was closer now. "I'll do it."

A sheen of sweat slicked my forehead as the door-knob turned.

The shadow greeted me with an icy smile as she opened the door and stepped in the room, and a shiver rippled through me as the sweet-talker peeked his head in over her shoulder. She raised a fist and slammed it back, hitting him square in the nose without even turning to look where she was aiming.

"Fuck," the sweet-talker growled as he clutched his nose and watched the blood trickle through his fingers with widened eyes. "What the hell's wrong with you?"

A frigid burst of laughter trickled from the shadow's lips. "We don't have enough time for me to answer that question."

"You are wicked to the core, woman," he grumbled as he wiped the blood from his nose on his sleeve. "Why the hell am I with you?"

Her eyes locked with mine, draining every bit of warmth from my soul as she answered. "You're with me because you crave this, darling."

"I crave what, Payne?" he muttered, "A beating?"

The shadow winked at me as she slammed the door in his face without turning to look at him. "It's time for us to play."

She seemed to be waiting for me to respond, but I couldn't find my voice and I had no idea what she wanted me to say. With each step she took toward me, the temperature in the room seemed to drop several degrees and by the time she reached the bed, I was shivering convulsively. When she sat down on the bed beside me, my heart froze.

"I'm sorry I came here with him," I whimpered.

She let out another icy chuckle. "Don't be. I'm glad you're here."

"What?"

"Monogamy is so boring," she murmured. "Do you suppose I've never brought a lover of my own to this bed?"

"I..."

She traced a fingertip along the tether around my left wrist. "You're exactly what I hoped he'd bring home." All the air escaped my lungs as the shadow leaned toward me. "Do you want me to hurt you again?"

"No."

She reached across my torso and stroked a finger along the tether that bound my right wrist. "Do exactly as I say and I'll have no reason to. Are we clear?"

If I wasn't so dehydrated, I probably would've pissed myself and made her angry again. "Yes."

"Good." She placed a cold hand on either side of my head, and I squeezed my eyes shut and braced myself for whatever she planned to do. "Hosting parties always makes me so tense," she murmured as she stroked a thumb over my cheek, "and this one will be the grandest we've ever thrown, thanks to the special guest our leader has acquired for us. We are about to be in the presence of royalty. Isn't that exciting?"

I opened my eyes and waited for her to elaborate but when she just watched me, I nodded.

"Our guest of honor should be arriving very soon," she murmured, "You're going to help me let off a little steam while we wait and once I finish with you, we'll get you ready for the party. Everything needs to be absolutely perfect. It isn't every day that a royal comes to one of our parties."

I nodded and prayed that I wouldn't do anything to anger her.

She leaned forward with a giddy smile and planted a kiss on my forehead. "This is going to be so much fun."

28

BOB

My jaw tightened as I watched the oversized retard wheel Nellie back into the room. She looked white as a ghost after her talk with the new doc. Whatever the fuck he said to her, it obviously hadn't made anything better. I smiled at her as the dimwit helped her onto the couch next to me. "Hey."

She answered with the saddest smile I'd ever seen. "Hey, yourself."

Seein her lookin so frail and hopeless like that made me tear up like a fuckin pussy. "You came back to me."

"Yes." A tear slipped down her cheek and she wiped it off with a shaky hand. "You asked me to, remember?"

I cleared my throat and took her wrinkled hand in mine. "How could I forget?"

She let out a laugh that sounded more like a sob. "You forget a lotta shit, you old fool."

I gave her hand a squeeze. "Maybe, but I'd never forget you."

She dropped her head to my shoulder. "I know."

I touched my head to hers and whispered, "Good." With her safely tucked beside me, it didn't take me long to nod off…

…I woke to the thunderous sound of a snoring troll. The air in our tree trunk hiding spot was thick with a pungent odor that I'd rather not recall in much detail. I brushed the dirt off the side of my face as I sat up and looked around. Pip was lying on his back a few feet from me with his mouth hanging open and his limbs sprawled at odd angles. His snoring was barely audible above Jack the troll's, but I still caught a faint whiff of his morning breath when he exhaled. Judging by the acrid taste in my mouth, I doubted my own breath was much better. I stood and stretched as I moved toward Pip, then knelt down beside him.

"I'm awake." He rubbed his eyes with the heels of his hands as he sat up. "But we're not going anywhere till that fat lump rolls away from the exit."

Jack's snoring came to an abrupt stop. "Who're you calling fat?"

Pip wrinkled his nose as he looked up at me. "Just testing to see if you're awake, old friend."

The troll rolled to his belly and peered in at us through the entrance. "We ain't friends."

I looked the creature square in the eye as I stepped toward him. "How in God's name do you fit in here?"

His snort of laughter spewed a massive gust of halitosis into our hiding place. "I don't, dummy." Next to this hefty creature, Pip's breath was downright delightful.

I moved closer to the opening, hoping Jack would back away so we could step out. "Then why do you call this your napping spot?"

To my surprise, Jack took the hint and scooted back. "Because I can nap at the opening and keep my next meal nice and fresh without worrying it'll escape while I'm sleeping."

I sincerely hoped Pip and I weren't on the breakfast menu. "Clever," I muttered as I stepped out and inhaled a glorious breath of fresh air.

Pip scrambled out the opening after me. "Any sign of my cousin?"

The troll coughed a few times and hacked up a monstrous glob of phlegm before answering, "You think I stayed awake watching for her all night?"

"No," Pip took a step toward him, "but I think you would've noticed if she got home."

Jack scratched his head as he stood up. "So?"

"So," Pip repeated in an unconcerned tone, "I think you owe it to us to answer my question."

The troll let out a snort. "Is that so?"

"Yes," Pip answered calmly.

"Or what?"

I lifted Pip and placed him in my pocket because I knew a challenge when I heard one, and that would hardly be a fair fight. "Or you can find out what else I'm good at gutting."

The troll narrowed his eyes at me, but he didn't laugh off the threat. Quite the contrary, he seemed to measure me up and decide it wasn't worth the confrontation. "Aubrey got back a few hours ago."

Pip shot me a grin then turned to Jack, "Lead the way, fatso."

Jack grumbled under his breath as he started marching.

"Don't push your luck," I whispered as I fell into step behind him.

Pip let out a faint chuckle. "Sorry. Couldn't help myself." He watched Jack stomp down the path ahead of us for a minute before whispering, "Where have you been all my life, Bob?"

"Missing all the fun apparently."

"You and I make a pretty good team," Pip whispered. "If things don't work out—"

"Don't say it." Just the thought of what I might encounter when I found Nellie turned my stomach.

Pip seemed to deflate a little. "Sorry."

His change in posture made me regret the harshness of my tone. "Who's to say we can't remain a team if things turn out for the best?"

"If your life goes back to normal, why would you want to keep me around?"

"I've always wanted a sidekick," I whispered, paying careful attention to our surroundings. For all we knew, the troll could be leading us into a trap. I had never known trolls to be a particularly honorable bunch.

"Bob and Pip," he whispered, "Brawn and brains."

A burst of laughter sprung from my mouth before I could contain it. "Excuse me?"

"Well," Pip muttered as his cheeks flushed a deep shade of crimson, "you're obviously the muscle of this operation. You've gotta give me *something*."

"I suppose you were the one who got us this far," I whispered.

Ahead of us, Jack stopped and scratched his head as he looked right and then left.

A smug grin spread across Pip's face. "You lost, big guy?"

"Which way is left?" Jack muttered to himself.

Pip and I pointed and answered in unison as if we'd rehearsed our response, "That way."

"Yeah. That's what I thought," Jack muttered, "You'll find her up that way then." With that, the troll turned around and started back in the direction we'd come from.

"Thanks," Pip called after him.

"Thank your friend," Jack grumbled without turning back to look at us. "I was gonna fix ya for breakfast."

The two of us watched the troll in silence for a few minutes. Only when we were certain that he was out of ear shot did we look at each other and burst into laughter.

As our laughter died off, I headed left and Pip turned in my pocket to look up at me. "Thanks."

I shook my head. "I'm the one who should thank you for helping me get this far."

"No. I'm serious," Pip muttered, "Thanks for all of this—taking me along, listening to my advice, giving me a reason to get up in the morning. Really... thanks."

It didn't seem appropriate to dismiss his gratitude as unnecessary, given the sincerity of his tone, so I nodded and walked in silence for a bit before whispering, "We do make a pretty good team, don't we?"

We hiked in silence until I rounded a massive moss-covered boulder that had seen fit to park itself on our path, and a weather-beaten cottage appeared up ahead.

"That's gotta be her place," Pip muttered.

"What now?"

"Walk up and knock on the door," Pip whispered with a shrug.

It didn't take long to cover the short distance to the cottage. My heart was in my throat as I approached the door and knocked. If this turned out to be a dead end, what on earth would I do?

We heard movement inside the cabin, but no voices. There was no response for so long that I began to doubt anyone would ever answer. Just as I was about to say as much, the door opened. A plump female troll stood at the opening dressed in a grease-stained apron and a comparably filthy frock. She noticed me first because of my larger stature, and studied me from head to toe and back up again before her beady eyes met mine. "Well, what do you know? Dreams do come true."

Since I was at a temporary loss for words, it was Pip who answered, "Hello, cousin."

The troll's eyes widened as they dropped to my shirt pocket. "Melvin? It's good to see you."

"You too, Aubrey."

Her attention was now solely focused on Pip, as if she'd completely forgotten that I existed. "I'm sorry about—"

"Don't mention it," Pip interrupted, "Really. It's fine."

"I wanted to come—"

"This is my friend, Bob," Pip interrupted again.

It was clear to me that he didn't want to talk about whatever this troll was so keen to bring up, but she didn't seem to take the hint. "I just—"

I didn't want poor Pip to have to keep this up, so I took it upon myself to interrupt this time. "It's a pleasure to meet you, Aubrey."

ERIN A. JENSEN

Thankfully Pip's cousin took the hint and dropped the subject. Her eyes shifted back to mine. "The pleasure's all mine, Bob. Why don't you boys come in and rest for a while? You look tired."

She moved from the doorway and motioned me in, and I stepped inside and wiped my feet on the doormat. "We haven't got time to rest, but we would appreciate your help."

Aubrey shut the door with a playful grin. "Sure. How can I help?"

I followed her to a rustic sitting room with a stone fireplace and sat down on the couch she pointed me toward. "The woman I love was taken from me, and I was hoping you might help me find her."

The smile slipped from Aubrey's face as her eyes dropped to Pip. "Why would you think I could do that?"

"Godric took her," Pip replied in a hoarse whisper.

Aubrey's eyes moved back to mine. "I am sorry to hear that, but what exactly do you think I can do about it?"

I took a deep breath and forced myself to remain calm. "I'm searching for a friend of mine who's been training with the Dragon King. I was told to find him and ask him to inform the King that his Princess is in danger. Godric plans to take her, too."

The troll let out a gasp. "Do you know where to find Godric?"

"I was led to believe that my friend Charlie could help us find him."

"Charlie," the troll muttered, "You mean, the lost dragon?"

"No." A rising sense of terror burgeoned inside me. Enlisting this troll's help had been my only hope of locating Nellie, but this conversation seemed entirely pointless.

"Bob is Unsighted," Pip muttered.

"Then," Aubrey glanced down at Pip, then back up at me, "how do you know any of this? Who told you to search for these people?"

"The woman who was taken from me."

"How?"

"I hear her whispering in my head when I wake. She is Sighted, and she's been trying to guide me to my friend and this King he's been training with."

"Can you help us?" Pip whispered. "Take us to your buddy and let us plead our case to him. Please? For old time's sake."

"I was planning to head to work soon anyway," Aubrey muttered. "My friend at the tavern works for the Dragon King, and he brought your friend Charlie to the tavern not all that long ago."

Tears filled my eyes as I whispered, "Thank you."

29

ROSE

I couldn't do anything right. When the Princess fainted mid-sentence, I just stood there in the doorway and watched her drop to the floor. A burning sensation crept up my throat as the initial shock subsided. Leaving her lying in the hall to go get help seemed like the wrong thing to do, so I crouched down beside her and called out to anyone who might hear, "Help!"

The Princess didn't even stir when I hollered right next to her.

"Someone, please help!" Realizing it might evoke a quicker response, I added, "The Princess needs help!"

My mother dried her hands on her apron as she came rushing up the stairs. For one jealous instant, I couldn't help wondering whether she'd come faster because it was the Princess who needed help.

Dr. Price raced up the stairs a few steps behind Isa. "What happened here?"

As Doc knelt beside the Princess and lifted her wrist to check her pulse, I stood and backed away. "She, um... I woke up because the Princess was pounding on my door. When I opened it, she collapsed before she even finished a sentence."

"Damn it," my mother muttered. "I should've known better than to put you in that room. With everything that was going on... I just wasn't thinking."

I didn't want to sound dense, but I didn't get what the problem was. "What's wrong with this room?"

"When Emma first came home from the facility, this is where the Sarrum moved all his things because he didn't want her to feel pressured to share a bedroom."

My stomach dropped as I glanced at the unmade bed I'd just hopped out of. "I was sleeping in the Sarrum's bedroom?"

"Sort of," Isa muttered as she wiped her already dry hands on her apron. "He never actually spent a night in there, but I suppose technically it could be considered his room because his things are in there."

Doc shook his head as he lifted Emma's eyelids. "What did she say before she lost consciousness?"

"She was starting to ask who the hell I was," I whispered, "but she collapsed before she finished the question."

"Damn it," Isa muttered again.

Doc carefully lifted the Princess off the floor and stood up with her in his arms. "Isa, would you open the door to her room for me please? I'm going to lie her down in there."

"Of course." My mother darted to open the door directly across the hall from the room I'd been sleeping in—*the Sarrum's bedroom.*

As Doc carried Emma's limp body into the room and placed her on the bed, my mother turned to me. "Let's give her some privacy. You and I can go talk somewhere else."

I nodded, then glanced down at my pajamas. They were a bit on the skimpy side, but Emma Talbot was the most gorgeous woman I'd ever seen. Next to her, I was painfully average no matter what I was wearing. How could the Princess think the Dragon King would want *me* in his bed? "I should probably change first."

"Alright," Isa whispered, "I'll meet you in the kitchen."

"Sure." I stepped back into the King's bedroom and shut the door. Then I hastily gathered my clothes, changed into them and raced from the room like an intruder who feared getting caught where she had no right to be.

I descended the staircase, entranced by the pictures hanging in decorative silver frames on the wall beside me. They looked like the perfect pictures that come in the frames when you buy them. The Princess was in all of them—looking every bit as gorgeous as a supermodel—laughing on the beach with the wind blowing through her hair, standing in front of an ivy-covered building in a graduation cap and gown with her arms around Brian and Tristan, dancing in the Sarrum's arms as they gazed adoringly into each other's eyes. How on earth could this perfect creature of Light possibly think the King of the world would want *me*, when he had *her*? I mean, I knew she'd lost her Sight and didn't remember who she really was...or who her husband was. Still, in what universe would any man choose me over *her*? As I stepped off the staircase and moved toward the kitchen, I was already starting to regret feeling jealous of a woman whose entire world was crumbling around her. The Princess had looked so heartbroken when I opened the door, so utterly lost and confused.

My mother smiled at me as I stepped in the kitchen. "Would you like some hot cocoa?"

I nodded and sat down across the table from her, where a mug of hot chocolate already sat waiting for me. "Thank you."

"You're not a horrible person for feeling jealous of her."

"What?" When I looked up from my cocoa, there were tears in my mother's eyes.

"I raised her," Isa whispered as a tear slid down her cheek, "and I left you in a foreign country to be raised by someone else...you—my own flesh and blood."

Witnessing Isa's tears felt oddly like spying on a private moment that wasn't any of my business. "That's ancient history."

"No," Isa reached across the table and placed her hand on top of mine, "it's *our* history."

I shifted in my chair and dropped my eyes to the mug in my hand. "I'm sure you had your reasons. It's really none of my business."

"None of your business?" Isa stood from her chair, rounded the table and sat down in the seat next to mine. Then she gently placed a hand under my chin and lifted my head so she could look me in the eye. "It's your life, Rose. How could that possibly be none of your business?"

"You don't have to explain why you didn't want me." I closed my eyes because it hurt too much to look at her. "You were young. You had your whole life ahead of you, and I was something that was never meant to be. I'm thankful enough that you risked your life to bring me into the world."

"Is that what you think?" my mother whispered as her hand dropped from my chin, "That I didn't want you?"

I opened my eyes and felt foolish when they filled with tears. Thankfully, Isa wasn't looking at me any-more. "Why would you want me? I was just some-thing horrible that was forced on you."

"No." Isa lifted her head to meet my eyes. "The shadow who fathered you was something horrible that forced itself on me. I never thought *you* were horrible, and I didn't give you up because I didn't want you."

A lump in my throat made my voice come out fainter than I meant it to, "Then why did you?"

"I was young and unmarried," Isa whispered. "My parents were incredibly strict and extremely religious, and my parents and siblings were all Unsighted. The only other Sighted member of our family was my grandmother Rosa, who served as my guide. When I told my grandmother what the shadow had done to me, she brought me to the Sarrum to ask for protection so the Purists couldn't take you when you were born. My grandmother insisted that telling the rest of our family would only lead to disaster. The shadow who forced himself on me was a high-ranking Purist who intended to create a new dragon to fight for the would-be king. If I told my parents I was raped, they'd expect me to press charges against my attacker and they wouldn't understand why he was so untouchable. How could we explain why the bartender in the hotel where I worked as a maid had powerful connections who would eliminate me before they'd allow him to get sent to jail? And if I didn't tell my parents who fathered you, they would disown me for getting pregnant out of wedlock.

I wanted to do things differently, but I couldn't do anything on my own—the Purists would've taken you from me as soon as you were born, and that was assuming I even survived your birth. Fortunately, Benjamin took pity on me when I showed up at the palace pleading for help, and he agreed to protect me and my child. After weighing all the options the Sarrum presented to us, my grandmother convinced me that the best course of action was to tell my family that a wealthy lawyer had hired me after one of his employees was impressed with me during a stay at the hotel. I told my parents that my new boss was very particular and he wanted to send me to England to be trained to do things precisely as he was accustomed to having them done. It seemed excessive, but it was logical enough for my parents because they believed the upper class did everything to excess. The Sarrum had offered to take me into his home and pay for me to go to college, become a lawyer and join his firm—but my grandmother convinced me to decline the offer and explain that it just wouldn't make sense to my parents. They'd assume I was sleeping with him in exchange for all of that. In the end, we all agreed that the only way to make things appear logical to my parents was to send me off to England before my pregnancy showed, keep me there for the duration, then bring me back just as childless as they thought I was when I left.

I honestly believed it was the right thing to do for everyone concerned. The Sarrum and Benji would've taken me in and protected us both here in America, but there would've been no explaining that to my family. You have to understand...I came from a different generation. Making our actions seem logical to the Unsighted was of the utmost importance. I had to honor my family's traditions. My grandmother also convinced me that Louise Talbot could do a better job of raising you than I ever could—you'd be a dragon, after all. What did I know about raising dragons? My grandmother assured me that an upbringing surrounded by royal dragons would be best for you, but my grandmother was wrong...and I was wrong to listen to her. By the time I realized that, I feared you'd have no desire to come live with me and leave behind everything that you knew—everything Louise had to offer."

I mulled my mother's words over while I took a few sips of cocoa. "Louise always said that I would've been a burden to you. She raised me to believe that the greatest goal I could ever hope to achieve would be bringing a new dragon into the world. I...well... Louise and I were both under the impression that the Sarrum brought me here to make him an heir since his Princess was too weak and too precious for the task."

"You can accomplish whatever you set your mind to," Isa whispered. "You have no obligation to anyone but yourself, and your life is just as precious as any other. I am so sorry that I wasn't around to teach you that while you were growing up."

I nodded and straightened in my chair. Desperate to change the subject, I muttered the first question that popped into my head, "How could the Princess possibly believe that the Sarrum would touch another woman? I've never seen the two of them together, and even I can tell how deeply he treasures her."

"She isn't herself. Her mind has been altered and filled with lies."

"I failed at my task," I whispered. "I collapsed while I was holding her mirage."

"But it still stands."

"No thanks to me," I muttered. "Charlie caught the burden when I collapsed."

"Yes, and you shouldered it while he was struggling with everything that being a dragon entails." Isa took a deep breath then whispered, "I can tell that you have feelings for Charlie. You light up whenever he's around."

My cheeks flamed as I muttered, "It doesn't matter how I feel about Charlie. He loves the Princess... Doesn't he?"

"Their relationship at the facility was clouded by factors that neither of them consciously understood."

"Meaning?"

"When Emma was admitted to the facility, she immediately caught Charlie's eye—and not just for the obvious reason. She may not have remembered it, but the Princess is extremely talented at charming other creatures into doing what she wants them to. It's not an innate skill for a fairy like it is for a succubus, but it is a magic they're capable of mastering and Emma was especially well suited to it because of her beauty. The Sarrum trained her to harness that manipulative ability and make it her strength. She may not be physically strong, but the strength to bend the will of others is an equally powerful attribute.

Emma didn't remember any of that because she was blind to what she was, but she knew in her heart that she needed her dragon—and somewhere deep inside, she recognized what Charlie was. She was drawn to him because he *felt* like her husband in some inexplicable way. Without consciously realizing it, she used her charm to capture Charlie's attention. Since Emma needed her dragon more than anything, she unwittingly woke something dormant in Charlie that longed to be exactly what she desired. It was a vicious cycle. He further endeared himself to her because he instinctively knew what she needed, and he provided it. She didn't do it intentionally, but she charmed Charlie into falling in love with her—but Emma's heart will only ever belong to the Sarrum. What drew her to Charlie was the faint echo of a dragon's heartbeat, and she clung to it desperately because it reminded her in some small way of her soul mate. I'm afraid poor Charlie was greatly misled. Emma will never be capable of loving any man but the Dragon King. She just doesn't remember that at the moment."

"Charlie started exuding his scent in the clearing," I whispered without looking up at Isa. "That's why I collapsed. It divided my focus."

"Was I correct in assuming that you have feelings for him?"

"Yes," I muttered, "How pathetic is that?"

"It's not pathetic at all," Isa whispered. "Charlie is a good man, and his feelings for Emma are based on their mutual deceptions. For him to exude his scent in reaction to your presence while still under her influence, he must feel something quite genuine for you."

"Benjamin would never let anything happen between us," I whispered. "He's made that very clear."

"That isn't Benji's decision to make. Besides, his opinion is biased."

"Because he's in a relationship with a Sighted woman?"

"Our relationship was extremely strained for many years," Isa whispered. "I married an Unsighted man in the waking world because my parents expected me to get married, and I gave birth to his Unsighted child because they expected me to raise a family of my own. It was painful for both of us, but Benjamin sat back and endured it because he didn't dare endanger me with a physical relationship in the waking world. You are my Sighted child, so Benjamin cares for you as if you were his own. He doesn't want to see you suffer by denying yourself a physical relationship for the waking half of your life, or risk your life by being with a man who could kill you just by fathering your child."

"It doesn't matter," I muttered. "Charlie is too hung up on the Princess."

"That will soon change, assuming she remembers who she is in time and we get her away from Godric. Right now, rescuing the Princess needs to be everyone's priority. Relationships and feelings can be sorted out later, but Emma is running out of time."

30

DAVID

When Brian and I set off in opposite directions to search for the Purists' cabin, I chose my direction with a specific purpose in mind. The Dragon's Lair was hardly the sole place to gather information, and the Purists' meeting place was unlikely to be anywhere near the tavern, so I paid little attention to the terrain below as I took flight and headed for Devil's cove. Nomads never lingered long on the isolated beach because a dense population of crimson-colored algae made the Waters that washed ashore appear to be drenched in blood. However, there was one vile creature who considered those surroundings to be quite ideal. Since no passersby ever stayed long enough to ask questions, it was the perfect location for this sweet-talker to conduct his unscrupulous experiments.

The winds died off as I approached the cove, and a silent bloodbath welcomed me as it spilled from the sea and bled onto pure white sand. A short distance from the beach, the demon's dilapidated cottage hid amongst an overgrowth of brier patches and rotting trees. The silver-tongued demon who resided there possessed the ability to coax most creatures into doing whatever he willed them to, and he considered this isolated wasteland the perfect place to test the limits to which he could bend others to his will. The moron went by the name of Lucifer and believed himself to be quite untouchable. He was moments away from discovering just how far from the truth that was.

I touched ground without the slightest disturbance to the air current or the silence that engulfed the demon's hideaway. Masking myself in human form, I moved to the door and kicked it in.

A high-pitched squeal greeted me as I stepped inside, and a wicked grin spread across my face. I could not have timed things better if I'd purposely aimed to. The sweet-talker's wife was a satori—a demon capable of viewing the memories of others through physical contact. She was in the kitchen mindlessly fixing something insipid for dinner. The mixing spoon slipped from her hand as I stepped toward her. "What is this?"

My grin widened as I picked up the spoon, placed it back in her hand and wrapped her trembling fingers around the handle. "I've come to pay your husband a visit, satori."

"What…" she whispered, "what's he done?"

"Plenty, my dear," I leaned closer to her ear and added, "but you're well aware of that."

The satori was so focused on maintaining control of her bladder that the ability to speak momentarily escaped her. She answered with a timid nod without meeting my eyes.

"I believe your husband possesses information that could prove useful to me."

The woman's lifeless eyes drifted to a door on the far side of the room.

"Call him," I snarled.

"Lou!" she managed to screech, "You've got a visitor!"

The door swung open a few seconds later and a slender demon stomped into the room. "Woman, what the hell—"

Behind me, his wife exhaled a sigh of relief as I took a step in his direction.

The demon dropped to his knees the instant I moved toward him. "To what do we owe this honor, my King?"

A molten burst of laughter trickled from my lips and singed the demon's eyebrows. "Haven't you even got the guts to own up to your allegiance?"

Beads of perspiration erupted on his brow and upper lip as he muttered, "What?"

"Do not insult my intelligence, sweet-talker. Every creature in this room is aware that you are a Purist."

The demon reluctantly dipped his head in agreement.

"Although," I took another step toward him, "I would be willing to wager that not everyone in this room is aware of how you recently paid your dues to the would-be king."

The satori behind me took a step closer. "What's he talking about?"

I turned toward her with a morbid grin. "Your sixteen year old son went missing right around the time that Godric's raids along the fringe began, did he not?"

The woman's hateful glare shifted to her husband. "Yes."

"And did your spouse explain why?"

Her widened eyes searched mine as she shook her head.

"This spineless miscreant donated his own stepson to the Purists' latest effort. He enlisted him to take part in the raids in exchange for a few sinful favors for himself."

The woman's eyes filled with tears as she whispered, "Is he dead?"

The sweet-talker's heart began to race as I stepped toward him while my eyes remained locked with his wife's. "No, he is not. The boy is in my possession, and your cooperation this evening shall determine his fate."

"Anything," the woman's voice was ripe with despair as she reached a hand toward me. "I'll do anything you ask of me, Sarrum."

"You are a satori." I motioned for her to come closer. When she nodded, I took her hand and tugged her over to her kneeling spouse. "I simply ask you to do what you do best. View this man's memories, and share the images you pull from his mind with me."

She nodded and reached a tentative hand toward her husband.

When he tried to scurry away, I seized him by the neck and dragged him back. The demon attempted to shake his head in protest, but my hand was wrapped too tight around his neck. "You are *pathetic*. You sent a boy off to be slaughtered in exchange for your own selfish gain. At least show some dignity in front of the wife whom you wronged."

The air soured with the stench of fresh urine as it soaked the front of the sweet-talker's trousers, and my stomach dropped. This piece of filth wasn't afraid of upsetting his wife with his scandalous memories. She already knew about his numerous infidelities and the twisted experiments he performed on the premises, and there was no hope of salvaging their marriage now that she knew he had sold her child into slavery. Only one possibility remained—he feared *my* reaction to the images she was about to extract from his head. I bent close to his ear without loosening my grip on his neck. "You're already a dead man, but you can determine how painful that death will be."

His only response was to soil himself a second time.

Thoroughly disgusted, I grabbed the satori's hand and pressed it to the crown of her pathetic excuse for a husband's head. "Show me the cabin in the forest where the Purists congregate." A rush of images poured from his head to his wife's—and from hers into mine—and our collective minds traveled the winding route from Devil's cove to the Purists' cabin at lightning speed, but that was more than enough time for me to commit every inch of the journey to memory. I tightened my grip on the sweet-talker's neck and snarled, "Now show me the shadow and sweet-talker who boasted about selling my wife to the highest bidder."

The spineless coward began to twitch convulsively in a desperate attempt to guard those images from us. I squeezed his neck tighter and his wife mirrored my action by tightening her hold on his head. A rush of images raced through our collective minds, peppered by frequent glitches as he fought to regain control of his memories—a dark-skinned male sweet-talker and a pale female shadow with platinum blonde hair laughing and drinking at the

Dragon's Lair...sweaty palms exchanging money as various creatures filed into the Purists' cabin in the forest...all sorts of terrified female creatures getting manhandled and dragged off...all went dark as the sweet-talker lost consciousness in a last ditch effort to escape our mental invasion. I lifted him off the floor with an infuriated growl. I had neither the time, nor the patience for such nonsense.

Any Sighted idiot with a modicum of training can pick stray thoughts from an untrained mind, but stealing guarded memories is a far less common skill. Dragons do not lack the ability to extract visual memories from the minds of others but unlike the satori, we don't do it neatly. Our extractions rip the images from the minds of our victims and leave their bodies lifeless—and those are the best-case scenarios. Needless to say, it was a technique that we dragons typically avoided. However, I had no intention of letting this parasite live and no time to waste on more humane methods.

The satori kept her hand on her husband's limp body as I lifted his face to mine and forced my way back inside his perverse mind...ripping and tearing through images of playgrounds...and grade school...and his first job in the waking world...his wedding day...an unfortunate image of his wedding night that would now be forever seared into my mind... adulterous candlelight dinners with scores of females and a few males of questionable age...sweaty nights with stupefied victims in his workshop full of medieval torture devices...family ballgames and church services in the waking world, spent fixated on the bodies of the females in front of him...him jerking off next to shackled women who'd been grossly mutilated...kneeling before the would-be king...trading his own stepson in exchange for fresh subjects for his experiments...slipping money into an ogre's palm as he entered the Purists' cabin in the forest—even in unconsciousness, he fought me at this point...desperately erecting makeshift mental shields to keep the next images hidden. Enraged, I trampled past the barriers and barreled through the disjointed images...him handing gold coins to a half-breed demon with a jagged scar slashed across his face...the half-breed walking him to a door that his mind refused to step through, even torn to shreds as it now was...I pushed forward...and my mind stalled for an instant, refusing to recognize the female shackled to the bed...he locked the door, then stepped toward her...both our minds fought what came next, but there was no stopping it at this point...him grabbing her perfect face and slamming the back of her head against the headboard to stop her from crying...tearing off the gown they'd dressed her in...unzipping his pants...fury paralyzed me for an instant too long, forcing me to witness a glimpse of what he did to my sweet Princess...her tortured screams rang in my ears as my rage erupted...and the rest of the memory burst into flames... I set fire to every image inside his head...one by one...I ignited them and watched them blacken and melt away...but his shrieks did nothing to lessen my grief.

In a fit of blind fury, I unmasked and tore into him—puncturing organs, gushing venom into open wounds, watching them blister as my poison scorched its way through his insides, splintering bones, tearing him limb from limb—how long this went on, I cannot say. When I regained enough composure to consider my actions, the room was drenched in blood. It dripped from my lips and claws, it soaked the rugs and painted the walls, and it spattered the front of his newly widowed wife. I took human form and stood from the floor without the slightest trace of remorse. Then I stepped toward the trembling female covered in her own husband's blood.

Tears filled her eyes as she whispered, "What happens to my son now?"

It took me a few seconds to find my voice. "You did as I asked, and I am a man of my word." I waved a hand and a Waterfall poured from the ceiling of her macabre dwelling. "Step through, ask for Demetri and repeat these words to him, 'The Sarrum declared that the young warrior's debt has been paid.' Demetri will take it from there."

The woman took a step toward the Waterfall, then turned back to me and dropped to her knees. "Thank you, my King. You are truly merciful."

I narrowed my eyes at her. "I just ripped your husband to shreds right in front of you."

"Yes," she whispered, "but he deserved it. I realize you did it because of what he did to your wife, but I thank you all the same for destroying the monster who sacrificed my son…and for sparing my son's life."

I gestured toward the Waterfall. "Do you remember the words I told you to say?"

As she stepped in the Waters, she whispered, "I will never forget."

31

EMMA

I honestly couldn't recall everything that had happened to me since Isa first woke me and informed me that it would be dangerous to sleep. A substantial portion of that time was nothing but a dark gaping hole that throbbed if I ventured anywhere near it, so I kept my distance from those memories. Some ordeals must be forgotten if we wish to survive them because at a certain point, we reach our limit and our minds are just incapable of processing the rest. I was cowering far beyond that limit—somewhere beyond sleep, but not quite awake. I was lying on a bed, but I couldn't remember how I'd gotten there. *I wouldn't remember.* My heart was pounding because something had happened—something that ought to horrify me—I was sure of that, but what'd happened…I couldn't say.

There was an unbearable ache in my head. I wanted to cry out in pain and beg for someone to make it stop, but it seemed important not to draw attention to myself. I could feel the mattress beneath me, but I couldn't move or even lift my eyelids. I was stuck…suspended between worlds, but that didn't frighten me. I knew it ought to, but all I felt was a sinking feeling deep inside that made my heart throb with an intensity that I couldn't quite comprehend.

Adrift in this in-between place—just beyond everything waiting to break me—my thoughts drifted to a lesson when I was fourteen…

…The smile the Sarrum greeted Demetri with almost made me feel sorry for the dungeon keeper. The King was obviously enjoying this. David always said Demetri was the most stoic elf he'd ever encountered, and he said it with the utmost respect. Unfortunately for Demetri, the Sarrum believed that the elf's iron will made him an ideal subject for me to practice on.

There was no trace of amusement on Demetri's face as he stepped from the Waterfall with a respectful nod to the King. He squared his broad shoulders as he crossed the floor of the great hall. When he reached the base of the stairs, Demetri flashed me a warm smile. "Good evening, Princess."

My stomach knotted as I whispered, "Good evening."

The Sarrum stood from his throne and gestured for me to stand from mine and descend the stairs with him.

"There is no need for you to feel guilty, Princess. You are simply sharpening your skills in a safe environment. Demetri may not look happy about this, but he did agree to serve as your guinea pig for the evening."

Demetri nodded as I stepped off the stairs. "You must learn somehow, Emma. My displeasure with this particular training exercise is the reason that I was chosen."

"Quite right." The Sarrum turned to me and put a hand on my shoulder. "Now I want you to think of something that Demetri would never do, then make him do it."

I shot Demetri an apologetic frown. "What should I make him do?"

A hint of amusement glinted in David's blue eyes. "Whatever you like. If we speak your intention aloud, Demetri will either prepare to fight it or cooperate because he is assisting with your lesson. However, if he has no preconceived notion of what you wish him to do, his response will entirely depend on your ability to manipulate his will."

I nodded as I locked eyes with Demetri and flashed him a dazzling smile. Then I focused on envisioning him doing exactly what I wanted him to.

A tremor rippled through Demetri's muscular frame as he shook his head. "I am not doing that."

"Alright," I whispered, "I'll try something else."

"No," the Sarrum interjected in a stern tone that demanded our attention, "Stick with the first command. The fact that Demetri has no desire to do it, makes it the perfect task. Concentrate, and make him do it."

My eyes drifted back to Demetri, and he shook his head but he didn't shy away from the eye contact. I smiled again and willed him to do the same thing, but with greater force this time. Demetri's head continued to shake, but I kept pushing.

After a few minutes of this, I was about to give up when he reached up, took the jeweled tiara off my head and placed it on his own. I couldn't stop myself from giggling as he headed to the corner of the room where Benji and Isa sat watching. When he reached them, Demetri dropped to one knee at their feet. "Would you do me the honor of dancing with me?" When Isa started to stand, Demetri shook his head. "Not you, Madame. I was speaking to Benjamin."

Benji's glare shifted to me. "Not on your life."

I giggled as I took a step toward them. The Sarrum was about to stop me and remind me that my persuasive skills were no match for the Darkness's will, but I'd heard that a hundred times. How would I ever get better if I didn't challenge myself? I locked eyes with Benji and focused on dazzling him with my smile. I could feel him fighting my influence, but I continued to push with every ounce of force I possessed. When Benji rose to his feet and fixed me in a death glare that would stop a weak heart, I didn't giggle. I couldn't afford to lose focus for a second with a creature as powerful as the Darkness. I slipped into an almost trance-like state of concentration—willing Isa to stand and sing, Demetri to rise from the floor and Benji to take the dungeon keeper into his arms and waltz him around the great hall. I orchestrated every movement and choreographed every step with unshakable focus—until the Sarrum's laughter stole my attention.

His voice was close to my ear as he whispered, "You know he's going to make you pay for that later during your self-defense lesson."

The rest of my focus slipped away as I giggled. "It was worth it."

"I imagine it was." The pride in David's eyes was worth any amount of extra repetitions it would cost me later during my lesson with Benji.

"Well, how did I do?" I whispered as I watched my three disgruntled puppets march toward us out of the corner of my eye.

"Excellent." David put a welcome, albeit unnecessarily protective arm around my shoulders as he took the tiara from Demetri's head and slipped it back on mine. "You have obviously been practicing the techniques I taught you last week."

"Yes, I have."

"It shows." He kept his arm around my shoulders as he headed toward the nearest Waterfall, sweeping me along with him. "Now, let's get to dinner and replenish your strength whilst your self-defense instructor cools off."

I giggled at the grimace on Benji's face as David stepped into the Waterfall ahead of me. "Love you, Benji."

Even he couldn't keep a straight face as he whispered, "Love you, too. You did well, Princess."

I felt my cheeks flush at the unexpected compliment. "Thank you."

Benji kissed my forehead and whispered, "I'm still going to make you pay for it later."

I flashed him one last dazzling smile as I stepped into the Waterfall. "I wouldn't expect anything less."...

...As much as I wanted to remain in that memory, reality wouldn't allow it. The ache in my head was so blindingly intense that it was becoming difficult to focus on anything else. I knew I couldn't hide much longer in this in-between place, but the alternative was just too unthinkable.

32

BOB

I was far too impatient to sleep. Nevertheless, Pip's cousin had insisted that the two of us rest for a few hours before we took off for her workplace because we both looked exhausted. After lying in her guestroom staring at the ceiling for over an hour, I gave up on pretending that I was asleep. I was too anxious to set out for the tavern where we might find this friend of Aubrey's who worked for the Dragon King.

By the time Aubrey emerged from her room, I had dinner ready and waiting for us in the kitchen. Aubrey licked her lips as she eyed the feast I'd spread out on her table. "It smells delicious. Where did you get the meat?"

I nodded toward the bow I'd propped against the windowsill.

"Damn," Aubrey whispered, "I really wish you weren't spoken for."

I smiled at her and slid a chair back from the table. She plopped into it with a suggestive smirk, and as I slid her closer to the table, Pip stumbled into the room half-drunk on sleep and the small nips of brandy Aubrey had given him before we retired.

Pip shrugged at me as his cousin picked him up and sat him on the table in front of the saucer I had set for him. "I'll be fine," he muttered in response to my unspoken concern that his hangover might slow us down.

I settled into my own seat. "I'd leave without you if you weren't."

"Ouch." Pip winced as if I'd struck him, but a mischievous smile spread across his face.

"You know what's at stake," I mumbled around a mouthful of venison.

"Yeah, I do," he muttered, "and I wouldn't jeopardize your mission."

Aubrey giggled as she picked up her goblet of mead. "Don't worry about my cousin, Bob. Melvin can handle his liquor surprisingly well for someone his size. I think it's the troll in him."

I swallowed the meat in my mouth before answering because I realized it was rude of me to talk around it in front of a lady, even if she was a troll. Manners are manners after all. "Good to know. I apologize for my impatience, but I fear what may happen with each passing second that my Nellie and her child are in that monster's hands."

Aubrey dropped her fork to her plate. "Why didn't you tell me a child was involved?"

A spark of hope ignited within me. "Does that make a difference?"

"Of course," she whispered, already sliding her chair back from the table. "I'll go get changed and we'll leave right away. Dinner can wait if a child's life is at risk."

I reached across the table, took her pudgy hand in mine and gave it a squeeze. "Thank you."

She grinned at me and started to stand, then seemed to think better of it and plopped back down in her chair. "I should probably warn you about my friend at the tavern first."

I couldn't help chuckling at her concerned expression. "I'm sure I can handle whatever sort of creature your friend is. I've encountered my fair share of terrifying blokes."

Amusement twinkled in Aubrey's eyes as she glanced at Pip. "Tristan's not terrifying. Well...not unless you're a homophobe."

"Why should I care about this man's preference of bed partners?"

"You shouldn't," the troll chuckled, "but you might be a bit shocked by yours when you meet him."

In no mood for games, I narrowed my eyes at her. "Come again?"

There was a glint of mischief in her eyes as she whispered, "Yeah. You might."

"Could we skip the games and cut to the chase?" I took a deep breath to rid the irritation from my voice because she was trying to help us. "I'm in a bit of a hurry. What exactly are you trying to say?"

Aubrey's playful expression morphed to a somber one. "Sorry. I'm being insensitive. I just wanted to warn you that Tristan's an incubus. Have you ever encountered one of those before?"

"Not that I recall."

"But you know about them?"

"Of course."

"Just be prepared to find yourself drooling over him," her eyes dropped from me to Pip, "both of you."

Pip let out a few grunted syllables around a mouthful of bread, swallowed it and added, "Fat chance."

Aubrey responded with an unladylike snort. "Care to wager on that, cousin?"

My blood was boiling too much to stop myself from snapping, "What does it matter? I've encountered plenty of menacing foes in my day. I'm not about to shy away from this fellow just because he has a pretty face."

"And a smokin hot body," Aubrey muttered.

"I don't really give a damn what he looks like."

"Alright," Aubrey whispered, "just remember I warned you when you come face to face with Tristan and suddenly find you have less room in your trousers."

"Not likely," I muttered, "and certainly not appropriate dinner conversation for mixed company."

"Sorry," Aubrey whispered, "I didn't realize you were a prude."

"If it's prudish to be proper," I grumbled, "then yes, I am."

As I stormed from the table and swung my bow over my shoulder, Aubrey whispered, "Then he's really not going to like Tristan."

Too weary to debate the matter further, I turned and pushed my chair to the table a bit more forcefully than necessary. "I don't *have* to like him. He could be a salacious tutu-wearing nymphomaniac goblin for all I care! If he can help us, I'm perfectly fine with that. Now, can we please get on with it?"

"Sure." Aubrey stood from her chair and headed to her room without looking up at me.

When I looked across the table at Pip, he was scowling at me. "Did you have to be such an ass?"

I started toward Aubrey's room, but spun around and headed back to the table without knocking on her door. When Pip just continued to scowl, I let out a regretful sigh. "Sorry. I know she's been nothing but kind to us. I don't mean to be rude, but my mind occupies every quiet second with thoughts of what that dragon could be doing to the woman I love. I've seen too much violence in my lifetime to blindly believe that it will all turn out fine just because I want it to. He could be violating her, or torturing her, or God knows what else at this very second…and every other second we waste. I need to get to her, Pip. Can you imagine what it's like to be powerless to stop a monster from harming the woman you love?"

Dead silence fell over the room as Aubrey stepped into the kitchen. The look on her face told me all I needed to know. Pip didn't have to imagine. *He'd lived it.*

"We'd better get moving," he muttered as he moved to the edge of the table.

Tears swam in Aubrey's eyes as she lifted her cousin, slipped him in her apron pocket and moved to the door. The three of us left the cabin in silence, and I followed her to a stone path behind her cottage that led downhill to a narrow stream. When we reached the Water, she stepped in and I followed without questioning it—although I did fear she might be unaware that I couldn't travel through the Waters like the Sighted. As we waded toward a Waterfall that poured from a rock ledge several feet above, I broke the silence, "You do realize I can't travel through the Waters like you Sighted folks, don't you?"

Aubrey smiled at me as she took my hand and led me to the Waterfall. "Hold on tight and we won't get separated."

I nodded and tightened my grip on her fat hand as I stepped into the Waterfall after her. I stepped out the other side and marveled at the quaint little village before me, with charming cobblestone streets and wisps of smoke wafting from the chimneys of various shops. When I turned to look at the Waterfall we'd just stepped from, there wasn't one. I followed Pip's cousin toward the stone tavern with a wooden sign—identifying it as the Dragon's Lair—swaying in the breeze. I eyed the dragon silhouette painted on the sign and muttered, "Well, I'm certainly out of my element."

"Yeah," Pip whispered, "Me, too."

Aubrey exhaled a defeated sigh at the lost puppy look her cousin eyed me with. Shaking her head, she gently extracted him from her pocket and slipped him into mine.

I grinned as his comfortably familiar weight settled against my chest, certain that I could get used to having a pint-sized sidekick.

Several feet ahead of us, Aubrey frowned at the entrance to the stone structure then picked up her pace and raced for the door. Recognizing trouble when I saw it, I sped up and reached the door the same instant she did. The monstrous solid oak door had been splintered and savagely ripped from its hinges. I couldn't imagine what sort of creature could cause that much damage but whatever it was, it must have been massive.

The door cracked in two as Aubrey pulled it open and stepped inside. "Holy shit."

I stepped in after her. I'm not a particularly squeamish man, but the carnage sprawled out in front of us turned my stomach—blood spilled from bodies that had been ripped clean apart, skulls were bashed in, burnt bodies still smoldered from the fire that had cooked their flesh while they still drew breath, this evidenced by the agonized expressions on their partially charred faces. A ripe blend of odors choked the air—blood and piss and burning flesh—but one pleasant aroma hung heavier than all the nauseating ones. I'm ashamed to admit that despite the carnage, the delicious combination of exotic spices made my mouth water. Then it hit me—if one of these mangled corpses was Aubrey's friend, all would be lost. The trail would grow cold and I'd have no hope of ever finding Nellie. Misery strangled my voice as I whispered, "I am so sorry, Aubrey."

"I don't understand…" She shook her head, her expression dazed. "What happened?"

"The Sarrum came to interrogate the Purists," a voice like liquid silk replied from the shadows behind the bar at the far end of the room.

"Holy Jesus," Aubrey muttered as she moved toward the bar.

The most beautiful man I had ever set eyes on moved into the light, and my heart damn near sang as he stepped out from behind the bar and met Aubrey halfway across the floor. He wrapped his muscular arms around her as her head dropped to his shoulder. "It'll be alright. We'll rebuild."

The troll looked up at him and touched a hand to his chiseled cheekbone. "Did anyone other than the Purists get in his way?"

His gorgeous green eyes glimmered with kindness as he smiled at her. "No. Only the bastards who deserved to die."

"Thank God," Aubrey muttered.

"You know him better than that," the Adonis murmured, "He wouldn't harm an innocent soul."

Something between a sob and a laugh gurgled from Aubrey's throat. "He's a dragon who has been robbed of his greatest treasure, Tristan. I don't think there's a line he would hesitate to cross to get her back."

The living, breathing work-of-art that the gods had carved out of flesh and bone let out a troubled sigh as he wrapped his muscular arms a little tighter around her. Then he looked over her shoulder and flashed the two of us a mesmerizing smile. "Aren't you going to introduce me to your friends?"

Aubrey frowned as she turned toward us, as if she'd forgotten all about us. "Oh...right. They came here to see you, Tristan."

I repressed the desire to drop to my knees and weep as he grinned and stepped toward us. "Well, this day just took a turn for the better."

"Damn," Pip rasped from my breast pocket, "I wish he was talking about me."

Tristan flashed my miniature sidekick a breathtaking smile. "Who says I wasn't?"

A thin trickle of drool dripped from Pip's lips as he muttered, "Please tell me you're looking for a portable sidekick."

I gave him a gentle flick upside the head. "Am I so easily replaceable?"

Pip shrugged without even turning to look at me. "As far as I'm concerned, this godlike creature could replace anyone or anything."

Aubrey let out a laugh as she stepped beside Tristan. "I think you owe me some money, cousin."

"I'll pay whatever you want if I can take a ride in your muscular friend's pocket."

I gave my traitorous sidekick another flick to the head. "Oh for fuck's sake! What the hell is wrong with you?"

Aubrey narrowed her eyes at me. "I didn't think you swore."

"Well I normally don't, but this is fucking ridiculous! Why are we wasting time drooling over this man's body?" Sick with worry to the point of breaking, I yanked up my shirtsleeve. "I have well defined muscles, too. Hooray for the both of us! Now can we *please* get on with our lives?" I locked eyes with Tristan as I took a step toward him. "I have traveled a long way to seek your help, and I'm praying I haven't wasted my time. I don't give a damn how green your eyes are or how spectacularly rippled your abdominal muscles are," I tugged up my shirt to display my stomach, "mine are too, and I'm sure your lips taste like chocolate and your cock is humongous, but I don't particularly give a fuck about any of that! All I care about, is finding out if I have wasted God knows how much time searching for you only to discover that you can't help me find the woman Godric took from me!"

A knowing smile tugged at the corners of Tristan's perfect lips. "This woman you're looking for is the love of your life, isn't she?"

I exhaled a slow breath as I wiped my brow with my shirtsleeve. "Yes, she is."

"How did you know that?" Pip whispered from my pocket.

The incubus flashed Pip a swoon-worthy smile. "Because it's one of the only reasons why my charm would have no effect on an Unsighted man."

Aubrey nodded as she whispered, "And it's extremely rare for *any* creature other than a dragon to be completely unaffected by the charms of a pure incubus."

Tristan nodded without breaking eye contact with me. "I've only encountered it twice before."

Still hanging on the incubus's every word, Pip whispered, "In who?"

Genuine respect permeated Tristan's liquid tone as he replied, "One person from my past, and one Princess."

33

DAVID

As I took flight to trace the route to the Purists' cottage that the recently deceased sweet-talker had unwillingly divulged, my vision of the forest below was obscured by the flames that raged in my eyes. Whilst I eyed the treetops through the haze, the inclination to set fire to everything beneath me was too dire. I couldn't afford to dwell on what I had witnessed—the things I had watched that deviant do to her—doing so would inevitably lead to a death toll too catastrophic to fathom. The Waters would burst into flame, the forests would burn and every corner of Draumer would suffer for my agony. The image of that vile beast's hand grabbing her perfect face and bashing her head against the headboard would haunt me till my dying breath.

My heart was fracturing within my chest and I couldn't allow that to continue. My wife was still out there waiting for me to rescue her, regardless of whether or not she remembered me after what they'd done to her. As my mind lingered on the images I had plucked from the sweet-talker's head, the crushing weight upon my chest was a thousand times worse than the weight I had shouldered since Emma's birth. This was no time for my fool heart to give out, not while she still drew breath—and I knew that she did, I would have felt it if her heart stopped beating. Those nightmarish images rose to the forefront of my mind again, and I grimaced at the terror and agony etched on her face as the crushing weight intensified. If I continued to picture her frightened and helpless like that, the perverse images I had plucked from the sweet-talker's mind would be the death of me.

The only way to press onward was to suppress that horrific memory of his and replace it with one of my own. I needed to remember how vibrant and strong she had been before all of this began. For some reason unbeknownst to me, a memory from her fourteenth year was the first that came to mind…

…Emma's excitement during dinner as she marveled at her own accomplishment filled me with pride. Her enthusiasm was certainly warranted. Manipulating Benjamin's will was no small feat. As usual, I suppressed my outward reaction because it was far too easy for a perfect creature such as herself to succumb to vanity. Yet here she was, fourteen years old—lovely and brilliant

ERIN A. JENSEN

and full of life—and still entirely humble and selfless. I made no attempt to hide the pride in my eyes as I sat my napkin on the table and smiled at her. She deserved to feel joyous after such an accomplishment. "Perhaps you should go rest for a while before Benjamin comes to collect you for your self-defense lesson. I suspect you'll need your full strength tonight."

"I don't care," she whispered, grinning from ear to ear. "I'm not going to give up my time with you to go take a nap."

I feigned a disapproving frown. "Well then, what shall we do till he comes for you?"

A hint of mischief crept into her grin. "I want to practice some more."

In no particular hurry for our time together to come to an end, I slid my chair back from the table and reclined a bit. Strict as I normally was about sticking to her training schedule, I was extremely tempted to cancel her lesson for the evening to extend our leisure time. "With whom? Demetri has gone back to the dungeon, and I doubt Benjamin would volunteer to join us."

She fixed those magnificent green eyes of hers on me and practically blinded me with her dazzling smile. "Then let me practice on you."

I couldn't help grinning at her enthusiasm. "The skill you demonstrated today was quite impressive, but you are still no match for me, my dear."

Something wicked glinted in her eyes. "Then, what's the danger in letting me try?"

"It is not my safety that concerns me."

She sat up a bit straighter. "I'm not afraid of you."

My God, how this sweet creature tugged at my heart-strings. "You're the only living thing who isn't."

"I'm the only living thing who has no reason to be," she whispered, "I know you'd never hurt me."

"You've a clever answer for everything tonight, haven't you?"

"You've got yourself to blame for that. You taught me to be clever."

I'd always gone to great lengths to avoid reading her thoughts. Yet, it was impossible for me to refrain from sensing her desires—attempting to would be as futile as sticking a pungent odor beneath a bloodhound's nose and instructing him not to pick up the scent. What my Princess wanted this evening, was to demonstrate her strength to me—not by showing me how she could manipulate another creature—by letting me feel the strength that flowed through her. "Very well then," I whispered, "just don't be too disappointed when you fail to manipulate me."

She slid her chair close to mine and threw her arms around my neck. "Thank you!"

I breathed in the sweet scent of her innocence as I wrapped my arms around her, committing each molecule of her being to memory. Our days together were numbered and those numbers were dwindling far too quickly. "Don't thank me yet," I whispered as I released her and leaned back in my chair, "I don't intend to let you succeed."

A wicked grin spread across her face as she leaned back in her chair. "We'll see."

"Yes, I suppose we will." I felt her tug at my mind and released the mental barriers I had erected to keep her thoughts guarded from me. I had warded her mind long ago because stray thoughts were far too easy for me to pick up without consciously intending to. It was sinful enough that my blood inked her flesh. I had no intention of compounding that intrusion by invading her thoughts. However, for this attempt of hers to achieve any modicum of success, the barriers had to be temporarily loosed. I grinned at her as her eyes locked with mine, and a touch of wickedness darkened her dazzling smile as she pushed against my mind with impressive force. The pressure increased as the image of what she intended to make me do formed in my head. I chuckled and leaned a bit closer as I gently pushed back. "You would have the King of the world get up and curtsy for you?"

"Why not?" she giggled, losing a bit of focus, "There's no one else around to see." Connected as I had allowed our minds to become, her disappointment in herself for slipping up echoed like a silent scream inside my head.

It pained me to see how much influence her biological father had on her self-esteem. Years of my threatening him in Draumer, coupled with constant headaches whenever he contemplated laying a hand on her in the waking world, had turned Albert into a bitter alcoholic who took his frustrations—at not being able to touch her body—out on her mind with subtle forms of verbal abuse.

I loathed the fact that he had any influence over her at all. I gave her a mental tug and whispered, "Don't give up so easily, Princess."

Her timid smile was grateful and devoid of mischief as she began a fresh attempt. I had no intention of allowing her to bend my will, but I was bursting with pride at the progress she had made. My sweet child of fourteen would undoubtedly be a force to be reckoned with in the near future. It came as no surprise that her manipulative power was this substantial. It would have to be for her to bend the Darkness's will.

What did come as a surprise, was the subtle subconscious intent that she herself was unaware of. This was quite a different intent than her silly desire to make me **curtsy.** *Kiss me... stand up... take me into your arms... and kiss me.* **My eyes widened as an image of me doing just that, and by no means in a fatherly way, flitted through her subconscious mind. It lasted for just an instant, yet fighting this command required a far greater effort. This repressed desire was something she wasn't even aware existed. Yet, I found myself gripping the arms of my chair to brace myself against the tremendous force that it pressed upon me with. This primal longing buried deep inside her spoke to a feral part of me that would always be desperate to provide what she desired.*

For a brief instant that seemed to stretch to eternity, I warred with my conflicting intentions as I struggled to resist the lustful command she was entirely unaware she had issued. Fleeting as the moment was, I marveled at the enormity of it. If she were ever to realize this power she held over me and consciously attempt to wield it, I would drop to my knees at her feet. A few thunderous heartbeats later, reason took over and an entirely foreign sense of genuine panic gripped me. This would be the end of everything...the end of us. In the throes of panic, I slipped undetected into her mind and walled off her subconscious desire. Then I gently severed our mental connection and buried my own memory of the occurrence, willing myself to suppress it and forget it entirely so that nothing would be jeopardized between us—and for two years, I succeeded.

34

CHARLIE

After Benjamin finished his story about how he met the Sarrum, the two of us had settled into an uneasy silence beneath the dome that encompassed Emma's clearing. I let my eyes droop shut as I lay on my back, and I focused on sucking air into my lungs and blowing it out. Each breath required a little more effort than the last as the weight of the mirage continued to crush me. I stayed like that for hours with Benjamin sitting on the ground beside me, lending his strength to keep me from crumbling.

We'd been silent for so long that when Benjamin finally spoke, it startled the crap out of me. "Heads up, kid. We've got company."

I expelled a groan that was worthy of an eighty year old arthritic as I opened my eyes and pushed myself to a seated position beneath the crushing weight. "Who?"

Benjamin didn't have to answer because Isa and Rose had already stepped from the cave and were heading toward us. I raked a hand through the tangled strands of my sweat-soaked hair as I watched Rose walk beside her mother. When her eyes met mine, a warmth spread through me and that blatant scent started leaking from my pores.

Benjamin let out a low growl and glared at me as the two women sat down on the grass in front of us.

Isa narrowed her eyes at him. "Can I talk to you over by the cave, Benji?"

The Darkness's expression softened as his eyes met hers. "Why?"

"Because chaperoning two grown dragons is not your appointed task."

"No," Benjamin growled, "but seeing that neither of them loses focus is."

"You know there's another way," she whispered as she stood from the ground, "but that's not all I need to discuss with you."

He shot me another glare as he stood, then he turned to Isa. "Alright. Let's go talk." *Don't lay a hand on her when I step away, dragon.* The thought was obviously directed just at me because neither of the women reacted to it, and I was pretty sure that Isa would have if she'd heard.

Isa smiled at Benjamin as she took his hand, and they started toward the cave.

Rose watched them for a minute before she turned to me. "I'm so sorry I dropped the weight of the mirage on you like that earlier."

"You don't have to be sorry," I whispered, "I'm just glad you're okay. Besides, if anybody should be sorry, it's me. I left you to shoulder the weight alone for too long because I can't seem to stop acting like a crazed animal."

That exotic floral scent of hers wafted toward me as she whispered, "It's not easy to keep your dragon impulses in check."

The scent leaking from my pores intensified in response to her intoxicating scent. "Yeah. I'm finding that out pretty quickly."

"If it's any consolation, you're doing much better than I did the first time I unmasked."

I smiled at her and marveled at the fact that the burden seemed lighter with her beside me. "Yeah, but how old were you, like nine or ten?"

Something stirred inside me at the sound of her soft feminine laughter. "Three, actually."

Despite the agony I was in, I let out a laugh. "Great, so I'm doing better than a toddler. That's a huge accomplishment."

"You're doing a lot better than you think." Rose's eyes darted across the clearing to Isa and Benjamin.

"The Princess isn't doing well at all, Charlie. She just collapsed right in front of me in the waking world."

"Does Emma even know who you are?"

"No," she whispered as her eyes filled with tears, "and apparently, the bedroom that I was sleeping in has been the Sarrum's unofficial room since the Princess came home from the facility. I woke up to her banging on the door and when I answered it, she took one look at me in my pajamas in her husband's bedroom and she passed out."

A spark of terror ignited inside me. "Doesn't that mean she's in *this* world with Godric now?"

"I think so," Rose whispered as she watched Isa and Benjamin head back toward us. "My mother says we're running out of time."

"Is that why the two of you came here?" I muttered in a hoarse rasp.

Rose nodded, but Benjamin and Isa stepped beside her before she could say anything more. It felt like Benjamin was staring straight through me. "We're gonna have to change up our plans, kid."

"Okay?"

"Stand up," Benjamin growled as he motioned for us to get to our feet. I was about to protest that I didn't have the strength, but I didn't dare question him because of the urgency in his tone. So I attempted the impossible, and somehow managed to get to my feet.

For a split second, I saw the worry in Benjamin's pitch black eyes and it terrified the hell out of me. He stiffened the instant he noticed me watching. "It's time for you to shoulder the weight without me, Charlie."

"But...you promised the Sarrum you wouldn't leave me alone," I croaked, shocked at how terrified I was at the thought of doing any of this without him.

Benjamin narrowed his eyes at me as the four of us started toward the cave. "The Sarrum needs me to assist with Emma's rescue."

"But—"

"If we don't get her back soon, there'll be no need to keep her home intact," Benjamin snapped. Then his expression softened. "You can do this, kid. You won't be doing it alone. Isa and Rose will be here to help you."

Worry flashed in Benjamin's eyes again, and my stomach dropped. "Does the Sarrum know where Emma is?"

"Yeah." Benjamin blew out a breath before adding, "He got a pretty good lead on where they're keeping her. I'm supposed to meet up with him and Brian to help with her extraction."

"So—"

"You need to focus on learning how to shoulder the weight of this mirage beyond the walls of this dome, in both worlds."

"How?"

Benjamin touched a hand to my shoulder as we stopped at the entrance to the cave. "The same way you've learned to do everything else of consequence. Sink or swim."

My voice was barely more than a whisper, "What if I sink?"

"You won't."

"How can you be so sure of that?"

"Because the Princess is gonna be in rough shape when we get her back and if you don't protect her home, we may not be able to save her."

"No pressure there," I croaked as my eyes filled with tears.

"I have no doubt that you can do this, Charlie. When it really matters, you always come through. You shine under pressure." At that, Benjamin stepped inside the cave.

Rose and I exchanged worried glances as we followed Isa into the cave. The instant we stepped in, the weight of the mirage grew ten times heavier. The splintering crack of breaking ribs accompanied my shriek as I dropped to my knees on the stone floor, and the world around me became nothing but one gigantic blur that was just too much to process. The next thing I knew, my face was between Rose's hands. She tilted my head up and planted a sweet kiss on my lips. The ache that permeated every fiber of my being heated as her warmth spread through me, and the weight grew a bit more bearable. When she let go of my head, the world around me was in focus and Benjamin was already gone. I turned to look at Isa. "What's happening with Emma? Do you know where she is?"

Isa's voice was thick with unshed tears as she whispered, "They're keeping her in a cabin. The Sarrum is headed there now…"

When her voice trailed off, I cleared my throat. "What have they done to her?"

"You don't want to know," she whispered as she wiped a stray tear from her cheek.

"Yeah," I muttered, "I do."

Isa's eyes dropped to the floor of the cave. "They've already hurt her, Charlie. They've done horrible things."

The world slipped back out of focus. "What things?"

"You don't need to know."

"Yeah," I muttered as I tried to focus on Isa's face, "I do."

Isa sat down on the stone beside me. "Charlie, your feelings for Emma are as misguided as her grasp on who she is. Your relationship is clouded by factors that neither of you understand, it always has been. You need to understand that Emma will never love any man but the Sarrum. She's forgotten that for the time being, but that doesn't make it any less true."

ERIN A. JENSEN

Even as close as she was, Isa's face was a blur. "Why are you saying all that?"

"Because you will never be able to pledge your loyalty to a ruler you believe you're competing with for a woman's love. But there is no competition. There never could be. I promise you, Emma will never love anyone but the Sarrum."

"You…" The world was beginning to sway. "You can't know a thing like that."

Isa touched a comforting hand to my cheek, and I had to fight the impulse to smack it away. "I can. Deep in my heart, I know it. I've never been more certain of anything."

The weight crushed me with more force than I'd ever imagined a soul could withstand, forcing me to lie down on the stone. "What the hell am I supposed to do?"

Rose's face was in perfect focus as she laid down on the stone floor beside me. "Keep doing what you're doing now, shouldering the weight."

Tears slipped from my eyes, but I was in too much physical and emotional agony to be embarrassed. "I can't. It's too much. It's all just too much, and I'm tired."

"I know, Charlie." She took my hand in hers and that comforting warmth spread through me again. "But you're doing great."

My words came out like sobs, "I can't do this."

She slid closer and touched her forehead to mine. "Focus on me, Charlie. Look in my eyes."

I did as she said, but couldn't bring myself to speak.

The heat of her spiced breath caressed my face as she whispered, "You don't have to do this alone."

Warmth spread through me as her scent washed over me. "I don't want to do it at all."

She swept my sweat-soaked hair off my face with her fingertips. "Let me take some of the weight now."

Tears streamed down my cheeks as I sobbed, "How?"

She slid a bit closer and pressed her soft lips to mine again. This time, I kissed back. The flavor of our scents mingled on my tongue as my body radiated heat, and the weight pressing down on me shifted. It was still all there but like this, the weight seemed to distribute itself between us. Lost in a swell of agony and grief, I clung to her warmth like a lifeline—pulling her closer and pushing my tongue into her mouth, greedy for more of the sweet taste of her. She welcomed the intrusion, greeting my tongue with hers and everything including the weight of the mirage faded away until there was nothing but the two of us and the delicious heat blossoming between us.

It suddenly occurred to me that Rose's mother was still in the cave with us. Even so, it took me a full minute to pull my mouth away from hers. I needed the taste of her, more than I needed to breathe. Rose let out a soft whimper as I pulled back from her and turned toward where Isa had been sitting. For a split second, the fact that she wasn't there filled me with panic, but as I scanned the rest of the cave and saw no one else, a heated thrill began to swell inside me. I turned back to Rose, desperately fighting to keep my head. As much as I wanted to latch onto her and devour the warmth that lay there waiting for me, this didn't seem right. Hadn't I been heartbroken over what Isa said about Emma just a few minutes ago? For some reason, that no longer seemed to matter, which made it all seem that much more wrong.

Rose slid closer to me as I met her eyes, clearly eager to pick up where we left off.

Despite my mental reservations, I slid my fingers through the strands of her sleek dark hair. "This doesn't seem right."

Rose smiled at me as she whispered, "Who cares how it seems. How does it *feel*?"

It took a couple seconds to stop focusing on the feel of her hair. "Wrong," I forced myself to whisper.

"Does it really feel wrong? Or is that just how you think it's supposed to feel?"

"Doesn't it bother you that I was just pining away for Emma a few minutes ago?"

"No."

"Why?" I muttered. "And why don't I feel devastated by the idea that Emma will never love me? I was crushed by it a few minutes ago."

"My mother lessened the effect of Emma's charm."

"Charm? What...like an incubus's charm? Emma's a fairy."

"She's extremely skilled at manipulating other souls."

"So, are you saying Emma was just manipulating me all that time at the facility?"

"Not consciously," Rose whispered, "She didn't have any idea what she was doing or even that she was capable of doing it. She just desperately needed someone to watch over her and make her feel safe, and she sensed what you were—how you were like her husband."

"I'm nothing like David Talbot."

"You're a dragon," Rose whispered. "Emma sensed the dragon's heart beating in your chest, and she latched onto you because she needed a dragon—her dragon—even though she didn't know it at the time."

"So...it was never about me?"

"You were an echo of the creature she needed."

"And she suckered me into playing along."

"No. She had no idea what she was doing. It was all just desperate instinct."

"Then why did I fall for it so hard? I thought dragons were immune to that sort of thing."

"We are when we want to be."

"Why wouldn't I want to be?"

"Because you needed someone to love you."

I sat up and raked a hand through my hair as a long-buried ache flared in my chest, truer words had never been spoken. "That makes me sound so pathetic."

"We all need that, Charlie." Rose sat up and slid closer to me, and I saw the desperation in her eyes as she whispered, "I need that."

As I witnessed the ache that mirrored my own, the scent leaking from my pores intensified and I shook my head. "Yeah, but why would you want it from a fool like me?"

"You're not a fool. You wear your heart on your sleeve, despite how much you try to hide that behind your sarcasm—it's obvious to me," she let out a little sob as she whispered, "and you have the kindest eyes I've ever seen. Why would I want it from anyone *other* than you?"

A fierce need to mend the hurt in her eyes swelled inside me as I wrapped my arms around her. "Where have you been all my life, Rose Salazar?"

She wrapped her arms around me and whispered, "Waiting for you."

35

BOB

Tristan wasn't at all the narcissistic sexual deviant that Aubrey had prepared me for. I got the feeling that a fair portion of his behavior was just an act he put on for the world because that was what everyone expected from him. The rush of elation that filled me when I first set eyes on the incubus had nothing to do with his outward appearance. It had everything to do with the hope that swelled inside me when I realized he hadn't been slaughtered and I'd finally found the man who might be able to help me. Once Tristan realized his charm had no effect on me, he seemed to develop an almost profound respect for me.

I wasted no time in explaining how Nellie was taken from me and that she'd been guiding me with a few whispered words each time I woke. I told Tristan that Nellie had instructed me to find

Charlie, who could in turn take me to this Dragon King he'd been training with, then I explained that I needed to warn this King that Godric also meant to abduct his Princess. Tristan's hypnotic green eyes filled with tears as he informed me that it was already too late for that, Godric had in fact kidnapped the Princess and they were running out of time. Despite the urgency of our mission, Aubrey insisted that Pip and I eat a quick meal before heading off with Tristan to speak to Charlie. While she prepared our food, Tristan explained that the King couldn't be bothered because he was already on his own quest to find Godric and rescue his Princess.

As Tristan and Aubrey headed out back to go over a few plans for the tavern, Pip and I finished our meal. When Pip swallowed his last bite, he reclined against the cushion Tristan had placed on the table for him. "It's been a real pleasure, Bob."

I tossed my napkin to the table and settled back against the cushions of the booth. "You say that as if we're about to part ways. Have you tired of being my pocket-sized travel companion?"

There was no trace of amusement on Pip's face as he shook his head. "No, of course not. It's just that I figured you'd probably be better off without me at this point. I mean, you've got Tristan to help you now. I imagine he'd be a hell of a lot better choice to stand beside during a fight, and your friend Charlie sounds a lot more capable than me—especially now that he's been training with the King's men."

"And why would that mean I'd need you any less?"

Pip rolled his eyes as he licked the last traces of meat juice from his fingers. "Come on, Bob. Be serious. I can't compare to those guys. I'd just slow you down."

"I don't see how. You ride in my pocket. It's not as if we'd have to worry about your running speed."

"You are without a doubt the noblest man I've ever met, Bob," Pip whispered with a wistful smile, "but I don't want you to feel obligated to drag me along for the rest of this journey just because I started it with you. I was the only help you could find at the time, but you've got powerful allies to stand with you now. Don't saddle yourself with me just to spare my feelings."

A wide grin spread across my face. "You know, I can be rather dense at times. Are you trying to get rid of me?"

"Yeah," Pip chuckled. "You're really holding me back from my dreams."

I dropped the smile and lowered my voice, "And what are your dreams, my friend?"

Pip's expression darkened the instant I stopped smiling. "No dreams for me. They only lead to heartbreak. It's better to face the world one day at a time with no attachments. There's nothing to lose that way."

I lowered the mouth of my goblet and nodded toward it, offering him a sip of my wine. "What happened to her?"

Pip downed a sizable gulp, considering his size. Then he wiped his mouth on his sleeve without meeting my eyes. "Who?"

"You know who," I whispered.

"It doesn't matter."

"It certainly does." I tipped my glass and offered him another sip. "It matters to me because I know it matters to you, and I would not be sitting here if it weren't for you. At least let me lend an ear to repay the favor."

Pip clutched a hand to his chest as if bracing for an impending heart attack. "Why dredge all that up?"

"Because it's the only way to move past it. My friend Charlie recently helped me realize that. I spent years of my life running from my nightmares, but now that I've faced them, I'm a new man. Life has new purpose, and I have a wonderful woman to share my life with."

A melancholy grin curved his lips for a second. "I used to have one of those."

"What happened?"

"Godric happened," he muttered. "Godric and his Purists…"

I waited in silence because it was his choice whether or not to tell the tale. I just wanted to offer him the option of unburdening a fraction of his pain.

"She was more than I ever deserved," he whispered. "I don't know why she never realized that."

"Probably because you undervalue your own worth."

"I'm a mutt," he muttered, "a half-troll, half-imp freak of a creature who's never fit in anywhere."

"You fit in just fine with me," I whispered, "and it sounds like you fit in with her, too."

"She was a beautiful breath of fresh air in my filthy little life."

"What was her name?"

"Elizabeth," the name lingered on his tongue for a moment, as if he hadn't said it in some time and was in no hurry to let it go.

"That's a lovely name."

"She was a lovely girl," he whispered, "but she didn't realize it."

"No?"

"Well... I suppose she did in this world, but not in the other one. She was Unsighted, like you."

"Where did you meet her?"

"In the forest," he whispered. "She wandered in during a game of hide and seek with the other elf children and somehow lost her bearings, and she got frightened because it was almost nightfall."

"How old was she?"

"She was ten at the time, and I was twelve. I'd skulked off to find a quiet spot because the trolls were bullying me, and I found her hugging her legs to her chest and sobbing. When I saw her sitting there, all my troubles melted away. I led her to a hollow tree trunk where she could hide from the creatures who wandered the forest after dark, and I stayed with her till morning. I made up silly stories to make her smile and actually managed to make her laugh and forget her fear for a while. In the morning, when it was safe, I led her back to the edge of the forest by the shore where her nomadic tribe had set up camp. She thanked me and headed back to the other elves.

I figured that was the last I'd see of her, but I started spending a lot more time in the woods near her shore. I was just hoping to catch an occasional glimpse of her, but a week later, she wandered in and spent the afternoon laughing and talking with me. After that, she started coming all the time and telling me secrets she said no one in her tribe would understand. It didn't take me long to decide to leave the trolls I'd never fit in with anyway and move to the forest by her shore.

Her tribe moved twice in the years after that, but she convinced me to relocate to the woods near their new camp both times. She was the light in my otherwise dark little life, and I never expected her to be anything more than that. I mean, I was a pocket-sized freak, and she was a beautiful elf. Then one day, when I was twenty-seven, I was eating lunch in my favorite diner in the waking world when a girl walked through the door. She didn't look anything like she did in Draumer, but I recognized her right away. I would've known her anywhere. Feeling the need to do something, I asked the waitress to bring me her bill. I paid it anonymously and left without thinking anything more would come of it."

"Why did you pay for her lunch if you didn't intend to get to know her?"

"I already knew her," Pip whispered, "but I didn't want to spook her by walking up to her. I mean, she was Unsighted. I was a total stranger to her in that world."

I felt the need to prompt him for more, "But…"

"But she came back the next day for lunch, headed straight for my table and asked if she could join me. The rest—as they say—is history."

"She became your girlfriend?"

"She became my wife."

"And?"

"And, she was timid and soft spoken and didn't think much of her own appearance. It always killed me that she never believed she was good enough for me. I think a small part of her always feared that I'd find somebody better to replace her. She had no idea that there was no one better in either world. She was my soul mate, and I loved her with all my heart, and in one of these worlds, I was lucky enough to build a life with her."

"What happened?"

Pip shook his head. "It's too soon."

"Godric hurt her recently?"

"He didn't hurt her directly," Pip muttered, despite the fact that he said he couldn't talk about it. "His followers did when they raided the fringe."

"They killed her?"

"No," Pip whispered, "they killed her entire tribe right in front of her... and they did... other things to her."

I waited for him to continue but when he didn't go on, I whispered, "I'm so sorry, Pip."

"I was right there in the woods when it happened. Useless as I was, I raced out there and tried to stop the three shadows who..."

I tipped my glass and he gave a grateful nod and took another sip of wine.

"I watched it all happen," he muttered, "and I was so insignificant that they didn't even bother to kill me. They just let me race around like a pathetic fool, trying to grab at them and pull them away from her.

She lasted almost a year after that. In this world, she moved into the woods, and I helped keep her hidden and safe when the forest was dark. I led her to food and watched over her as best I could. But in the waking world, it was even harder for her to deal with. She slipped into a deep depression that no medication could fix. Unsighted doctors think depression is a chemical imbalance that they can treat with more chemicals, but it never is. There's always a reason for the depression—a trauma or the death of a loved one—it's just not anything they consciously remember in that world, but they still feel the pain.

I tried everything I could think of to help her get through it, but eventually it was just too much for her. I came home from work and found her note on the kitchen table, apologizing that she couldn't be the woman I needed... and I found her in the bedroom with my shotgun in her hand...and a hole in the back of her head."

No condolence I could offer would be enough, so Pip and I just sat there in silence. Eventually I whispered, "You have to come with us, Pip. You have every reason in the world to want Godric and his followers to pay for what they did to your wife. Like it or not, you're a part of this battle, and I would be honored to fight beside you."

"Weren't you listening to my story?" he whispered. "I'd serve no purpose in a battle."

"Everyone serves a purpose, my friend. You just haven't found yours yet, but I have no doubt that we'll find it together."

36

ROSE

The instant my mother lessened the effects of the Princess's charm, I could see the difference in Charlie. He still cared about Emma's safety—the way we all cared—but he didn't seem crushed by the notion that she'd never love any man but the Sarrum. It all made so much sense once Isa explained their relationship. How else could Charlie look at all the signs in that house and still be blind to the depth of their love? I'd never even seen the Sarrum and his wife in the same room, but I saw it in all the pictures of the two of them together. The way they looked at each other personified the sort of undying love that you read about in fairytales. Except in the fairytales, the Princess never lives happily ever after with the dragon. Then again—if a dragon looked at you the way the King looked at Emma in those pictures—how could you not fall head over heels for him?

After giving us a bit of time alone, my mother came back into the cave to see how Charlie and I were holding up. Our goal was to shoulder the weight of the mirage without having to stay there twenty-four hours a day, but we planned to accomplish that goal in baby steps. We sat in the cave for a few hours, getting used to the feel of sharing the burden. There was quite a trick to it. You had to remain synchronized so that one person didn't end up shouldering more weight than the other and knocking everything off balance. It sounds like an abstract concept, but nothing had ever felt more real to me.

We were about to attempt heading inside the palace when Tristan came rushing into the cave. When he noticed how close Charlie and I were sitting, he stopped dead in his tracks and grinned at us. "Now there's a power couple if I ever saw one."

Charlie's cheeks flushed as he shot Tristan a dopey grin. "Shut up. Did you come here just to gawk at our magnificence, or was there a reason you came barging in?"

Tristan's playful grin spread from ear to ear. "I've got a visitor in the palace who traveled pretty far to see you, Charlie."

Charlie combed his fingers through the disheveled locks of his hair. "To see me? I don't know anyone who isn't already here."

Tristan winked at me, and when Charlie's scent hit the air, Tristan grinned at him. "Just follow me."

Charlie started to stand, then plopped back down on the floor of the cave beside me. "Can I go out there without dropping the weight?"

"You'll have to," Isa whispered, "If you can't, Emma may not survive."

Charlie exhaled a tired sigh as he touched his head to mine. "Maybe I'd better stay here."

"Trust me," Tristan insisted, "you're gonna want to talk to this visitor."

"Sure," Charlie muttered as he carefully got to his feet. "Why not?"

I stood up beside him and took his hand. "You can do this, Charlie."

"Are you coming with me?"

"Yes," I whispered. "Where you go, I go. We have to stay close to share this burden."

"I like the sound of that," Charlie muttered under his breath as the three of us followed Tristan down the stone corridor to the Waterfall at the far end. Tristan winked at Charlie as he stepped into the Waterfall, then Charlie and I followed with my mother close behind.

We stepped out into a small room that was comfortably furnished in muted shades of blue. A ruggedly handsome man sat on a couch against the far wall. When he saw Charlie, he hopped to his feet and moved toward us.

"Bob?" Charlie muttered as the man pulled him into a muscular bear hug.

The mystery man smiled at Charlie. "How are you, my friend? It's good to see you again."

Charlie hugged the man back, then they both broke the hug with a manly clap on the shoulder. "It's good to see you, too. But what the heck are you doing here, and how did you find me?"

The handsome stranger's face fell. "Godric kidnapped Nellie and Lilly."

"Shit, Bob," Charlie whispered. "I'm so sorry."

The handsome stranger's eyes dropped to the floor. "It seems I failed to best her dragon in the end."

"This isn't the end," Tristan whispered as he put a hand on Bob's shoulder. Then he turned to Charlie. "Nellie has been whispering in Bob's ear in the waking world to guide him toward you. She told him you were training with the Dragon King and instructed him to find you and ask for help. She also told him to warn the Dragon King that Godric intended to abduct his Princess."

Charlie's eyes widened as he studied Bob. "How did you hear her?"

"I heard her whispers in the breeze when I woke each morning."

Charlie nodded. "Do you think Nellie could describe the place where Godric is keeping her?"

"I couldn't say," Bob whispered, "We can't exactly communicate the way things are now. Anyway, what good would that do? We would have to find the place before we could ask her and by then, there'd be no point."

"I think it's time to pay the facility a visit," Tristan whispered as he started toward the Waterfall.

Charlie followed him with a pensive nod. "I can't go far from Rose," as an afterthought he added, "Oh…by the way Bob, this is Rose."

The man politely but distractedly dipped his head to me as Tristan murmured, "Rose can come."

Bob stepped up to the Waterfall with us, but Tristan put a hand on his shoulder. "I'm afraid we'll have to make this trip without you, Bob. You're Unsighted, so you wouldn't have any idea what we were talking about in the waking world. Besides, *old you* is already there."

"Well," Bob muttered, "that makes no sense at all."

Charlie looked at Bob with an apologetic frown. "Is there a message you'd like me to deliver to Nellie for you?"

"Tell her I love her with all my heart, and I won't give up searching for her till she's back in my arms."

"Will do, Bob," Charlie whispered, "See you there."

37

NELLIE

It was all going to shit. I had no way of knowing if whispering in the ear of the old man sitting next to me was doing a damn bit of good. I was still Henry Godric's captive in the Dream World. I hadn't seen Lilly in either world for days, and I was sick to my stomach over what he'd done to Emma after he separated us. I'd drifted in and out several times since then. At one point, I overheard two filthy demons laughing about what a struggle the King's precious little Princess had put up when they "took their turns" with her. The larger one even bragged about how broken she was by the time he finished with her. As much as I disliked Emma, no creature deserved to be violated in the ways the demons had cackled about in horrifically descriptive detail. For all I knew, I'd be next. The demons had hinted as much on more than one nightmarish occasion. I was beginning to think my best option was to goad Godric's demons into killing me. I'd have to be careful about it though. Godric wouldn't allow that to happen if he knew I was planning it. Why the hell didn't I see how evil Henry Godric was when I was younger? This man had no heart—he wasn't even a man, for that matter—he was a monster.

Tim the troll flashed me a toothy grin as his Cro-Magnon shoulders squeezed through the doorway into the main common room. "You've got visitors, Nellie."

"Fuck off," I grumbled, "There must be moths between your ears. I don't get visitors."

"You haven't changed a bit," a familiar voice chuckled behind Tim.

For the first time since Godric abducted me, I felt a glimmer of hope. "Charlie?"

The troll stepped aside, and Charlie headed toward our couch with a bouquet of daisies in his hand and a goofy grin on his face. "Did you miss me?"

I couldn't stop myself from tearing up as he bent down to hug me and hand me the flowers. "Believe it or not, I did." Then I noticed the visitors he'd brought with him—a pretty young Hispanic girl and a gorgeous chocolate-skinned specimen of male perfection that would've taken my breath away fifty years earlier. "Well, you've certainly traded up from me and Bob. Who are your new friends?"

Charlie's cheeks flushed as he stood upright and touched the girl's arm. "This is Rose." The girl nodded to me with a shy smile as Charlie pointed to the godlike male, who I was pretty damn sure was an incubus. "And this is Tristan."

Tristan flashed me a dazzling smile as he bent, took my wrinkled hand and pressed it to his lips like a perfect gentleman. "It's a pleasure to meet you, Nellie."

"You probably figured this out already," Charlie whispered, "but Bob came to see me in Draumer. He told us Godric took you and Lilly."

I couldn't find the words to answer, so I just nodded as the tears spilled down my cheeks.

"We're going to find you and get you out of there, Nellie," Tristan whispered, "Any information you can give us about where Godric is keeping you would be a tremendous help."

I stole a glance at Tim, who was standing by the door, staring at Rose with a dopey, lopsided grin on his face. "He's keeping me somewhere Dark."

"We figured as much," the incubus murmured.

"The room he first brought me to looks like a parlor from the Victorian age," I muttered, "but he moved me to some filthy old dungeon."

Tristan nodded with a sympathetic frown. "Can you tell us anything else?"

"Well…the yard outside the window in the parlor is crawling with demons…way too many of them to count." For some stupid reason, the new doctor's face suddenly popped in my head. "Oh, and that snot-nosed investigator of yours tried to intimidate me earlier today."

Tristan's flawless brow furrowed. "What investigator?"

"The doctor you sent here to deal with me for leaving my beach without permission."

"That should be something I get punished for," Charlie whispered. "I'm the idiot who took you out of there."

"There's no punishment," Tristan muttered. "With everything that's going on, do you really think the Sarrum gives a damn about sending somebody to punish you for leaving your mirage?"

My throat constricted as I whispered, "He's not with you?"

The incubus shook his head. "No. He's not with us, but I'm going to look into that right now."

The color drained from Charlie's face as he watched Tristan walk out the door. "What happened to Spenser?"

I gave him my best *you're a moron* scowl. "You know what happened. He pissed off the King."

"No," Rose whispered, "He hurt the King's wife. There's no walking away from an offense like that."

I smiled at Charlie's pretty new friend. "Well said." After a short pause, I added, "How is Emma holding up in the waking world?"

"Not good," Charlie whispered, "Have you seen her with Godric in Draumer?"

"Once," I replied with a nod, "before his demons took me to the dungeon. I haven't seen her since they separated us...but I overheard a couple of demons in the dungeon bragging about, um...'taking their turns' with the Princess."

The old man beside me on the couch roused himself from sleep with a grizzly-bearish snort. His old eyes were dim with confusion until they landed on Charlie. "Hey, kid. What brings you back here?"

Charlie's face was so green, I half-expected him to vomit. He shook his head to snap himself out of it as he sat down on the couch next to Bob. "I came to pay you guys a visit. How are you doing, Bob?"

"Fine," Bob grumbled as his eyes drifted to Rose. "Who's the girl? What happened to the Barbie doll whose pants you were so hot to get into when you lived here?"

A horrified expression spread across Charlie's face as he looked up at Rose, but she just grinned.

"This new one's a peach, too," Bob muttered.

"Oh shut up, you old pervert." I gently smacked him upside the head. "This young thing doesn't want to hear what you think."

"Shut yourself up, woman," Bob grumbled.

"Nellie," Charlie muttered in a voice too low for Bob's deaf old ears to pick up, "do you think you could tell us how to find this place where Godric's keeping you?"

"No," I whispered, "He took us through the Waters. There's no path to retrace."

A wide grin curved the incubus's perfect lips as he reentered the room and sauntered toward us. "The doctor won't be bothering you again, Nellie."

"How can you be so damn sure?"

No more than a few seconds later, the doctor tip-toed in the room and eyed Tristan like a crazed teen-ager would eye the latest television heart-throb.

Tristan winked at the fool, and his cheeks flushed the deepest shade of pink I'd ever seen anyone turn. "I'm pretty damn sure."

I wrinkled my nose. "Do I want to know?"

"I'd be happy to share the details," Tristan mur-mured, "but if you'd rather skip them, let's just say he'll be too busy fantasizing about me to remember why the Purists sent him here."

"Huh," I muttered as I watched the doctor smooth a hand over his even messier than usual hair, "I wouldn't have pegged him as gay."

"He might not have either," Tristan whispered as he flashed the doctor a smile that would make any creature go weak at the knees, "but he's gonna be questioning it for a while."

I grinned at the incubus. "You're a pretty handy fellow to have around."

"That's what they tell me," Tristan chuckled. Then he turned to Charlie. "Did you pass young Bob's message on to Nellie?"

"Oh yeah," Charlie muttered, "Bob wanted me to tell you that he loves you with all his heart, and he won't stop searching for you till you're in his arms again."

I smiled at the wrinkled old fool sitting beside me with his eyes glued to the television screen. "Tell him I don't doubt it for a second."

Charlie clapped Bob on the shoulder as he whispered, "Will do."

Then, Tristan sat down on the coffee table in front of me and pulled something small from his pocket. When he held it out, I was surprised to see that it was nothing but a dime store bracelet. He leaned forward and pressed it into my palm. "Wear this night and day. It will lead us to the house where Godric's keeping you, so don't take it off and don't let lover boy over there take it from you."

"How am I supposed to stop him?"

Tristan grinned as he stood and placed a gentle kiss on my cheek. "Leave that to me. It was lovely to meet you, Nellie. I'm sure we'll meet again soon. Until then, I promise to take good care of your soul mate."

A fresh swell of tears filled my eyes. "Henry always said *he* was my soul mate."

"He was wrong," Tristan whispered. With that, the incubus stood and moved toward the door so slowly that the doctor was drooling with anticipation by the time Tristan reached him.

The doctor lit up as Tristan leaned close to his ear and whispered something. Then Tristan slipped something into his hand, leaned a little closer and shot him a look that I was amazed didn't make him faint dead on the spot as he walked out the door.

The doc made a hasty retreat to his office the second Tristan was out of view, but I didn't want to give that too much thought.

38

DAVID

The Purists' cabin was just a short distance from where I waited in the forest for Benjamin and Brian. It would have been infinitely faster and more efficient to coordinate our arrival through the Waters, however the Purists would've sensed us coming had we formed a temporary portal and the element of surprise would have been lost. So I waited within the trees, half-crazed with hunger for traitorous blood as I watched for them through the flames that blazed in my eyes. An image of my Princess's suffering flashed through my mind and a throb of pain seared my heart.

I pressed a hand to my chest, desperate for a memory to occupy my mind till Benjamin and Brian arrived. Fearing that any memory of her would evoke too much pain, I chose the day I first met Brian...

...I shifted impatiently on my throne's velvet cushions and wondered for about the hundredth time whether this was in fact the ridiculous waste of time I suspected it to be. When Walter Mason had shown up at the palace three days prior, announcing that he was on his deathbed and pledging his eldest son's life in service to me in order to settle his own debts, Benjamin had convinced me to let him track the young man down and size up his worth. In retrospect, I wasn't quite sure how Benjamin had talked me into it.

Walter Mason was a good-for-nothing incubus who had squandered his life and left a string of broken hearts and illegitimate offspring in his wake. Yet even at a tender age, his eldest son had a vastly different reputation. Stubborn, headstrong and honorable as the day was long, the half-incubus had forsaken any favors that his charms might have granted him and devoted himself to training for a life of nomadic knighthood. Summoning the young man to the palace to consider working for us instead made no sense whatsoever to me, but Benjamin felt differently. Of course none of us had any intention of holding the young man accountable for his father's debts, but Benjamin believed that Brian's honor should afford him an invitation to join our family. Perhaps the fact that we all knew something of cold-hearted fathers—who lived their lives with little concern for the well-being of their offspring—convinced me to grant Walter's singular legitimate son an interview.

Benjamin's well intentioned plan had been further complicated when he tracked the half-incubus down at a training camp up North and discovered that he had little interest in serving the palace. Stubborn as he was, Benjamin had insisted that the young man at least come for an interview.

They were now an hour overdue, and the cushions on my throne were growing less comfortable by the minute. The only thing keeping me from exiting the great hall and abandoning the foolish notion altogether was the eagerness I had witnessed in Benjamin's eyes. Having originated from humble beginnings himself, Benjamin relished any opportunity to discover a diamond in the rough, polish him to perfection and gather him into our fold. Of course being a shadow, the Darkness hid that soft heart of his behind a hefty façade of terror-inducing intimidation.

"We're here," Benjamin shouted as he stepped from the Waterfall at the far end of the hall.

A strapping young man—whose handsome features were somewhat obscured by the permanent scowl that was pasted on his face—stepped out after Benjamin and crossed the floor beside him. Brian Mason carried himself with an air of sturdy confidence and a graceful stride that affirmed his elven heritage every bit as much as his pointed ears. He had the muscular physique of a warrior-in-training and the unshakable determination of an elven nobleman. Sizing the young man up gave me great confidence that he would indeed be well qualified to guard the Princess on campus where Benjamin or myself would stick out like a sore thumb, and I had no qualms about his character—Benjamin was an excellent judge of such things, and he'd already deemed him worthy. All that remained of the decision process was for me to interview him and the Princess to determine whether he was right for the job.

Brian halted at the foot of the stairs with a respectful nod. When I motioned for him to approach, he ascended the steps and settled into the seat beside mine, completely at ease in his opulent foreign surroundings.

I gestured toward a goblet of wine on the table beside him as I picked up my own. "It's a pleasure to meet you, Brian. Benjamin has had nothing but good things to say about you."

He picked up his drink, out of polite obligation rather than thirst. "Thank you, Sarrum. It's an honor to meet you."

"I assume you already know why you're here?"

"You have a position to offer me," his voice remained steady as he shifted in his seat, "but I have no interest in any scraps my father left behind for me."

"Actually, your father offered you up in servitude to pay a debt that he failed to repay before passing."

There was no trace of emotion on Brian's stoic face as he nodded. "Yeah. That sounds like my father."

"You are nothing like him," I remarked as I set my goblet back on the table.

A faint smile curved his lips. "I take that as a tremendous compliment."

"I have no intention of holding you accountable for your father's debt."

"I appreciate that, Sarrum."

"Although from what I hear, you would honor the debt if I did."

The faint hint of a smile slipped from his face. "I would."

"Honor is quite important to you."

"It is," he agreed. "May I be honest with you, sir?"

"Please."

"I don't think I'm the man for this job."

"And why is that?"

"What do I know about guarding a Princess?"

"Would you like to meet her before you determine you have nothing in common with her?"

He took a deep breath before replying, "With all due respect Sarrum, why would you want a half-incubus to guard your future wife?"

I answered with an amused grin, "You suspect I have something to fear?"

"There's a certain measure of charm that can't be dampened, Sarrum," he replied with an apologetic nod. "I'd certainly never intentionally do anything to—"

"Do I look concerned?"

"No, sir," he replied, "but perhaps you should be."

"Why don't we leave that up to her?"

"Sir, fairies are extremely susceptible to our charms."

I picked up my goblet and eyed him as I took a sip. "Yes. I am well aware of that. I assure you, my education on the characteristics of various creatures was quite adequate."

"But?"

"But I am not concerned."

Brian nodded and took a sip of wine. "Maybe meeting her would be best then."

"Excellent." I stood from my throne and gestured for him to follow me down the steps.

"What?" he muttered as he rushed down the stairs after me. "Now?"

"Unless you have something better to do."

"No, sir," he muttered, "it's just that...I would've dressed differently had I known I'd be meeting a Princess."

I looked him over with absent disinterest. "You are dressed just fine." Before he could argue, I stepped through the nearest Waterfall.

He stepped through the Waterfall and entered the atrium a few seconds after me. The Princess was seated on a nearby bench reading a book with her legs tucked beneath her, much like a grade-schooler perched on a piece of furniture that was too spacious for her size. Having just finished her fencing lesson, she was dressed in form-fitting black pants and a fitted emerald blouse that allowed for ease of movement whilst emphasizing the magnificent green of her eyes and showing off each gorgeous curve of her body. Despite his concerns about her potential reaction to his charm, it was Brian's heart that skipped a beat when her eyes met his.

Stubborn as she was to prove that she had no need for any guard because she was perfectly capable of protecting herself, the Princess flashed Brian a dazzling manipulative smile. It was a rather tumultuous time in our relationship due to the fact that I had been guide and guardian to her since birth and we now found ourselves engaged to be married. Despite the evolution of our relationship, there was a certain measure of protection that I was unwilling to forgo. Her gaze shifted to me, and she shot me a look that challenged me to resist taking her into my arms and ravishing her right then and there.

I narrowed my eyes at her. Regardless of whether or not we choose this fellow for the job, you are not setting foot on that campus without a suitable guard.

She narrowed her eyes right back at me. Fine. You can be such a bully sometimes.

Yes? Well, feel free to commiserate with your new classmate after I leave the premises.

She let out a throaty chuckle that caused Brian to raise an eyebrow. "Sorry," *she whispered,* "that was rude."

"Not at all, Princess," he muttered with far less composure than he had shown in the great hall.

She stood from the bench and extended a delicate hand. "You must be Brian."

Brian took her hand with a respectful nod and shook it as he whispered, "It's an honor to meet you."

A wide grin spread across her face. "Are you always this serious?"

His scowl dissolved and a curious grin took its place. "I suppose I am."

"We'll have to fix that," she whispered.

He looked over his shoulder at me and suddenly seemed to realize that he was still holding her hand. He cleared his throat and let her hand slip from his as he turned back to her.

But her eyes were locked with mine.

"Wow," he whispered, "I've never met a fairy who was unaffected by my charm."

Her eyes lingered on mine for a moment before drifting to his. "No?"

"No, usually fairies are easy…" he cleared his throat as he shot me an awkward glance, "…to um, get to know."

Mischief glimmered in Emma's eyes. "I'm sure they are."

The knight-in-training's serious façade crumbled in a burst of laughter. "Wouldn't you rather have someone less serious keep you company?"

She glared at me over his shoulder. "You mean babysit me?"

"You certainly don't look like a baby to me," he muttered.

She leveled me with a sinful grin. "Tell that to my overprotective daddy over there."

A perverse thrill coursed through me at the term of endearment I had so desperately longed to hear when she was a child, but a disciplinary growl rumbled in my throat as Brian's jaw dropped in response to her words.

Emma simply giggled and shot me a sinful grin.

I narrowed my eyes at her. Shall I take you over my knee, young lady?

Oh God, yes.

Though our exchange was private, the incubus was instinctively aware of the charge in the air between us. The fact that Emma knew this made her behavior all the more wicked. "I should probably go," he muttered.

"I'm sorry," Emma whispered with an apologetic frown. "I didn't mean to make you uncomfortable."

A play-boyish grin replaced Brian's somber scowl. "I'm half incubus, Princess. There isn't a sexual comment you could utter that would make me uncomfortable."

She winked at me with a devilish grin. "Well, I do love a challenge."…

…An unbearable sense of guilt gripped me as the fond memory dissipated into a rush of sinful images of what transpired in the atrium after Brian left. It seemed wrong to picture her like that after what I had witnessed.

Thankfully, Benjamin's thoughts stole my attention just as my guilt began to conjure images of the way she'd been violated. *I left the mirage in good hands,*

Boss. Charlie and Rose are shouldering the weight together, and Isa is overseeing their efforts.

I masked myself in human form as I stepped toward Brian and Benjamin.

Benjamin narrowed his eyes as he watched me approach, but the look on my face cautioned him not to question anything. "There are twelve heartbeats within the cabin," I informed them in a venomous whisper. "Nine strong and healthy, and three faint ones at the back of the structure."

Rage flashed in Benjamin's eyes. "How do you want us to proceed, Boss?"

"I'll take the front," I whispered, "whilst the two of you secure the creatures in back."

Brian's eyes filled with tears as he glanced toward the cabin. "You can count on us, Sarrum."

"I know." Another stab of pain pierced my heart as I touched a hand to his shoulder. "I'll storm in once the two of you are positioned behind the building."

Without another word, the two men nodded and took off.

I waited till their pounding hearts flanked the rear of the cabin, then I unmasked and knocked the door down in one flying leap.

Startled screams bounced off the walls as I barged inside the cabin—smashing support beams and caving in walls—whilst being careful to leave the rear of the structure undamaged. I trampled two sorrows and snapped the neck of a shadow with a swift flick of my tail, and the six remaining demons raced for the kitchen. My furious roar echoed through the cabin as a male fairy grabbed a knife from the counter and rushed toward me in a moronic act of misplaced bravery. I caught him by the throat with my teeth and shook his body till the blade dropped from his lifeless hand. Then I snarled at the five remaining deviants who cowered on the floor in a tight huddle. "Where is Godric hiding? Does the coward not have the courage to face me?"

"He doesn't want the fun to end too quickly," a blonde shadow rasped from the corner.

A wisp of smoke wafted from my nostrils as I stepped toward the loathsome creature I had seen laughing at the Dragon's Lair in the sweet-talker's vision. "Is that so?"

Payne let out a throaty chuckle. "It is. Are you having fun yet, Sarrum?"

I smashed a claw into the cupboard behind her, trapping her by the neck. "Not nearly as much as you soon will be."

"Bring it on," she whispered, "I dare you to make me scream."

A flicker of fear glinted in her eyes as I snarled, "Oh, I intend to."

"Sarrum." It took a moment for Brian to capture my attention. It wasn't until I realized which bedroom he had rushed out of that I stepped away from the shadow.

Brian's voice barely registered as he muttered something about keeping an eye on the filth in the kitchen. In fact, all sounds dimmed but the pounding of my own heart as I moved toward the door that I had entered in the sweet-talker's memory. Bile crept up my throat as the images of what he'd done to her flashed through my mind and my heart throbbed with an intensity that should have dropped me to the floor, but there was no time for that. My Princess was beyond that door. Broken as she had already been for far too long, this was different. There could easily be nothing left of the Princess I had treasured since the day she was born, and all of this was my fault. For the first time in my life, I regretted taking her. I should have appointed her a more suitable guide and watched over her from afar. What I had done was unforgivable, and this was the cost. She had always been destined to pay the price for my actions. If I had it to do over...

I drew a ragged breath as I reached a trembling hand toward the door. Then I barreled through the crippling pain and stepped inside the room.

For a brief instant, a morbid ripple of relief washed over me as I stepped toward her. Battered and broken as she was, I had found her. These monsters could no longer harm her. I suppose my eyes refused to see the truth because I needed this to be over—I needed her to be safe with me—but reason soon replaced the deception.

This poor battered creature tied to the bed wasn't her. It was her face and her body, but it had all been a massive distraction to lead me down the wrong path whilst the real trail went cold.

Shattered as my heart was, I stepped toward the injured changeling who lay trembling on the bed. The rage that swelled within me had nothing to do with her. The violation I had witnessed had been hers. Some inhumane part of me thanked God for that as I sat down beside her and ripped apart the shackles that bound her wrists and ankles.

She whimpered and shrunk from me as best she could in her battered state.

"It's alright," I whispered. "We've come to get you out of here. No one will harm you again. You have my word."

"You're him," she whimpered.

I tilted my head and raised an eyebrow, unsure how to respond to that.

"You're the guest of honor."

Her words turned my stomach despite the fact that I wasn't quite sure what she meant.

"You're the Dragon King," she whimpered.

"I am."

"They said you'd come for her."

"They were correct."

"I'm sorry...she...isn't here."

"You have nothing to be sorry for."

"They told me to tell you..." she winced, whether from pain or fear I couldn't say, "you will never find her."

39

BOB

It frustrated the hell out of me being left behind while they went to speak to my Nellie. It also made no sense. I was the one who needed to get her back, who loved her with all my heart, who would've given anything to hold her in my arms and reassure her that I was coming for her and everything would be alright. Charlie and Tristan's assurance that I was already there only made it all seem more ridiculous. They had gone to speak to Nellie in the waking world, where she and I were patients in a psychiatric facility. They were all Sighted and could remember the world they weren't in, but I couldn't. Even though I was right there beside Nellie—and I'd been there beside her all this time—I couldn't remember a word of what she said to me. I wouldn't even be able to pick her older self out of a crowd, or my own self for that matter.

When I grew tired of pacing back and forth—in what was basically the palace waiting room, as far as I could tell—I dropped into a chair near the Waterfall, which apparently served as a door.

"You're there, too," Pip whispered from my pocket. "It's not like you're deserting her because you didn't feel like going along for the visit."

"That gives me no comfort."

"We made it here," he whispered as he crawled from my pocket and settled onto a pillow in the chair beside me. "That should give you some comfort."

"It does," I muttered, "and I have you to thank for that, my friend."

Pip closed his eyes with a tired sigh. "She understands, Bob."

"And how exactly do you know that?"

"I know," Pip opened his eyes and looked up at me, "because I've been in her position. I know what it's like to love a person who doesn't remember who you are to them in the other world."

"Did you ever tell your wife about your Sight?"

"No," he whispered, "She wouldn't have understood. She probably would've had me committed. It's an unspoken rule among the Sighted, we don't tell the Unsighted things that they were never meant to know."

"But... I know."

"Yeah. Why do you think everybody's so shocked about that? It just isn't done. You don't speak to the Unsighted about the world you aren't in."

"Charlie is the one who told me," I muttered.

"From what I picked up from the conversations around here, your friend Charlie didn't know what the hell he was until pretty recently. You met him in that mental institution. He probably just thought he was nuts."

I couldn't help chuckling at that. "How nuts was I for believing everything he told me?"

Pip let out a pensive chuckle. "You're nuts for a lot of reasons."

"Says the man who's too afraid to peek out of my pocket and introduce himself to anyone here."

"Yeah," he muttered, "I was kinda surprised you didn't mention me."

"I took the fact that you've stayed hidden since we arrived at the palace to mean that you weren't ready for introductions."

He punched at the pillow behind him to fluff it up. "Guess I'm nuts, too."

Thankful to have something other than my threadbare nerves to focus on, I smiled at him. "You live in the forest. Have you ever been anywhere like this before?"

"Nope," he whispered as his eyes looked over the room, "this is extreme culture shock for me."

"Me too," I cast a glance at the Waterfall door, "I can't recall ever being anywhere but the shore I used to guard."

"Used to?"

I nodded. "I left it behind to rescue Nellie, and since it's no longer anyone's home, I don't see much point in going back once this is all over."

"Where will you go when this is over?"

"Something tells me that this won't be over anytime soon, regardless of whether or not we retrieve Nellie and Emma."

"This is gonna start a war," Pip agreed. "You don't abduct the Dragon King's wife and walk away without a fight."

"This fight could end when we locate the women."

He cocked his head to one side and studied me with a curious frown. "You don't say that like you believe it."

I shook my head. "These sorts of issues are never resolved that quickly. No matter who walks away from our rescue mission, there will be enemies on both sides who'll feel the need to retaliate."

"Then we should get the hell out of here and find a safe place to tuck away until the battle is finished."

"I've never been one to walk away from a fight."

"No one would doubt that," he muttered, "but you don't know a thing about the politics of this fight. How could you be certain which side you should fight for?"

I narrowed my eyes at him as I shifted in my seat. "One side kidnapped the woman I love. The other plans to help me get her back. How could I possibly question which side to fight for?"

"There's more to it than just the way this affects your personal life."

"How can you say that? The Purists were responsible for the death of your wife's entire nomadic tribe and her resulting suicide."

The color drained from Pip's cheeks as he whispered, "I hate Godric, but there are a lot of creatures out there who question the Sarrum's priorities."

"And do you count yourself among them?"

"No." Pip stretched and shifted his weight on the pillow. "I just figured you should know, Godric has a lot of supporters."

"There'd be no need for war if he didn't."

Pip elbowed the pillow behind his back. "I suppose that's true enough."

Being careful not to knock him over, I slid the pillow out from behind Pip and fluffed it as he'd been attempting to. "Plenty of contemptible men have risen to positions of power throughout history. There will always be people who are easily swayed to side with the wrong man because they believe it will suit them better. Personally, I side with the man who is worthy of ruling."

"And how do you know that the Sarrum is worthy? You've never even met him."

"I'm an excellent judge of character, and every worthy fellow I've met stands behind this Dragon King. If Charlie and Tristan stand with the King, that's good enough for me."

40

CHARLIE

We raced through the forest, guided by nothing but Tristan's vague intuition of his older brother's whereabouts. After leaving the facility, we'd rushed straight back to the palace to get Bob and fill him in on what he'd missed. Then we started our search at the edge of the forest where Tristan and Brian had met with the Sarrum before he sent Tristan to the Dragon's Lair to wait for possible leads. The Sarrum, Benjamin and Brian didn't know it, but they were on a wild goose chase. Wherever this cabin in the forest was, it wasn't where Godric was keeping Nellie, and unless he'd taken her elsewhere since Nellie last saw her, it wasn't where Emma was either.

With each passing hour we spent combing the woods, the hearts of every member of our search party beat louder and faster. I could hear them clearly now that my dragon instincts had kicked into overdrive. Whether that was due to the danger, or my progress in mastering my abilities, or my bond with Rose, I had no idea. Bob, Rose and I stuck close together on one side of the woods while Tristan branched off to cover the far side, hoping he'd eventually feel his brother's pull and be able to fine tune our search.

I thanked my lucky stars that my night vision had improved now that my dragon instincts were fully operational because the woods were pitch dark. Rose was equally capable of navigating her way in the dark, but Bob moved between us, blindly trusting us to warn him of any obstacles that he couldn't see. Being a creature of Darkness, Tristan also had no trouble navigating without light, although he seemed to be guided by an entirely different sense that was drawing him toward his brother.

The silence in the Dark Forest was deafening. Focused as I was on the beating of our hearts, I nearly jumped out of my skin when something sneezed inside Bob's shirt pocket.

"Bless you," Rose whispered in a casual tone that suggested the creature who'd sneezed was no surprise to her.

"Thanks," a small voice muttered from Bob's shirt.

I frowned at Bob's utterly calm expression. Apparently, I was the only clueless dummy who was surprised by the stowaway in his pocket. "What the hell was that?"

"Hey," a small, ugly creature whispered as he poked his head from Bob's pocket, "I'm Melvin, but my friends call me Pip."

A smile spread across Bob's face as he looked down at the creature in his pocket.

"Hey, yourself," I muttered, "How long have you been in there, and who the hell are you?"

Pip glanced up at Bob with a raised eyebrow. "Is your friend slow? I already told him who I was."

"Sorry," I muttered, wondering how exactly I was the weirdo in this scenario, "Guess I'm not accustomed to *whatever the hell you ares* popping out of people's pockets in the middle of the woods. What the hell are you anyway?"

Again, Pip looked at Bob rather than me. "And you thought I was rude when we first met?"

"Alright," I muttered, realizing I probably had come off sounding a little rude, "*Who* the hell are you?"

"I'm—"

"Pip. Yeah, I got that." I narrowed my eyes at Bob. If Pip could ignore me, why shouldn't I do the same? "Who the heck is this guy?"

Bob smiled at both of us in turn. "Pip is my new traveling companion and pocket-sized sidekick." When I just stared at him, he added, "If it weren't for him, I'd still be stumbling around with no clue how to find you or rescue Nellie."

"Huh," I narrowed my eyes at Bob's pocket-sized traveling companion, "then I guess it's lucky you met up with him."

Judging by the look on his face, Pip was opening his mouth to say something smart-ass-y when Tristan snuck up beside me. All interest in our little exchange vanished as the incubus motioned for us to stop moving. "The cabin is up ahead. We need to go slow because there's no way of knowing what we're walking into."

As we started forward, Bob gripped the hilt of his sword, and Rose and I took dragon form. Loud as I'd have guessed the two of us would be stomping through the trees in our ginormous bodies, we were the quietest members of our little band of misfits. I would've grinned with pride at being so awesome if this wasn't such a serious situation we were blindly tip-toeing into.

It wasn't long till the cabin came into view. As we inched toward it, a deafening roar shook the ground beneath our feet and shattered every window in the cabin. Horror movie-worthy screams echoed from inside the cabin, but Tristan just kept moving forward, and we kept following.

We stayed within the cover of the woods as we followed Tristan toward the back of the building. Then without a single word of warning, he rushed from the woods and slipped in the back door. Before we could debate whether or not to follow his lead, Benjamin came rushing out of the cabin toward us.

His pitch black eyes raked over Rose and me as he dipped his head. "This was a false lead intended to throw us off course."

My throat constricted as I forced out the words, "We know." As the Darkness's eyes drifted to Bob and his mini sidekick, I muttered, "This is Bob and his portable sidekick, Pip."

The fury in Benjamin's eyes was all the reminder I needed that this was no time for humor.

"Bob is Nellie's soul mate," I muttered, "He traveled a long way to warn us that Godric abducted Nellie and planned to take Emma."

"You're late," Benjamin snarled.

Bob didn't even flinch. "Yes? Well, it's a bit difficult to succeed at a quest when you aren't blessed with this Sight that everyone keeps raving about."

Benjamin narrowed his eyes at Bob. "You're Unsighted?"

Bob nodded and said nothing, but the look on his face said *Duh.*

"Then how the fuck did you find your way to us?"

"I followed the instructions my soul mate whispered in my ear as I woke in this world each morning."

A glimmer of respect flickered in Benjamin's eyes as he nodded. "We need to go speak to Nellie Godric at the facility."

"We already did," Rose whispered beside me.

"Did she tell you where Godric's keeping her?"

"No," Rose whispered, "All she could tell us is that Godric brought her to a room that looked like a Victorian sitting room with a yard full of demons outside the window, but Tristan gave her a trinket to wear so he can find his way to her when she falls asleep."

The morose smile that crept onto Benjamin's face sent a shiver down my spine. "Has Nellie seen Emma there?"

"Yeah," I muttered. "She said she saw her once."

"Did she say how recently that was," Benjamin whispered, "or whether the Princess had been hurt?"

As I was working up the courage to answer, another roar shook the ground so hard that it nearly knocked us all over. A few seconds later, Brian came running out the back door of the cabin leading two trembling females along with him. Tristan rushed out next, carrying another female. Even at a distance, it was obvious that she was badly injured. My stomach clenched as the battered victim lifted her head from Tristan's shoulder. "Emma?"

"It's not her," Benjamin whispered.

I could barely squeak out a whisper, "What are you talking about?"

"She's a changeling," the Darkness replied in a deep soothing tone that seemed completely at odds with his pitch black eyes, "They forced her to take

Emma's form to lead us on a false trail—bragging about selling her in public places, and prostituting her at a gathering they held here the other night."

"What…" I couldn't even finish the sentence. The look on the poor changeling's face as Tristan reached us made me want to burst into tears, and yet some selfish part of me was thankful as hell that it wasn't really Emma in his arms.

"The Sarrum witnessed a vision of what they did to the changeling and believed it to be the Princess," Benjamin growled.

Pathetic as it was, I doubled over and puked on the ground right in front of the poor creature who'd actually suffered the horrors that perverse plan entailed.

I was about to apologize for being so weak when another roar shook the ground beneath us. This one was so bad that Rose and Bob fell on their asses. The two shell-shocked females Brian had herded toward us also lost their footing, but he caught them before they hit the ground.

I looked at the cabin's shattered windows and muttered, "Are there Purists in there?"

"Yeah," Brian whispered. "Five are still breathing."

"Then…" I scowled at Brian, then Benjamin and wondered why the hell they weren't in there helping the Sarrum deal with the Purists. With the way I reacted to this, I could only imagine how David must be feeling. "Why aren't we in there helping him?"

Brian shook his head, but before he could speak, another roar echoed through the forest. This one knocked us all to the ground and resonated inside my head with such ferocity that I half expected it to split open. As I pushed myself to my feet, a blinding burst of light lit the Darkness and for a moment the Dark Forest was light as day. I heard the hiss a second before the heat barreled into us, but I was too shocked to react. A second later, the cabin ignited in a ball of blue flames and the flames spread like wildfire, devouring the forest as it barreled toward us.

As the flames approached at lightning speed, my life flashed before me—my father teaching me how to survive along the fringe, my mother's vacant eyes as we stood by his casket while they said the final blessing, monster after monster, facility after facility, Emma walking through the door during a group therapy session, Nellie confiding that she also saw the monsters, Frank reaching for Emma like a man possessed, me rushing at the Dragon King when I first saw Emma in his arms, him smashing me against the wall of his home with his eyes full of flames, Benjamin driving us off a bridge, Frank and Spenser and that doctor who let the Purists hurt Emma shackled in stone cells, Isa waking from her coma as the Sarrum knelt over her and breathed life back into her, Godric taking Emma—but as the flames reached us, they parted like the red sea did for Moses. I watched, stupefied as the flames engulfed everything else while we stood in the center of the massive inferno, unharmed. Completely at a loss, I turned back toward the raging fire where the cabin had been and watched the flames climb to impossible heights. Our collective heartbeats pounded in my head as the heat from the flames drenched us all in sweat. It was just too much to process. The weight of the mirage crushed down on me and robbed the breath from my lungs, and my vision blurred for an instant. Then a rush of power surged through me. I was about to ask Rose if it'd come from her when that glorious black dragon that'd shadowed Emma at the facility emerged from the center of the inferno where the cabin had been. To say that he walked calmly from the center of it wouldn't do his exit justice. He sauntered from it with menace rolling off of every rippling muscle of his massive torso. The fear that his presence induced made Benjamin at his worst seem like nothing more than a toddler in the throes of a tantrum. I was so far beyond worrying about pissing myself, and so drenched in sweat from the flames that I doubted anyone would've noticed if I did. My eyes filled with tears as a crippling dose of fear gripped me, and I actually felt my heart stop for a few beats. I'm not certain, but I think *he* was the only thing that restarted it. In fact, it was a collective reaction—I felt all our hearts stutter and then reboot in unison. I wept at the awe that this creature inspired without even caring who witnessed my tears.

As the Sarrum stepped from the flames, Benjamin's voice barely registered, "Behold the Dragon King in all his venomous glory. *This* is what I meant when I said you didn't want to make an enemy of David Talbot."

41

MIA

There was something far worse than being invisible. I knew that now. If only I'd understood it earlier and stayed invisible, I wouldn't be trapped in this nightmare—bloody and broken and shackled to a bed—and it wasn't even my nightmare. This should have been the Princess's hell, not mine. They had forced me to take her form and endure more pain and humiliation than I ever would have believed a soul could survive. After they'd all finished with me and left me lying broken and discarded on the bed, the female shadow came in and smiled at me. Then she told me that the "guest of honor" would be coming soon. She explained that this was all for the Sarrum, and my one remaining task was to inform him that he would never find his precious Princess.

I have no idea how long I waited, but it was long enough for the blood to cake and the bruises to ripen to deep purple splotches on the pale skin I'd been forced to clothe myself in. The shadow had warned me not to change my form. If I did, she said they'd hurt me all over again. So I stayed in that beautiful broken body I loathed so much, wanting nothing more than to transform into something as plain and invisible as possible. It should've been her on the bed, not me.

After drifting in and out for what felt like days, thunderous roars and smashing walls and blood-curdling screams outside the room jarred me awake, and I knew he'd finally come—the guest of honor I'd been forced to wait for. A man noiselessly slipped in my room while all the commotion was going on, but this man wasn't the Dragon King. He was an elf and a warrior, with pointed ears, well defined muscles and tattoos that marked him as a member of the royal guard. I recoiled as he stepped closer, terrified to have any man come near me in my vulnerable state. Tortured affection and genuine sorrow swam in his eyes as he touched a finger to his lips, warning me to stay silent. He looked at me like we were old friends and he was heartbroken to see me this way, but I'd never met this man before. Then I realized he must be close to the woman who should be lying on the bed in my place. I stilled as he leaned

toward me and kissed my forehead with more tenderness than I'd ever witnessed in any man's eyes.
A tear slid down his cheek as he whispered, "I'm so
sorry we failed you."

Stunned and terrified as I was, I was also sad-
dened by the knowledge that nobody would care
what'd happened to me once they knew what I really
was. How nice it must be to have people genuinely
care for you. Before I could even find my voice, the
man slipped out the door. A few moments later, another man stepped in the room.

Until that moment, I had no idea what true heartache looked like. There was no doubt that this man
was the King I'd been forced to wait for. The grief
in his eyes was every bit as boundless as my own. As
he moved closer, I saw the realization in his eyes. *He
knew.* He saw through the deception and realized I
wasn't the Princess who inspired that infinite grief in
his eyes, yet he continued to step toward me and sit
down on the bed. The rage in his fiery eyes didn't
petrify me because I knew it wasn't meant for me. It
was for the monsters who had hurt me and tricked
him into believing they'd hurt his Princess. With a
few concise movements, he tore off the shackles that
bound my wrists and ankles.

The instant he freed me, I shrunk back from
him.

"It's alright." The kindness in his eyes was just
as intense as the rage. "We've come to get you out

of here. No one will harm you again. You have my word."

"You're him," I whispered, shocked that his tone was still so gentle now that he knew what I really was.

He cocked his head and stared at me, waiting for me to say more.

"You're the guest of honor," I muttered. "You're the Dragon King."

"I am," he whispered.

"They said you'd come for her."

"They were correct."

The grief in his eyes prompted me to mutter, "I'm sorry she isn't here."

His tone softened even more as he whispered, "You have nothing to be sorry for."

"They told me to tell you," I winced, bracing myself for his fury, "You will never find her."

But there was no rage, none directed at me anyway. Although he called to no one, a Dark and terrifying shadow entered the room as if responding to a call. I'd never seen him before, but there wasn't a doubt in my mind that this was the Darkness. The heartbreak in his eyes as he looked at me made it clear that he knew I wasn't the Princess. "Stay with her," the Dragon King whispered. With that, he slipped from the room.

The Darkness looked at me as a roar shook the foundation of the cabin, and I felt him retract the fear he projected. "We're going to get you out of here. Just hang on a little longer."

Screams and crashes and nightmarish sounds echoed through the cabin as I nodded.

The Darkness watched over me intently, like a protective father keeping an eye on an injured child who wasn't his but deserved his protection all the same. "What's your name?"

I didn't want these people to know my name. I wanted to slink away nameless and invisible, and yet I answered, "Mia."

"Mia," he whispered, "I'm Benjamin. We'll be making our exit any second now."

"I can't walk," I muttered.

"You don't have to," a voice like liquid silk murmured from the doorway.

The incubus bartender from the Dragon's Lair stepped in the room, and I thanked God that he wouldn't recognize me in the Princess's form. The way he looked at me—in that other form on the night I was abducted—was the memory I'd clung to for days before the monsters broke me. I didn't want my memory of that look to be replaced by a look of pity...or disgust. I wanted to run away from all of this and crawl in a hole with that one perfect memory. Not this...I couldn't handle him seeing me this way. He was so beautiful and perfect, and for one brief moment, he'd looked at me like I was, too. Now even that would be lost to me.

ERIN A. JENSEN

The incubus stepped in the room, nodded to Benjamin and approached the bed at a tentative pace as the Darkness slipped out the door. Another roar shook the cabin, followed by more screams as I watched the incubus move toward me. He stopped beside the bed but didn't sit. "It's you," he whispered.

A tear slid down my swollen cheek as I shook my head. "I'm not the Princess."

"No." He extended a hand as if he meant to wipe the tear from my cheek, but retracted it without touching me. "You're the changeling from the Dragon's Lair."

Whatever words I meant to utter stuck in my throat.

"I looked for you when I came back inside." I could've sworn there were tears in his gorgeous green eyes. "But you were already gone. When they told me you left with the sweet-talker...I searched the woods for you. I should've searched harder. I'm sorry I didn't."

Numb and speechless, I just stared at him.

"We can continue this conversation later," he murmured. "Right now, we need to get you out of here before this place goes up in flames."

Another tear slipped down my cheek. "Just leave me."

This time, he reached out and brushed the tear from my cheek with a fingertip. "Not a chance."

"I'm broken."

354

"We're all broken in our own way," he whispered.

"I'm…ugly," I choked between sobs.

"Physical beauty is nothing but a curse."

"Right," I sobbed, "You must live such a cursed life."

"Don't judge a book by his cover," the incubus whispered. "You don't know my story, and I don't know yours."

"Why would you want to?"

"Because," he whispered, "you remind me of someone special."

At a loss for words, I searched his beautiful eyes.

He lifted me off the bed with a tenderness that brought more tears to my eyes. "We need to get you out of here now."

Too overwhelmed and confused to think any-more, I dropped my face to his chest and sobbed, "I can't…"

"Just trust me," he murmured in my ear as he started toward the door. "My name's Tristan, by the way."

"I'm Mia," I whimpered against his collarbone.

"Beautiful name for a beautiful girl," he mur-mured as he stepped from the cabin.

His words stung like salt in an open wound, un-til I looked up and saw the sincerity in his gorgeous eyes. Those eyes mirrored the flames that erupted in the cabin as he broke into a sprint, and I buried my face against his chest.

"It's alright, Mia," he murmured. He didn't sound the least bit winded, which wasn't all that shocking, considering the shape he was in. "I promise you, you're safe now."

42

BOB

I stood in the center of the raging inferno with my mouth hanging open as I watched the dragon step from the flames and advance toward us. No one had to announce this beast. There wasn't a doubt in my mind that this was the Dragon King. Inside my pocket, Pip was trembling so hard that the lip of my pocket vibrated in his grip. "Shit," he muttered, and I worried for a second that he actually might have. It'd be understandable of course, but it was my only shirt and I didn't want to rescue the love of my life reeking of feces. I looked down at him, and he glanced up and shook his head. "No," he whispered as if reading my mind, "I didn't."

My eyes drifted back to the monstrous creature heading toward us. "I almost wouldn't blame you if you did."

Everyone was silent as the Sarrum joined us in the eye of the firestorm, where we stood—protected by an invisible barrier—from the flames that blazed through the rest of the forest with a vengeance. In the blink of an eye, the Dragon King took human form but his human form was only slightly less terrifying than his dragon form. Sapphire blue flames raged in his human eyes and blue smoke billowed from his flared nostrils. I normally didn't succumb to fear, but even I found myself trembling at the sight of this man. He narrowed his eyes at me and spoke to everyone but me. "Who is this?"

"This is Bob, my friend from the facility," Charlie muttered, clearly still feeling the aftereffects of the Sarrum's fury. "He was Emma's friend, too."

The King's eyes remained locked with mine. "He is Unsighted."

I nodded but couldn't seem to find my voice, which never happened. I didn't get frightened speechless.

"Then what is he doing here?" he asked, still staring at me but addressing anyone else who dared answer.

"He came to warn us that Godric planned to abduct the Princess," Charlie muttered.

The King narrowed his eyes and finally spoke to me, "A little late to the party, aren't you?"

Shocked that I still couldn't bring myself to speak, I nodded.

The King shot Charlie an inquiring glance. "Is your friend mute?"

"No," Charlie muttered. "He's probably feeling a little overwhelmed by what he just witnessed."

"I see."

Despite my desperate urge to turn away from this King and flee straight into the flames, I swallowed and took a step forward. "The love of my life was also taken by Godric. I came to seek your help in getting her back."

"I'm a bit busy searching for my own female," the Sarrum replied icily.

"Godric is keeping them in the same place," I muttered, disappointed in myself for sounding so pathetic.

That certainly captured his attention. "How do you know this?"

"She's been whispering to me when I wake each morning," I muttered, "and when Charlie, Rose and Tristan paid her a visit at the facility, she told them she saw your Princess."

The King stepped toward me and I resisted the urge to flinch when he took my face in his hands and kissed me on the forehead. "You just became my new best friend."

"Ouch," the shadow beside him muttered.

A smirk played at the edges of the King's mouth as he released my head. "Tell me she told you how to locate her."

"She didn't," Tristan murmured, "but I gave her a trinket during our visit and instructed her to wear it at all times."

Being careful not to touch the injured girl in Tristan's arms, the King took a step toward the incubus and planted a kiss on his forehead. "You beautiful man, I knew there was a reason I kept you around."

Tristan winked at him. "There are lots of reasons."

"You wish."

Anxious to steer the conversation back to our dire circumstances, I cleared my throat. "May I ask how the trinket that you gave my soul mate helps us?"

"I'm an incubus," Tristan murmured. "If we press a token of remembrance to our lips in the waking world and instruct our intended conquest to wear it to bed, it will lead us to them in this world."

"For what purpose?" I whispered, although I was fairly certain I knew the answer.

"Typically," Tristan whispered, "so we can have our way with them. The Unsighted wake from the experience giddy from what they believe to be a blissfully sinful dream, and the Sighted often don't mention it to anyone else because they're hoping for a repeat visit."

"You track the Unsighted for sex?"

"Not personally," he murmured. "I don't really need to, but it's a technique we can use to locate anyone we might wish to cross paths with at some point."

"And you intend to use this technique to find my Nellie?"

"And my Princess." The Dragon King eyed me curiously for a moment. "This is good news, Bob. It means that we now have a way to find our soul mates and rescue them."

I stared at the dragon in human form for a moment, sizing him up and wondering what to make of him. "I want to take part in the rescue mission."

The King nodded. "I wouldn't dream of excluding you."

"Then," I looked at each face in turn as I muttered, "What are we waiting for?"

Tristan glanced at the frightened creature in his arms and exhaled an apologetic sigh. "It won't work until Nellie falls asleep."

43

MIA

I called the diner and quit my job in the waking world the day the Sarrum rescued me from that nightmarish cabin. I didn't care how I'd get by. There was no facing the world after what I'd been through. In fact, it would probably be best if I just stayed in bed till I died of hunger or thirst. In Draumer, they brought me back to the palace with them after the Sarrum burned down the cabin that would haunt me for the rest of my life. The Sarrum burned the entire forest—not because of me, but because of what'd been done to me—because they led him to believe it had been done to his wife. The Princess was gorgeous, but I couldn't shed her form fast enough. I transformed into the mousiest form I could think of—my own plain form in the waking world that practically rendered me invisible. I

wanted nothing more than to be invisible for the rest
of my short life.

Tristan, the incubus who'd carried me out of the
cabin, seemed unfazed by my transformation into
the invisible girl—just as he'd seemed unfazed to
find me in the Princess's form. I wasn't sure what
to make of him, and I honestly didn't care anymore.
I just wanted to crawl into a dark hole, curl up and
starve myself till my heart gave out.

Tristan didn't seem to grasp that. Actually,
that's not true. I think he grasped it too well,
and that was tough to stomach. He stayed with
me and kept a gentle hand on my arm while the
witchdoctor and the Sarrum's sorceress tended to
my injuries. He'd offered to step outside the room
while they treated me, but he was the only familiar face in a sea of potential abusers. Somehow,
I knew with absolute certainty that this gorgeous
man would never hurt me and he'd never allow
another to harm me. It had nothing to do with
his looks. After everything I'd endured, I didn't
want to be touched in an intimate way by anyone
ever again. I wanted Tristan to stay close because
of the kindness in his soft voice and the pain in
his eyes that went beyond sympathy. He *knew*, because he had suffered at some point. He understood what I was going through in a way that only
a fellow victim could. Of course, Tristan didn't

say any of that, but I'd never been more certain of anything. Someone had hurt this beautiful man at some point in his life—and not just emotionally—he'd been an abuse victim. I would bet my battered life on it, not that anyone would want such a worthless prize.

Whenever Tristan did have to leave to assist the Sarrum with the ongoing search for the Princess, the doctor was kind enough to sedate me until he got back—or maybe Doc just didn't have the heart to listen to my whimpering and screaming. Of course there was no guarantee that the witchdoctor wouldn't abuse me after he drugged me, but I wouldn't remember it. After everything I'd endured, that had to be enough. Death would be better, but until I could find a way for death to claim me, I had to settle for *enough*.

I was just starting to drift back to consciousness as Tristan's voice echoed, "How is she?"

"Resting comfortably for the most part," the witchdoctor's voice echoed back.

The incubus who had once been the star of my raciest daydreams let out a troubled sigh. Even that sounded sexy coming from him. "How long do you need to keep her for observation?"

"I can't say for certain." I lifted my eyelids and watched the blurry skull-faced witchdoctor shake his head. "She's certainly not ready to go out in the forest and resume her old life."

"I doubt she'll ever be able to resume her old life," Tristan murmured with a sorrow born from personal experience. I didn't turn my head in his direction. It hurt too much to look at his beautiful face and be reminded of the butterflies in my stomach that I was no longer capable of feeling.

The doctor's soft voice was laced with regret. "Then what do you plan to do with her?"

My stomach dropped at his ominous choice of words, but I couldn't be sure whether fear or relief prompted the response.

"That's up to her," Tristan whispered.

I turned my head on the pillow and chanced a peek up at him.

He smiled at me with a tenderness that would've melted the old unbroken me. "Hey, how are you feeling?"

"Hopeless," I croaked, hating myself for dissolving into tears.

Tristan didn't try to quiet me or stop my tears. He just touched my arm in a completely platonic, comforting way. "Doc, would you excuse us?"

The doctor's bony features relaxed as he let out a sigh, nodded and turned toward the Waterfall to make his exit. "I'll stay close by in case you need me."

"We won't," Tristan whispered as he watched the witchdoctor step through the Waterfall and exit the room. His expression softened as he turned back to me.

I was sobbing and trembling like a pathetic fool, and I was too broken and emotionally exhausted to care that this perfect man was there to witness my meltdown. He'd already seen me at the lowest point in my life, and I didn't have any desire to impress him or any other man ever again. "What do you plan to do with me?" I whimpered. "You should put me out of my misery and stop wasting your time feeling sorry for me."

"I'm not wasting my time." He gave my arm such a gentle squeeze that I probably wouldn't have noticed if his touch didn't elicit a warm tingling sensation. A slight tingle was all I could detect of this godlike creature's charm after everything that'd been done to me. "Tell me where to find you."

"What?"

"In the waking world," he whispered.

"Why would you want to find me there?"

He took his hand off my arm, and I felt much colder for the lack of it as he dragged a chair to my bedside. "You shouldn't be alone there either."

"Why do you care?" I croaked as I watched him settle into the chair.

He touched his hand to my arm again, and the comforting tingle chased away the shiver that'd developed in its absence. "Does it matter?"

"Yes."

"I know what it's like to feel all alone in that great big terrifying world."

I swallowed and worked up the courage to mutter, "What happened to you?"

A sorrowful smile lit up his face in an achingly beautiful way. "What makes you think something happened to me?"

"I see it in your eyes." Embarrassed for admitting it, I dropped my head and focused on the bed sheet. "And I feel it when you speak to me. Someone hurt you, too."

"That's a story for another time," he whispered, "Right now, we need to bring you somewhere you can feel safe."

"There's no such place," I muttered as my eyes drifted to his hand, resting comfortably on my arm.

"It's not about a place," he whispered. "It's about being in the company of people you know you can trust."

"Who can I trust?"

"Me." He gave my arm another gentle squeeze, and the tingling sensation warmed me a bit more. "You know that, right?"

"Yeah," I muttered. "I do."

"So tell me where to find you."

I reached under my pillow and pulled out the thin silver bangle I'd found on my wrist when I first woke in the palace. "You already know how to find me."

"Yes," he whispered, "but I'd like your permission to pay you a visit."

"I never realized incubi were so honorable."

I looked up just in time to watch his gorgeous green eyes brighten as he smiled at me. "This one is."

"I still don't know why you'd want to find me," I muttered, "but you have my permission to."

"Good," he murmured, "then I think you should wake up and let me in."

"What?"

Sorrow clouded his perfect features as he grinned at me. "I know you're feeling pretty weak after spending so many days in bed. All you have to do is get to the door of your apartment. I've got you after that."

"I…" Despite the fact that I shouldn't care, my eyes flooded with tears as I sobbed, "I'm filthy. I don't even know how long it's been since I showered. You don't need to—"

"No," he whispered, "I don't, but I want to. Now wake up and let me in before one of your neighbors walks down the hall of your apartment building and wonders what the hell I'm doing sleeping on the floor outside your door."

"I don't know what to say."

"Don't say anything," he whispered, "Just wake up."

He touched a hand to my cheek—the same barely perceptible gentle way he touched my arm—and the next thing I knew, my eyes were open and I was staring at the ceiling of my bedroom in the apartment.

I felt filthy—downright oily skin and fuzzy-mouthed filthy—as I sat up and glanced at my refection in the mirror across the room. I looked like death warmed over. Shit. Why did I even care? He already knew how unattractive I was. I took this ugly form in Draumer as soon as I was able to transform.

A knock at the front door of my apartment gave my heart a jolt. What if it wasn't Tristan? He could've been trying to make it less traumatic for me when they came to eliminate me. I was nothing but collateral damage. It'd make more sense to just get rid of me than go to all the trouble of trying to mend an un-mendable soul.

Another knock at the door had me clumsily scrambling to my feet. If this was the cleanup crew, at least it would all be over soon.

I combed my fingers through my greasy hair as I crossed the bedroom and unsteadily stepped into the living room. Relief washed over me as I moved toward the front door. Was the Darkness on the other side? Or would they send some unknown demon to tie up an insignificant loose end like me?

My hand shook as I grabbed the doorknob. *Just please don't let it be Tristan.* I could handle death, but I couldn't face it coming from him...anyone else... but not him. I drew a shallow breath as I unlocked the door and opened it, steeling myself for whatever executioner waited on the other side.

Tristan's gorgeous green eyes glistened with tears as he smiled at me, and I broke down in tears like a blubbering idiot.

He wrapped his muscular arms around me and whispered something unintelligible as he half-carried me back into the apartment and shut the door.

"Why does it have to be you?" I whimpered as he guided me to the couch and sat down beside me.

"Who else would it be?"

"Death at your hand won't be better..."

"I'm here to help you," he whispered, "You're disoriented, but I need you to remember. You trust me. Do you remember that?"

"I..."

"I came to take you somewhere safe," he whispered.

"Where?"

"Fifty-five Sycamore Drive," he murmured, "We'd like you to join the family."

"You're not making any sense," I muttered. "What family?"

"The royal family," he whispered, "We're a beautiful band of misfits who've pledged our life in service to the Sarrum."

"I don't have anything to offer the Sarrum," I muttered.

"He expects nothing from you," Tristan whispered, "but he owes you everything. We all swear to protect you."

I shook my head. "I don't…"

"*I* swear to protect you," he whispered.

"Why?"

"You don't have to understand it, or trust it yet. Just trust me and we'll take it from there, alright?"

"Alright."

44

NELLIE

I resisted falling asleep for as long as I possibly could, and I actually managed to avoid the Waters for two painfully exhausting days, but nobody can stay awake forever. Failure was inevitable at some point…

…Henry's charming British accent greeted me as I opened my eyes and blinked the room into focus. "Welcome back."

The instant my eyes adjusted, I regretted resisting sleep for as long as I had. Lilly was seated on the couch between Henry and me, looking just as lovely and cheerful as ever. I reached out and smoothed a wrinkle from her dress. Enduring any form of torture would be worth it for another chance to see her.

"You ladies have certainly kept me waiting long enough."

I assumed Henry was referring to Lilly and me till I followed his line of sight across the room. Emma must have also just come through the Waters because she was blinking at the dragon enchantment above her, as if she were trying to get her bearings. "Why don't you be a man," she muttered as she turned toward Henry, "let us go and fight my husband face to face?"

"What?" Henry murmured as he stood from the couch, "And abandon all this fun?"

A tear slid down Emma's cheek as she met his eyes. "You're a coward."

I wanted to warn her not to provoke him, but I didn't dare draw attention to Lilly or myself.

Henry locked eyes with Emma's dragon as he stepped toward them. "Says the girl who cowers beneath this whisper of her husband."

Emma looked up and seemed to draw strength from the enchantment above her. "Would hurting me make you feel powerful?"

Godric grinned as he knelt in front of her. "Don't try my patience, Princess."

Emma jutted her chin forward and regarded him with utter contempt. "You disgust me. You hide behind women and children and your demon minions because you're too weak to face my husband outright."

"I believe the holes in your memory are affecting your judgment," Godric growled. "You would do well to mind your tongue when you speak to me."

ERIN A. JENSEN

Defiance flashed in Emma's eyes as she whispered, "Says the man who threatens women and children."

Henry reached a trembling hand toward her, but said nothing.

"You're pathetic," Emma continued, "Thank goodness the Talbot family was smart enough to see that and pass the throne to David's father instead of you. What a weak ruler you would've been."

Wisps of pale blue smoke wafted from Henry's flared nostrils as a vein on his forehead began to bulge. I'd never seen anyone rattle him like that, and I was terrified to find out how he'd respond.

Emma crossed her arms over her chest. "The Talbots saw straight through you, didn't they? A coward like you could never rule this world."

A perverse grin darkened Henry's chiseled features as he glanced over his shoulder at Lilly. "Do you recall my warning that you weren't as untouchable as you believed yourself to be?"

A spasm of queasiness churned my stomach as Emma shook her head. "I don't believe you'd really harm that child. Even monsters have their limits."

"My limits shattered the day your husband entered the world," Godric growled.

"If you truly treasured David's mother," Emma whispered, "how can you justify terrorizing her son?"

Crystal blue flames flared in Henry's eyes as he snarled, "*He* was never meant to be."

"But he's the only remaining piece of your sister that still draws breath," Emma whispered. "Why don't you treasure him for that?"

"Treasure the monster who tore apart the person I loved more than anything?"

"Treasure the child she brought into the world," Emma whispered. "He's your nephew."

"Yes." Henry turned his head toward the door and growled something in a harsh demonic dialect. "And that girl on the couch is my daughter."

A split second later, the door opened and five gaunt demons with jagged teeth and oil-slicked skin filed into the room. Their blood-shot eyes raked over each of us in turn, as if we were part of a succulent feast that'd been spread out just for them.

"You're bluffing," Emma insisted in a confident tone, though her eyes seemed far less certain.

Henry spoke another demonic command and two of the beasts licked their lips and eyed Lilly as they stepped toward our couch.

My heart hammered in my chest as I drew Lilly closer. "Emma, shut up and do as he says!"

"No," she muttered, "He wouldn't harm his own child. No man is that heartless."

"My heart shattered when your husband drew his first breath," Henry whispered as the demons grabbed Lilly's fragile little arms and yanked her to her feet.

Emma's eyes widened as she watched the demons drag my daughter toward her and Henry. "No one would harm their own child."

I wanted to warn her to shut up again, but I couldn't summon the courage to speak.

Henry took one of Lilly's tendrils and smoothed it between his fingers. "Perhaps if she had resembled my sister instead of her mother, things might have been different."

"What about David?" Emma muttered.

Godric narrowed his eyes at her. "What about him?"

"Does he resemble your sister?"

"No," Henry growled, "He is the spitting image of his father."

"You can't blame a child for their own appearance," Emma whispered.

"Can't I?" Henry absently let Lilly's curl slip through his fingers. "A child with my enemy's face is nothing but a constant reminder of the wrongs that were done to me."

Tears glistened in Emma's eyes as she glanced at Lilly. "And what wrongs could your daughter possibly have done?"

"She was supposed to be a son," Henry muttered, "a son to fight at my side, help me take back the throne that was rightfully mine and rule this world after I passed."

"Why couldn't a daughter do all those things?" Emma whispered.

Henry's eyes seemed to glaze over as Lilly sat down on the floor beside him. "What?"

"A daughter could fight at your side and take the throne after you passed," Emma whispered. "Why blame her for being female?"

"Females are weak," Henry muttered, "I refuse to love another weak creature, only to watch this world destroy her."

"But you could protect this female," Emma whispered.

I wanted to tell her to shut her mouth, but I still couldn't find my voice and her words seemed to be having a bizarre hypnotic effect on Henry.

"You could redeem yourself and right the wrongs that were done to your sister by loving and protecting your daughter."

A gust of steam spewed from Henry's nostrils as a growl rumbled deep in his throat. "It's too late for that."

Emma shook her head. "It's never too late."

"Enough," Henry snarled as he nodded to the demons, "The only sound I wish to hear from your lips is a command for your dragon to stand down."

The demons each grabbed a fistful of Lilly's tendrils and dragged her toward the windows by her hair, but the bloodcurdling scream that I wanted to let out stuck in my throat.

Emma's eyes darkened in horror as she shook her head. "You're bluffing. You can't be that much of a monster."

A nauseating burst of laughter trickled from Godric's perfect lips. "You have no idea what a monster I am."

"She's your child," Emma muttered as the shorter demon forced Lilly to her knees, "you're supposed to protect her. You're supposed to love her."

Godric's foul laughter echoed through the room as the shorter demon forced Lilly's head to one side and trailed the tip of his thin tongue up the side of her face. "Just as your daddy loved you?"

"No." Emma's voice was thick with tears, but my eyes stayed on my daughter and the demons who were just itching to violate her. "You..."

"What's the matter, Princess?" Godric whispered, "Have I rendered you speechless?"

A hushed sob escaped Emma's lips as the taller demon grabbed Lilly by the ear, tugged her head back and raked his jagged teeth over the porcelain skin at her jaw.

"Well, that won't do," Godric murmured, "I need you to speak to that dragon of yours and instruct him to stand down."

"Why are you doing this?" Emma sobbed.

"That's a good start," Henry whispered, "The desperation in that sweet voice of yours is music to my ears. All that defiance just didn't suit you. You are a weak creature, and I expect you to behave accordingly."

"What do you want from me?" Emma whimpered as one of the demons raked a claw through Lilly's hair.

"Everything," Godric whispered, "Your husband destroyed everything that mattered to me. I intend to return the favor."

"Then why would I tell my dragon to stand down?"

The taller demon tore the bow off Lilly's dress, leaving a gaping hole in the pure white fabric.

I wanted to leap from the couch and offer to take her place, but I couldn't move a muscle or utter a sound.

"You will tell that enchantment of yours to stand down," Henry snarled, "or watch this child suffer and die a horrific death that you could have prevented."

The demons let out a collective burst of laughter—that could best be described as a disconcerting chorus of droning insects, howling wolves and wailing infants—while the shorter beast clamped his jagged teeth down on a mouthful of Lilly's tendrils and ripped them clean off her head. My sweet child made no sound, but tears streamed down her cheeks as her eyes pleaded with me to make it stop. Still, I couldn't make a sound or move a muscle to help her.

"Please don't do this," Emma whimpered.

"How many have suffered and died so that your precious King could keep you as he does?" Godric snarled. "Have you ever stopped to consider that, Princess? Your daddy would still be alive today if David hadn't ripped out his heart."

"He was going to hurt me," Emma muttered.

"So your dear dragon hurt him first," Henry whispered, "but how many times has your husband hurt *you*?"

"What are you talking about?"

"How many women has he taken to his bed?" Godric whispered. "He constantly plays you for a fool. You are nothing but one female in his impressive collection of conquests."

"That's not true."

"No?" Henry whispered, "What about Sophie?"

An agonized sob escaped Emma's throat as she dropped her chin to her chest.

"Or that lovely young thing you caught in David's bedroom the other day?"

"How could you know about that?" Emma whispered, "That was just a dream."

Godric let out a laugh and the demons' laughter mingled with his as the taller demon stroked Lilly's face with his claw. "*This* is just a dream, Princess."

"What are you talking about?" Emma whispered.

"This is all just a nightmare," Henry assured her in a mock-soothing tone, "but you'll wake from it—unable to forgive yourself for letting this child suffer in your place when you could have prevented it—even in a dream, you know that isn't right."

"You're insane," Emma whimpered as the shorter demon traced a claw over Lilly's collarbone, drawing a trail of blood that dripped down and drenched her white collar.

"Perhaps," Henry whispered, "but you'll blame yourself all the same for allowing an innocent child to be violated in your place."

"You're a monster."

"Yes. You're finally getting it." A disturbingly cheery grin spread across Godric's face. "When you think about it, it's actually rather fitting. You should have been violated a thousand times over, had your husband not prevented it from happening. You have no idea how many men desired to do perverse things to you, or how many men your dear Sarrum's guards killed to keep you from harm."

Emma's body convulsed as she let out a silent sob.

"A creature of Light was never meant to be kept in the heart of the Darkness," Henry whispered. "Darkness and Light were never meant to coexist."

Emma's pupils grew unnaturally large as she looked up at Godric. "What did you say?"

"I'm done playing nice," Godric whispered as he nodded to the demons.

At his cue, the shorter beast knocked Lilly to her back on the floor. A string of drool trickled from his lips as he knelt over her and bunched a fistful of her dress in his clawed hand.

"No!" Emma's scream of protest was so loud that she actually managed to tear my eyes away from Lilly. She looked up at the dragon above her, and smoke wafted from his nostrils as he shook his head. "I'm sorry," Emma whispered, "but I can't let this happen. You taught me better than that. I can't allow a child to suffer in my place."

Bile crept up my throat as my eyes drifted back to Lilly. The face of the demon kneeling above her was now only inches from hers, and her porcelain skin was slick with his drool. I knew I should tell Emma not to call off her protective enchantment because that wasn't really my Lilly on the floor. My daughter had already died a very long time ago. I opened my mouth to warn her...

But I couldn't bring myself to do it. How could I just sit back and watch them hurt my child? It would be like enduring my baby's death all over again. Everybody suffered. Maybe this was supposed to be Emma's turn. After all, how many men *had* died because of her? Maybe letting this happen was for the best. I didn't honestly believe that, but a mother whose child is in danger can justify anything that will protect her from harm.

So, I said nothing.

45

A long forgotten ache gripped my heart as Godric's words rang in my ears. *Darkness and Light were never meant to coexist.* I had heard those words before. As they echoed inside my head, Godric's voice morphed into David's—he spoke those same words a long time ago—right before he left me...

...My seventeenth birthday was only two months away. It had been almost a year since David walked away from me and disappeared into the cave. I hadn't set eyes on him since, at least not in Draumer. There had been a few times when it had been impossible for him to avoid me in the waking world but on those occasions, David had gone out of his way to keep his distance. He made sure to stay where there were lots of other people so I'd have no opportunity to speak to him in private. Although on most occasions, he just came up with a

flimsy excuse for his absence: he was sick, or working on a case that needed his immediate attention, or—the excuse that hurt the worst—he had a date. The thought of him touching another woman never failed to deliver a crushing blow to my heart. The more time passed, the clearer it became that David didn't intend to change his mind. He was over me, but I would never get over him.

I slipped into the nightgown I wore the night David gave me the pendant—the night he walked away from me forever. I'd worn the nightgown every night since because I saw the way he looked at it that night. His jaw had tensed and his nostrils had flared as a whisper of his scent washed over me, but what did that matter now? It'd been almost a year, he still hadn't set foot outside the cave, and I couldn't go on like this anymore. The ache in my chest was unbearable, my lungs felt impossibly heavy and every breath just took too much effort. I crawled into bed, wrapped my fingers around the pendant, then summoned the Waters and jumped in…

…As I stood and moved toward the barrier, the night breeze seemed to blow straight through me as if I were nothing but a faded whisper of a person who had once stood there. I could feel David's presence inside the cave, but after spending the better part of a year praying that he'd come out and talk to me, I was no longer stupid enough to believe that he might.

How could he expect me to just uproot myself, move to the Light and leave the clearing behind? There was nothing for me in the Light. My heart was in the

Darkness—whether or not he ever let me near him again, I couldn't walk away—there was no life for me without him. Why couldn't he understand that?

As I pressed my forehead against the barrier that prevented me from getting any closer to him, the futility of it all finally struck me, and my heart just shattered. I hated myself for needing him this desperately. I hated him for making me love him more than I could ever love anyone else and then tossing me aside when he grew tired of me.

It was time to end this agony while he still cared enough to sit in the cave and watch. I wanted him to feel some small fraction of the pain that I'd felt all year. He deserved to hurt for what he'd done to me. Tears filled my eyes as I fumbled to take off the pendant with trembling fingers. Broken and exhausted and utterly lost, I outstretched an arm and held the pendant away from my body as I stared at the entrance to the cave. "I don't need something to remind me of you," I sobbed in a broken whisper, "I need something to help me forget you."

I opened my hand and let the pendant drop to the grass with a resounding thud that seemed impossible given its size.

A chorus of growls echoed beyond the mirage, but I was too consumed by my own grief to notice. It was the nearness of a deep-throated growl that startled me from my trance-like state. When I turned toward the sound, the contours of a monstrous face pressed inward from the fabric of the sky, like the features of a face straining *against the material of a nylon stocking. As the demon's face stretched toward me, other growls sounded and other faces pressed in from all directions. A shiver coursed through me, but I didn't run. I meant to end my life. I needed to silence the anguish that had consumed me for the better part of a year. Even torture and death at the hands of these monsters would be better than the unending hell he'd condemned me to. I only hoped that watching these demons destroy me in the most horrific way possible might make David regret toying with my heart. I wanted him to ache—if only for a moment—the way I'd ached all these months.*

I swallowed, strengthening my resolve. Then I lifted a hand to the base of my neck and gripped the tie to my nightgown. If these were my final breaths, there was no point to modesty because I'd soon be nothing but an empty husk. For a brief glorious moment before he walked away from me that night, David had looked at me like he wanted me—not to play the role of his child, but to take to his bed. If some small flicker of that desire remained, I wanted him to see what he'd tossed away. Let this be David's last memory of me. I yanked the tie and let the white satin fabric slip down my body and puddle at my feet. Then I took a deep breath—the final breath that would belong just to me—threw my head back and chanted the words I'd memorized from Isa's book of forbidden incantations, "I offer myself up to the Darkness...to be bound to it forever...and claimed by whomever would have me."

Tears streamed down my cheeks as the growls intensi-fied. Then a sound like wet fabric ripping at the seams echoed through the clearing as the magic that warded the mirage faltered and failed, and the sky tore apart...

...A tear slid down my cheek as I looked up at my dragon and whispered, "I'm sorry."

The sapphire flames in his eyes blazed brighter as he lunged toward Godric, but I didn't give him a chance to touch him.

"I dismiss you," I sobbed, "You are no longer needed here."

A furious bellow shook the room as my dragon dissipated, leaving me to face this nightmare on my own.

A wicked grin spread across Godric's face as he nodded to the demons who were crouching over Lilly. He growled something in a guttural tongue, and they backed away and left her trembling body curled up in a fetal ball on the floor by the windows. Nellie moved to go to her, but her muscles seemed to lock in place as she dropped back down on the couch. "Do not go near her," Godric snarled. Then he turned to me. "Well, isn't this interesting?"

I wanted to tell him how much he disgusted me, but I couldn't summon the courage to speak now that my dragon had left me.

"What shall I do with you?" He reached out and stroked my cheek with a false sincerity that soured my stomach. "So many possibilities."

Another bellow—even more furious than the one my enchantment had let out as he vanished— shook the building and Godric's eyes drifted to the window. "Your husband is beginning to irritate me."

I followed his eyes to the window.

The Darkness beyond the windowpane had intensified, so I could only make out vague shadows of the creatures outside. They were rushing at each other from all directions as if a haphazard battle had broken out amongst them. *Then I felt him.* David was out there—not my enchantment, but the real flesh and blood Dragon King—my husband was coming for me.

I looked back at Godric and laughed despite my dire circumstances. "I suppose you'll have to fight him now."

He let out a snarl that was in no way human as he clutched the back of my neck. "Yes. It's a pity you'll be in no shape to witness that." He tightened his grip, digging the tips of claws that I couldn't see into my flesh until a feeble whimper escaped my throat.

As my vision began to dim, David's voice sounded in my head. ***We are coming for you, Princess. Stall him for as long as you can.***

How?

Remember your lessons. Manipulate him.

I'm not strong enough.

You are stronger than you think.

I…

Trust me.

I do. I always have.

You can do this.

David's faith in my ability summoned a courage that I would never possess on my own. I looked up at Godric and shot him a dazzling smile. *You don't want to harm me.* As I thought the words, I pictured him allowing Nellie to get off the couch and comfort her daughter while I mentally nudged her to do it.

Godric narrowed his eyes at me. "What the fuck are you smiling at?"

Out of the corner of my eye, I watched Nellie get to her feet and move toward her daughter, but two of Godric's demons caught her by the arms and dragged her back to the couch. Manipulating their simple minds would be easy, but it would require pulling some of my focus away from Godric, and he was too powerful to be swayed by anything less than my full effort. *Allow Lilly and me to sit down on the couch beside Nellie while you attend to the battle outside.*

Godric winced and blinked at me. "What are you doing to me?"

"Nothing," I whispered, reinforcing my words with more mental manipulation. *You don't want to hurt me. Let me go sit on the couch with Nellie and her daughter.*

It wasn't working. Godric looked mildly irritated, but I certainly wasn't in control of his actions. He was too powerful...but maybe I could use that to my advantage. He didn't view me as any sort of threat. In his eyes, I was nothing but a weak female. If I tread softly, maybe I could penetrate his mind and get a look at his thoughts without him noticing the intrusion. If I knew what motivated him, it might help me sway him.

I reached out tentatively, mentally tip-toeing past his defenses, and a spark of hope spurred me onward when he didn't seem to notice. The trick was to proceed extremely cautiously. It was sort of like walking through a minefield. Disturb the wrong thought and the results could be catastrophic. I just hoped to God David reached us before Godric caught on to what I was doing. I wasn't searching for concrete memories. That was beyond the scope of my abilities, but I could access dormant feelings—sensations, longings, deep desires—those were all I needed. What drove this madman to do the things he did? *Obsessive love* for the sister he'd lost. She was the reason behind everything he did...his purpose...his obsession. When she was taken from him, a massive void was left in her place, and he desperately desired to fill that void. I remembered the way he'd looked at me the day I found that girl in David's room. I'd been desperate for comfort, and so had he. For a few minutes, he'd let down his guard because some repressed part of him wanted to replace the object of his obsessive love.

I withdrew from his mind undetected, fixed him in a dazzling gaze and let my eyes fill with tears. I had no desire to earn this monster's affection, but I knew how it felt to ache for someone who had left you—someone you desperately needed.

Godric's claw still gripped my neck, but he had loosened his hold while I was probing around in his mind. He tilted his head back to get a better look at me. "Why are you looking at me like that?"

A tear slid down my cheek as I recalled the pain I felt when David walked away from me all those years ago. "I can't go back to the way things were."

Godric's hold on my neck loosened a bit more. "What other options do you have?"

Feel my pain. See how it mirrors your own emptiness. "Don't let him take me back," I replied in a hoarse whisper. *Keep me with you. Let me fill that void inside you.*

Godric's voice was just as hoarse, "Why would you want to stay with me?"

"Because he hurt you, too. You understand the pain he's caused me."

His grip grew so lax that I could've easily slipped away. "You're not making any sense."

"He's hurt us both," I sobbed, aching at how true it was, "You said it yourself the other day."

"Do you really expect me to believe that you wish to betray the husband whom you love so obsessively and stay here with me?"

I can fill the void inside you. Look in my eyes. You know it's true. "Yes."

"Why?"

Everything else dimmed—the sounds of the battle raging outside the window, the others in the room. This was draining me, but it was working. *You need me. You want to keep me, and you would never harm me.* "I can't take the heartache anymore," I whispered. "You said you never once hurt the woman you treasured. I want someone to love me like that, and I want it to be you…because that would kill him."

Godric's face dropped the instant I mentioned love, and the trance was broken. I'd gone too far— I poked the spot I wasn't meant to touch—asking for his love was too much. His treasure was dead. He would never love again. I knew enough about dragons to know that, but I'd been so caught up in keeping him distracted that I made a catastrophic mistake. The tips of his claws pierced my flesh as he grabbed the goblet of wine on the floor beside me. "Do you really think I'm that stupid?"

I tried to knock the goblet from his hand, but my muscles locked in place. As much as I struggled to move, I couldn't do a thing to stop him from pouring the foul mixture into my mouth. *His blood wine.* It was a burning violation that bled down my throat with a vengeance. David's blood already inked my flesh. Now his worst enemy's blood was coursing through my insides, possessing me with its venomous intent. He drained every drop of the blood wine into me. It singed the flesh of my chin as it dripped from my mouth, but my muscles were still frozen and I couldn't even wipe him from my lips. I tried to make myself vomit—to bring it back up—but his blood wouldn't have it.

You disappoint me, Princess. Godric's voice thundered inside my head. *Your husband doesn't love you anymore. Other women fill his bed. You want to hurt him back? Take my side over his. Let me slip away whilst you distract him by threatening to slit your throat with this.* The room around us blurred as he placed a dagger in the palm of my hand and closed my fingers around the hilt. It felt heavier than it looked like it ought to. *Then once I'm gone, slice your throat open while he watches. It will devastate him, and we will win.*

Everything else seemed distant and out of focus as Godric's voice echoed inside my head... His words felt so wrong... *No...*

Godric's words felt true.

46

DAVID

It took two days for the old woman to succumb to sleep so that Tristan could locate her, but we didn't squander the time. Unlike Nellie, the doctor who had replaced the sorrow at the facility slipped through the Waters at the first opportunity and Tristan wasted no time in leading us to him. It was imperative that we reach the doctor before he informed any of his fellow Purists that Charlie and Tristan had paid Nellie a visit. If Godric were to learn of this, he would know we were coming. Thankfully, Tristan realized that. Before he left the facility, he charmed the hell out of the sorry fellow, slipped him a trinket and instructed him to keep it on his person at all times so that he could pay him a visit in Draumer. Charmed as he was, the doctor never even considered the possibility that it might be a trap. After we brought him to the palace for safekeeping,

Benjamin and I put our talents to work interrogating the lust-drunken Purist. It took little time to break him and determine just how insignificant his knowledge actually was. The new doctor was merely a low ranking spy whom the Purists had planted at the facility to keep an eye on Godric's discarded possession, just as the sorrow had done before him.

Charlie and Rose continued to shoulder the weight of the mirage whilst we waited for the estranged Mrs. Godric to succumb to sleep and return to Draumer. It was imperative that I conserve my strength so that I would be ready to fight my way to the Princess the instant the opportunity arose. Besides, the virgin was eager to make up for his past transgressions and I was more than willing to let him suffer after what he had let happen to Emma. Naïve and impulsive as the boy was, he had led Godric to the clearing out of sheer stupidity. He would never intentionally allow any harm to come to Emma, and his strength had increased tremendously since he had assumed the burden of her mirage. Even I had to admit that he could prove useful in our efforts to rescue my wife, and he was certainly determined to do so. He was also smart enough to keep his distance from me whilst we waited.

After nearly two days of waiting, I was practically crawling out of my skin. Everyone was keeping their distance from me. Having no desire to interact with anyone, I had retreated to the cave to wait in solitude. As I sat there watching the vacant clearing, my thoughts strayed to the past…

…I sat in the cave, watching over the empty clearing with a heavy heart. Emma's seventeenth birthday was only two months off, and she still showed no indication that she intended to move on.

A crippling jolt of desire roused me from my musings as she materialized by the lake at the far end of the clearing. The urge to go to her was maddening by this point, but I fought it, as I always did. She stood and moved toward the barrier with such purpose that I found myself rising from my chair and moving to the Waterfall to get a better look at her. She touched her head to the barrier and the growls of the demons beyond the mirage intensified, but she seemed too lost in her own thoughts to notice.

A chill crept down my spine as she removed the pendant from her neck. When she held it at arm's length, I had to physically brace myself to keep from rushing out to ask what the hell she thought she was doing. After all these months of separation, approaching her would be a grave mistake. It would get her hopes up—and more likely than not, for good reason. My desire to claim her was unbearable even at this distance. If I were to get close enough to touch her, there would be no stopping me. Even my self-restraint had its limits and I had already pushed them much farther than it was prudent to. If she only knew the things I wished to do to her, and the torture she inflicted upon me each hour she remained in my sight.

Her voice was barely a whisper across the clearing, but it rang in my ears with perfect clarity, "I don't need something to remind me of you. I need something to help me forget you." With that, she let the pendant slip from her hand.

I felt the blood diamond hit the ground, as surely as if my body had dropped from a rooftop. It sunk to the earth with such force that it robbed the breath from my lungs.

Tears stung my eyes as the face of a massive beast pressed inward. Now that the walls were thin enough for them to see her, they were all desperate to get at her. I blinked back the tears and focused my strength on bracing the walls of the mirage. Other demons pressed in from all sides, declaring how much they hungered for her in a plethora of languages that she didn't speak. I had seen no need to include lower demonic dialects in her childhood lessons because the demon-tongues were crude and uncivilized, and I presumed she would have no reason to interact with the creatures who spoke them. As the perverse threats that spewed from their mouths echoed through the clearing, I thanked God that she couldn't understand their words.

She reached back to the base of her neck and grasped the tie of her gown, and I stilled for a moment, as did the demons beyond the walls. Then she tugged it with a resolute sigh, and my breath caught in my throat as the snow-white satin slipped down each exquisite curve and pooled in a puddle at her feet. An unbearable ache gripped me as she outstretched her arms and threw her head back, and the pressure on the walls of the dome increased a hundredfold as the demons strained against them, desperate to taste the Light creature's virgin flesh.

I pushed back, matching their collective force until her words dissolved the wards that protected the mirage, "I offer myself up to the Darkness...to be bound to it forever...and claimed by whomever would have me."

There was no holding them back after that...

..."Boss?" Waves of menace rolled off of Benjamin as he stepped in the cave.

His pounding heart had me on my feet in an instant. "Has the dragon mother succumbed to sleep?"

Benjamin's pitch black eyes Darkened as he nodded. "Tristan is gathering everyone."

I felt a bit like a snake—coiled and aching to strike—as I followed Benjamin through the Waterfall to the great hall of the palace. The assembled rescue party stood ready and waiting beside the steps to my throne. Brian and Tristan were dressed in the traditional black uniform of the royal guard, each with a sword belted at his side. The Unsighted knight stood between them, entirely focused on the mission and not the least bit distracted by their charms. His bow and the quiver full of poison-tipped arrows that Brian had equipped him with was confidently slung over one broad shoulder. The knight's miniature companion still cowered in his shirt pocket, under the misconception that his presence was unbeknownst to me. Rose and Charlie stood hand in hand at the other end of the steps. As I moved toward them, the virgin met my gaze without hesitation. I no longer detected any hatred toward me in his eyes. Instead, the young dragon greeted me with a respectful nod and an apologetic frown.

I nodded to the assembled rescue party as I stopped in front of the Mason brothers. Then I traced a hand through the air to summon a Waterfall and gestured for Tristan to enter the temporary portal. "Lead the way."

Wasting no time with words, Tristan stepped through the Waterfall. I followed and stepped out beside a wrought iron fence that was more decorative than functional in purpose. The sky was pitch black and the breezeless air was sweltering. Hordes of demons roamed the grounds within the fence, most of them mindless and starving for flesh, many of them Unsighted and all of them unburdened by matters of conscience. They had clearly been positioned there to serve as entirely disposable bestial guards. A large Victorian estate stood well within the borders of the fence line. I recognized it as a meticulous replica of the Godric family's homestead, having seen pictures of the actual house in my mother's old photo albums. Callous as my father had always been toward me, he'd never had the heart to discard any of his treasured late wife's possessions. When I was a child, I used to sneak into the sitting room that my father preserved as a shrine to her, look through her things and try to decipher some connection to the woman who brought me into the world. This obviously wasn't the actual Godric home. The magic that warded it was too new. This was simply a mirage that my deranged uncle had constructed in its likeness to serve as a hideaway.

I stepped toward the fence as I surveyed the area it encompassed. Demons lingered mere inches from us, but thanks to Benjamin, they were not wise to our presence. His ability to cloak himself—and any others whom he chose to include—in Darkness was an invaluable tool during missions such as this. I wagered there were nearly a thousand demons within the perimeter, not to mention several hundred beating hearts inside the building—but one heartbeat called to me above all the others. The familiar hummingbird-like flutter of her precious heart was like a fingerprint unique to her. I would know it anywhere.

We are coming for you, Princess. Stall him for as long as you can.

A faint smile curved my lips as her lovely voice sounded in my head like a beloved song I'd been desperate to hear. *How?*

Remember your lessons. Manipulate him.

I'm not strong enough. Her telepathic voice was thick with panic. My enchantment no longer guarded her. Godric had somehow persuaded her to dismiss it.

My stomach knotted at the realization of how dangerous our approach would be without her enchantment to watch over her. As soon as the would-be king sensed us coming, he would direct his anger toward her. **You are stronger than you think.**

I—

His hands were on her. I could sense it in her fearful tone. Rage darkened my vision as the flames flared in my eyes. **Trust me.**

I do. I always have.

You can do this. She could. My Princess was a force to be reckoned with—at least, she would be when she was mine once again.

"We need to spread out," I whispered as the last of our group stepped from the Waterfall, "and clear this yard as swiftly as possible. Godric is aware that we are here, and he has already dispatched Emma's protective enchantment."

"What?" Even cloaked in shadow, the fury in Benjamin's growl caused some of the nearest demons to flinch.

I shook my head. "No time for explanations. Sweep the yard by whatever means necessary, and spread out to cover more ground."

ERIN A. JENSEN

Benjamin turned to Charlie and Rose. "You two take the far end, and spread as far apart as you can without severing your connection."

Charlie and Rose unmasked and trampled the metal fence posts like twigs beneath their dragon limbs as they rushed into the yard.

"Tristan and Brian, take the left," Benjamin growled. "I'll take the center and keep Bob cloaked beside me."

Bob shook his head as the incubus brothers drew their swords and entered the yard. "Save your cover. I face my enemies head on." Without waiting for an answer, the fearless knight rushed in through the trampled section of fence.

"Fucking idiot," Benjamin snarled as he rushed in after Bob with a grin of approval that didn't match his words. He spread out from the knight to cover more distance and wasted no time attempting to cloak our Unsighted friend.

As I unmasked and moved toward the house, my thoughts turned to the day my bride forsook the Light and bound herself to the Darkness forever. Pure unadulterated fury guided my movements, just as it did all those years ago.

47

BOB

I no longer moved blindly through the eternal Darkness. The Dragon King's shadow had touched my shoulder as we followed Tristan through the Waterfall, and suddenly the darkness seemed less absolute. It wasn't daylight by any means, but I could see well enough to maneuver. I could see enough to fight. I stepped over the downed portion of fence that Charlie and Rose had trampled when they took dragon form. Nothing much shocked me, but when Charlie first told me that he was a dragon, I didn't believe it straightaway. Then when he unmasked and revealed his dragon form to prove it, I nearly pissed myself.

I drew an arrow from the quiver and lifted it to my bow.

"Why the hell didn't you stay with the Darkness and let him keep us cloaked?" Pip whispered from my pocket.

I let the arrow fly, and it took down a fat ugly beast with massive teeth that protruded past his chin. "I don't hide from my enemies."

"You aren't like the rest of these creatures," Pip squeaked.

"I've told you before," I whispered as I drew another arrow, "it's all in your state of mind."

"I think you're just plain *out* of your mind," Pip grumbled, "Maybe I should've hitched a ride in the Darkness's pocket.

I released the second arrow and hit a hefty troll square in the eye, dropping him to his knees with a resounding thud. "You're welcome to jump ship at any time."

"Funny."

"Just go with it—"

A wiry demon who moved on all fours like a jungle cat rose onto his hind legs and lunged at me, but I caught him by the throat and slit it with my sword before he could sink tooth or claw into either of us.

Pip let out a startled squeak as the beast's inky blood spattered his face. "Holy hell! Alright...I'll admit that was impressive."

I ran my blade through a gaunt beast's chest as he reached for me. "Does that mean you're going to stop whining now?"

Pip squealed as a reptilian demon rushed at us with a double-edged cleaver. "Maybe," he grunted as he watched me run my blade through the beast's throat. "Shit."

Words escaped us both after that as I fought my way toward the house where Godric was keeping my soul mate, stabbing and slicing and slinging arrows at every manner of hellish creature who crossed our path. All around us, the battle raged. Charlie and Rose were at the far side, crushing demons beneath their feet, lighting them up with their fiery breath, chomping them with massive jaws. Brian and Tristan slayed everything that rushed at them with awe-inspiring grace. Many of the beasts simply stopped dead in their tracks when they saw them coming and stood there drooling while the incubi ran their blades through their hearts. A few even turned their blades on themselves simply because Tristan told them to. I couldn't see what Benjamin was doing because he was still cloaked in Darkness and I was no longer under his protective shield, but I could see the demons he attacked seemingly ripping in half for no apparent reason. I could hear their horrified shrieks as he touched them and enveloped them in fear. I saw them bleed from their eyes as they desperately scrambled to flee, but to no avail.

As we advanced, I kept pace with the rest of them and took down nightmarish foe after foe. While all of this took place, the Dragon King effortlessly took the lead. A great majority of the demons rushed at him, but none of them so much as slowed him down. He destroyed every beast that rushed at him from every side. Not one of them caught him off guard. He split the skulls of the demons who rushed up behind him with one perfectly aimed flick of his massive tail without even turning to look at what he was doing. He crushed smaller beasts underfoot and caught larger ones in his teeth and chomped them in half. His pace never slowed, and his eyes never strayed from the house where his soul mate was being held captive. Inspired by his incredible prowess, I reached the house soon after he did.

He greeted me with a nod of approval. "Remind me to offer you a job when this is all over." Then he turned to the door and let out a rage-filled bellow.

Chest heaving, I muttered, "What is it?"

"It's warded," he snarled. "This will take time that we don't have to spare."

Pip poked his head from my pocket and squeaked, "I've got this."

"How in God's name do *you* have this?" I muttered, noting that the Dragon King didn't seem at all surprised by my miniature sidekick's impromptu appearance.

"The wards only protect the outside of the building," he whispered. "I can slip under the door and unlock it from the inside."

I raised an eyebrow. "How are you going to slip in if it's warded?"

"No one wards the crack under the door," Pip whispered.

"And how will you unlock the door?" I whispered. "The door knob is too high for you to reach."

"All these old houses have lock releases at imp level," he muttered with a grin, "for the servant imps who tended to their housekeeping."

"But this isn't a real house," Charlie muttered as he and Rose joined us, "It's just a mirage."

"A thoroughly authentic one," the King whispered. "Your friend is correct. Set him down."

I wasn't quite so ready to sacrifice the friend who had gotten me this far. "What if something grabs him before he unlocks the door?"

Benjamin pulled an arrow from my quiver, snapped off the tip and handed it to Pip. "Stab them with this. The venom takes effect almost instantly."

"This isn't exactly a fool-proof plan," I muttered.

"Your soul mate is in there, Bob," Pip whispered, "This is what we came here for. I couldn't save my soul mate, but I'll be damned if I'll just stand by and watch you lose yours. Now put me down and let me do something to help for once."

I took him from my pocket and sat him on the step, and he slipped beneath the door before I even had a chance to wish him luck. A few seconds later, the door opened without a sound.

"Well done," the King whispered. "I may just have to offer you a position, as well."

48

CHARLIE

As we waited for Bob's pint-sized sidekick to unlock the door, I prayed to God that this wasn't just another false lead. Was it possible for the Purists to trick Tristan and lead him somewhere besides where they were actually keeping Nellie? I wasn't sure I could take another dead end. Emma's abduction was my fault. I needed to get her back, and Godric needed to pay for tricking me into helping him kidnap her.

Penny for your thoughts. As Godric's voice sounded inside my head that familiar rush of warmth washed over me until I could practically taste the crimson-colored liquid he'd served whenever we met in his mirage. A quick glance at the faces around me confirmed that I was the only one hearing voices, which was just fucking wonderful. Wouldn't that be just my luck to break down and lose it for real in the middle of Emma's rescue mission? *What in God's name are you still doing with these people, Charlie?*

Who else should I be with? You?

The door swung open and Bob's mini travel buddy ushered us into the house with a smug grin on his grimy little face. The Sarrum stepped in first, followed by Benjamin, Brian, Tristan and then Bob.

I gestured for Rose to go ahead of me, then stepped in after her. *You tricked me into putting Emma in danger.*

Come now, Charlie. Let's be honest. You did her a favor by getting her away from the Sarrum. He doesn't deserve her, but you do.

You're damn right, I do.

By all appearances, the dark house seemed deserted but I knew that was a deception. I could hear the heartbeats of at least a hundred creatures within those walls.

Join me, and I'll let you have Emma.

Bullshit.

Fight at my side, and she can be your Queen, Charlie.

I kept expecting the Sarrum to pick up on our telepathic exchange, but I guess he was too focused on tracking the faint flutter of Emma's heartbeat to notice.

Why the hell would I listen to you after what you tricked me into doing?

Because you were meant to fight beside me.

I hoped David wouldn't notice the way my heart was racing or that if he did, he'd just chalk it up to our current circumstances. Although I wasn't exactly sure why I was worrying, since I hadn't done anything wrong. I didn't initiate this unspoken conversation. *What the hell are you talking about?*

You were always meant to fight at my side.

The Sarrum signaled for us to stay put while he peered around a corner, then he nodded and motioned us forward.

I took a deep breath as I blindly followed Rose around the corner. *Says who?*

It is what I created you for.

As our little parade followed David Talbot down the narrow corridor, Godric's last words reverberated inside my head with enough ferocity to make it ache. *What?*

Why do you think I took such an interest in you, Charlie? Haven't you ever wondered why I tracked you down in the first place, or why I spent all that time getting to know you?

My throat constricted as we caught up to David. *You did it to gain my trust so you could steal Emma.*

I told you, you can have Emma. I don't want her.

I tried to swallow, but my throat was too dry. *What the hell do you want?*

I want the rightful rulers to take possession of this world. I want you to fight at my side.

It felt like the temperature inside the house was spiking, but I couldn't tell for sure whether it was because we were getting closer to Godric or if it was just *my* temperature that was rising. *Why the hell would you want that?*

Because you are my son, Charlie.

Yeah, he lost me there. That was just over the top. *Really? That's what you're going with? Isn't it a little too Star-Wars-ish?*

Excuse me?

You know... Star Wars? Darth Vader? Luke, I am your father? Star Wars? Come on. You can't seriously expect me to believe you didn't steal the I-am-your-father bit from Star Wars.

Are you serious?

No, not usually.

Honestly, I can't believe I sacrificed some of my power to bring you into the world.

You're not serious about the whole dad thing?

I am DEAD serious. My blood courses through your veins, Charlie. I know you felt it when you drank my blood wine. My blood recognized you, and it strengthened you.

Then...why not tell me this sooner?

I wasn't sure I could trust you to take my side.

And you're sure now?

I have no other options now. The Sarrum will kill me if you don't help me.

We turned another ominous blind corner and followed David down another poorly lit corridor. With each step, it felt a bit more like we were venturing toward the climactic scene of a horror film. *Why the hell would I help you?*

Because you have far too many unanswered questions to let it end this way.

I was trying to come up with a snide response as the Sarrum led us through an open door, but whatever smartass comment I meant to make slipped from my mind as I stepped in the room.

Nellie was closest to the door. She was seated on a red velvet couch surrounded by three greasy drooling demons. Two more of the same species of demon were crouching over Lilly, who was curled up in a ball on the floor near the windows. Emma was standing on the other side of the room with Godric behind her and a dagger at her throat, but Godric wasn't holding the blade—Emma was. Blood red liquid stained her lips and dripped from her chin. For a second, I thought she'd been injured and had coughed up the blood. Then I saw the broken glass and spattered drops of crimson liquid on the floor at her feet and realized it was Godric's blood wine on her lips.

Every member of our rescue party froze at the sight.

"Princess," David pleaded in a measured whisper, "Toss the dagger to me."

Tears streamed down Emma's cheeks as she shook her head. "Don't come any closer. I'll slit my throat if anyone takes another step toward us."

A menacing snarl reverberated in the Sarrum's throat as his glare shifted to Godric. "What sort of ruler hides behind a young woman? You wish to take my throne? **FIGHT ME FOR IT!**"

Amusement flickered in Godric's cunning blue eyes. "You occupy MY throne, David. I don't wish to take anything of yours. Well..." His eyes dropped to Emma's hand, tightly gripping the blade at her throat. "I suppose that's not entirely true."

David's enraged growl thundered through the room, making it suddenly seem much too small to contain him even in his human form. "You are too weak and cowardly to rule this world, Henry."

Godric's disconcerting burst of laughter echoed through the room—magnifying to a much greater volume than it ought to—and the room felt even smaller. "But I don't stand alone." As he wrapped an arm around Emma's waist, I could *feel* the rage radiating from David, but Emma gave no indication that it bothered her.

"Get your hands off her!" David snarled as he moved to step forward.

Emma increased the pressure of the blade against her flesh. "I will slice my throat open if you come any closer."

David's voice was ripe with sorrow as he stilled and met her eyes. "You don't want to do this."

"Yes, I do," she sobbed. "I can't take any more of this. I need it to end."

The Dragon King exhaled a sigh of frustration, and Emma's eyes glazed as his scent hit the air.

Penny for your thoughts. My focus shifted to Godric as his voice sounded in my head, and his crystal blue eyes filled with flames as they met my gaze. *It's time to come stand beside me, Charlie. You belong with me.*

The temperature in the room skyrocketed and everything took on an orange glow as my eyes filled with flames in response to his words. "I…"

Godric nodded at the fire in my eyes with a grin of approval. *You were meant to fight beside me.*

I sure as hell didn't want to, but my feet started moving toward him anyway. The drink he'd served me each time we talked—ever since I learned about Nellie… and the blood wine… and the way Godric had used it to control her—I knew he'd fed me his blood, too, but it never seemed to have any effect… except to warm me. "No…" I was already halfway across the floor. "I don't…"

Focus on my voice, Charlie. Benjamin's voice inside my head was like a slap to the face, anchoring me back to my senses.

What do I do?

Fight it.

He fed me his blood.

Doesn't matter. You're a dragon. He can't make you do anything against your will.

I wasn't so sure Benjamin was right about that. My feet were still moving. I was closer to Emma and Godric than I was to our rescue team. *He says he's my father.*

That's beside the point, Benjamin's voice growled.

I tried to turn and look at Benjamin, but I was no longer in control of my body. It felt like somebody had switched me to autopilot. *Is it true?*

What if it was? Benjamin's voice growled. **Would that be enough reason to take his side?**

IS IT TRUE?

YOU HAVE TO FOCUS ON FIGHTING THIS, DRAGON!

It is true... isn't it?

What does that matter?

Answer the question!

Yeah. It's true.

Great! That's just great! What the hell am I supposed to do now?

It's time, kid.

Time for what?

Time for you to choose a side.

WHAT?

Remember our conversation in the clearing?

Yeah...but you've all lied to me...and I don't know enough about any of this to pledge my allegiance to anybody.

Yeah, you do.

I fought like hell against whatever was in control of my body. My muscles screamed in protest and sweat dripped from my brow, but I managed to turn my head enough to look around the room. Nellie was sobbing on the couch, surrounded by demons. Lilly was curled in a ball on the floor with demons hovering over her. Rose, Bob, Tristan and Brian stood frozen watching me, but the Sarrum's eyes were glued to Emma. An involuntary grunt barreled up my throat as I forced my head to turn back to look at her. Tears were streaming down her cheeks. She wasn't holding that dagger to her throat by choice. Godric had forced her to drink his blood, and my stupid mistakes had gotten her into this royally fucked up situation. None of the rest of it mattered. I took another step toward Godric and Emma, and Godric shot me a satisfied grin. Enraged by his arrogance, I growled, "I choose the Sarrum, you son of a bitch."

Flames erupted in Godric's eyes as a command hissed from his lips in an ugly demonic dialect, and a shower of broken glass littered the room as the horde of demons in the yard came crashing through the windows.

49

EMMA

An endless stream of demons spilled into the house through the broken windows, and the world around me blurred until everything was distant and out of focus, but I didn't care. This would all be over soon, and I welcomed my approaching death because I couldn't take any more of this. David had hurt me too deeply, too many times. I just needed it to end.

I stood there motionless with the cold steel of the blade pressed against my throat as a surreal pageant of bloodshed swirled around me. Distant screeches and growls and demonic snarls echoed through the air, but I just stood there—and so did David. No one touched us as we stood there with our eyes locked. It was almost as if the two of us were encapsulated within some sort of protective bubble.

It was too loud for spoken words, so David spoke inside my head. *You don't want to do this, Princess.*

Yes, I do. I need this to end.

Put down that blade, and I promise you, it will end. I'll take you home and everything will be alright.

You can't promise that.

You don't belong here, Emma.

Then where do I belong?

You belong with me. You are mine, and I've come to take you home. Listen to my voice, Princess. Focus on my words. You know I speak the truth. YOU BELONG TO ME.

It was true. He would always come for me because I was his. He had claimed me a lifetime ago, when I forced his hand and left him no choice…

… I meant to keep my eyes shut after the walls of the mirage tore apart, until there was nothing left of me and the agony of being discarded like a useless plaything finally came to an end. That was the plan, but as the chorus of demonic growls magnified inside my head, my eyes flew open and I watched in detached horror as the scene around me unfolded like a slow-motion massacre in a movie.

That initial monstrous face that had pressed inward when I dropped the pendant to the ground was the first to break through the mirage. He rushed toward me with a speed and ferocity that I couldn't comprehend as I stood there with my arms outstretched—naked and

vulnerable—eager for physical pain to blunt the unbear-
able heartache that had gripped me for far too long.

A moment later, I was lying on my back in the grass,
unsure exactly how I'd landed there. The Sarrum
reached me seconds later, at the same instant the demon
did. Before I could even work out what was happen-
ing, David was standing over me in dragon form with
the demon in his jaws. As I lay there on my back—star-
ing up at the pitch black scales of the monstrous belly
above me, listening to the wailing of the demon who was
meant to end my suffering—I wanted to scream. This
was supposed to bring an end to my agony. How could he
deny me a release from the suffering he had caused? My
anger intensified as I watched the demon's lifeless body
sail through the air, slam against a tree trunk across the
clearing and drop to the ground in a mangled heap.

Menacing shapes were closing in on us from all sides.
It was difficult to make them out now that darkness was
spilling into the clearing from the gaping holes in the
mirage. The creatures snarled and howled and rushed
at us until it was all too much to process. It seemed to
occur—both extremely fast and in slow-motion—like an
artfully choreographed work of unending violence.

There must have been thousands of them pouring
in through the holes in the walls in a steady stream—
desperate to claim me—but none of them reached me.
David snatched them in his mouth and caught them with
his massive claws and tore them to shreds, spattering the
clearing with their Dark oily blood. I watched the scene

unfold in a state of transfixed fascination. Despite my thorough education on the innate characteristics of dragons, I was in absolute awe of the Sarrum's power. As much as I'd known he was capable of, this seemed impossible. No single creature should be able to defeat these odds. Yet there David was—stopping every demon who rushed at us, tearing them apart, dousing the only home I'd ever known in their blood.

I couldn't say how long it lasted, but it was long enough for me to wonder whether this was my own personal hell. Maybe that first demon had actually killed me, and this endless onslaught of demons was my eternal punishment for ending my own life in such a spiteful and violent manner. After a while it began to fade into one gigantic blur—an endless attack that was exhausting just to witness—still, David never weakened or even slowed his pace. He just kept tearing them to pieces, smashing their bodies against the stone walls of our cave with flicks of his massive tail, stomping them underfoot and somehow, he managed to do it all without getting a single drop of blood on me.

When it started to wind down—the demons still approaching, but more warily—his massive roar shook the ground beneath me. In fact, the thunderous sound must have shaken every corner of Draumer. Then his voice thundered aloud and inside the heads of every creature who still drew breath. I CLAIM THIS CREATURE! SHE IS MINE AND ANYONE WHO DARES TO GO NEAR HER SHALL ANSWER TO ME!

A rush of molten air swept through the clearing as he turned in a circle above me, bathing the walls of the dome in his fiery breath. Sapphire flames blanketed the heavens and the night sky burned until the Darkness was bright as day.

I was too mesmerized by the brilliance of the flames to notice when he masked himself in human form but the next thing I knew, the only man I would ever love was crouching above me on his hands and knees. I had just witnessed the depths of his fury for a brief eternity, but there was no rage in the human eyes that locked with mine. Instead, every feature of his beautiful face was etched in sorrow. I had caused that pain. I'd wanted him to feel it, but I never meant to force him to keep me. I just wanted to end my suffering.

He touched a hand to my cheek with a tenderness that brought tears to my eyes. "My sweet girl, what have you done?"

"You didn't have to do that," I whimpered in a small uncertain voice. "I just wanted it to end. I wasn't trying to force you to keep me when you didn't want me."

Tears filled his beautiful blue eyes as he whispered, "Didn't want you? Is that what you think?"

"Yes."

"You are all I have ever wanted. The agony that I suffered over giving you up..."

I opened my mouth to say something, but nothing came out.

"It killed me to walk away from you," he whispered, "Dragons do not leave their treasures behind, and I treasure you above all else. I let you go to spare your life."

I reached up with a hesitant hand and traced his cheek with the tips of my fingers. "Don't you remember what I said? I'd rather spend one day in the Darkness with you than a million days in the Light without you. I'm old enough to know that. I've always been old enough to know that. It could only ever be you. I'd rather die a horrific death than live a life without you."

A tortured grin tugged at the corners of his mouth. "Yes, I see that."

"Good."

He lowered his head and brushed his bottom lip against mine, and a rush of heat washed over me. His lips gently nudged mine apart and his tongue slipped between them, gentle and reverent.

I kissed him back with a needy fervor that had built over ten months' time, but he slowed my frantic movements without ever breaking contact with my mouth—like a dancer leading his partner—expertly, exquisitely, deliciously. His kiss gradually deepened at a leisurely pace that was so much better than my greedy desperation.

I felt the heat spread to my wings, wings I'd never known I had or felt in the slightest until that moment. I could feel them singeing and burning—dying—but I didn't care. He could have them. He could devour every piece of me one by one, and I would enjoy every precious second of my demise. This was how it was meant to be...

...I remembered everything now.

Everyone had always believed that he stole me, but I chose him. I captured his heart—the instant he first looked into my eyes—on the day I was born. There was something about him that I needed. I had always felt it, and I would always need it. David and I were meant to be together. Nothing else mattered... and none of it was true... Sophie... that girl in the guestroom across the hall... he would never touch any other woman. There *was* no other woman for him, just as there could never be any other man for me.

David and I were drawn to each other like a moth to a flame.

But who was the moth and who was the flame? That was the part everyone got wrong. I was his undoing, just as surely as he would be mine.

50

DAVID

The potion was working. Connected as we were, I felt Emma's memories come flooding back to her.

My thoughts traveled in tandem with hers to the day I claimed her in the clearing...

...I kissed her sweet lips, and a rush of adrenaline surged through my body as the Light from her wings seeped into mine. As Emma's snow-white wings withered and died, my massive black wings absorbed their radiance. The shimmering brilliance—that had so resembled newly fallen snow in the morning light on her gossamer wings—now brought to mind a billion stars scattered across the night sky on my pitch black wings. Each new spot of radiance on my wing mirrored a blotch of decay on hers. If I could have prevented it, I would have. However, I could no more stop it than night can stop itself from extinguishing the light of day. My Darkness would

devour her Light little by little until nothing remained of her.

She was still a child, not yet seventeen. Honorably as I had forced myself to behave up to this point, there was nothing I could do to protect her now that she had bound herself to the Darkness. If I didn't claim her, the creatures lurking in the Darkness would gladly risk their lives to do so. The only way to cement our bond and keep her safe was to claim her often, both verbally and physically. Necessary as it was to stake my claim, I felt like a monster hovering on hands and knees above this innocent young creature clothed in nothing but a pair of lace trimmed panties.

I gently broke our kiss and whispered, "You are mine." Was it possible to refrain from claiming her physically and simply declare this verbally—often enough to protect her from what lurked in the Darkness—till her eighteenth birthday? Tears filled my eyes and strangled my voice as I repeated my claim, "You are mine."

I knew full well it would be impossible to refrain from touching her for a year whilst repeatedly declaring ownership of her body and soul as she looked up at me with such longing.

"Please," she pleaded in a breathless whisper, "Don't hold back. Whatever you need, take it from me. Whatever Dark desires lurk in your dragon heart, they are a part of you and I want nothing less than all of you till the day my fairy heart gives out. Don't love me like

a human. I want you undiluted, Dark and fierce as you truly are. Love me like a dragon."

Never allow yourself to lose control. **It is the first rule we dragons are taught, practically since birth. Dragons must exercise control in all things. If we do not, the consequences may be catastrophic. We dragons love as fiercely as we hate, and because of our possessive nature, loving what we treasure without restraint may very well cost us our sanity. My uncle was living proof of that, just as my father had been. Losing the woman whom they both treasured had driven the two of them mad.**

I had vowed long ago never to make such a mistake, to exercise control in all things—but I never stood a chance of keeping that vow. I knew it the moment I first locked eyes with this precious creature of Light beneath me.

Everyone always assumed that I had fallen for Emma's striking appearance. Exquisite and perfect as she was, how could they think otherwise? In truth, it was her actions that stole my heart. When I first unmasked for her on the day she was born, she didn't cry. By all accounts, throughout all of history, she should have cried. The mere sight of me should have traumatized her for months. Yet, she nestled contentedly against my chest, cradled in my arms as she looked up at me and accepted me for exactly who and what I was. That was all she had ever asked of me. She loved me entirely—not just my human form, not just my gentle nature—she had witnessed the worst of me over the years and she loved me in spite of it or dare I say, because of it.

As this creature I had treasured since the day of her birth lay beneath me, pleading with me to love her without limits, I looked at the tears in her eyes and felt my heart fracture.

I dropped my mouth to hers and growled, "You are mine," against her lips.

"I'm yours," she whispered as I scattered tender kisses along her jawline and trailed them down her neck.

Doubt gripped me when my lips reached the base of her neck. I lifted my head to look into those magnificent green eyes as my desire to protect this innocent creature warred with my desire to take her, immobilizing me.

"Please, David." She arched her back so the smooth flesh of her breast brushed against my chin. "Don't hold back. Just love me."

I shut my eyes and touched my cheek to her chest. Within the confines of her ribcage, her precious heart fluttered at a hummingbird's pace.

"I'm yours," she whispered. "That's all I've ever wanted to be."

I turned my head and brushed my lips against her flesh as I murmured, "You have no idea the power you hold over me."

"If you don't mark me as yours, they'll seek me out in the waking world."

She was right, of course. And yet I hesitated, unwilling to strip her of her innocence.

"I knew it," she muttered as she pushed my head away and sat up. "You really don't want me."

I watched in stunned silence as she reached for her gown, the gown I had longed to strip her of since the day I first saw her in it. As she picked it up, her eyes filled with tears.

I balled my hand around her fist that gripped the gown. "You cannot possibly believe that I don't want you."

"If I'm wrong," she sobbed in a broken whisper, "then prove it to me."

The fear in her eyes was like a blow to the chest, deepening the fractures in my heart. She truly believed that she had trapped me into claiming her against my will. What sort of monster was I to let her doubt the depth of my love for her? That was a far greater crime than breaking some other world's law. In this world, I was the law. It was time to stop playing by human rules. I had what she desired, and I wanted nothing more than to satisfy her needs. It was as simple as that.

I tossed the gown aside and snarled, "You belong to me." Then I covered her lips with mine and kissed her like a man possessed, devouring her as I lowered her to the grass.

As I kissed my way down her neck, an intoxicating bouquet of scents rose from her flesh—ripe fruits and the nectar of exotic flowers mingled with a decadent blend of Dark spices and sweets—our scent, hers and mine.

I took my time bathing her in my scent, worshipping her body with my lips and tongue as I kissed my way down her slender torso. When I stopped and lifted my head, she let out a disappointed moan that morphed into a hitched exhalation as I captured the lace waistband of her panties between my teeth. Eager as I was to tear them off, I drew them down slowly and reveled in the whimpers of desperation that escaped her sweet mouth.

As I slipped my hands under her hips and trailed the sheer fabric lower, I exhaled through flared nostrils, scenting and staking claim to each tender inch of her flesh as I bared it.

An animalistic moan barreled up her throat as the heat of my breath whispered over her, and I nearly lost control. Don't hold back. Please. Love me like a dragon.

Frenzied by her unspoken plea—coupled with the mental pressure she was exerting with all her might— I yanked the lace panties the rest of the way down her legs and tossed them aside. "You are mine," I growled as I gently coaxed her legs apart, positioned my head between them and settled onto my elbows with my fore- arms hooked around her thighs. Maddened by the lust in her eyes and the suggestive images she fed into my head with her mental manipulation, I dipped my head and caressed her sweet flesh with one broad upward stroke of my tongue.

A primal cry escaped her mouth as she gripped my head, holding me exactly where I was, as if she feared I would change my mind and stop.

I took my time, savoring the taste I had craved for so long. Growling against her ripe flesh, I reveled in each spasm that overtook her as she writhed against my mouth and cried my name over and over at the top of her lungs. As her movements began to still, I shed what clothing I could without taking my mouth from her. Then I released her, peeled off my shirt and cast it to the grass as my mouth moved to hers.

I was about to pull back and ask if she wanted me to stop when her voice sounded loud and clear inside my head, Don't you dare stop now. Don't hold back.

"You are mine," I growled as I pressed my lips to hers.

Never allow yourself to lose control. It was the cardinal rule I had lived by since childhood—the law all dragons swore to uphold—but as I slowly sank into her, inch by delicious inch, Emma moaned my name and my control shattered.

A blaze of blue flames erupted in my visual field as I lost myself inside her, till there was no telling where I ended and she began. No world existed beyond our clearing. This exquisite creature of Light beneath me was all that mattered. I would burn heaven and earth to the ground if she but whispered the command in my ear.

Hours passed as we lost ourselves in each other's flesh—over and over, our bestial howls erupting in perfect unison—an unending symphony of carnal ecstasy. The sky above us darkened and still we remained entwined as I scented her—inside and out—until her sated body finally demanded rest.

In that blissful state of exhaustion, she nestled her head against my chest. "I don't care how long I live. Each breath—until my dying breath—belongs to you. I would trade a thousand nights in the Light for this one night beneath the stars in your arms. My heart belongs to you, David. It always has, and it always will."

The world could have stopped in that instant, and I doubt I would have even noticed. My world was right there in my arms.

As she drifted off to sleep, I kissed the top of her head and whispered, "I will treasure you till my dying breath, Princess. My heart is yours. It has been since the day you were born."...

...The crushing weight in my chest retreated the instant I saw the recognition in Emma's eyes. Isa and Doc's potion had worked. My wife was whole again. She remembered all of it—every moment she had forgotten—but there was no time for celebration. I still had to get her home.

Godric was gone. He'd slipped away while his demons were pouring into the room through the broken windows. I knew of course, but this was the only choice I could make. If I had gone after the would-be king, Emma would have slit her throat with that blade. Godric's intent was screaming through her veins, compelling her to devastate me by slitting her own throat. My eye contact and my voice were the only things capable of grounding her, and getting that dagger out of her hand was all that mattered. The rest would have to sort itself out later. ***Drop that blade to the floor, Princess.***

My muscles are locked in place. I can't. It's impossible.

You found your way back to me. Nothing is impossible now.

But... you found me.

Physically, yes—but you fought your way back to us. You remember us.

I do.

Then you know that I would never touch any other woman.

Yes.

And you know that you belong to me.

I do.

Then I command you to drop that blade.

I—

Don't say that you can't. You are capable of miraculous deeds, Princess.

I used to be...

Then just do one thing for me, and I will take care of the rest.

What do you want me to do?

Drop that blade.

I can't.

Do not focus on Godric's command. His blood is a temporary violation, and his intent is an insult to our bond. My blood inks your flesh. Listen to my words, and do as I say. Drop the blade. I knew she was incapable of doing what I asked, but focusing on my voice was distracting her into an almost catatonic state. When I was satisfied that she was sufficiently lulled, I pounced and knocked the dagger from her hand. Then I caught her in my arms, raked a claw across my wrist and placed the cut to her lips as she collapsed against my chest. "Drink."

At first, her response was weak. She simply swallowed the drops of blood that trickled into her mouth. I felt the war raging within her as my blood neutralized his. My blood began to strengthen her and she gripped my wrist—first with one weak hand, then with both—until she was suckling on the cut, eagerly diluting Godric's blood with mine.

All around us, the battle raged—my warriors slaying Godric's, one by one. The Unsighted knight fought valiantly and with far more skill than he should have possessed. Even the half-breed imp who traveled in the knight's pocket discovered a new-found courage. He rushed at the demons' ankles, stabbing them with the poison-tipped arrowhead Benjamin had snapped off for him before he entered the house. With each beast the tiny creature dropped to the floor, his confidence grew. Benjamin and Brian and Tristan circled the room, defeating demon after demon with deft precision. Charlie and Rose fought fiercely and impressively well, considering they were simultaneously shouldering the weight of the mirage. For the first time, I understood why Benjamin had such faith in the boy. He would be capable of greatness, once he dropped the sarcasm and committed himself to learning all that he had yet to learn. In the thick of it all, he had chosen our side—just as Benjamin had been certain he would—even with the knowledge that he was created for a vastly different purpose. The boy was not yet ready, but he soon would be. With my guidance, he could become the dragon that he was destined to be.

My heart soared as Emma dropped my wrist and grinned up at me. "Take me home."

I hugged her to my chest and whispered, "I thought you'd never ask."

Tears streamed down her cheeks as she opened her mouth to answer, but she never got the chance.

A blood-curdling scream stopped us all dead in our tracks. Even Godric's demons stilled and turned toward the sound.

The only creature who didn't freeze was the Unsighted knight. He rushed across the room at the sound of his soul mate's cry, dove onto the couch beside her and searched for the wound that had prompted her scream. "Are you hurt?"

The dragon mother shook her head as she sobbed heart-wrenching, hopeless sobs that shook her whole frame, but produced no sound.

For the first time since I had met him, the knight's eyes shone with fear. "What is it?"

The number of remaining enemies was marginal at this point, and the rest of our party swiftly dispatched them to rid the distractions. As the room cleared of upright enemies, the half-imp cried out. "Bob!"

I couldn't see the impish creature past the litter of fallen demons from my vantage point, but Charlie unmasked and raced toward the shattered windows. A horrified sob hiccupped from his throat as he knelt and stood with a small mangled body in his arms.

The stoic knight let out an agonized groan as Charlie approached the couch, cradling the lifeless enchantment—of the sister he had never known—in his arms.

Tears streamed down Charlie's cheeks as he placed her broken body between the grief-stricken couple with the utmost care and touched a hand to Nellie's shoulder.

"Lilly." Nellie gently scooped the inert enchantment into her arms and clutched the child's body to her chest as she collapsed into Bob's arms. "My baby."

"I'm so sorry," Bob whispered, "I failed you. My God, I'm so sorry."

51

I jumped out of bed and raced for the door the instant my eyes popped open. It must have been torture for David, living with only half his wife for all those months—with me so broken and vulnerable, gullible enough to believe Sophie's lies, attempting to kill myself, putting Isa in a coma when she tried to stop me, getting admitted to the facility where he wasn't even allowed to visit—and all the while, me hating him for sins he'd never committed. As I opened the door to our room, his Dark spiced scent barreled into me. Shocked that I hadn't been able to detect him when he'd been so near the whole time, I followed his scent down the hall and found the door to the bedroom just three doors down from ours wide open.

David was sitting up in bed, attached to a jumble of tubes and wires. Jeremy was in the process of detaching him, but he stopped to look up at me when he sensed me standing in the hall. The doctor flashed me a knowing grin, then returned his attention to the task of disconnecting my husband from the monitors and IV fluids beside the bed.

As I stepped in the room, David flipped his palm upright and gripped Doc's arm. "That's enough for now, Doctor."

Deep frown lines creased Jeremy's brow as he glanced up at me. "Your reunion can wait, Sarrum. You've been out for days. We need to get you unhooked and have you eat a proper meal—"

"I don't believe I asked for your opinion." David's eyes were on me as he spoke, and his velvet tone and hooded eyelids made it clear that Jeremy was already gone as far as he was concerned.

"Yes, of course." Doc let David's arm drop to the bed, still attached to the medical equipment. "I'll come back in a bit."

David's nostrils flared as he watched me approach the bed. "No need."

"You need me to—"

David bunched the remaining tubes and wires in his free hand and detached them all with one swift tug. He didn't even flinch when they ripped from his arm, but I did.

Jeremy exhaled a frustrated sigh. "You need to—"

"You need to leave before I lose my patience," David all but growled, "and shut the door on your way out."

The doctor started toward the door, then hesitated and turned back. "When do you plan to eat?"

A wisp of blue smoke wafted from my husband's nostrils and every nerve ending in my body tingled as his Dark scent saturated the air. "You've kept me nourished through these tubes, have you not?"

"Yes," Jeremy muttered, "but—"

"I have far more important needs to attend to," David murmured as I sat down on the bed beside him.

"Yes," Doc muttered as he stepped into the hall and started to close the door, "What do I know? I'm just the doctor…" The rest of his sentence was muffled by the door as he pulled it shut behind him.

Sapphire flames danced in David's eyes as he stroked a thumb over my cheek. "There you are."

"Here I am." My cheek flamed at his touch as I slid closer to him. "I'm so sorry for everything you went through…" my voice trailed off as my eyes flooded with tears.

"None of it was your fault," David whispered, "I should have told you about your father years ago."

I shook my head and swiped a stray tear off my cheek. "You were protecting me. I don't blame you for that."

ERIN A. JENSEN

"Thank God," he replied in a thick whisper as he brushed a tear from my other cheek with a tenderness that bordered on reverence. "I'm not sure I could take any more tension between us."

"I'm so sorry for every second I spent doubting you," I dropped my eyes to his pillow as I added, "and hating you…"

"There's no sense in wasting more time regretting what has already transpired." He shifted toward me and gently lifted my chin till I met his eyes. Then he brushed his bottom lip against mine, and everything blurred until nothing existed but the two of us.

His tongue possessively slid into my mouth, but I clamped it with my teeth to break the kiss. "So," I whispered as I pivoted to face him, swung one leg over both of his and sat down, straddling his thighs, "how fragile are you?"

He gripped my waist with such unexpected fervor that I let out a startled gasp. Answering my wide-eyed gaze with a throaty chuckle, he slid me up his legs and aligned my arousal perfectly above his. "How fragile do I feel?"

The heat at that single blissful point of contact kindled a spark that burst into flames inside me as I murmured, "It's been far too long since we did this properly."

A wicked grin spread across his face as the flames in his eyes blazed brighter. "There is nothing proper about what I plan to do to you, Princess."

"I was hoping you'd say that." I shot him a dazzling smile, and a thousand brazen memories from our years together flitted through my head as I exerted my mental pressure for all its worth. *Show me what I've been missing all these months. Don't love me like a human. Love me like a dragon.*

A snarl reverberated up his throat as he slipped a hand in my hair, gripped the strands to bring my head closer and covered my mouth with his. **I thought you'd never ask.**

His lips coaxed mine apart and his tongue greedily pushed inside my mouth. Then he flipped me off his lap and onto my back in one swift motion without ever taking his mouth from mine. His kiss was deep and passionate and dizzyingly unhurried as he crouched over me…devouring me…licks of fire rushed down my throat…and I lost myself in the moment…moaning against his mouth…as his heat rushed through me… the world disappeared…time stopped…and I forgot that anything had ever existed beyond that bed.

I closed my eyes and inhaled deeply, drinking in his scent as his lips whispered over my jawline and traveled down my neck. I was too impatient to move this slowly, and he knew it.

He always knew exactly what I wanted…but more importantly…he understood what I *needed*… often better than I understood it myself. **Anticipation heightens the experience, Princess. We've all the time in the world now.**

That's not true... Forget about mental manipulation. I could barely get my words out when I only had to *think* them. It was impossible to think straight when his mouth was on me. *There's a war to prepare for...*

Not today, Princess. Today I re-stake my claim. The demons that lurk beyond the clearing seem to have selective memories when it comes to our bond lately. I don't intend to leave this room until you are thoroughly drenched in my scent. I want it to seep from your pores, so they drop to their knees and worship the ground you walk on for fear of what I will do if they so much as think of looking in your direction. Is that alright with you?

Oh God, yes.

52

CHARLIE

The silence was hard to stomach as we sat by the balcony railing on wrought iron chairs and watched the massive Waterfall several stories below, but there was nothing I could say to break the tension. Bob had been quiet since we got back to the palace. Doc had taken Nellie to a guestroom and sedated her the instant we returned from Godric's hideout, because she was inconsolable to the point of hysteria over what'd happened to Lilly. Bob wanted to sit at her bedside, but Doc insisted it'd be best to give her some time. I'm not sure how long Bob, Pip and I had been sitting on the balcony. Everyone else had rushed off to attend to urgent matters when we got back to the palace, but the three of us were adrift in a sea of anguish in a place where we didn't exactly belong. After a bit of aimless wandering, I had led us through a Waterfall out onto the balcony. It'd seemed as good a place to tuck out of the way as any. So we'd settled into a restless silence, each of us lost in our own troubled thoughts.

Godric was my father. That hadn't quite sunk in yet. Stupid as it sounds, I was still hoping somebody would crack a smile and tell me it was all just a big, fat, incredibly cruel joke. If I really was Godric's son, Lilly was my sister. It was hard not to think of her as the baby sister I'd never gotten to meet, but she actually died before my time. Lilly would've been my big sister. How different would my life have been if I'd had one of those? And how the hell had I ended up with the couple who'd raised me as their child? My birth father was the devil incarnate, but he was still alive. So, was my real mother still out there somewhere?

My head ached with unanswered questions as I scooted my chair back from the railing and started pacing the balcony. "How much time do you suppose we've got to kill before anybody comes looking for us?"

Bob blinked a few times as he shifted in his chair to face me. "I haven't the faintest idea."

The anguish in his eyes stopped me dead in my tracks. "You and Nellie are gonna be okay, Bob."

"Yes," he whispered, "I suppose eventually...we will be."

"She loves you more than anything," I muttered as I stepped toward the railing.

"And I her," Bob whispered.

Pip cleared his throat and chimed in from his perch on the middle chair, "Nellie and the Princess would still be Godric's hostages if you hadn't helped the Sarrum find them, Bob."

Bob gave a slight nod as he blinked the tears from his eyes.

"It's gonna take some time," Pip muttered, "That's all."

I was trying to think of something uplifting to add to Pip's words when Benjamin stepped through the Waterfall. He locked eyes with me as he headed toward us. "Time for you to come with me, kid. There are a couple conversations you need to attend to."

Not quite sure what to make of the Darkness's vague statement, I nodded, took a deep breath to slow my pounding heart and followed him across the balcony to the Waterfall. As Benjamin stepped in, I looked back over my shoulder. "See you soon, Bob."

Bob nodded and turned to the railing without a single parting word.

I couldn't stop my eyes from tearing as I followed Benjamin through the Waterfall. Bob was a freaking rock. Seeing him all torn up like this was heart wrenching.

Benjamin kept a steady pace as he headed down the stone corridor. Lost in thought as I was, I kept up but paid little attention to where he was leading me.

Sunlight and the melodious chirps of songbirds extracted me from my mental fog as the dimly lit corridor opened up, depositing us into the cave that led to Emma's mirage. I froze and gawked at the clearing beyond the mouth of the cave. The paradise outside would've rivaled the Garden of Eden itself.

I turned to Benjamin and did a double take. He looked downright respectable in his sleek black warrior getup, aside from the soulless black eyes and menacing-as-hell aura. "You're not a sock monkey anymore."

Benjamin leveled me with his finest *you're a fucking idiot* stare. "Well, give the dragon points for being observant."

"Sorry," I muttered as my eyes drifted back to the clearing, "It looks so perfect."

"Yeah," Benjamin agreed in an uncharacteristically hushed tone, "The damage has all been repaired. Since the wards had to be reformed, the Sarrum dropped the children's plaything look that Isa and I had been stuck sporting for years—not much need now that the Princess's childhood innocence is a thing of the past."

As if on cue, Emma strolled into view near the lake at the far end of the clearing. She looked radiant. Even at this distance, the difference was palpable. She looked healed and whole, back home where she belonged.

Benjamin's voice was a distant echo beside me, "She wants to talk to you."

I nodded and muttered a barely audible, "Thanks," as I ventured out of the cave.

I blinked, adjusting my eyes to the sunlight as I stepped onto sweet spring grass. As soon as she saw me, Emma started toward me. It didn't take us long to meet in the middle of the clearing.

She greeted me with a brilliant smile. "Hey, Charlie."

I smiled at her despite the storm cloud that had settled over my heart after we returned from our rescue mission. "Hey."

"Thanks for coming to see me," she whispered.

"Yeah... um, I'm kinda surprised I'm not banned from this place," I muttered as I took in our utopian surroundings, "My last visit didn't exactly go well."

A tender smile tugged at the corners of her mouth. "Bygones."

"Bygones," I echoed in a hoarse whisper. Incredible as it felt to be with Emma again, there was a marked difference that I couldn't quite put my finger on.

She motioned for me to follow her to a blue blanket that was spread out over the grass a bit closer to the lake. "I owe you an apology, Charlie."

I frowned at her as we both sat down. "You owe *me* an apology?"

ERIN A. JENSEN

She dropped her eyes to the blanket. "Yes."

"What the hell for, Em? I led Godric to your safe haven," my voice cracked on the words, and I had to stop talking for a second as the magnitude of my fuckup hit me. "I'm responsible for your abduction. If anyone owes an apology, it's me."

She shook her head. "It wasn't your fault. You had no idea who he was or what he was capable of. Godric is manipulative and incredibly persuasive."

"That doesn't matter," I muttered, "Please forgive me for putting you in danger, Em. If I'd known…"

She leaned closer and wrapped her arms around me. "There's nothing to forgive."

Instead of the elation that I used to feel in her arms, I actually found myself flinching because the benign contact had a curious sting to it.

Her soft laughter was every bit as glorious as the songbirds' melodies that echoed through the clearing. "You feel it now, don't you?"

"Yeah," I muttered, suppressing a shiver. "What exactly am I feeling?"

"Him." Color rushed to her cheeks at the vague mention of her husband.

"How?"

She blushed a deeper shade of pink as she whispered, "He reinforced his scent about a hundredfold."

I couldn't help grinning at the unadulterated joy in her eyes. "So…what did you want to apologize for?"

"I mislead you at the facility. Not intentionally," she muttered as her eyes dropped to the blanket, "I had no idea I was doing it, or even that I could do it, but I charmed you into protecting me. You felt fond of me and protective of me because I willed you to."

My smile widened as I touched her hand and ignored the resultant sting. "I'm betting I would've felt the same without the charm."

"Not with that intensity," she whispered, "I needed a dragon's heart. I didn't understand that in my altered state, but something inside me recognized yours, and I latched onto you for dear life because I was drowning. What I felt for you…" she stopped to wipe a tear from her cheek, "I love you, Charlie. I always will. You saved me during the darkest time of my life. But I love you like a friend. Anything I felt beyond that was a desperate grasp at what I truly needed… *who* I truly needed. I needed a dragon's heart, but there will only ever be one dragon for me. I forgot so much of my history with David when my memories split. David never cheated on me, Charlie. He was no pedophile, and he didn't steal my innocence—I stole him. I backed him into a corner and left him no choice but to claim me or watch me die."

"Yeah," I muttered, "Benjamin kinda hinted at something like that, but I figured he was full of crap at the time."

She let out a subdued chuckle as she dabbed at the corners of her eyes. "I'm sorry for the way

I mislead you and toyed with your heart, Charlie. Please forgive me."

I gave her hand a squeeze and resisted the impulse to jump back when an electric current raced up my arm. "I get why you did it. Isa explained why our connection was as immediate and intense as it was when she lessened the effect that your charm had on me. Honestly, if I had it to do over again, I wouldn't change a thing. It might've been the darkest time in your life, but it was the beginning of a new chapter in mine. If it wasn't for you, I'd still believe I was mental."

"I think we're all a bit mental," she whispered with a sweet smile, "Just imagine how boring life would be if we weren't."

A burst of laughter hiccuped from my mouth. "Yeah. My life sure as hell hasn't been boring."

"What will you do now, Charlie?"

"Did your husband put you up to asking that?"

"My husband doesn't put me up to anything," she whispered with a coy grin. "If he has questions for you, he'll ask them himself. He isn't shy."

"No shit," I whispered, "He definitely is not."

"He's waiting for you in the great hall. Go when you're ready."

I wrapped my arms around her, pulled her into a bear hug and ignored the sparks of electricity warning me to step the fuck away from the Sarrum's soul mate. "Thanks, Em."

She squeezed me back and the resulting jolt stole the breath from my lungs as she whispered, "For what?"

"For loving me and believing in me… when nobody else ever had," I whispered in her ear, "and for seeing me as something more than just a mental patient."

"We all amount to more than our labels, Charlie. We are what's in our heart, and your heart is noble and kind."

"Yeah, I'm not so sure about that," I muttered as I slipped from our electrically charged embrace.

"I am," she whispered. "Go talk to the King."

I saluted her with a playful grin as I hopped to my feet. "Yes, your majesty."

My chest felt lighter as I crossed the clearing, entered the cave and headed down the stone corridor solo, since Benjamin was nowhere to be found.

I wandered through the dark corridors, took a few questionable turns and soon realized I had no idea how to get to the great hall from where I was. Then I remembered what Doc said, the day we sat on the balcony drinking funky wine and chuckling over Benjamin's broodiness. Space wasn't linear in Draumer. You couldn't necessarily get from point A to point B by going in a straight line. So I marched up to the nearest Waterfall and stepped through, picturing the great hall in all its grandiose magnificence on the other side.

"Took you long enough," the Sarrum's voice mused behind me.

I mentally patted myself on the back for finding my way there as I turned and headed toward the wide set of steps that led to the King's throne. "Better late than never?"

To my absolute shock, the Sarrum responded with a genuine smile as he gestured for me to climb the steps and sit in the chair beside his throne. "Yes, I suppose you're right."

I ascended the stairs, dropped into the chair and sunk against the sumptuous black cushions. "Emma said you wanted to talk to me."

"She was correct," he agreed curtly.

"So," I muttered, "what happens now? Do I stand trial for royally fucking up, or do you just sentence me to death on the spot?"

"What do you think ought to happen now?" His regal posture and stoic expression gave nothing away. He could be seconds away from offering me a job or sentencing me to life in a dank cell with my putrid guts spilling from my stomach.

"Well," I muttered, "I'd kinda like to keep breathing."

The Sarrum narrowed his eyes at me without lessening the intensity of his burning stare. "You would do well to drop the sarcasm from time to time."

"And is this one of those times?"

He raised an eyebrow, but didn't dignify my stupid question with a verbal response.

"Right," I muttered, sitting up a little straighter, "Sorry."

"You have great potential," the King went on, ignoring my apology. "If you tempered that smartass attitude, there is much that you could learn from us."

"You mean, you still want to keep me on after everything I've done?"

"You fucked up royally, as you so eloquently put it. No one would argue that, but you also did everything within your means to atone for your errors. You shouldered the burden of the mirage. You helped us locate Nellie Godric. You joined us on the retrieval mission and fought admirably." He shifted in his seat without easing up on his intimidating stare for a second. "And when it came right down to it, despite your misgivings and suspicions, you chose to take our side. Considering the fact that you'd just learned your father led the opposition, that was no minor decision."

"Yeah," I muttered, fighting the impulse to squirm in my seat, "I mostly did it because of the position I was responsible for putting Emma in."

"Yes," he replied with a pensive nod, "Loyalty to the Princess is a perfectly acceptable reason to serve the crown."

"I'm sorry for all the pedophile comments," I muttered, resisting the overwhelming urge to drop eye contact, "Emma explained that she forced the shift in your relationship by putting you in a position where you had to choose her or let her die. Why didn't you just tell me to shut the fuck up and put me in my place by explaining that?"

"Because it was none of your fucking business," he replied matter-of-factly, "and it still isn't."

"Right. Sorry. So... if Godric is my dad, then that makes you and me—"

"Cousins," he interrupted with a nod. "Yes. Why did you suppose you were able to break through the prison I'd sealed Nellie Godric into?"

"I figured it was because I had mad skills."

His nostrils twitched as he replied, "It was because we share the same blood, Charlie Oliver. Your father's blood created that mirage, and your cousin's blood warded it shut. Believe it or not, a tremendous amount of power flows through your veins because you are a royal."

"I'm a royal dragon, seriously?"

"You're a royal bastard," he agreed with a dry smile, "but a royal dragon nonetheless."

"So... do you know who my real mother is?"

"I do."

"Great," I growled a little louder than I meant to, "Care to let me in on the secret?"

"In time."

"Well," I took a deep breath and did my best to mask the irritation in my voice, "is she still alive?"

David shook his head. "We would address all your questions during your future lessons."

"*Would*?"

"You chose to align with me during the heat of battle. Now, you must decide whether you wish to pledge your undying loyalty to the throne or part ways with us."

After everything I had witnessed, there was no way I was ever going to align myself with my shit bag birth father. Benjamin said the Sarrum was a man worth binding yourself to for life, and the King himself confirmed that loyalty to the Princess was a perfectly good reason for joining them. "So, where do I sign up?"

53

BOB

Pip had spent the better part of our last hour in the sparsely furnished sitting room pacing back and forth across the tabletop beside me. Needless to say, his anxiety was doing nothing to calm my nerves. Although I wasn't a bundle of nervous energy like he was, I couldn't help wishing for a sign to assure me that the path I was about to take was indeed the right path.

Charlie stepped from the Waterfall with Rose following close behind him, and their untroubled grins actually did quell some of my misgivings. Rose hung back by the Waterfall, while Charlie crossed the room to me and Pip.

When he reached us, Charlie extended a hand and grinned from ear to ear as I shook it. "It's kinda nice to be strong enough to shake your hand without worrying you'll cripple me with that power grip of yours."

I answered with a polite smile, but I'm sure he could tell that my heart wasn't in it. "Why didn't you just ask me to ease up on the grip?"

Charlie let out a laugh, but his keen eyes swam with concern. "Are you kidding? I wasn't gonna tell the coolest guy I knew that his handshake was too manly for me."

"Yes," I muttered, "I suppose I see your point."

"Charlie," Pip moved to the edge of the table and tugged at Charlie's shirtsleeve, "Help me cheer this guy up, will you?"

The sorrow in Charlie's eyes cast a gloomy shadow over his otherwise cheerful expression. "That's a pretty tall order these days, Pip."

"If I knew for certain that this was where I was meant to go from here," I whispered, "perhaps I would be less glum."

Charlie exchanged a knowing look with Pip before meeting my eyes. "I'm pretty sure you're on the right track, Bob."

Brian stepped from the Waterfall before I could utter a syllable in response. The tattooed warrior's astute eyes swept over the room with a contemplative frown as he took a few steps toward the three of us. "You guys ready?"

"Hell, yeah," Charlie replied for the lot of us.

Brian nodded as he glanced at the silent majority. "Good. Because it's show time." He moved back to the Waterfall and stepped through without waiting for a response from anyone.

Rose flashed Charlie a beaming smile as she followed Brian out of the room.

Charlie grinned as he watched her leave, then expelled a pent up sigh as he turned back to us. "Ready?"

I glanced down at Pip and mimicked his half-assed nod. "Ready as we'll ever be."

"You're doing the right thing, Bob," Charlie whispered as he touched a hand to my shoulder. Then he crossed the floor and stepped into the Waterfall.

I lifted Pip off the table and tucked him in the breast pocket they had added to my sleek black shirt for just that purpose. "If only we were as certain."

"Where you go, I go," Pip whispered, "My only doubt stems from your uncertainty."

"Fantastic," I muttered as I crossed the room, "Now I have your future happiness riding on my decision as well."

Pip flashed me a sorrowful smile. "I'm happy sticking with you wherever you choose to go, big guy."

"Fair enough." A pang of doubt gripped me as I reached the silent cascade of Water, but I stepped in with a resolute sigh, wishing the sign I so desperately needed would hurry up and make an appearance.

I stepped out the other side and felt Pip burrow deeper into my pocket as several hundred pairs of eyes settled on us.

The grand set of steps to the King's throne stood at the far end of the great hall. A narrow, ornately embroidered black rug had been rolled out to form a path—from where we stood behind Brian—to the foot of the stairs. On either side of this walkway, neat rows of gold chairs with black cushions had been lined up and filled with an audience of all manner of creatures. At the base of the steps, the Dragon King stood in human form dressed in elegant black clothes befitting the ruler of an entire world. Benjamin stood to his right, in a sleek black uniform similar to the ones the four of us wore, but clearly indicative of a much higher rank. The Princess stood on the King's left side dressed in a white satin gown that shimmered like virgin snow bathed in sunlight. Her golden hair fell around her in silken waves and her cheeks—sunken and pale when we rescued her from Godric—now had a healthy pink glow. She flashed me a radiant smile when she noticed me staring, and I responded with a respectful nod.

Her beckoning eyes drifted to the audience members nearest to her, and my eyes filled with tears as I followed her gaze and found the sign I'd been desperate for. Nellie was in the front row, seated beside the girl the Sarrum and his men had rescued from the Purists' cabin. The girl was no longer masked in the Princess's form, but I recognized her new form. I had seen her in the medical ward while I was pleading with Doc to let me see Nellie. Tristan sat on the girl's other side with his hand on her forearm. He too was dressed in a uniform of the royal guard, similar to ours but also denoting a higher rank than the four of us.

"Ready?" Brian whispered beside me.

Nellie smiled and blew me a kiss, and I exhaled a muted sigh of relief as I nodded.

"We are now," Pip whispered from my pocket.

Ethereal a cappella music echoed from an unseen chorus of angels as Brian started down the aisle. Rose waited several beats then fell into step behind him, Charlie followed after her and I waited the proper number of paces before heading up the rear.

I paid little attention to the blur of faces I passed by as we headed toward the King and Queen. My eyes remained fixed on the porcelain-skinned angel with a lovely head of russet curls. As we neared Nellie, I mentally traced each delicate feature—sculpted cheekbones, full soft lips and adoring eyes brimming with tears. She looked genuinely happy and proud.

Nellie smiled at me as we reached the steps and arranged ourselves in a semicircle before the royal family.

My heart sang as I winked at her, then turned my attention to the monarch I would pledge myself in service to for the remainder of my days.

The Sarrum raised a hand in the subtlest of gestures and the unseen chorus immediately fell silent, as did every single spectator in the great hall. It was an eerie feeling—that much silence amidst that many creatures—but that was the utter respect the Dragon King's mere presence commanded. "Do all of you come before me of your own volition?"

"We do," we answered in unison—my voice confident and certain among the others now that Nellie was there to support my decision.

There was no other choice. The rightful rulers of the kingdom stood before us. This monarch led the rescue mission to retrieve Nellie from the bastard who'd taken her. The Sarrum's enemy was my enemy. There was no nobler course of action than pledging myself in service to the man who intended to crush Godric's army and force him to answer for his crimes.

The King's brilliant blue eyes stopped on each of us in turn before he nodded, satisfied that each of us belonged there. Then he turned to Brian. "Do you deem these four ready to join the ranks of the royal guard under your command?"

Brian took a step forward. "I do, Sarrum."

The King responded with a nod. "Whom do you bring before us today?"

"Rose Salazar Talbot." Rose stepped forward as Brian announced her. "Daughter of Isa Salazar Ramirez, the castle's royal sorceress. And ward of

Benjamin Shade, commander of the royal guard and shadow bound to the Sarrum of Draumer."

"Charles Oliver." Charlie stepped forward as Brian continued, "Dragon of royal lineage. Son of Henry Godric and cousin of David Talbot, Sarrum of Draumer."

"Robert Cassleman, night errant." I stepped up as Brian motioned to me. "Guardian of Nellie Godric, estranged wife of Henry Godric. And Unsighted protector of the Eastern Shore."

As Brian gestured toward Pip, I lifted him from my pocket and set him on the small marble pedestal they had positioned there for him. "Melvin Wise, Navigational Guide and partner to Robert Cassleman. And consultant in matters of magical security."

Pip, Charlie and I suppressed a smirk at Brian's creative description, mainly because Charlie's suggestions during preparations for the ceremony had included *Pocket-sized Sidekick Extraordinaire* and *Sneaky Little Bastard Specializing in Magical Breaking and Entering, desperately in need of a power scrubbing.* The Darkness narrowed his eyes at us, and our expressions quickly grew somber.

"Rose Salazar Talbot, step forward and state your reason for pledging your life in service to the crown." Rose stepped forward as the King spoke her name, and Benjamin beamed with parental pride as he placed a gilded sword in the Sarrum's waiting hand.

Rose smiled at Benjamin, then glanced back at her mother as she knelt before the King. "I wish to join the royal family, to train under the royal sorceress and serve the crown in whatever manner the Sarrum sees fit."

The Dragon King touched the blade of the sword to one of her shoulders, then the other. She remained kneeling as the Sarrum turned his attention to Charlie. "Charles Oliver, step forward and state your reason for pledging yourself in service to the crown."

Charlie stepped forward and smiled at Rose as he knelt beside her. "I wish to join the royal family, to train alongside Rose and serve the crown in whatever manner the Sarrum sees fit."

The King touched the blade to both of Charlie's shoulders, then fixed me in his sights. "Robert Cassleman, step forward and state your reason for pledging your life in service to the crown."

I stepped forward and knelt beside Charlie. "I wish to serve the royal family, to fight with the royal guard and help bring the Sarrum's enemies to justice in whatever capacity he sees fit."

I smiled at Nellie as the King touched the blade to both of my shoulders.

Brian slid Pip's perch closer to the King as he addressed him, "Melvin Wise, come forward and state your reason for pledging your life in service to the crown."

Pip knelt on his stand. "I wish to serve the royal family, to assist Sir Robert Cassleman in his duties and serve the crown in whatever manner the King sees fit."

The King gently touched the tip of the blade to both of Pip's shoulders. Then he took a step back and touched each of our heads in turn. "Arise, members of the royal guard and take your place among the ranks."

I stuck Pip back in my pocket as we got to our feet while a few hundred members of the royal army entered the hall through the Waterfalls along the walls and filed into the center aisle. We took our places at the front of the formation beside Brian as the King and Queen ascended the steps and settled into their thrones.

Benjamin stepped forward and spoke for a bit but I must admit, I missed most of what he said because my focus was on Nellie. Though Benjamin's words were lost on me, Nellie's expression would stick with me till my dying breath.

Her eyes swam with tears as she blew me subtle kisses and beamed with pride.

I smiled at my soul mate. Then I looked down at the partner in my pocket and at Charlie beside me, and I knew in my heart that I had chosen the right path.

54

NELLIE

As the King's shadow droned on about what the future had in store for all of us, I tuned out and focused on keeping a smile on my face as I blew discrete kisses to Bob. Despite how effortless I made it look, smiling was no easy task.

Everything felt wrong. I wanted to jump in the Waters and go back to set things straight, but there was nothing to go back to. My Lilly was gone, and so was the house where Godric had kept us. Charlie demolished it in a blaze of orange flames with one fiery whisper of his dragon breath. I'd watched from the yard—barely aware of Bob's arm around my shoulders—as it burned to the ground with the fallen demons still inside it.

Poor Bob. The grief that had filled his eyes when Charlie placed Lilly's lifeless body on the couch between us still haunted me. Bob knew Lilly wasn't

real.   That beautiful man and I had no secrets.
Once I realized I could trust Bob with anything, I'd
poured my heart out to him and shared my entire
life story beneath the stars on our beach.   He knew
what Henry had tricked me into doing all those years
ago, but the fact that the broken child on the couch
between us was just an enchantment—a faint echo of
the daughter I'd lost—didn't seem to lessen his grief
over failing to protect her.   Funny thing is, it wasn't
Bob's fault.   It was mine.

I kept that phony grin pasted on my face while
my eyes filled with tears as I recalled the nightmarish sequence of events that transpired inside that
Godforsaken house where Godric had kept us…

*…My heart sang as the Sarrum's thunderous roar
shook the room.   They'd finally found us.   The King of the
Dream World was outside the house, and Bob was with
him.   I'd bet my life on it.   My Unsighted knight in shining
armor had helped them get this far.   There was no chance
he'd stay behind while they rescued us.*

*Heart in my throat, I watched the gruesome battle
unfold outside the window and paid little attention to
Henry and Emma's exchange.   It wasn't any of my business.   She had dismissed her protective enchantment, but
that was hardly my fault.   Sure, I could have told her not
to do it and let the demons destroy my Lilly—but even
though she wasn't real, I couldn't bring myself to sacrifice my daughter to spare Emma Talbot.   I didn't owe
that Princess anything.   She was a stupid girl who'd wed*

a creature of Darkness, the King of the dragons no less. Emma was a dead woman walking. Her dear husband was slowly killing her—kiss by kiss—and unlike me, she'd willingly chosen that fate. I was probably doing her a favor by shortening her death sentence. Okay. I didn't really believe that, but I was a coward. So I let Emma wave off her protection, and I ignored what transpired after that and focused instead on the battle in the yard.

Eventually, Henry's agitated tone made it impossible to tune them out, so I turned and watched in horror as he poured his blood wine down Emma's throat. Once she was under his sway, Henry persuaded Emma to threaten to kill herself to distract the Sarrum and then slit her throat after he slipped away.

They arrived soon after that—the Dragon King, the Darkness, Charlie, the incubus and pretty young thing who'd come with Charlie when he visited the facility, another handsome man who appeared to be half-incubus-half-elf and my Bob. Most of what happened moved too quickly for me to follow, and there was a lot that I simply didn't understand. Somehow, Charlie fell under Henry's influence shortly after they entered the room. I watched the silent battle that was warring inside him play out on this face. In the end, Charlie chose the Sarrum's side, and Henry commanded the demons in the yard to storm the house.

A multitude of nightmarish beasts shattered the glass and spilled in through the broken windows, and I just sat there on the couch like a petrified twat watching the

Sarrum's men gloriously locked in battle with Godric's demons. I noticed when Godric slipped away, but I had more important things to worry about.

I wasn't completely helpless. Henry had taught me one defensive skill back in the days when we were young and happy—or at least, when I believed we were. In retrospect, I suspect he taught me how to charm people mostly out of boredom. His eyes always lit up during my lessons. He once confided during a particularly enjoyable session that it reminded him of his childhood, when he'd instructed his precious sister. Back then, I was too blissfully ignorant and drunk on his blood wine to question the nature of their relationship. I was also too stupid to heed the warning bells when he cried out his dead sister's name—more than once—in the throes of passion, but that's neither here nor there.

I wasn't powerful enough to manipulate a creature like Henry, of course, but the demons crouching over my Lilly were a different story. They were nothing but mindless drones. Once Henry was distracted, it was easy enough to manipulate them into sitting back and watching Lilly from afar without laying so much as a claw on her. In fact, they were so simple-minded that I didn't even have to keep an eye on them. So, I mentally focused on controlling them as I watched the battle swarm around us. Had I kept my eyes on Lilly, things would've ended differently.

No one could blame me for letting my eyes drift to Bob. His fearlessness and skill on the battlefield were magnificent to witness. My heart swelled to the point of bursting as I watched his muscular physique maneuver to fend off demon after demon with such valor and precision. It didn't matter how large the demon was or how many of them charged at him. He slayed them all as if it were nothing, and he was doing it to defend me. What in God's name had I ever done to deserve a man as honorable and decent as Bob?

I saw the innocente before anyone else did. When Henry taught me about these demons with the ridiculously misleading name during my lessons years ago, I was fascinated. They were small shape shifting creatures capable of transforming their physical appearance to something that their intended victim would never harm, usually a child or young woman. After manipulating their victims into dropping their guard, they would sink their teeth into them. A single bite from an innocente was a death sentence because their saliva was poisonous and there was no cure. I identified the creature immediately because I saw it scramble through the broken window and the instant it noticed me watching, it took Lilly's form. It kept its eyes glued to me as it raced past the couch, then it rushed on toward Bob.

My Unsighted hero was busy dispatching a pair of trolls when the innocente entered the room, so he didn't see its true form and he didn't see it race past me in Lilly's form. By the time Bob had run his sword through both trolls, the innocente had passed me and taken a new form. It was still a little girl, but this one was a bit older than Lilly and had no business walking upright—her limbs were bent at impossible angles, her clothes were torn and her face was badly bruised—she looked inches from death's door. As Bob dispatched the second troll, he looked up at the approaching child. His mouth fell open and the sword slipped from his hand. That's when I realized who she was. I first heard Bob's story during a group session at the facility. The doctor shared it because old Bob's Swiss cheese brain couldn't even recall the incident. The child that Bob lost his mind rescuing had haunted his dreams until Charlie reassured him that he'd saved that girl and her brother from their abductors in the waking world. Bob got shot in the head in the process of rescuing them, hence the Swiss cheese brain. This foul little demon had donned the likeness of the girl Bob sacrificed his life to save, and my heroic soul mate dropped his weapon to the floor the second he saw her.

It happened in an instant—the greatest moment of clarity of my entire life. I knew exactly what would happen if I did nothing. That demon-child would approach and Bob would just watch her walk right up and take a bite out of him, and I would lose the love of my life. Once upon a time, I believed that Henry was the love of my life. Then I met this beautiful, selfless honorable man who would lay down his life to protect another without giving it a second thought, and he healed what I thought was forever broken inside me. Lilly was my baby, and I loved her with all my heart, but she'd been gone for years. I killed her decades ago. That little girl on the floor was nothing but a clever bit of dragon magic that I'd clung to for most of my adult life. Lilly was my past, but Bob was my present. He was my future. Bob was my everything. Nothing was going to take that from me while I had a means to prevent it. So, I did the only thing I could do. I stopped focusing on the pea-brained demons who were drooling over my Lilly, and I focused like hell on the innocente who was brazenly approaching the man I loved. I pictured the vile little creature losing interest in my knight and going after the demon who'd raced through the window on her heels. The battered demon-child stopped and shook her head as she looked up at Bob, who was only a few feet away by that point.

Bob's eyes filled with tears as he crouched down and reached a hand out to her. "It's alright, child. I won't allow any more harm to come to you."

I focused with such force that blood started trickling from my nose, but I wiped it away and kept on manipulating that vile demon's mind till it turned away from Bob. Just as my knight moved to go after the demon-child, it caught sight of the demon behind it and transformed into a younger version of the skeleton-like creature with florescent eyes and bony, clawed fingers. Bob clutched his head as he glanced over at me.

The tortured expression on his face nearly stopped my heart. "It's a shape shifting demon, Bob! Send it back to hell!"

He only hesitated for a second before retrieving his sword and running it through the innocente and its new target in one precise jab...

...I knew exactly what would happen to Lilly when I did it and I stood by my decision, but it had crushed Bob for so many reasons.

I couldn't wait for this stupid ceremony to wrap up. I was impatient to reassure Bob that he'd done the right thing. I wanted to explain that I chose him and it was a choice I would never regret. If it took some time for Bob to come to terms with that, so be it. The alternative was just too unthinkable. I couldn't watch him die.

Despite all the odds, my Unsighted knight had tracked me down in the heart of the Dark Forest and he'd braved every nightmare that lurked within those trees to save me. Bob was real. He was the greatest truth I'd ever known, and I would love him till my dying breath.

55

DAVID

While Benjamin spoke, a lump formed in my throat as I looked out over the faces of the crowd and the royal guard assembled before us. I watched as looks were exchanged between brother and sister, parent and child, and lovers—both new and old. Tears filled Bob's eyes as he winked at his soul mate. Broken as that woman had been for decades, this Unsighted man with a heart of pure gold had managed to mend much of the damage that Henry Godric had caused. Nellie had sacrificed the enchantment—for which she once would have traded hordes of innocent souls—because this knight meant that much to her. Charlie and Rose allowed their fingers to brush in the subtlest of affectionate gestures as they stood side by side, beaming with pride over what they had accomplished together. Tristan laid a gentle hand on the arm of the changeling who had been forced to endure so much pain in my Princess's form for no other purpose than to deceive and enrage me. Despite the hell I had watched this girl suffer through the sweet-talker's memory, she smiled at Tristan with genuine trust and affection. I couldn't help but wonder if she sensed how much they had in common.

I took a deep breath as I turned to the woman seated in the throne beside mine. Part of me couldn't help fearing I would see the uncertainty that had clouded her eyes for so long, but she laid those fears to rest with a smile that spoke volumes of our history. I reached out with a knowing grin and took her hand, threading my fingers through hers.

Benjamin nodded to me as he finished his speech. Then he took his seat in the front row beside Isa as I stood from my throne.

I cleared my throat and the silence in the room intensified tenfold. "This is a celebration for all present. My Queen is back home where she belongs, and the royal guard is honored to receive four new members into its ranks. These warriors each fought valiantly to right the wrongs that the royal family recently endured. If it weren't for the valiant efforts of Sir Robert and Sir Melvin—braving the Darkest depths of the forest to bring word to us as to the whereabouts of the Princess and Nellie Godric—I shudder to think of what might have transpired. Charles and

Rose shouldered a massive burden throughout the entire ordeal and still trampled many a foe, as did Robert and Melvin. Our family is that much richer because they are now a part of it. Yet however joyous this occasion is, a heaviness weighs on our hearts this day.

I realize that many of you believe I am a monster because of the lengths I went to in order to track down the Princess, and you are not wrong. I am indeed a monster, but I make no apologies for my recent actions."

Hushed murmurs erupted from the audience, but quickly died off as I continued.

"I stand behind my decisions, just as I always have. Lawlessness shall not be tolerated in this kingdom. Violate our laws and prey upon the innocent, and I will gladly show you just how much of a monster I am. The creatures whom I executed in the Dragon's Lair were all Purists who played a role in the abduction of the Princess and committed various other crimes, preying upon the Unsighted along the fringe. Those who were burned in the Dark Forest at the site of the Purists' meeting place all took part in the sex trafficking of both Sighted and Unsighted creatures. They were punished for their crimes, violently and without mercy because they showed no mercy to their captives. The demons who were put to death at Godric's home, for their role in the abduction of the Queen and Nellie Godric, understood full well the magnitude of their crimes and the possible consequences of their actions.

If you are a creature capable of such heinous crimes, then you should fear the monster standing before you today because I will not hesitate to execute you just as I did those creatures.

Godric the would-be king and his army of Purists are no longer hiding in the shadowed corners of our world. They have marched into our midst and declared war on us all. Godric's troops have mounted countless attacks along the fringe, laying waste to peaceable settlements and violating the Unsighted inhabitants in unspeakable ways. Godric himself invaded the palace and abducted the Queen from her home.

For years, Godric has been quietly building an army of dragons in preparation for war."

Another murmur rippled through the audience, but hushed the instant I continued.

"Godric would have you revert to the ancient ways. The Purists view the Unsighted as worthless creatures because they lack all memory of the world beyond the Waters. The Purists see no wrong in stealing from these "inferior creatures"—their possessions, their property, their bodies, even their very lives—in the Purist's eye, all of it is theirs for the taking. They would sell the Unsighted into slavery, then mistreat and molest them without fear of consequence. I am quite sure I needn't remind you that the Unsighted live amongst us in the waking world. They are your coworkers, your friends, your lovers, and your own flesh and blood. Unsighted lives are no less precious than ours and should be protected with no less vigilance.

The Purists also maintain that a woman's purpose is to cater to man, satisfy his demands and populate the world with more dragons, whether or not they consent to do so. They have already violated the women of this world in countless ways." A spasm of pain seared my chest as the visions I had ripped from the sweet-talker's mind rushed back to me. I felt the changeling who had suffered horrific crimes at the hands of the Purists whilst in my wife's form shrink in her seat, but I did not shy away from her tortured stare. Instead, I spoke my next words directly to her. "These crimes shall not go unpunished. I intend to see to it personally that each of them suffers grievously for what they have done."

Mia held my gaze as she nodded and wiped a tear from her cheek.

"Women are not inferior creatures. Women serve as counsel to me, they defend our borders and they should take no backseat to man in either world.

Man or woman, young or old, mighty or frail, there is a place for you in this battle. Each of you have talents that may be harnessed to fight this evil that threatens to choke the good from our world— be it to clothe the troops, forge weapons, or join the ranks and fight alongside me—no one has any excuse to shrink from this war. You needn't be fierce to contribute, but you owe it to your friends, and neighbors, and loved ones to fight this poisonous weed that has sprung up amongst us, because the only feasible method of restoring peace to Draumer is war.

Godric has already declared war on all of us— Sighted and Unsighted, seasoned warrior and innocent soul alike—his actions have sent a message loud and clear, and it is high time that we send a message back.

THIS ENDS NOW.

We cannot idly sit back whilst this evil lurks in our shadows. I promise all of you that this monster standing before you today shall not rest until every trace of this insurrection has been extinguished. The Purists will no longer be permitted to occupy the Dark corners of our world. Godric began this battle. Now it is time for us to finish it."

Keep reading for an excerpt from Book Four of the Dream Waters Series

Excerpt from Book 4 of the Dream Waters Series:

CHARLIE

I shut the door to my room, shuffled to the armchair in the corner like a ninety year old man, then plopped into it like a hyperactive child. Dropping my head against the headrest, I took a peek out the window and instantly wished that I hadn't. Minutes after finishing my daily self-defense torture session, Benjamin was already setting up a hellishly complex obstacle course in the backyard to torture me with tomorrow. He was enjoying this way too much. Since Rose was raised among royal dragons and had been in training since birth, none of these sessions were beyond her capabilities and the Darkness knew I'd do anything to keep from looking like a weakling in front of my girlfriend.

I flexed a muscle and winced at the burn, although I couldn't help grinning at the results. There was no arguing the fact that I was in the best shape of my life. I mean, I wasn't gonna beat Tristan or Brian in a flexing competition anytime soon. Had they looked like regular guys before Benjamin got a hold of them? Probably not, mainly because they were never "regular guys." No regular guy could ever match up to an incubus in the looks department, but I didn't look half bad for me. Then again, I wasn't exactly a regular guy either. I was a dragon—and so was my adorable girlfriend and fellow trainee— which was why I was working so damn hard to kick ass during our training sessions.

I pushed myself out of the chair with a pitiful groan and peeled off my t-shirt as I headed to my bathroom for a much needed shower.

Unfortunately, a knock on my door suggested that someone had other plans for me.

I plastered my best *I'm not in excruciating pain* smile on my face as I crossed the room to the door. For all I knew, somebody I didn't want to look like a wimp in front of was on the other side of that door.

Tristan greeted me with a playful grin as I pulled the door open. Without waiting for an invitation, he nudged the opening wider and stepped into my room. He wrinkled his nose as he looked me up and down. "Damn. You stink."

I plopped down on my bed with a frustrated sigh. "Yeah, thanks. I was just about to take a shower be- fore I was rudely interrupted. Can I help you with something?"

"Yup." He tugged my aching arm and pulled me to my feet with a knowing grin. "You're gonna end up giving yourself a hernia, dragon. I doubt Rose would think any less of you if you eased up a little during your training sessions with Benjamin."

"Whatever." I glanced into the hall to make sure Rose hadn't been out there to overhear Tristan. Satisfied that the hall was vacant, I shut the door and dropped my voice a little lower. "I don't need relationship advice from a guy who looks like a Greek god. What the hell do you know about impressing a girl? For you, it's as easy as breathing."

"Not always," he muttered under his breath.

"Sorry," I whispered, feeling like a complete ass. "I'm just tired. What do you need my help with?"

"We've got a couple new housemates to chauffeur to the house."

"This house is filling up fast," I muttered as I grabbed a fresh t-shirt from the dresser and slipped it over my head. In addition to Brian, Benjamin, Isa, Doc, Rose and me, Tristan and Mia had taken up residence at fifty-five Sycamore. There were still plenty of empty rooms in the house, but privacy was getting harder to come by—unless you holed up in your bedroom. "Why do you need my help driving people to the house? That kinda sounds like a one-man job."

A wide grin spread across Tristan's perfect face. "Well, there's a bit of a catch."

"Alright," I muttered, "I'll bite. What's the catch?"

"They aren't exactly aware that they're moving in with us."

"So…" I raked a hand through my hair as I mulled that over. "You need my help kidnapping a couple people?"

Tristan shrugged his broad shoulders, rippling muscles that I was pretty sure I'd been born without. "I suppose you could look at it that way."

"Wouldn't Benjamin be better at helping with something like that?" Even as I said it, I wondered at the fact that my greatest concern was Tristan's choice of co-kidnapper rather than the fact that he needed help with something like that at all.

Tristan let out a chuckle that was beyond sexy. "Not with these two."

"For that matter," I muttered, reminding myself that I didn't have to let his charm affect me, "can't you just charm them into hopping into your car?"

"That's a negative," Tristan murmured, "Come on, dragon. Where's your sense of adventure?"

"In what universe is kidnapping an adventure?"

"It's not exactly kidnapping," Tristan whispered with a coy shrug, "It's more of an invite they have no choice but to accept."

"Yeah," I muttered, "That sounds like kidnapping to me."

"It's just the start of their grand new adventure," Tristan chuckled.

"Uh huh, and why exactly are we *insisting* that these people move in with us?"

"For their own safety," Tristan murmured as he opened the door, "If they're here, the Purists won't be able to get to them."

"Stop being so freaking mysterious," I growled as I followed him out the door and down the stairs. "Who the hell are these people?"

"Old friends of yours," Tristan whispered as he opened the front door and ushered me out.

"Okay?"

Tristan shook his head as he opened the driver's side door to the sleek silver vehicle parked in the driveway. "Just get in."

Against my better judgment, I opened the passenger side door, hopped in and buckled myself in. This wasn't my first ride as Tristan's passenger. The gas was his favorite pedal, and he considered the brakes optional in most instances. When you looked like him and could charm the pants off almost anyone, you didn't much worry about traffic tickets. He wouldn't do anything that'd cause an accident, but at an intersection with no traffic coming from the other direction, he saw no reason to wait around for a pesky green light to give him permission to go. I braced myself as he started the engine. Not surprisingly, it purred like a freaking kitten—which meant that his sweet touch on the gas pedal would quickly propel us to *oh my fucking hell* speed. "Where the hell are we going, Tristan?"

"The boss thinks your favorite elderly couple would be safer with us than they are at the facility."

I let out a laugh at the thought of Unsighted old Bob snoring on the couch in the midst of Benjamin's rigorous training regimen. "One look at the giant flat screen television in the living room and Bob will be in his glory."

"Good," Tristan muttered as he pressed the gas pedal a little closer to the floor. "That's why we need you. You know how to coax the ornery old bastard off that couch at the facility and into the car of a total stranger."

"Have you tried this already without me?"

"Yeah," he muttered as he fiddled with the radio, "It didn't go so well."

"What about Nellie? She knows who you are and she understands why they'd be safer with us. Couldn't she just convince Bob that it's for the best?"

"They both agreed to it in Draumer," Tristan grumbled, "and Nellie had him convinced before I showed up at the facility, but old Bob informed me that he had no intention of riding off into the sunset with some pretty boy who's liable to rape them and leave them both for dead."

I tried to stifle my laugh, but not successfully. "Seriously?"

"Nellie says he's hooked on criminal investigative dramas lately. Apparently, there's a real danger of devilishly handsome young men with elder-abuse fetishes absconding from institutions with dementia patients."

I suppressed my smirk because Tristan seemed genuinely frustrated. "Great. So Bob wouldn't listen to Nellie, but you think he'll listen to me?"

"He knows you, so he won't suspect you're there to rape them," he grumbled, "That'll start you off on a better foot than me."

"Just when I thought old Bob couldn't get any loonier," I muttered as we pulled into the facility parking lot. "Can't you just charm that doctor who couldn't take his eyes off you into letting you take Bob kicking and screaming?"

"As delightful as that sounds," Tristan murmured as he parked the car, "It'd be best if we got the pair of them to come willingly."

I battled the inevitable bouts of déjà vu as we crossed the parking lot and entered the facility. Lost in an onslaught of memories, I moved alongside Tristan to the front desk, then down the hall to the doors that could only be accessed by key. As we stepped in, I scanned the faces both painfully familiar and newly admitted. It was no shocker that we found Bob and Nellie on the couch in the big common room in front of the television.

I walked in and did the unthinkable. I stepped in front of Bob, blocking his view of the detective show they were watching. "Hey, Bob."

To my surprise, he grinned at me. "Hey, kid. Long time no see." The grin slipped from his face when his eyes moved to Tristan. "What's this pretty boy doin here again? I oughta bust that perfect nose of yours for comin back."

"Good to see you too, Grandpa."

Bob's wrinkled hands balled into fists. "Fuck off, pretty boy. I ain't your damn Grandpa."

"Whoa," I muttered as I took a step closer to Bob. "Tristan is a friend of mine, Bob."

"A friend of yours?" Bob echoed skeptically as he narrowed his eyes at Tristan. "What the fuck have you gotten yourself into these days, kid?"

I glanced at Tristan out of the corner of my eye and spoke in a voice too low for old Bob's ears, "Damn. He really hates you. Why doesn't your charm work on him?"

"He's too deeply in love with this lovely woman beside him to be affected by my charm."

Nellie's wrinkled cheeks blushed at the compliment, and I suddenly realized what the problem was. "Then stop flirting with his soul mate, you idiot."

"I'm not flirting," Tristan whispered, "It's called being polite. You should try it sometime."

"Trust me on this one. When *you* are polite to the love of someone else's life, it comes across as flirting whether you mean it to or not."

"What are you suggesting I do?" Tristan whispered, "Be rude to her?"

"It always worked for me," I muttered, earning a scowl from Nellie. I frowned right back at her and whispered, "Do you have to smile at him like that?"

"I didn't realize I was smiling," she muttered, "I can't help it. My heart belongs to this old coot next to me, but my body's not dead. When I see an Adonis like this, what am I supposed to do?"

"I'd suggest the old *picture him in his underwear* trick," I muttered, "but that wouldn't exactly help in this situation."

Nellie blushed a deeper shade of pink as she looked the incubus up and down. "No kidding."

Bob hopped to his feet faster than I would've guessed he could. "Get this sick fuck away from us."

I let out a sigh as I stepped closer to Bob. "My friend's not so bad, Bob. He came here to help me bring you to your new home."

"New home?" Bob muttered, "Will this asshole be there?"

I grinned at Bob and deflected the question the best way I knew how. "There's a flat screen television there that's big enough to knock your socks off."

ERIN A. JENSEN

Bob glanced back at Nellie and spoke the words I'd never have expected him to utter, "There's more important things than television."

"You and Nellie can share a room there," Tristan murmured.

I tensed, waiting for Bob to lunge at him, but if Tristan knew how to read any situation, it was that one. "Yeah?" Bob muttered as he eyed the incubus, "Can you promise that?"

"Yes," Tristan murmured. "I promise you, Grandpa. You and Grandma can share a room, and anyone who says otherwise will have to answer to me."

Bob relaxed his stance as soon as Tristan referred to Nellie as Grandma. I had to hand it to Tristan, he was the smoothest talker I'd ever met. "Charlie," Bob muttered, "You can vouch for this guy?"

"Yeah, Bob," I muttered as I glanced at Tristan. "This guy has a heart of gold."

Bob scrunched up his face as he mulled it over out loud, "Huge fuckin television...and an angel in my bed every night."

Nellie's face lit up ten times brighter when Bob called her an angel than it had when Tristan smiled at her.

Bob nodded his head as he looked back and forth between me and Tristan. "Well, what the fuck're we waitin for? I got a program to watch at five a'clock."

62097469R00295

Made in the USA
Middletown, DE
19 January 2018